LAUREL K. HAMILTON'S

ANITA BLAKE
VAMPIRE HUNTER

CIRCUS OF THE DAMNED
~ THE CHARMER

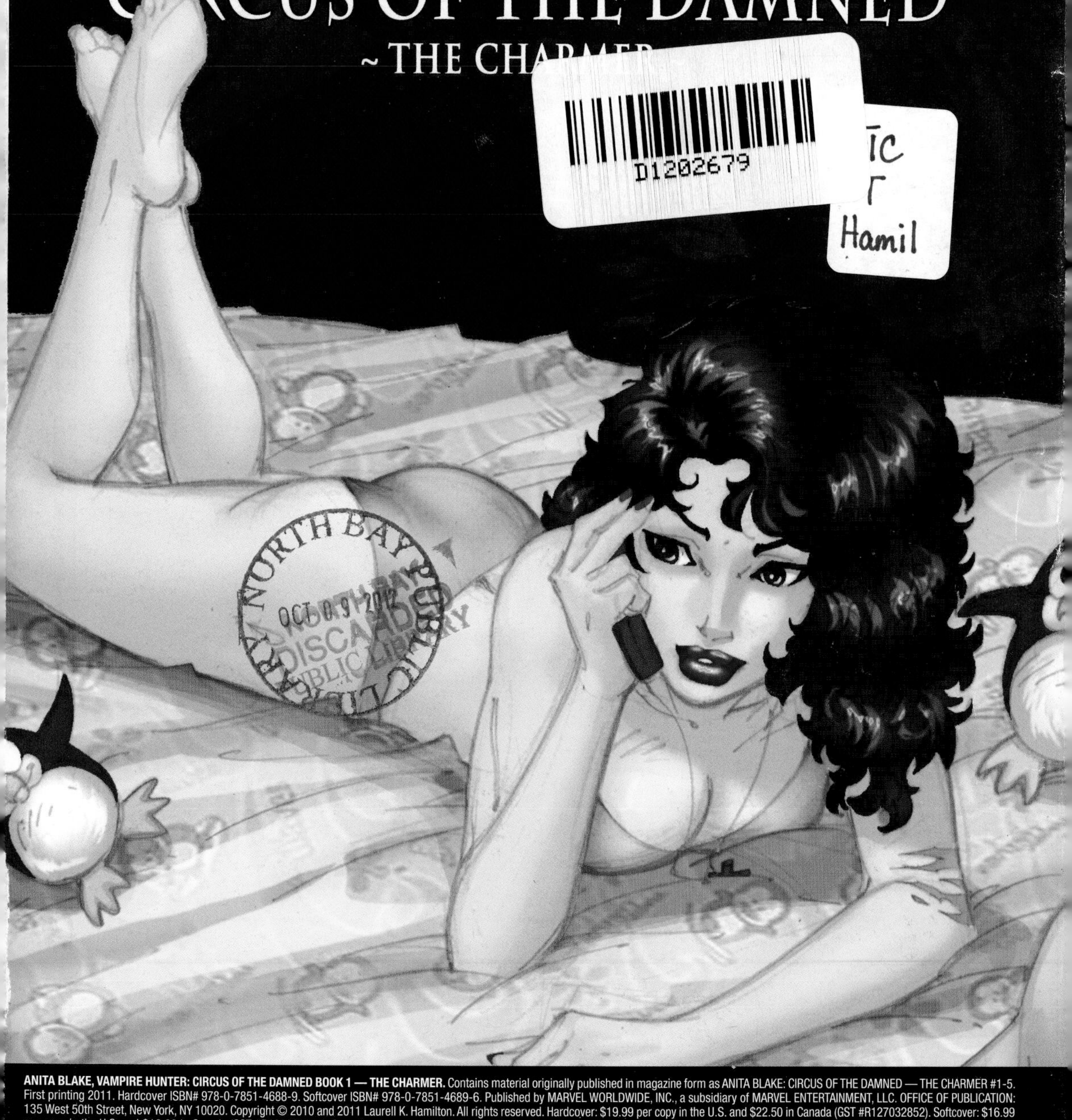

ANITA BLAKE, VAMPIRE HUNTER: CIRCUS OF THE DAMNED BOOK 1 — THE CHARMER. Contains material originally published in magazine form as ANITA BLAKE: CIRCUS OF THE DAMNED — THE CHARMER #1-5. First printing 2011. Hardcover ISBN# 978-0-7851-4688-9. Softcover ISBN# 978-0-7851-4689-6. Published by MARVEL WORLDWIDE, INC., a subsidiary of MARVEL ENTERTAINMENT, LLC. OFFICE OF PUBLICATION: 135 West 50th Street, New York, NY 10020. Hardcover: $19.99 per copy in the U.S. and $22.50 in Canada (GST #R127032852). Softcover: $16.99 per copy in the U.S. and $18.99 in Canada (GST #R127032852). Canadian Agreement #40668537. All characters featured in this issue and the distinctive names and likenesses thereof, and all related indicia are trademarks of Laurell K. Hamilton. No similarity between any of the names, characters, persons, and/or institutions in this magazine with those of any living or dead person or institution is intended, and any such similarity which may exist is purely coincidental. Marvel and its logos are TM & © Marvel Characters, Inc. **Printed in the U.S.A.** ALAN FINE, EVP - Office of the President, Marvel Worldwide, Inc. and EVP & CMO Marvel Characters B.V.; DAN BUCKLEY, Chief Executive Officer and Publisher - Print, Animation & Digital Media; JIM SOKOLOWSKI, Chief Operating Officer; DAVID GABRIEL, SVP of Publishing Sales & Circulation; DAVID BOGART, SVP of Business Affairs & Talent Management; MICHAEL PASCIULLO, VP Merchandising & Communications; JIM O'KEEFE, VP of Operations & Logistics; DAN CARR, Executive Director of Publishing Technology; JUSTIN F. GABRIE, Director of Publishing & Editorial Operations; SUSAN CRESPI, Editorial Operations Manager; ALEX MORALES, Publishing Operations Manager; STAN LEE, Chairman Emeritus. For information regarding advertising in Marvel Comics or on Marvel.com, please contact Ron Stern, VP of Business Development, at rstern@marvel.com. For Marvel subscription inquiries, please call 800-217-9158. **Manufactured between 12/13/10 and 1/10/11 (hardcover), and 12/13/10 and 6/20/11 (softcover), by R.R. DONNELLEY, INC., SALEM, VA, USA.**

10 9 8 7 6 5 4 3 2 1

LAURELL K. HAMILTON'S

ANITA BLAKE
VAMPIRE HUNTER

CIRCUS OF THE DAMNED
~ THE CHARMER ~

WRITER: LAURELL K. HAMILTON
ADAPTATION: JESS RUFFNER-BOOTH
ARTIST: RON LIM

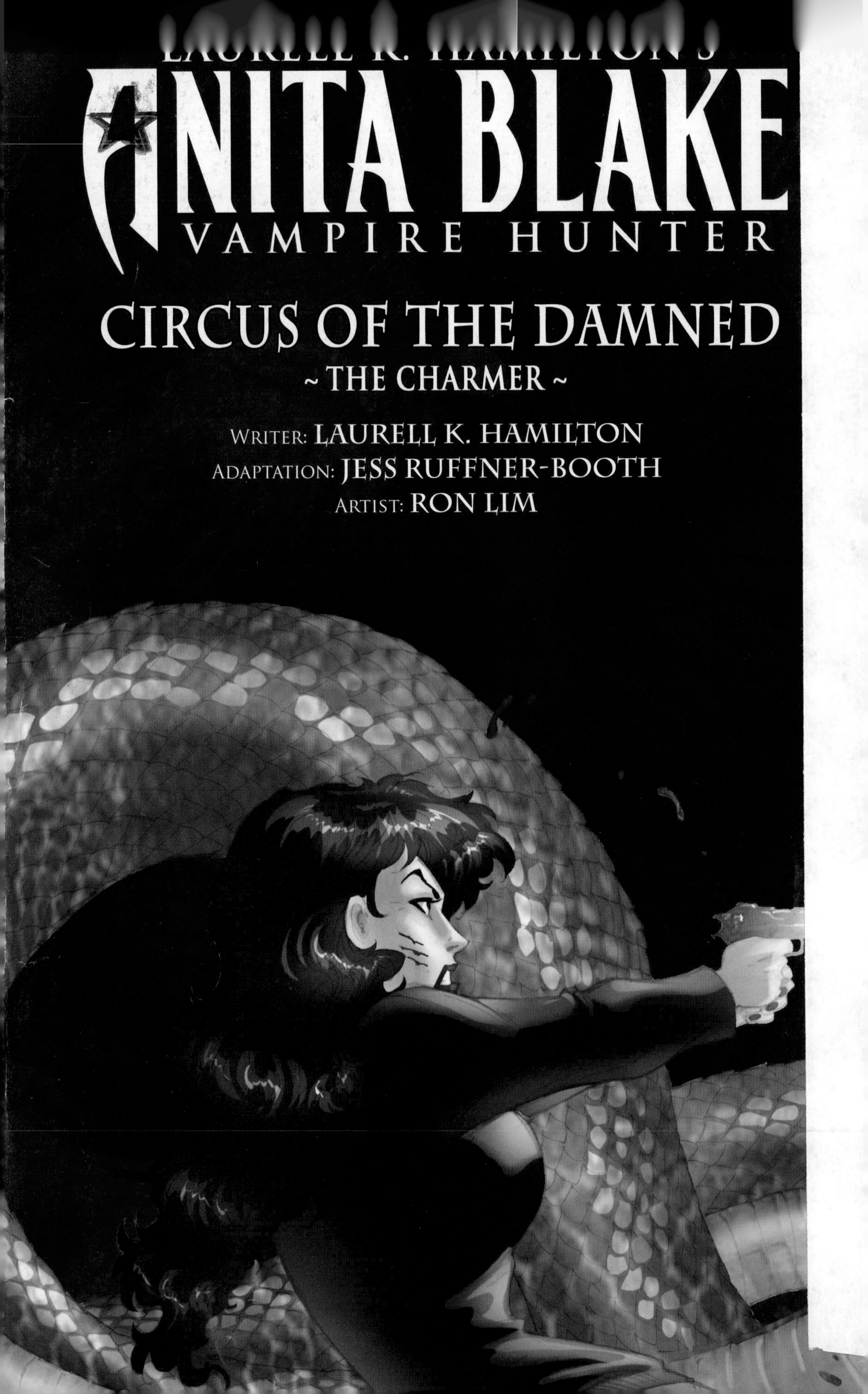

COLORIST: LAURA VILLARI
LETTERER: BILL TORTOLINI
COVER ARTISTS: BRETT BOOTH
WITH JESS RUFFNER-BOOTH (ISSUES #1-3)
& ANDREW DALHOUSE (ISSUES #4-5)
EDITOR: MIKE HORWITZ
CONSULTING EDITOR: MARK PANICCIA

SPECIAL THANKS TO JONATHON GREEN, CARRIE CLEAVELAND, MELISSA MCALISTER, JOHN DENNING & WENDY XU

COLLECTION EDITOR: CORY LEVINE
EDITORIAL ASSISTANTS: JAMES EMMETT & JOE HOCHSTEIN
ASSISTANT EDITORS: MATT MASDEU, ALEX STARBUCK & NELSON RIBEIRO
EDITORS, SPECIAL PROJECTS: JENNIFER GRÜNWALD & MARK D. BEAZLEY
SENIOR EDITOR, SPECIAL PROJECTS: JEFF YOUNGQUIST
SENIOR VICE PRESIDENT OF SALES: DAVID GABRIEL
SENIOR VICE PRESIDENT OF STRATEGIC DEVELOPMENT: RUWAN JAYATILLEKE

EDITOR IN CHIEF: JOE QUESADA
PUBLISHER: DAN BUCKLEY

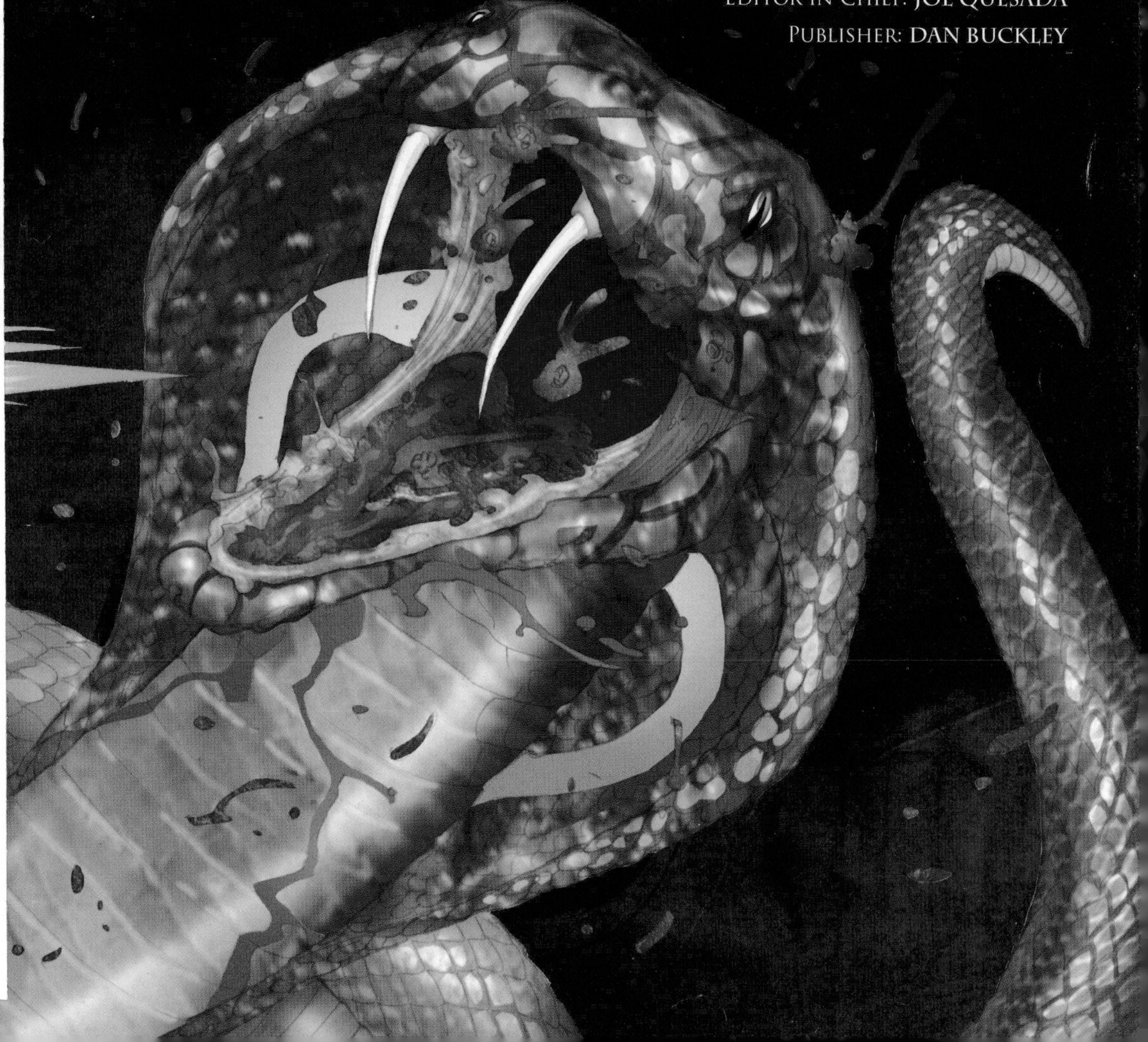

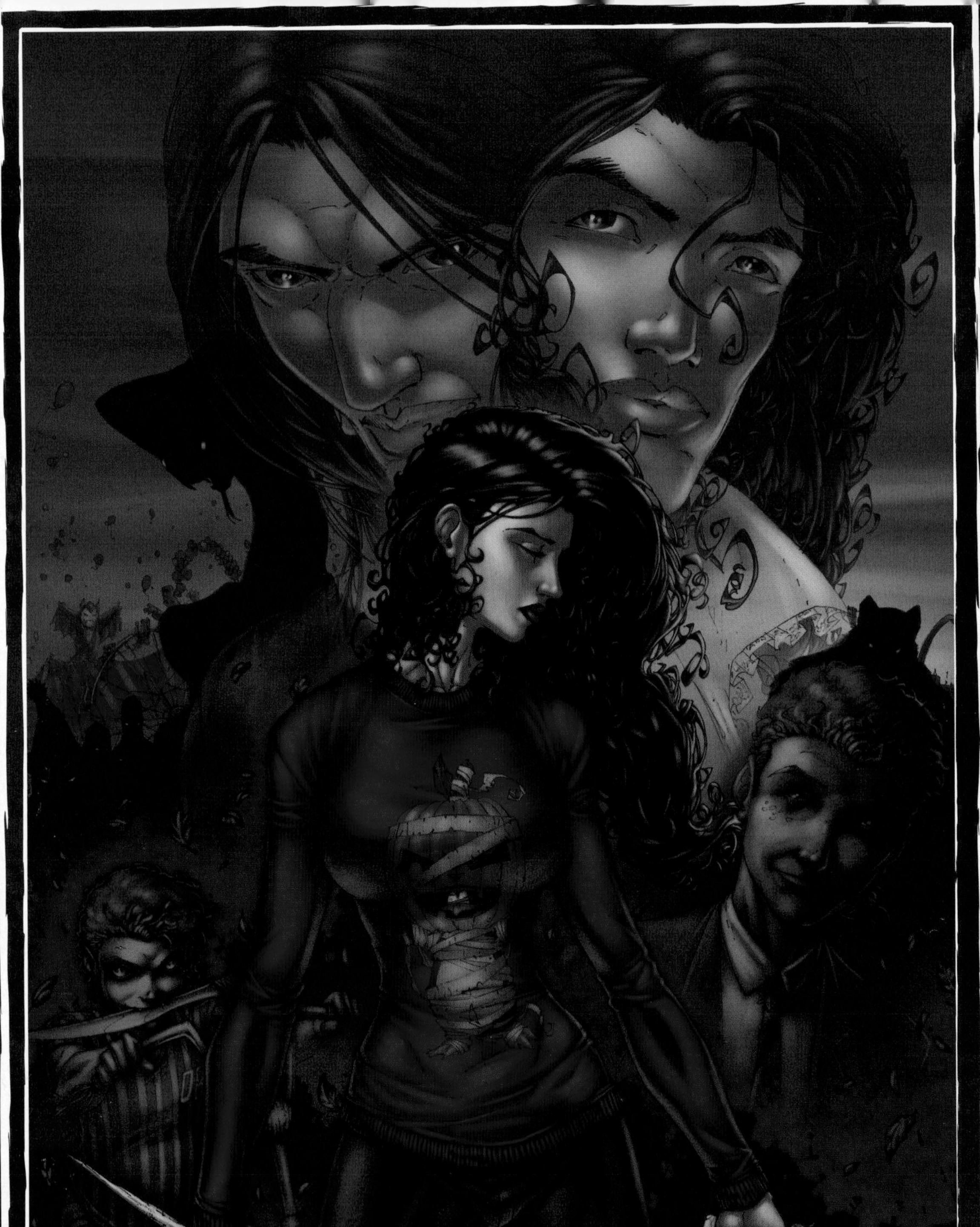

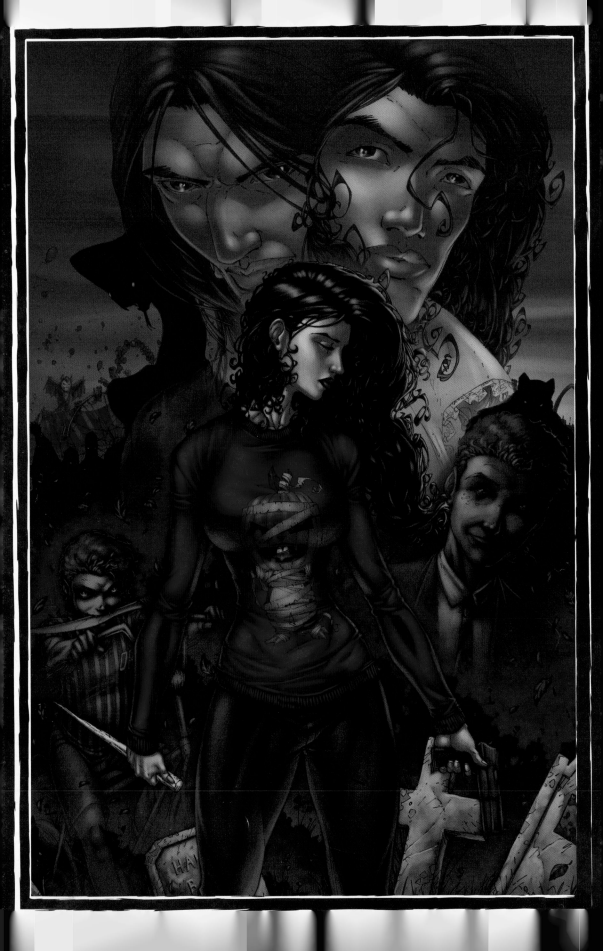

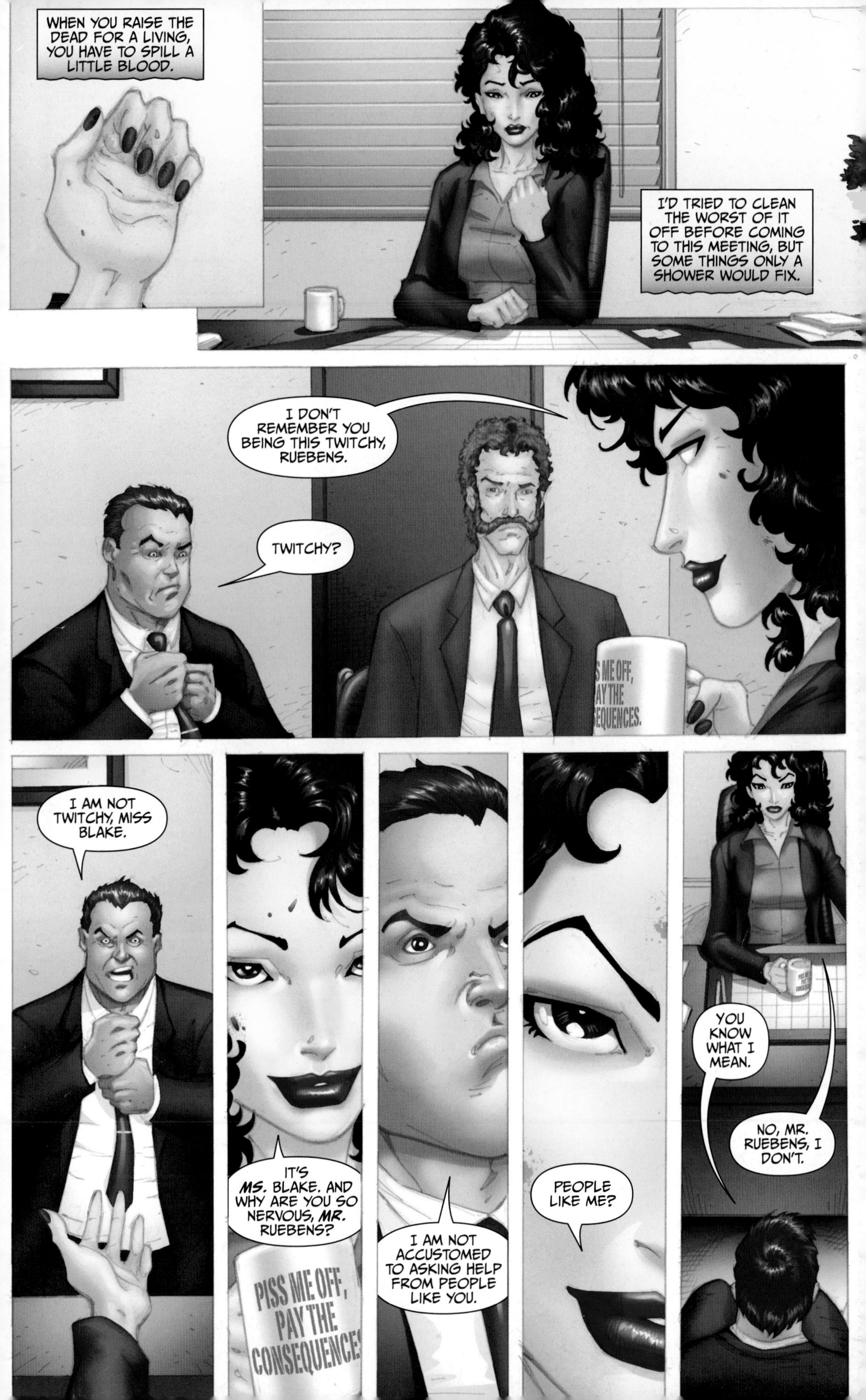
WHEN YOU RAISE THE DEAD FOR A LIVING, YOU HAVE TO SPILL A LITTLE BLOOD.
I'D TRIED TO CLEAN THE WORST OF IT OFF BEFORE COMING TO THIS MEETING, BUT SOME THINGS ONLY A SHOWER WOULD FIX.
I DON'T REMEMBER YOU BEING THIS TWITCHY, RUEBENS.
TWITCHY?
PISS ME OFF, PAY THE CONSEQUENCES.
I AM NOT TWITCHY, MISS BLAKE.
IT'S *MS.* BLAKE. AND WHY ARE YOU SO NERVOUS, *MR.* RUEBENS?
PISS ME OFF, PAY THE CONSEQUENCES
I AM NOT ACCUSTOMED TO ASKING HELP FROM PEOPLE LIKE YOU.
PEOPLE LIKE ME?
YOU KNOW WHAT I MEAN.
NO, MR. RUEBENS, I DON'T.

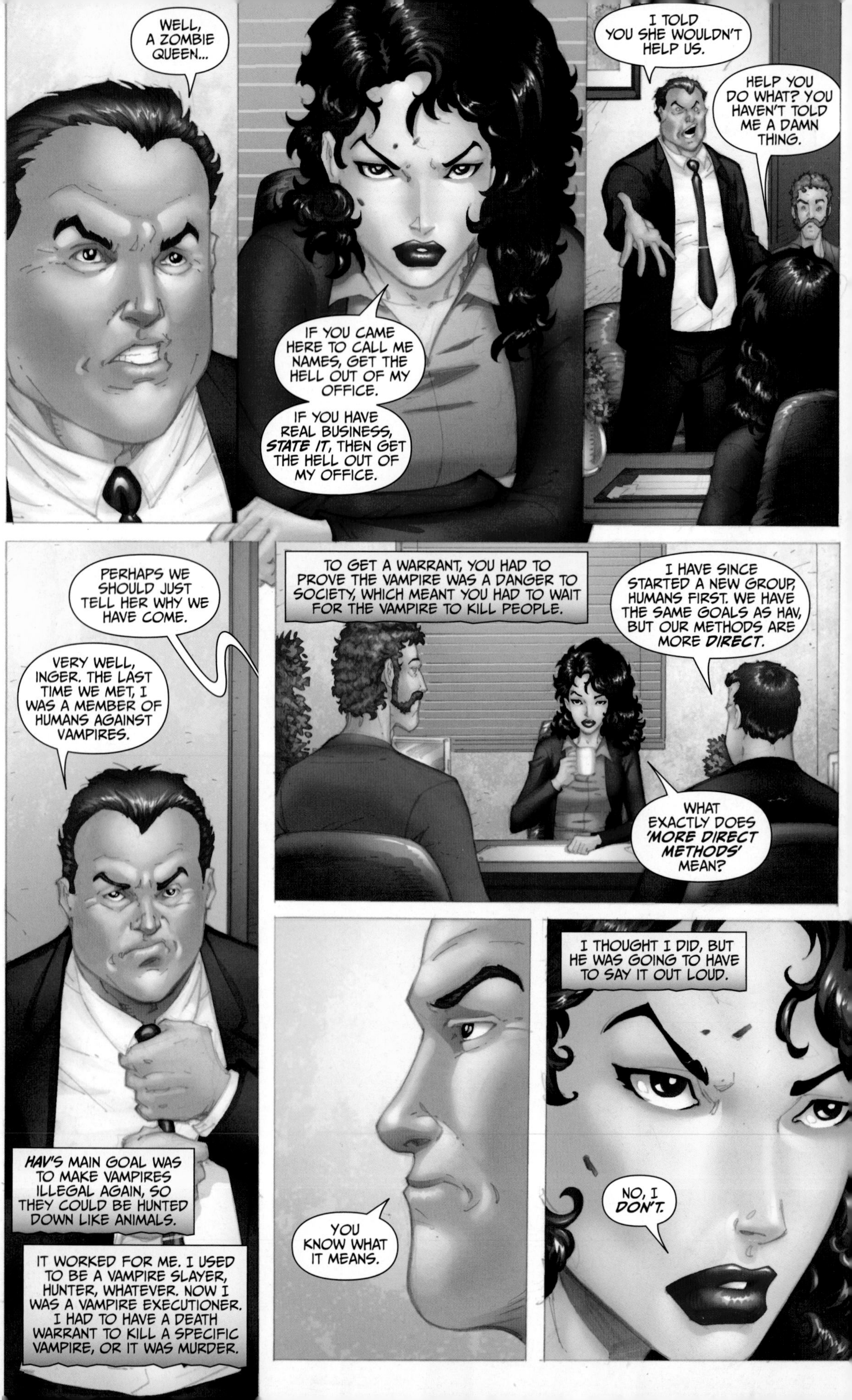
WELL, A ZOMBIE QUEEN...
IF YOU CAME HERE TO CALL ME NAMES, GET THE HELL OUT OF MY OFFICE.
IF YOU HAVE REAL BUSINESS, STATE IT, THEN GET THE HELL OUT OF MY OFFICE.
I TOLD YOU SHE WOULDN'T HELP US.
HELP YOU DO WHAT? YOU HAVEN'T TOLD ME A DAMN THING.
PERHAPS WE SHOULD JUST TELL HER WHY WE HAVE COME.
VERY WELL, INGER. THE LAST TIME WE MET, I WAS A MEMBER OF HUMANS AGAINST VAMPIRES.
HAV'S MAIN GOAL WAS TO MAKE VAMPIRES ILLEGAL AGAIN, SO THEY COULD BE HUNTED DOWN LIKE ANIMALS.
IT WORKED FOR ME. I USED TO BE A VAMPIRE SLAYER, HUNTER, WHATEVER. NOW I WAS A VAMPIRE EXECUTIONER. I HAD TO HAVE A DEATH WARRANT TO KILL A SPECIFIC VAMPIRE, OR IT WAS MURDER.
TO GET A WARRANT, YOU HAD TO PROVE THE VAMPIRE WAS A DANGER TO SOCIETY, WHICH MEANT YOU HAD TO WAIT FOR THE VAMPIRE TO KILL PEOPLE.
I HAVE SINCE STARTED A NEW GROUP, HUMANS FIRST. WE HAVE THE SAME GOALS AS HAV, BUT OUR METHODS ARE MORE DIRECT.
WHAT EXACTLY DOES 'MORE DIRECT METHODS' MEAN?
YOU KNOW WHAT IT MEANS.
I THOUGHT I DID, BUT HE WAS GOING TO HAVE TO SAY IT OUT LOUD.
NO, I DON'T.

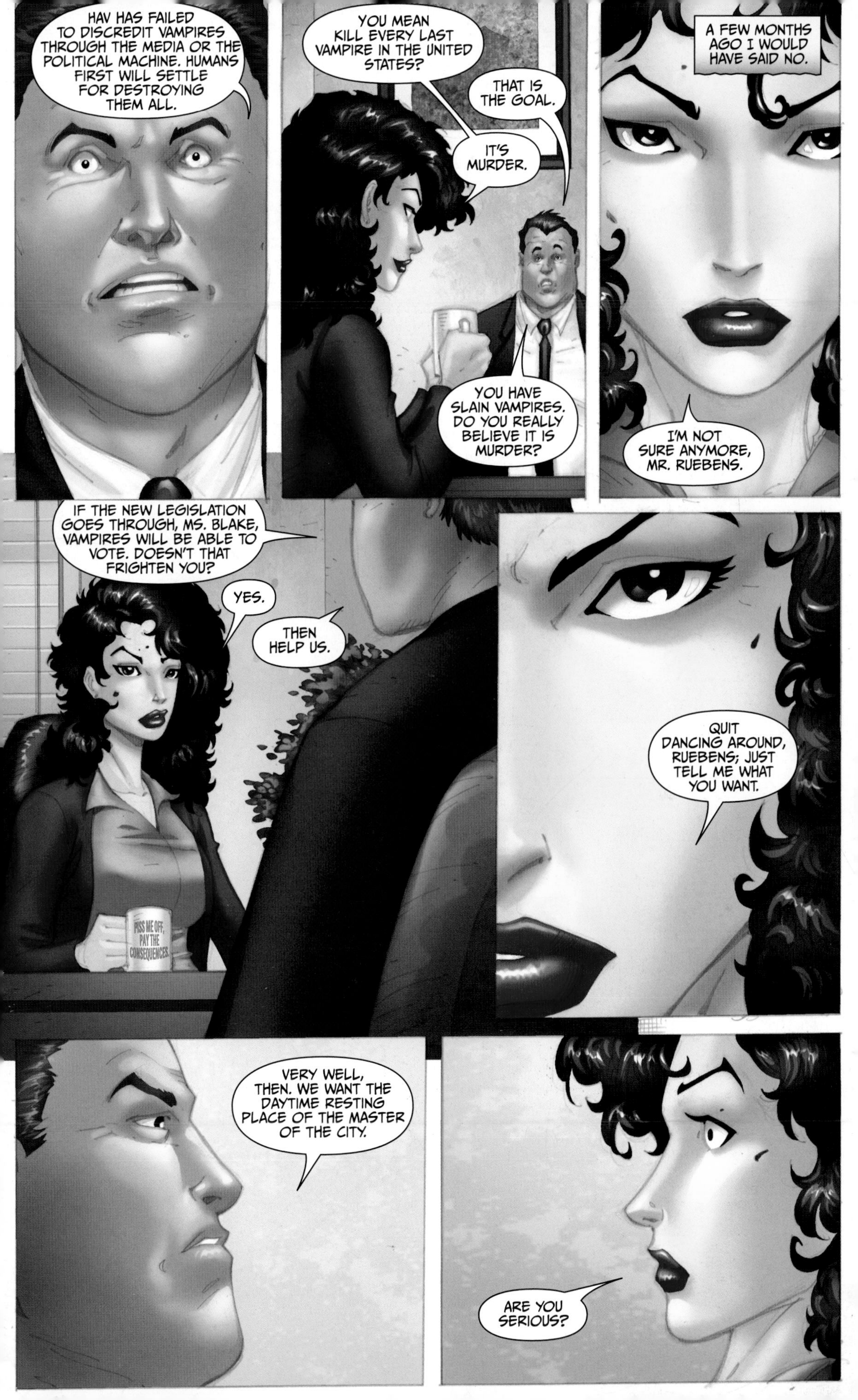
HAV HAS FAILED TO DISCREDIT VAMPIRES THROUGH THE MEDIA OR THE POLITICAL MACHINE. HUMANS FIRST WILL SETTLE FOR DESTROYING THEM ALL.
YOU MEAN KILL EVERY LAST VAMPIRE IN THE UNITED STATES?
THAT IS THE GOAL.
IT'S MURDER.
YOU HAVE SLAIN VAMPIRES. DO YOU REALLY BELIEVE IT IS MURDER?
A FEW MONTHS AGO I WOULD HAVE SAID NO.
I'M NOT SURE ANYMORE, MR. RUEBENS.
IF THE NEW LEGISLATION GOES THROUGH, MS. BLAKE, VAMPIRES WILL BE ABLE TO VOTE. DOESN'T THAT FRIGHTEN YOU?
YES.
THEN HELP US.
PISS ME OFF, PAY THE CONSEQUENCES.
QUIT DANCING AROUND, RUEBENS; JUST TELL ME WHAT YOU WANT.
VERY WELL, THEN. WE WANT THE DAYTIME RESTING PLACE OF THE MASTER OF THE CITY.
ARE YOU SERIOUS?

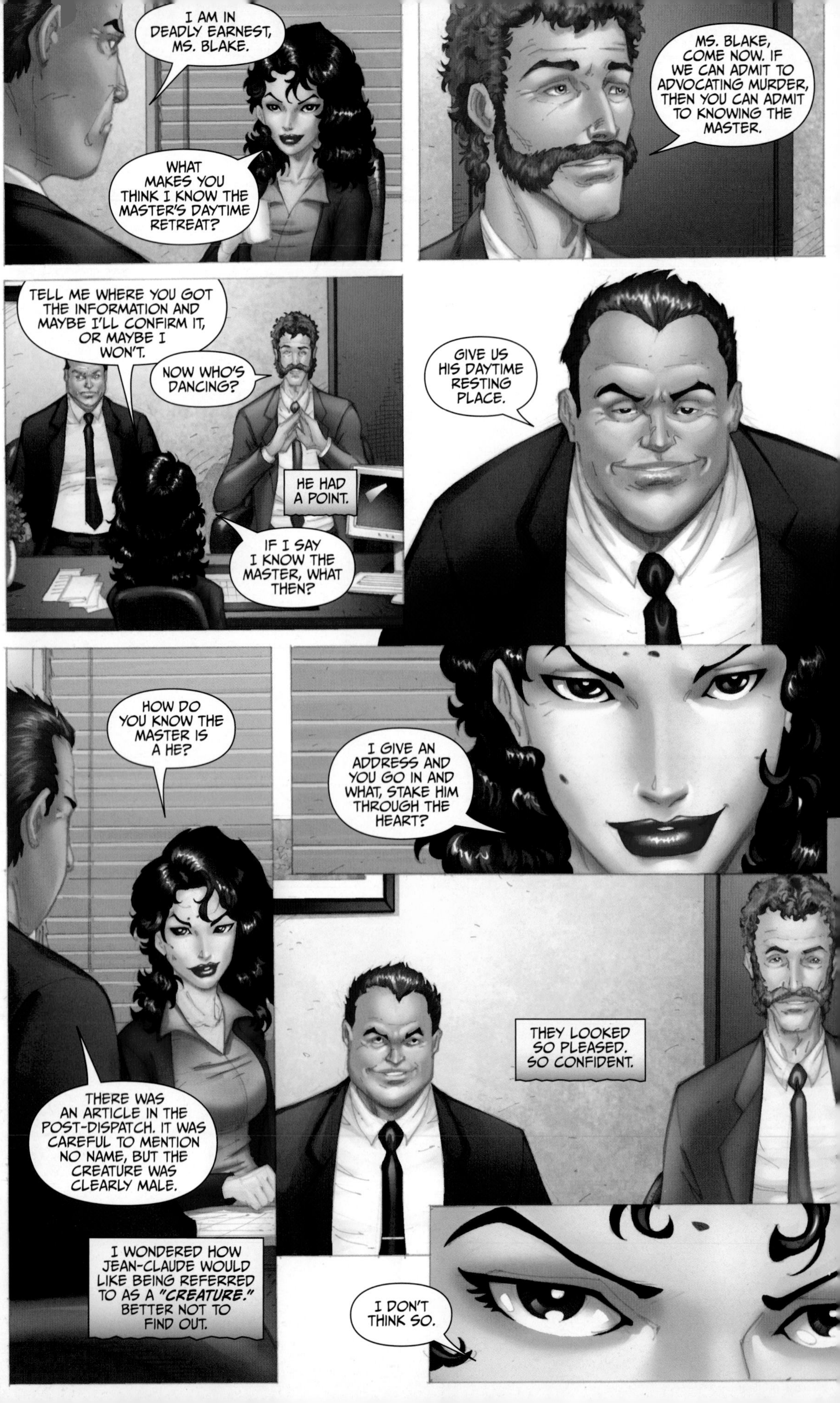
I AM IN DEADLY EARNEST, MS. BLAKE.
WHAT MAKES YOU THINK I KNOW THE MASTER'S DAYTIME RETREAT?
MS. BLAKE, COME NOW. IF WE CAN ADMIT TO ADVOCATING MURDER, THEN YOU CAN ADMIT TO KNOWING THE MASTER.
TELL ME WHERE YOU GOT THE INFORMATION AND MAYBE I'LL CONFIRM IT, OR MAYBE I WON'T.
NOW WHO'S DANCING?
HE HAD A POINT.
IF I SAY I KNOW THE MASTER, WHAT THEN?
GIVE US HIS DAYTIME RESTING PLACE.
I GIVE AN ADDRESS AND YOU GO IN AND WHAT, STAKE HIM THROUGH THE HEART?
HOW DO YOU KNOW THE MASTER IS A HE?
THERE WAS AN ARTICLE IN THE POST-DISPATCH. IT WAS CAREFUL TO MENTION NO NAME, BUT THE CREATURE WAS CLEARLY MALE.
I WONDERED HOW JEAN-CLAUDE WOULD LIKE BEING REFERRED TO AS A "CREATURE." BETTER NOT TO FIND OUT.
THEY LOOKED SO PLEASED. SO CONFIDENT.
I DON'T THINK SO.

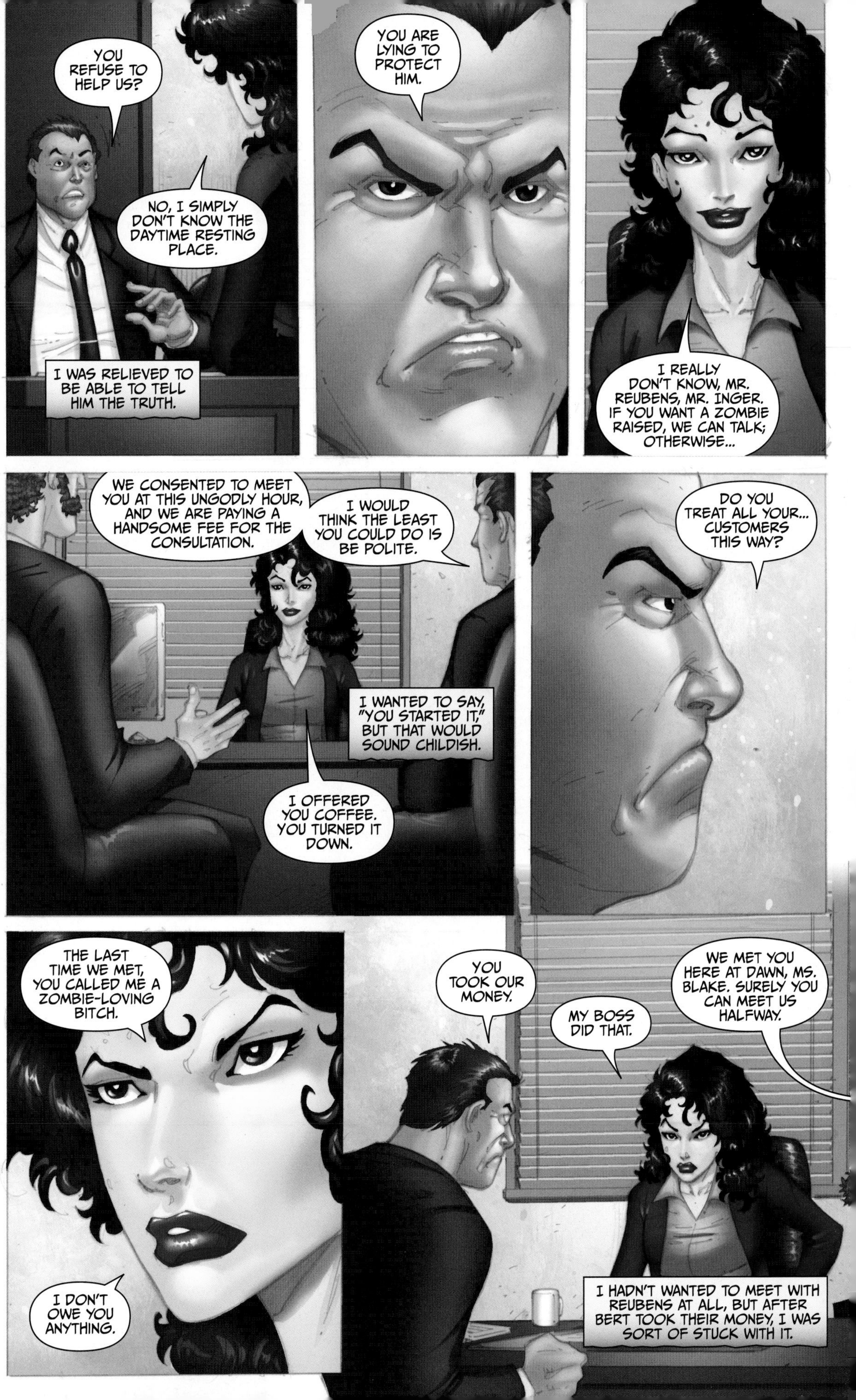
YOU REFUSE TO HELP US?
NO, I SIMPLY DON'T KNOW THE DAYTIME RESTING PLACE.
I WAS RELIEVED TO BE ABLE TO TELL HIM THE TRUTH.
YOU ARE LYING TO PROTECT HIM.
I REALLY DON'T KNOW, MR. REUBENS, MR. INGER. IF YOU WANT A ZOMBIE RAISED, WE CAN TALK; OTHERWISE...
WE CONSENTED TO MEET YOU AT THIS UNGODLY HOUR, AND WE ARE PAYING A HANDSOME FEE FOR THE CONSULTATION.
I WOULD THINK THE LEAST YOU COULD DO IS BE POLITE.
I WANTED TO SAY, "YOU STARTED IT," BUT THAT WOULD SOUND CHILDISH.
I OFFERED YOU COFFEE. YOU TURNED IT DOWN.
DO YOU TREAT ALL YOUR... CUSTOMERS THIS WAY?
THE LAST TIME WE MET, YOU CALLED ME A ZOMBIE-LOVING BITCH.
I DON'T OWE YOU ANYTHING.
YOU TOOK OUR MONEY.
MY BOSS DID THAT.
WE MET YOU HERE AT DAWN, MS. BLAKE. SURELY YOU CAN MEET US HALFWAY.
I HADN'T WANTED TO MEET WITH REUBENS AT ALL, BUT AFTER BERT TOOK THEIR MONEY, I WAS SORT OF STUCK WITH IT.

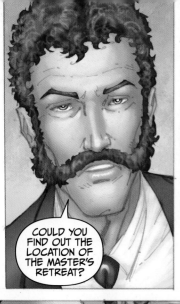

COULD YOU FIND OUT THE LOCATION OF THE MASTER'S RETREAT?

PROBABLY, BUT IF I DID, I WOULDN'T GIVE IT TO YOU.

WHY NOT?

BECAUSE SHE IS IN LEAGUE WITH HIM.

HUSH, JEREMY.

SHE'S--

PLEASE, JEREMY, FOR THE CAUSE.

WHY NOT, MS. BLAKE?

I'VE KILLED MASTER VAMPIRES BEFORE, NONE OF THEM WITH A STAKE.

HOW THEN?

NO, MR. INGER, IF YOU WANT LESSONS IN VAMPIRE SLAYING, YOU'RE GOING TO HAVE TO GO ELSEWHERE.

JUST BY ANSWERING YOUR QUESTIONS, I COULD BE CHARGED AS AN ACCESSORY TO MURDER.

WOULD YOU TELL US IF WE HAD A BETTER PLAN?

JEAN-CLAUDE, DEAD, REALLY DEAD. IT WOULD CERTAINLY MAKE MY LIFE EASIER, BUT...BUT.

PISS ME OFF, PAY THE CONSEQUENCES.

I DON'T KNOW.

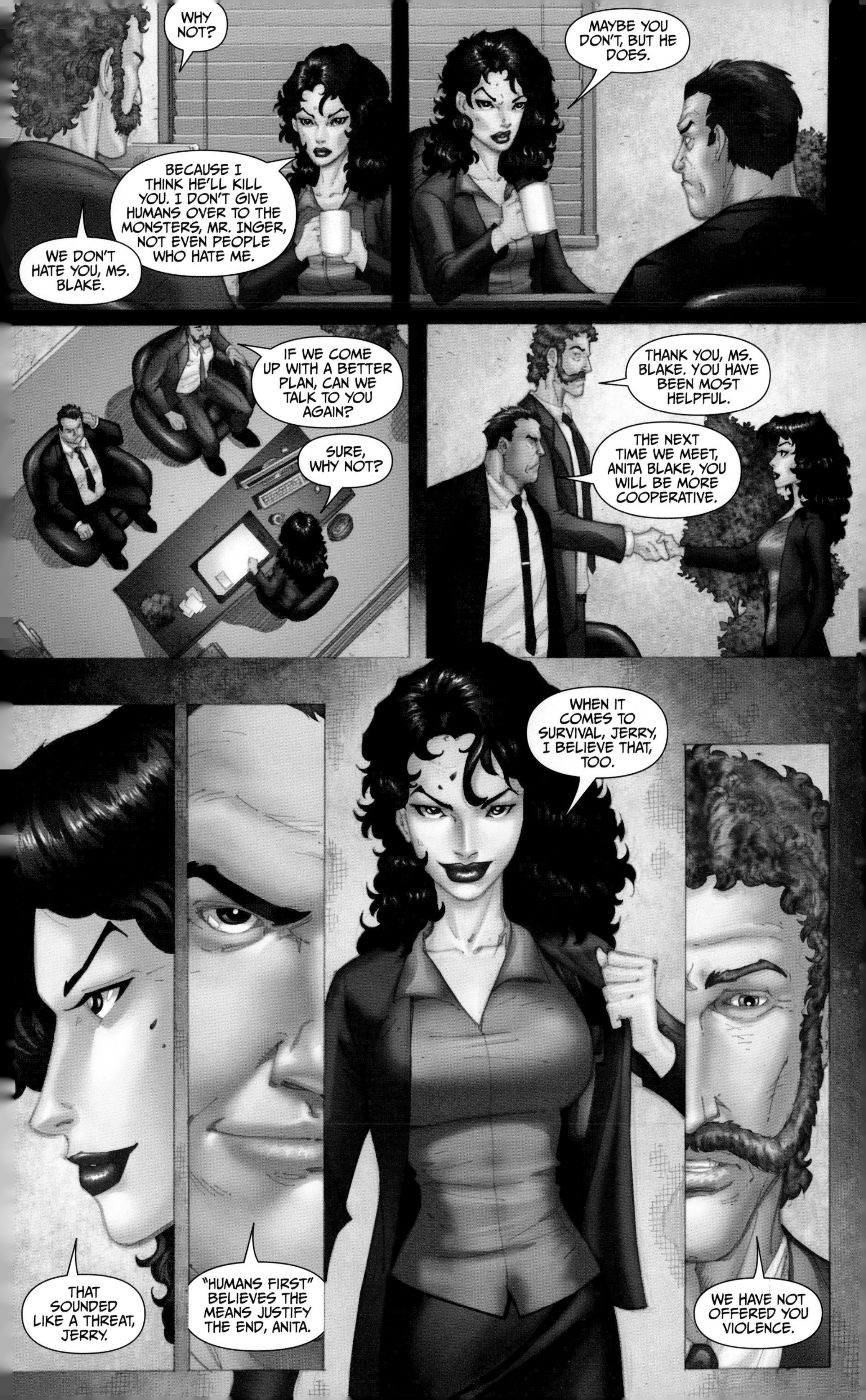
WHY NOT?
BECAUSE I THINK HE'LL KILL YOU. I DON'T GIVE HUMANS OVER TO THE MONSTERS, MR. INGER, NOT EVEN PEOPLE WHO HATE ME.
WE DON'T HATE YOU, MS. BLAKE.
MAYBE YOU DON'T, BUT HE DOES.
IF WE COME UP WITH A BETTER PLAN, CAN WE TALK TO YOU AGAIN?
SURE, WHY NOT?
THANK YOU, MS. BLAKE. YOU HAVE BEEN MOST HELPFUL.
THE NEXT TIME WE MEET, ANITA BLAKE, YOU WILL BE MORE COOPERATIVE.
THAT SOUNDED LIKE A THREAT, JERRY.
"HUMANS FIRST" BELIEVES THE MEANS JUSTIFY THE END, ANITA.
WE HAVE NOT OFFERED YOU VIOLENCE.
WHEN IT COMES TO SURVIVAL, JERRY, I BELIEVE THAT, TOO.

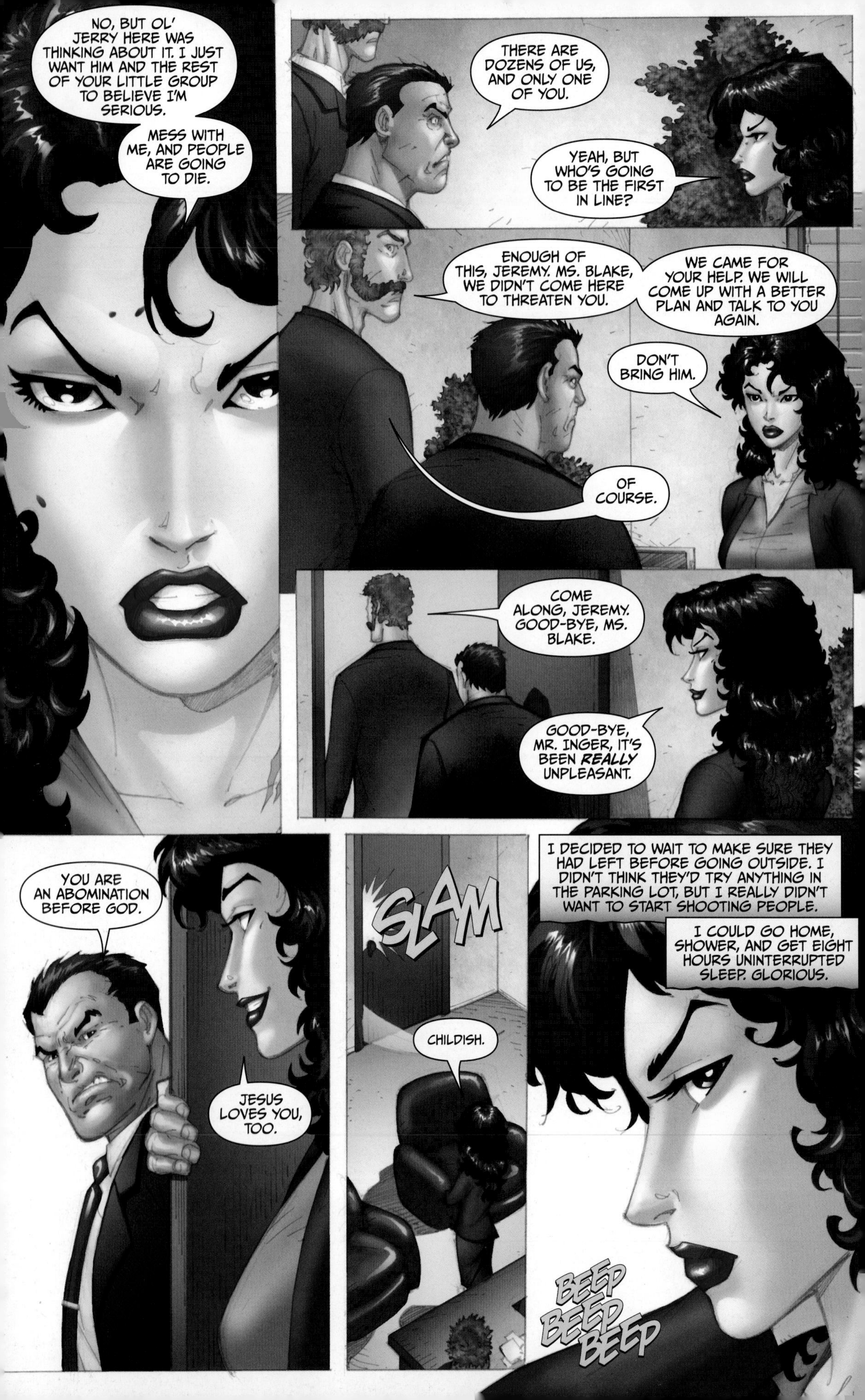
NO, BUT OL' JERRY HERE WAS THINKING ABOUT IT. I JUST WANT HIM AND THE REST OF YOUR LITTLE GROUP TO BELIEVE I'M SERIOUS.
MESS WITH ME, AND PEOPLE ARE GOING TO DIE.
THERE ARE DOZENS OF US, AND ONLY ONE OF YOU.
YEAH, BUT WHO'S GOING TO BE THE FIRST IN LINE?
ENOUGH OF THIS, JEREMY. MS. BLAKE, WE DIDN'T COME HERE TO THREATEN YOU.
WE CAME FOR YOUR HELP. WE WILL COME UP WITH A BETTER PLAN AND TALK TO YOU AGAIN.
DON'T BRING HIM.
OF COURSE.
COME ALONG, JEREMY. GOOD-BYE, MS. BLAKE.
GOOD-BYE, MR. INGER, IT'S BEEN *REALLY* UNPLEASANT.
YOU ARE AN ABOMINATION BEFORE GOD.
JESUS LOVES YOU, TOO.
SLAM
CHILDISH.
I DECIDED TO WAIT TO MAKE SURE THEY HAD LEFT BEFORE GOING OUTSIDE. I DIDN'T THINK THEY'D TRY ANYTHING IN THE PARKING LOT, BUT I REALLY DIDN'T WANT TO START SHOOTING PEOPLE.
I COULD GO HOME, SHOWER, AND GET EIGHT HOURS UNINTERRUPTED SLEEP. GLORIOUS.
BEEP BEEP BEEP

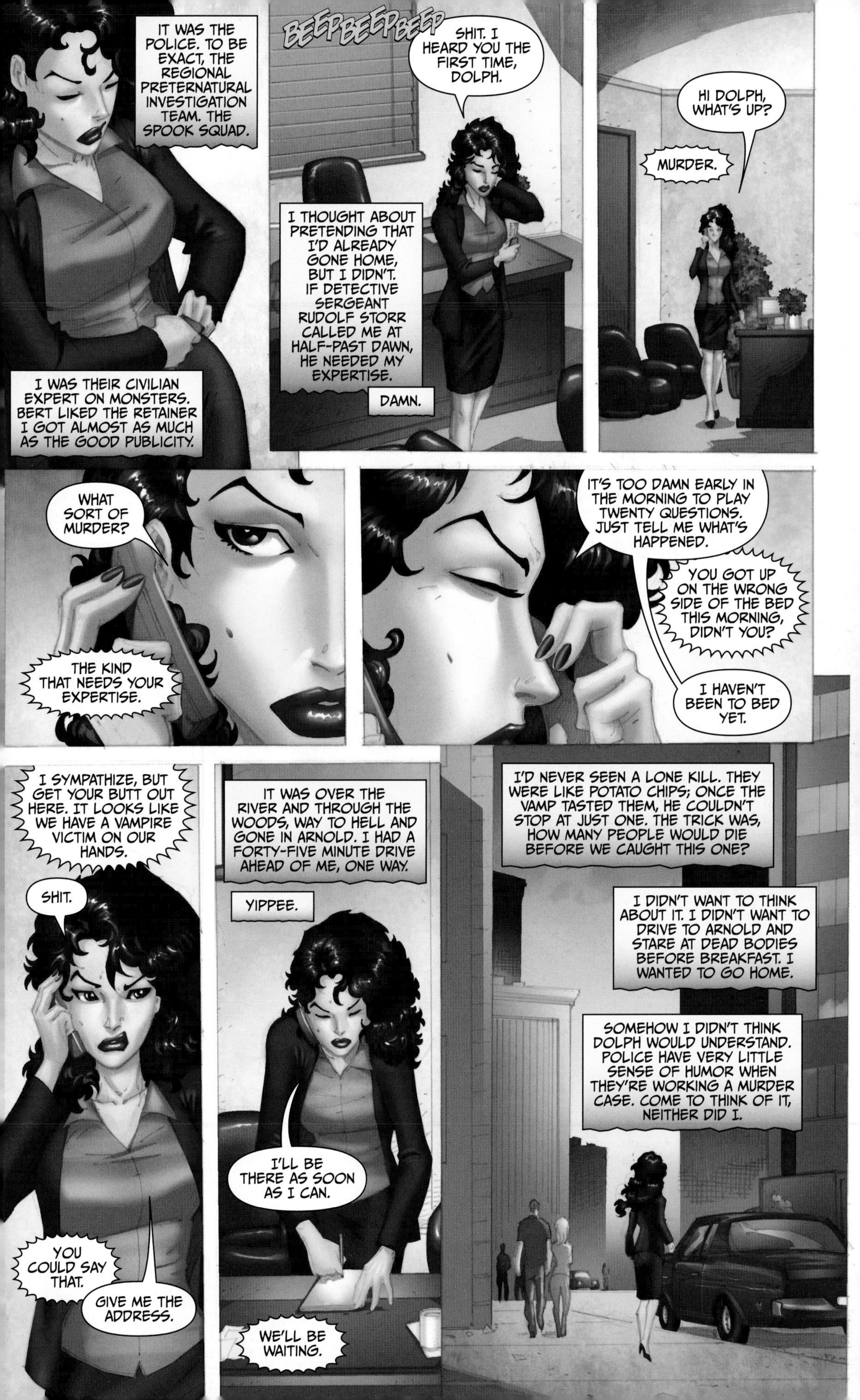
IT WAS THE POLICE. TO BE EXACT, THE REGIONAL PRETERNATURAL INVESTIGATION TEAM. THE SPOOK SQUAD.
I WAS THEIR CIVILIAN EXPERT ON MONSTERS. BERT LIKED THE RETAINER I GOT ALMOST AS MUCH AS THE GOOD PUBLICITY.
BEEPBEEPBEEP
SHIT. I HEARD YOU THE FIRST TIME, DOLPH.
I THOUGHT ABOUT PRETENDING THAT I'D ALREADY GONE HOME, BUT I DIDN'T. IF DETECTIVE SERGEANT RUDOLF STORR CALLED ME AT HALF-PAST DAWN, HE NEEDED MY EXPERTISE.
DAMN.
HI DOLPH, WHAT'S UP?
MURDER.
WHAT SORT OF MURDER?
THE KIND THAT NEEDS YOUR EXPERTISE.
IT'S TOO DAMN EARLY IN THE MORNING TO PLAY TWENTY QUESTIONS. JUST TELL ME WHAT'S HAPPENED.
YOU GOT UP ON THE WRONG SIDE OF THE BED THIS MORNING, DIDN'T YOU?
I HAVEN'T BEEN TO BED YET.
I SYMPATHIZE, BUT GET YOUR BUTT OUT HERE. IT LOOKS LIKE WE HAVE A VAMPIRE VICTIM ON OUR HANDS.
SHIT.
YOU COULD SAY THAT.
GIVE ME THE ADDRESS.
IT WAS OVER THE RIVER AND THROUGH THE WOODS, WAY TO HELL AND GONE IN ARNOLD. I HAD A FORTY-FIVE MINUTE DRIVE AHEAD OF ME, ONE WAY.
YIPPEE.
I'LL BE THERE AS SOON AS I CAN.
WE'LL BE WAITING.
I'D NEVER SEEN A LONE KILL. THEY WERE LIKE POTATO CHIPS; ONCE THE VAMP TASTED THEM, HE COULDN'T STOP AT JUST ONE. THE TRICK WAS, HOW MANY PEOPLE WOULD DIE BEFORE WE CAUGHT THIS ONE?
I DIDN'T WANT TO THINK ABOUT IT. I DIDN'T WANT TO DRIVE TO ARNOLD AND STARE AT DEAD BODIES BEFORE BREAKFAST. I WANTED TO GO HOME.
SOMEHOW I DIDN'T THINK DOLPH WOULD UNDERSTAND. POLICE HAVE VERY LITTLE SENSE OF HUMOR WHEN THEY'RE WORKING A MURDER CASE. COME TO THINK OF IT, NEITHER DID I.

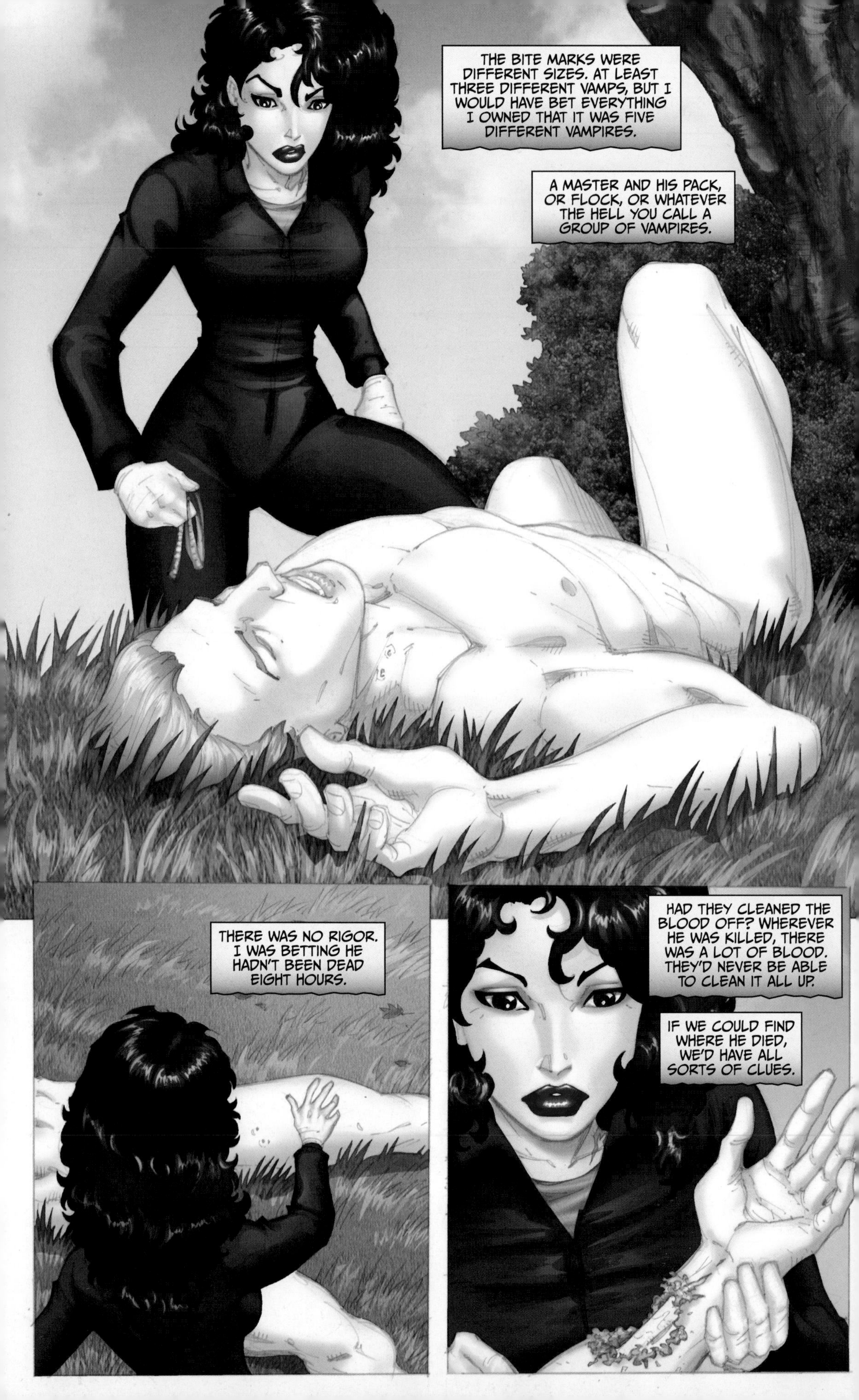
THE BITE MARKS WERE DIFFERENT SIZES. AT LEAST THREE DIFFERENT VAMPS, BUT I WOULD HAVE BET EVERYTHING I OWNED THAT IT WAS FIVE DIFFERENT VAMPIRES.
A MASTER AND HIS PACK, OR FLOCK, OR WHATEVER THE HELL YOU CALL A GROUP OF VAMPIRES.
THERE WAS NO RIGOR. I WAS BETTING HE HADN'T BEEN DEAD EIGHT HOURS.
HAD THEY CLEANED THE BLOOD OFF? WHEREVER HE WAS KILLED, THERE WAS A LOT OF BLOOD. THEY'D NEVER BE ABLE TO CLEAN IT ALL UP.
IF WE COULD FIND WHERE HE DIED, WE'D HAVE ALL SORTS OF CLUES.

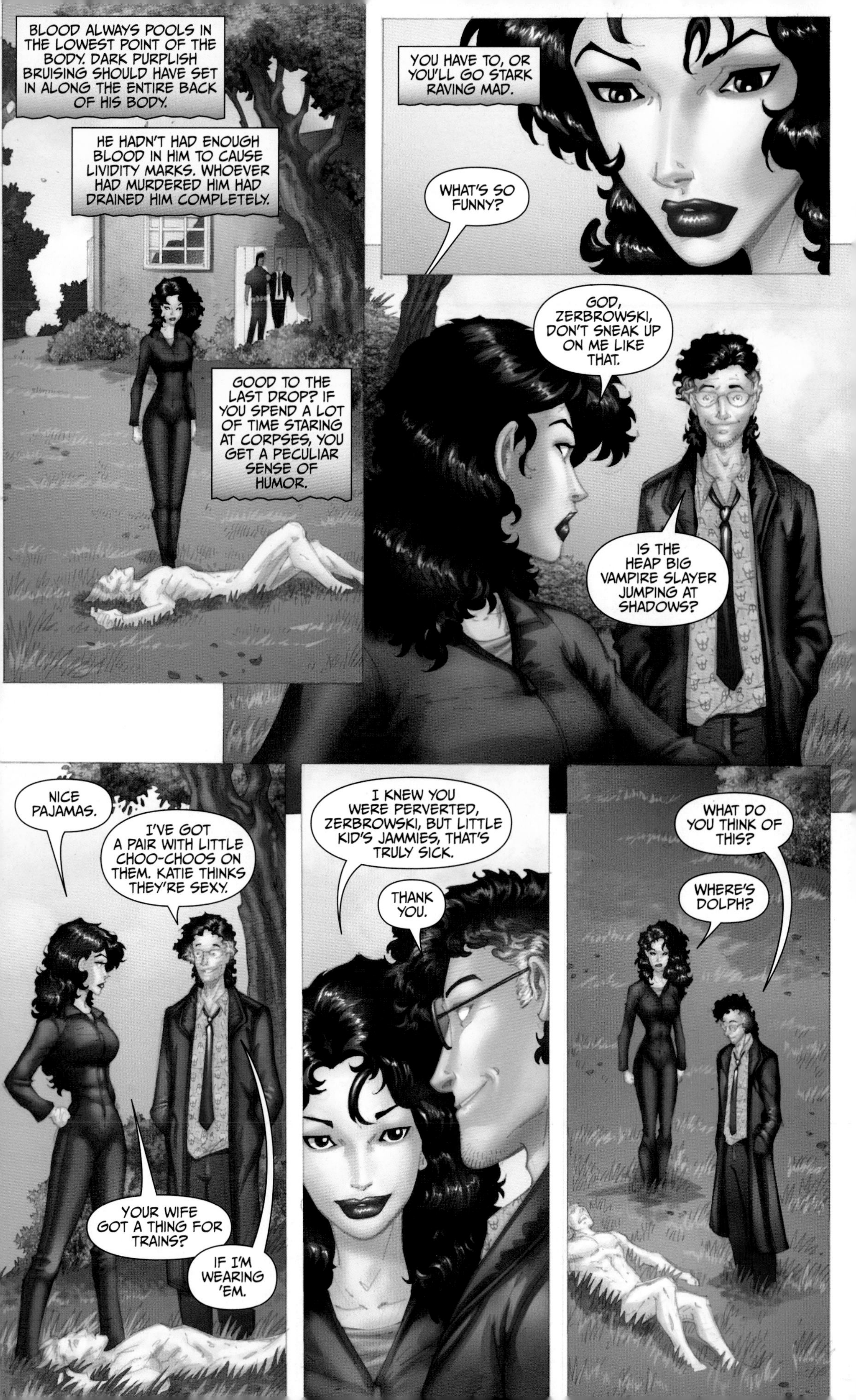
BLOOD ALWAYS POOLS IN THE LOWEST POINT OF THE BODY. DARK PURPLISH BRUISING SHOULD HAVE SET IN ALONG THE ENTIRE BACK OF HIS BODY.
HE HADN'T HAD ENOUGH BLOOD IN HIM TO CAUSE LIVIDITY MARKS. WHOEVER HAD MURDERED HIM HAD DRAINED HIM COMPLETELY.
GOOD TO THE LAST DROP? IF YOU SPEND A LOT OF TIME STARING AT CORPSES, YOU GET A PECULIAR SENSE OF HUMOR.
YOU HAVE TO, OR YOU'LL GO STARK RAVING MAD.
WHAT'S SO FUNNY?
GOD, ZERBROWSKI, DON'T SNEAK UP ON ME LIKE THAT.
IS THE HEAP BIG VAMPIRE SLAYER JUMPING AT SHADOWS?
NICE PAJAMAS.
I'VE GOT A PAIR WITH LITTLE CHOO-CHOOS ON THEM. KATIE THINKS THEY'RE SEXY.
YOUR WIFE GOT A THING FOR TRAINS?
IF I'M WEARING 'EM.
I KNEW YOU WERE PERVERTED, ZERBROWSKI, BUT LITTLE KID'S JAMMIES, THAT'S TRULY SICK.
THANK YOU.
WHAT DO YOU THINK OF THIS?
WHERE'S DOLPH?

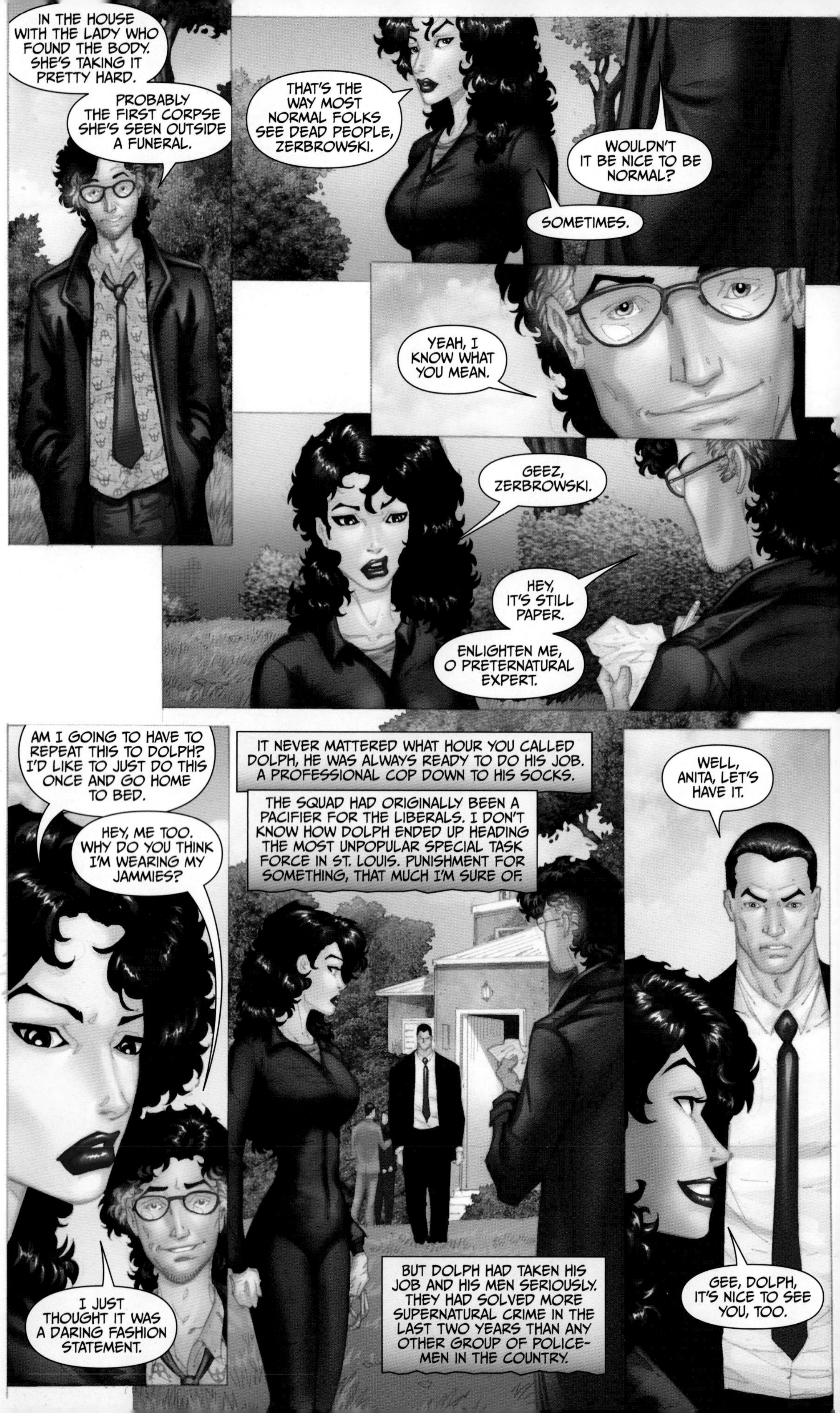
IN THE HOUSE WITH THE LADY WHO FOUND THE BODY. SHE'S TAKING IT PRETTY HARD.
PROBABLY THE FIRST CORPSE SHE'S SEEN OUTSIDE A FUNERAL.
THAT'S THE WAY MOST NORMAL FOLKS SEE DEAD PEOPLE, ZERBROWSKI.
WOULDN'T IT BE NICE TO BE NORMAL?
SOMETIMES.
YEAH, I KNOW WHAT YOU MEAN.
GEEZ, ZERBROWSKI.
HEY, IT'S STILL PAPER.
ENLIGHTEN ME, O PRETERNATURAL EXPERT.
AM I GOING TO HAVE TO REPEAT THIS TO DOLPH? I'D LIKE TO JUST DO THIS ONCE AND GO HOME TO BED.
HEY, ME TOO. WHY DO YOU THINK I'M WEARING MY JAMMIES?
I JUST THOUGHT IT WAS A DARING FASHION STATEMENT.
IT NEVER MATTERED WHAT HOUR YOU CALLED DOLPH, HE WAS ALWAYS READY TO DO HIS JOB. A PROFESSIONAL COP DOWN TO HIS SOCKS.
THE SQUAD HAD ORIGINALLY BEEN A PACIFIER FOR THE LIBERALS. I DON'T KNOW HOW DOLPH ENDED UP HEADING THE MOST UNPOPULAR SPECIAL TASK FORCE IN ST. LOUIS. PUNISHMENT FOR SOMETHING, THAT MUCH I'M SURE OF.
BUT DOLPH HAD TAKEN HIS JOB AND HIS MEN SERIOUSLY. THEY HAD SOLVED MORE SUPERNATURAL CRIME IN THE LAST TWO YEARS THAN ANY OTHER GROUP OF POLICE-MEN IN THE COUNTRY.
WELL, ANITA, LET'S HAVE IT.
GEE, DOLPH, IT'S NICE TO SEE YOU, TOO.

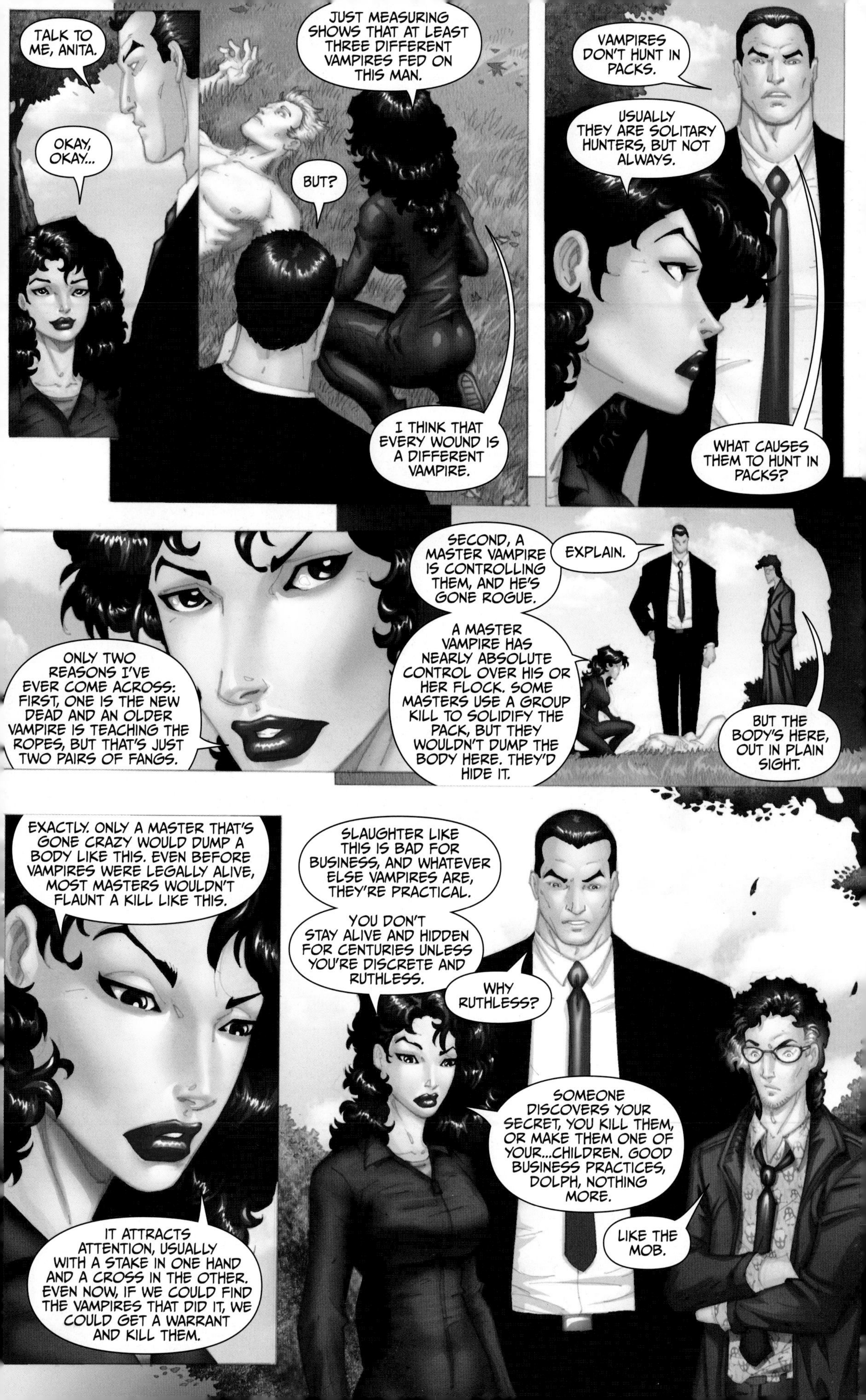
TALK TO ME, ANITA.
OKAY, OKAY...
JUST MEASURING SHOWS THAT AT LEAST THREE DIFFERENT VAMPIRES FED ON THIS MAN.
BUT?
I THINK THAT EVERY WOUND IS A DIFFERENT VAMPIRE.
VAMPIRES DON'T HUNT IN PACKS.
USUALLY THEY ARE SOLITARY HUNTERS, BUT NOT ALWAYS.
WHAT CAUSES THEM TO HUNT IN PACKS?
ONLY TWO REASONS I'VE EVER COME ACROSS: FIRST, ONE IS THE NEW DEAD AND AN OLDER VAMPIRE IS TEACHING THE ROPES, BUT THAT'S JUST TWO PAIRS OF FANGS.
SECOND, A MASTER VAMPIRE IS CONTROLLING THEM, AND HE'S GONE ROGUE.
EXPLAIN.
A MASTER VAMPIRE HAS NEARLY ABSOLUTE CONTROL OVER HIS OR HER FLOCK. SOME MASTERS USE A GROUP KILL TO SOLIDIFY THE PACK, BUT THEY WOULDN'T DUMP THE BODY HERE. THEY'D HIDE IT.
BUT THE BODY'S HERE, OUT IN PLAIN SIGHT.
EXACTLY. ONLY A MASTER THAT'S GONE CRAZY WOULD DUMP A BODY LIKE THIS. EVEN BEFORE VAMPIRES WERE LEGALLY ALIVE, MOST MASTERS WOULDN'T FLAUNT A KILL LIKE THIS.
IT ATTRACTS ATTENTION, USUALLY WITH A STAKE IN ONE HAND AND A CROSS IN THE OTHER. EVEN NOW, IF WE COULD FIND THE VAMPIRES THAT DID IT, WE COULD GET A WARRANT AND KILL THEM.
SLAUGHTER LIKE THIS IS BAD FOR BUSINESS, AND WHATEVER ELSE VAMPIRES ARE, THEY'RE PRACTICAL.
YOU DON'T STAY ALIVE AND HIDDEN FOR CENTURIES UNLESS YOU'RE DISCRETE AND RUTHLESS.
WHY RUTHLESS?
SOMEONE DISCOVERS YOUR SECRET, YOU KILL THEM, OR MAKE THEM ONE OF YOUR...CHILDREN. GOOD BUSINESS PRACTICES, DOLPH, NOTHING MORE.
LIKE THE MOB.

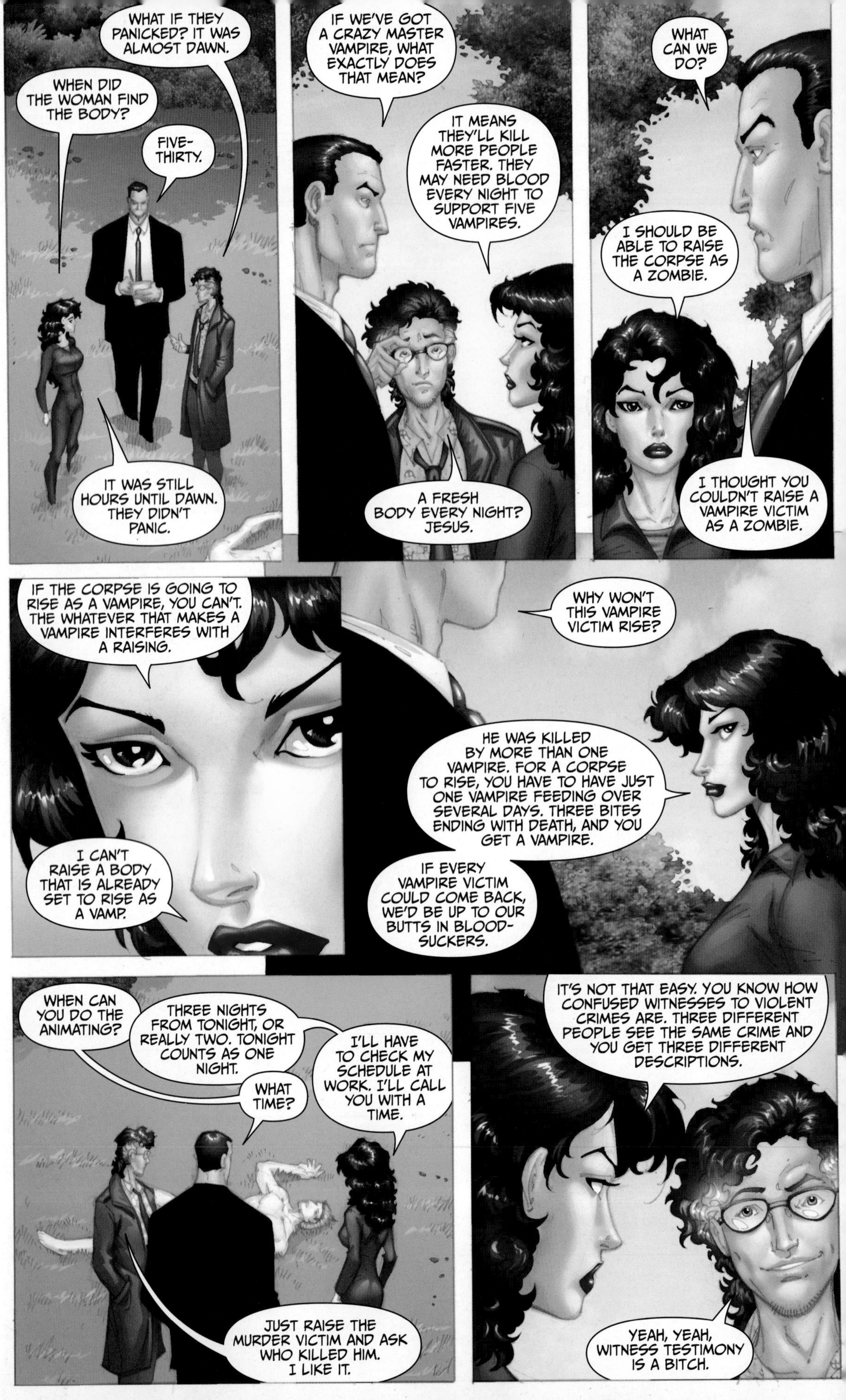
WHEN DID THE WOMAN FIND THE BODY?
FIVE-THIRTY.
WHAT IF THEY PANICKED? IT WAS ALMOST DAWN.
IT WAS STILL HOURS UNTIL DAWN. THEY DIDN'T PANIC.
IF WE'VE GOT A CRAZY MASTER VAMPIRE, WHAT EXACTLY DOES THAT MEAN?
IT MEANS THEY'LL KILL MORE PEOPLE FASTER. THEY MAY NEED BLOOD EVERY NIGHT TO SUPPORT FIVE VAMPIRES.
A FRESH BODY EVERY NIGHT? JESUS.
WHAT CAN WE DO?
I SHOULD BE ABLE TO RAISE THE CORPSE AS A ZOMBIE.
I THOUGHT YOU COULDN'T RAISE A VAMPIRE VICTIM AS A ZOMBIE.
IF THE CORPSE IS GOING TO RISE AS A VAMPIRE, YOU CAN'T. THE WHATEVER THAT MAKES A VAMPIRE INTERFERES WITH A RAISING.
I CAN'T RAISE A BODY THAT IS ALREADY SET TO RISE AS A VAMP.
WHY WON'T THIS VAMPIRE VICTIM RISE?
HE WAS KILLED BY MORE THAN ONE VAMPIRE. FOR A CORPSE TO RISE, YOU HAVE TO HAVE JUST ONE VAMPIRE FEEDING OVER SEVERAL DAYS. THREE BITES ENDING WITH DEATH, AND YOU GET A VAMPIRE.
IF EVERY VAMPIRE VICTIM COULD COME BACK, WE'D BE UP TO OUR BUTTS IN BLOOD-SUCKERS.
WHEN CAN YOU DO THE ANIMATING?
THREE NIGHTS FROM TONIGHT, OR REALLY TWO. TONIGHT COUNTS AS ONE NIGHT.
WHAT TIME?
I'LL HAVE TO CHECK MY SCHEDULE AT WORK. I'LL CALL YOU WITH A TIME.
JUST RAISE THE MURDER VICTIM AND ASK WHO KILLED HIM. I LIKE IT.
IT'S NOT THAT EASY. YOU KNOW HOW CONFUSED WITNESSES TO VIOLENT CRIMES ARE. THREE DIFFERENT PEOPLE SEE THE SAME CRIME AND YOU GET THREE DIFFERENT DESCRIPTIONS.
YEAH, YEAH, WITNESS TESTIMONY IS A BITCH.

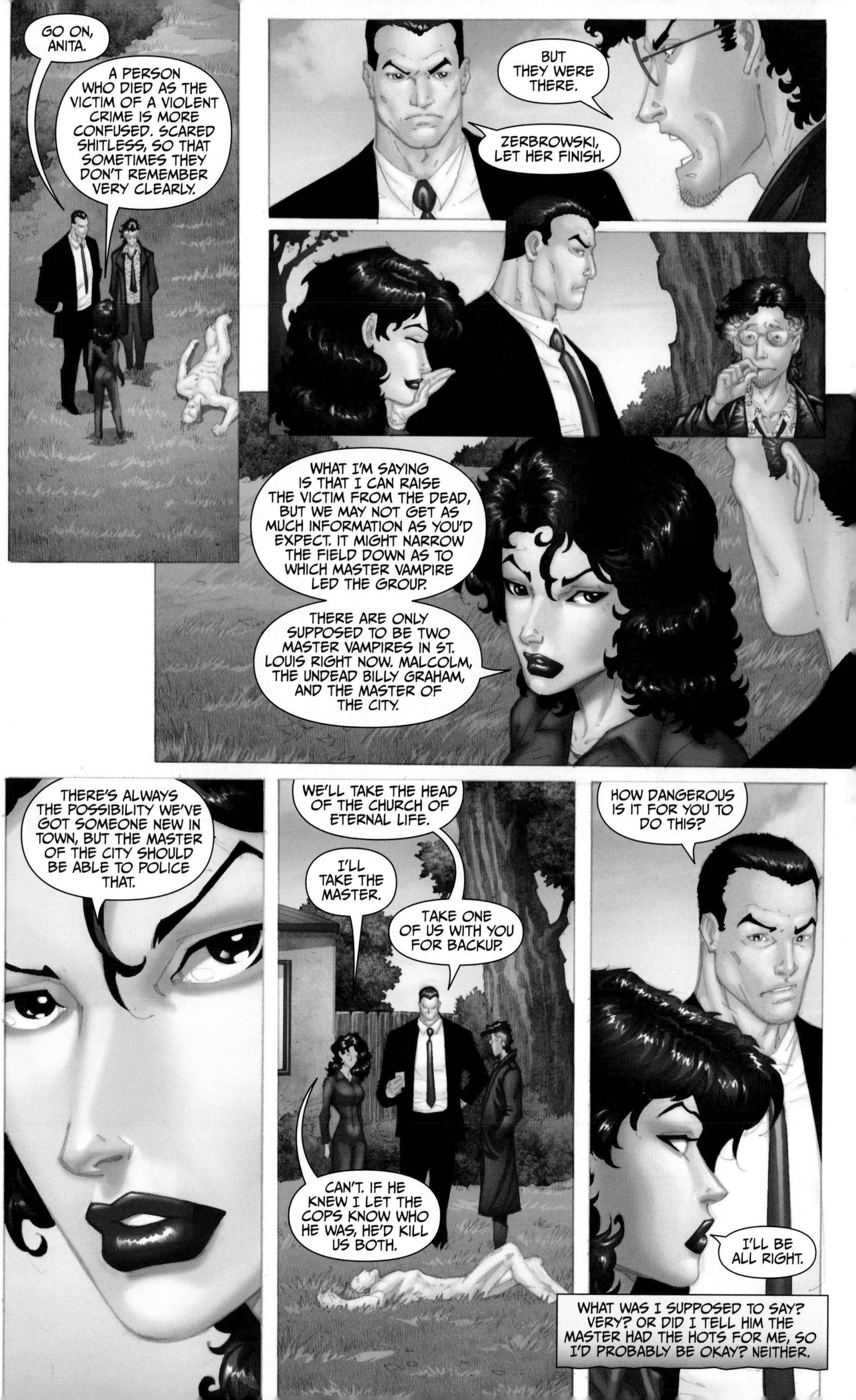
GO ON, ANITA.
A PERSON WHO DIED AS THE VICTIM OF A VIOLENT CRIME IS MORE CONFUSED. SCARED SHITLESS, SO THAT SOMETIMES THEY DON'T REMEMBER VERY CLEARLY.
BUT THEY WERE THERE.
ZERBROWSKI, LET HER FINISH.
WHAT I'M SAYING IS THAT I CAN RAISE THE VICTIM FROM THE DEAD, BUT WE MAY NOT GET AS MUCH INFORMATION AS YOU'D EXPECT. IT MIGHT NARROW THE FIELD DOWN AS TO WHICH MASTER VAMPIRE LED THE GROUP.
THERE ARE ONLY SUPPOSED TO BE TWO MASTER VAMPIRES IN ST. LOUIS RIGHT NOW. MALCOLM, THE UNDEAD BILLY GRAHAM, AND THE MASTER OF THE CITY.
THERE'S ALWAYS THE POSSIBILITY WE'VE GOT SOMEONE NEW IN TOWN, BUT THE MASTER OF THE CITY SHOULD BE ABLE TO POLICE THAT.
WE'LL TAKE THE HEAD OF THE CHURCH OF ETERNAL LIFE.
I'LL TAKE THE MASTER.
TAKE ONE OF US WITH YOU FOR BACKUP.
CAN'T. IF HE KNEW I LET THE COPS KNOW WHO HE WAS, HE'D KILL US BOTH.
HOW DANGEROUS IS IT FOR YOU TO DO THIS?
I'LL BE ALL RIGHT.
WHAT WAS I SUPPOSED TO SAY? VERY? OR DID I TELL HIM THE MASTER HAD THE HOTS FOR ME, SO I'D PROBABLY BE OKAY? NEITHER.

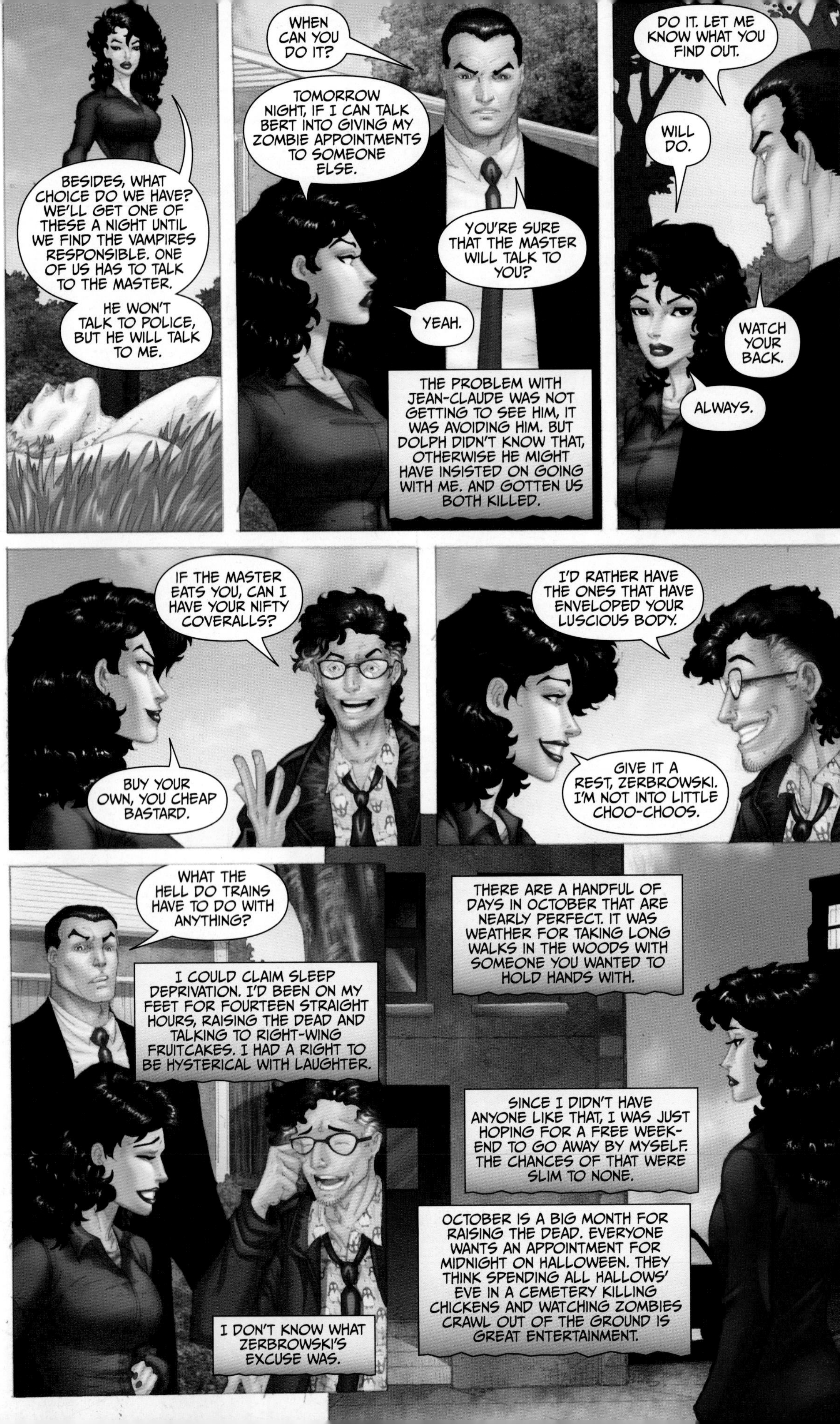
BESIDES, WHAT CHOICE DO WE HAVE? WE'LL GET ONE OF THESE A NIGHT UNTIL WE FIND THE VAMPIRES RESPONSIBLE. ONE OF US HAS TO TALK TO THE MASTER.
HE WON'T TALK TO POLICE, BUT HE WILL TALK TO ME.
WHEN CAN YOU DO IT?
TOMORROW NIGHT, IF I CAN TALK BERT INTO GIVING MY ZOMBIE APPOINTMENTS TO SOMEONE ELSE.
YOU'RE SURE THAT THE MASTER WILL TALK TO YOU?
YEAH.
THE PROBLEM WITH JEAN-CLAUDE WAS NOT GETTING TO SEE HIM, IT WAS AVOIDING HIM. BUT DOLPH DIDN'T KNOW THAT, OTHERWISE HE MIGHT HAVE INSISTED ON GOING WITH ME. AND GOTTEN US BOTH KILLED.
DO IT. LET ME KNOW WHAT YOU FIND OUT.
WILL DO.
WATCH YOUR BACK.
ALWAYS.
IF THE MASTER EATS YOU, CAN I HAVE YOUR NIFTY COVERALLS?
BUY YOUR OWN, YOU CHEAP BASTARD.
I'D RATHER HAVE THE ONES THAT HAVE ENVELOPED YOUR LUSCIOUS BODY.
GIVE IT A REST, ZERBROWSKI. I'M NOT INTO LITTLE CHOO-CHOOS.
WHAT THE HELL DO TRAINS HAVE TO DO WITH ANYTHING?
I COULD CLAIM SLEEP DEPRIVATION. I'D BEEN ON MY FEET FOR FOURTEEN STRAIGHT HOURS, RAISING THE DEAD AND TALKING TO RIGHT-WING FRUITCAKES. I HAD A RIGHT TO BE HYSTERICAL WITH LAUGHTER.
I DON'T KNOW WHAT ZERBROWSKI'S EXCUSE WAS.
THERE ARE A HANDFUL OF DAYS IN OCTOBER THAT ARE NEARLY PERFECT. IT WAS WEATHER FOR TAKING LONG WALKS IN THE WOODS WITH SOMEONE YOU WANTED TO HOLD HANDS WITH.
SINCE I DIDN'T HAVE ANYONE LIKE THAT, I WAS JUST HOPING FOR A FREE WEEK-END TO GO AWAY BY MYSELF. THE CHANCES OF THAT WERE SLIM TO NONE.
OCTOBER IS A BIG MONTH FOR RAISING THE DEAD. EVERYONE WANTS AN APPOINTMENT FOR MIDNIGHT ON HALLOWEEN. THEY THINK SPENDING ALL HALLOWS' EVE IN A CEMETERY KILLING CHICKENS AND WATCHING ZOMBIES CRAWL OUT OF THE GROUND IS GREAT ENTERTAINMENT.

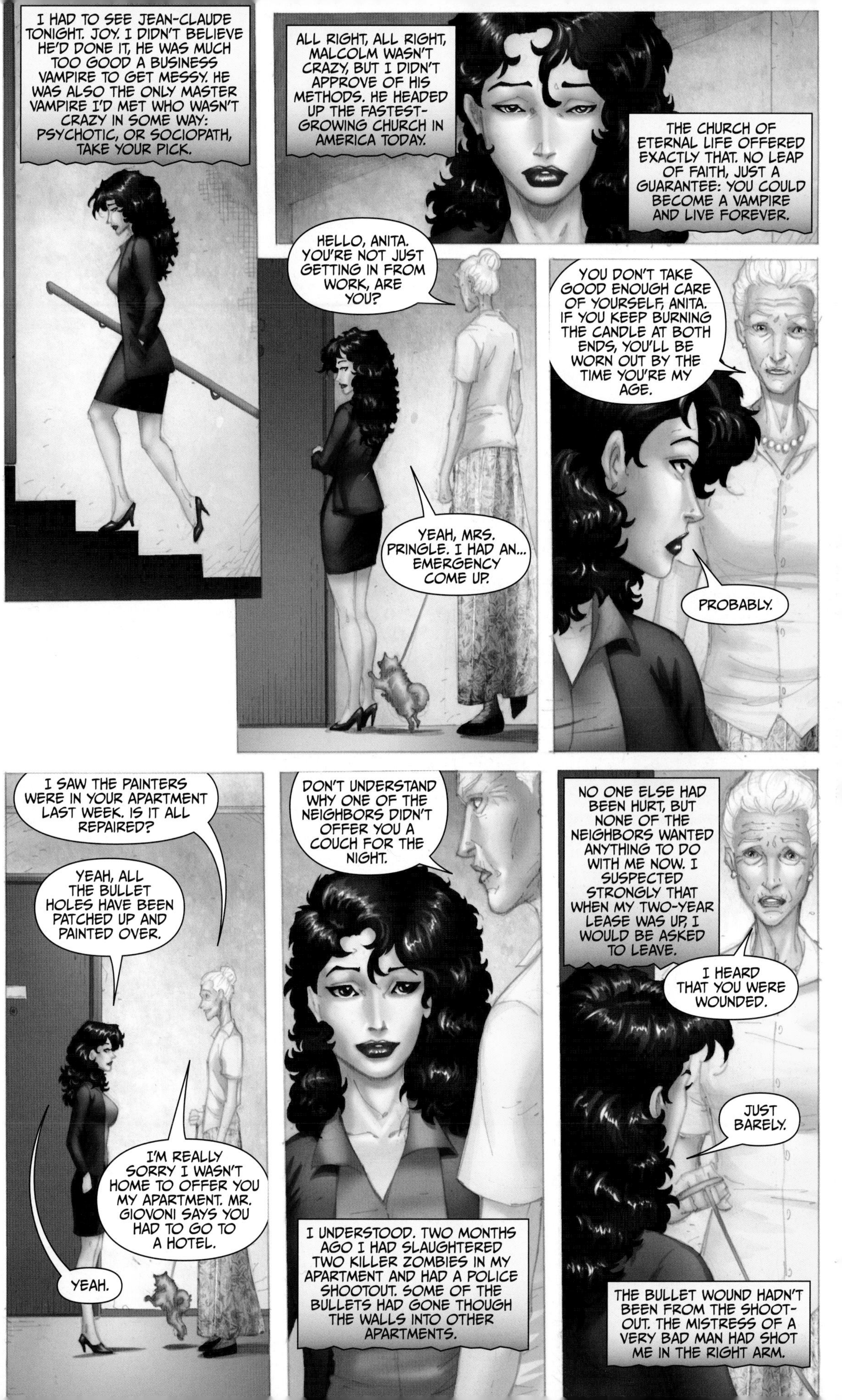
I HAD TO SEE JEAN-CLAUDE TONIGHT. JOY. I DIDN'T BELIEVE HE'D DONE IT, HE WAS MUCH TOO GOOD A BUSINESS VAMPIRE TO GET MESSY. HE WAS ALSO THE ONLY MASTER VAMPIRE I'D MET WHO WASN'T CRAZY IN SOME WAY: PSYCHOTIC, OR SOCIOPATH, TAKE YOUR PICK.
ALL RIGHT, ALL RIGHT, MALCOLM WASN'T CRAZY, BUT I DIDN'T APPROVE OF HIS METHODS. HE HEADED UP THE FASTEST-GROWING CHURCH IN AMERICA TODAY.
THE CHURCH OF ETERNAL LIFE OFFERED EXACTLY THAT. NO LEAP OF FAITH, JUST A GUARANTEE: YOU COULD BECOME A VAMPIRE AND LIVE FOREVER.
HELLO, ANITA. YOU'RE NOT JUST GETTING IN FROM WORK, ARE YOU?
YEAH, MRS. PRINGLE. I HAD AN... EMERGENCY COME UP.
YOU DON'T TAKE GOOD ENOUGH CARE OF YOURSELF, ANITA. IF YOU KEEP BURNING THE CANDLE AT BOTH ENDS, YOU'LL BE WORN OUT BY THE TIME YOU'RE MY AGE.
PROBABLY.
I SAW THE PAINTERS WERE IN YOUR APARTMENT LAST WEEK. IS IT ALL REPAIRED?
YEAH, ALL THE BULLET HOLES HAVE BEEN PATCHED UP AND PAINTED OVER.
I'M REALLY SORRY I WASN'T HOME TO OFFER YOU MY APARTMENT. MR. GIOVONI SAYS YOU HAD TO GO TO A HOTEL.
YEAH.
DON'T UNDERSTAND WHY ONE OF THE NEIGHBORS DIDN'T OFFER YOU A COUCH FOR THE NIGHT.
I UNDERSTOOD. TWO MONTHS AGO I HAD SLAUGHTERED TWO KILLER ZOMBIES IN MY APARTMENT AND HAD A POLICE SHOOTOUT. SOME OF THE BULLETS HAD GONE THOUGH THE WALLS INTO OTHER APARTMENTS.
NO ONE ELSE HAD BEEN HURT, BUT NONE OF THE NEIGHBORS WANTED ANYTHING TO DO WITH ME NOW. I SUSPECTED STRONGLY THAT WHEN MY TWO-YEAR LEASE WAS UP, I WOULD BE ASKED TO LEAVE.
I HEARD THAT YOU WERE WOUNDED.
JUST BARELY.
THE BULLET WOUND HADN'T BEEN FROM THE SHOOT-OUT. THE MISTRESS OF A VERY BAD MAN HAD SHOT ME IN THE RIGHT ARM.

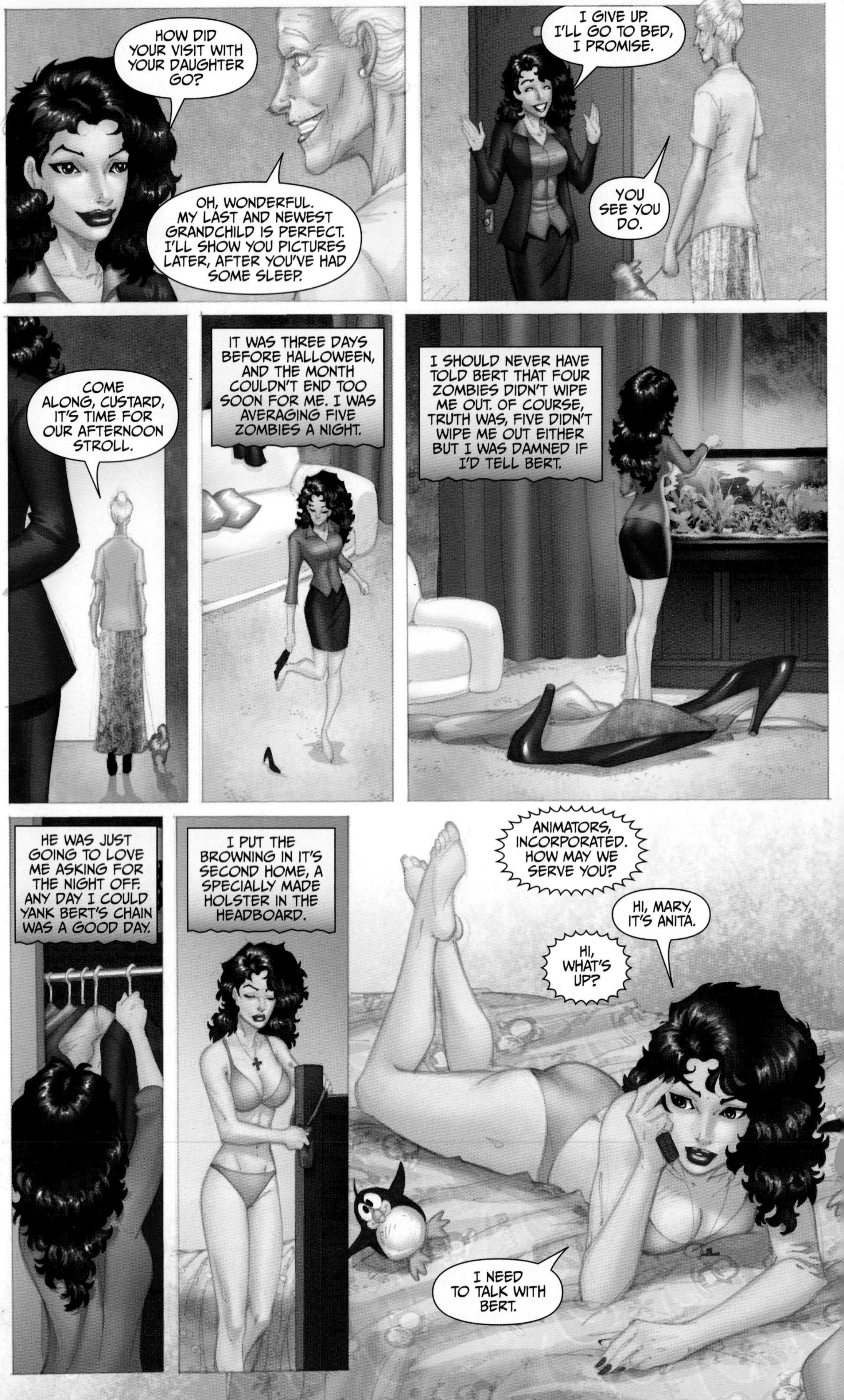
HOW DID YOUR VISIT WITH YOUR DAUGHTER GO?
OH, WONDERFUL. MY LAST AND NEWEST GRANDCHILD IS PERFECT. I'LL SHOW YOU PICTURES LATER, AFTER YOU'VE HAD SOME SLEEP.
I GIVE UP. I'LL GO TO BED, I PROMISE.
YOU SEE YOU DO.
COME ALONG, CUSTARD, IT'S TIME FOR OUR AFTERNOON STROLL.
IT WAS THREE DAYS BEFORE HALLOWEEN, AND THE MONTH COULDN'T END TOO SOON FOR ME. I WAS AVERAGING FIVE ZOMBIES A NIGHT.
I SHOULD NEVER HAVE TOLD BERT THAT FOUR ZOMBIES DIDN'T WIPE ME OUT. OF COURSE, TRUTH WAS, FIVE DIDN'T WIPE ME OUT EITHER BUT I WAS DAMNED IF I'D TELL BERT.
HE WAS JUST GOING TO LOVE ME ASKING FOR THE NIGHT OFF. ANY DAY I COULD YANK BERT'S CHAIN WAS A GOOD DAY.
I PUT THE BROWNING IN IT'S SECOND HOME, A SPECIALLY MADE HOLSTER IN THE HEADBOARD.
ANIMATORS, INCORPORATED. HOW MAY WE SERVE YOU?
HI, MARY, IT'S ANITA.
HI, WHAT'S UP?
I NEED TO TALK WITH BERT.

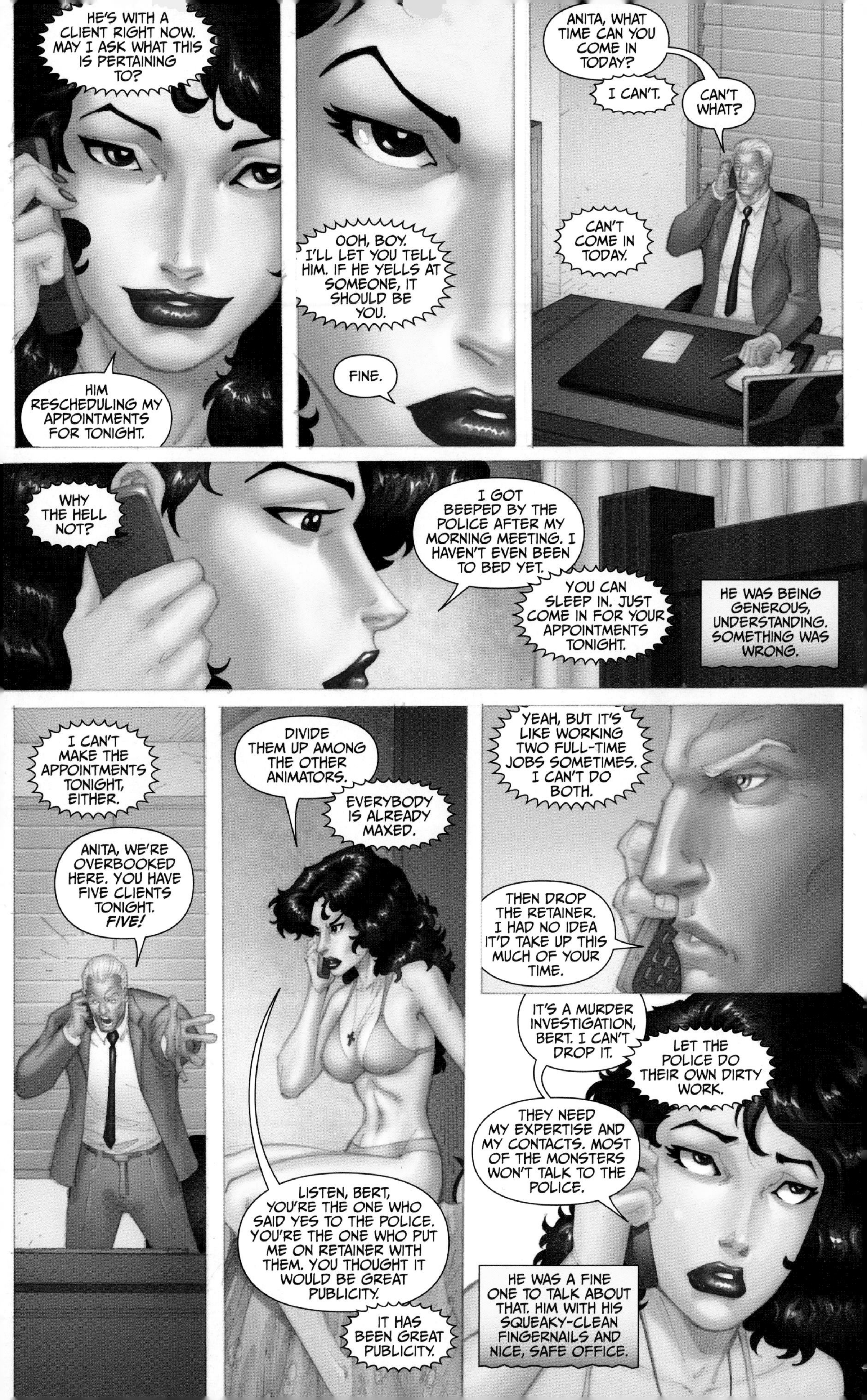
HE'S WITH A CLIENT RIGHT NOW. MAY I ASK WHAT THIS IS PERTAINING TO?
HIM RESCHEDULING MY APPOINTMENTS FOR TONIGHT.
OOH, BOY. I'LL LET YOU TELL HIM. IF HE YELLS AT SOMEONE, IT SHOULD BE YOU.
FINE.
ANITA, WHAT TIME CAN YOU COME IN TODAY?
I CAN'T.
CAN'T WHAT?
CAN'T COME IN TODAY.
WHY THE HELL NOT?
I GOT BEEPED BY THE POLICE AFTER MY MORNING MEETING. I HAVEN'T EVEN BEEN TO BED YET.
YOU CAN SLEEP IN. JUST COME IN FOR YOUR APPOINTMENTS TONIGHT.
HE WAS BEING GENEROUS, UNDERSTANDING. SOMETHING WAS WRONG.
I CAN'T MAKE THE APPOINTMENTS TONIGHT, EITHER.
ANITA, WE'RE OVERBOOKED HERE. YOU HAVE FIVE CLIENTS TONIGHT. *FIVE!*
DIVIDE THEM UP AMONG THE OTHER ANIMATORS.
EVERYBODY IS ALREADY MAXED.
LISTEN, BERT, YOU'RE THE ONE WHO SAID YES TO THE POLICE. YOU'RE THE ONE WHO PUT ME ON RETAINER WITH THEM. YOU THOUGHT IT WOULD BE GREAT PUBLICITY.
IT HAS BEEN GREAT PUBLICITY.
YEAH, BUT IT'S LIKE WORKING TWO FULL-TIME JOBS SOMETIMES. I CAN'T DO BOTH.
THEN DROP THE RETAINER. I HAD NO IDEA IT'D TAKE UP THIS MUCH OF YOUR TIME.
IT'S A MURDER INVESTIGATION, BERT. I CAN'T DROP IT.
LET THE POLICE DO THEIR OWN DIRTY WORK.
THEY NEED MY EXPERTISE AND MY CONTACTS. MOST OF THE MONSTERS WON'T TALK TO THE POLICE.
HE WAS A FINE ONE TO TALK ABOUT THAT. HIM WITH HIS SQUEAKY-CLEAN FINGERNAILS AND NICE, SAFE OFFICE.

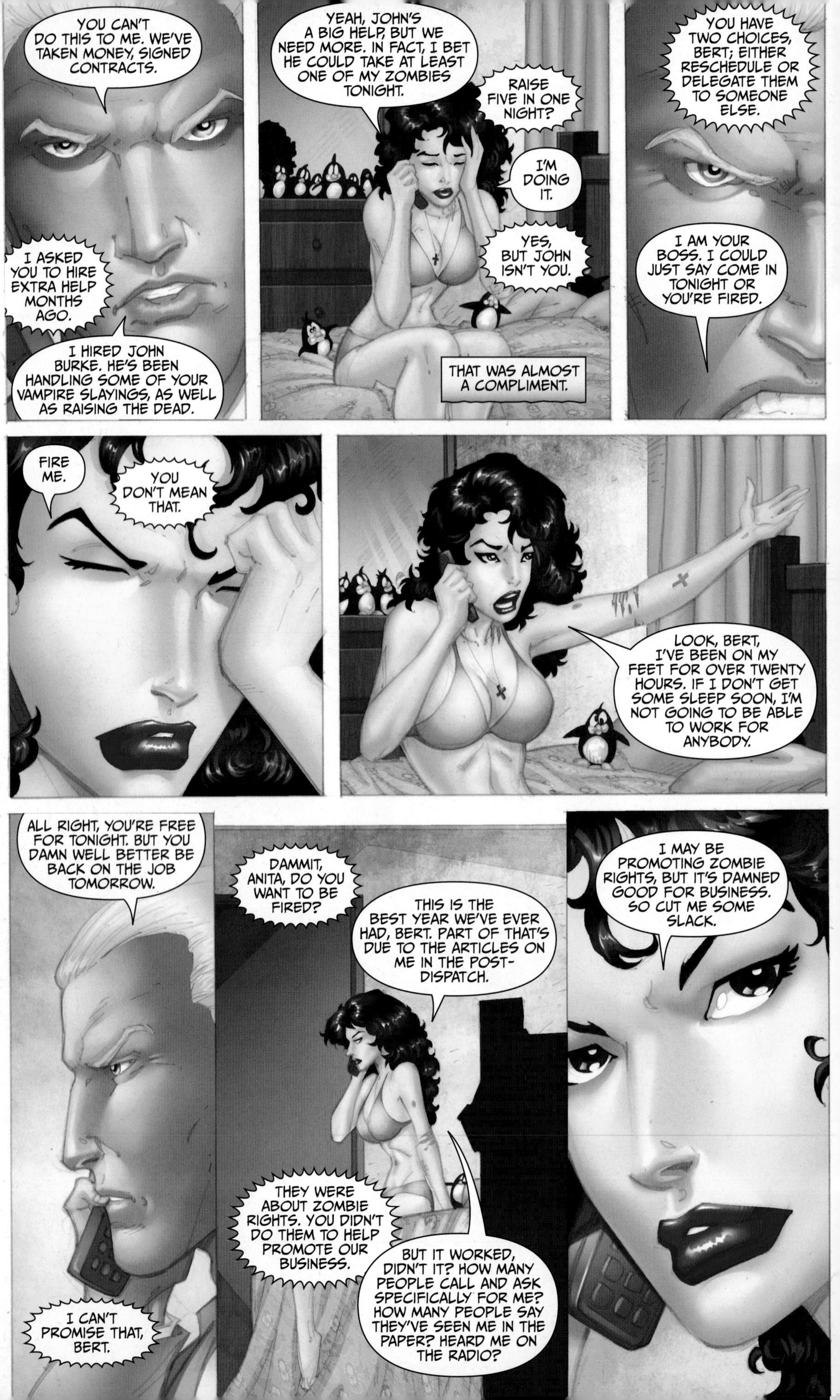
YOU CAN'T DO THIS TO ME. WE'VE TAKEN MONEY, SIGNED CONTRACTS.
I ASKED YOU TO HIRE EXTRA HELP MONTHS AGO.
I HIRED JOHN BURKE. HE'S BEEN HANDLING SOME OF YOUR VAMPIRE SLAYINGS, AS WELL AS RAISING THE DEAD.
YEAH, JOHN'S A BIG HELP, BUT WE NEED MORE. IN FACT, I BET HE COULD TAKE AT LEAST ONE OF MY ZOMBIES TONIGHT.
RAISE FIVE IN ONE NIGHT?
I'M DOING IT.
YES, BUT JOHN ISN'T YOU.
THAT WAS ALMOST A COMPLIMENT.
YOU HAVE TWO CHOICES, BERT; EITHER RESCHEDULE OR DELEGATE THEM TO SOMEONE ELSE.
I AM YOUR BOSS. I COULD JUST SAY COME IN TONIGHT OR YOU'RE FIRED.
FIRE ME.
YOU DON'T MEAN THAT.
LOOK, BERT, I'VE BEEN ON MY FEET FOR OVER TWENTY HOURS. IF I DON'T GET SOME SLEEP SOON, I'M NOT GOING TO BE ABLE TO WORK FOR ANYBODY.
ALL RIGHT, YOU'RE FREE FOR TONIGHT. BUT YOU DAMN WELL BETTER BE BACK ON THE JOB TOMORROW.
I CAN'T PROMISE THAT, BERT.
DAMMIT, ANITA, DO YOU WANT TO BE FIRED?
THIS IS THE BEST YEAR WE'VE EVER HAD, BERT. PART OF THAT'S DUE TO THE ARTICLES ON ME IN THE POST-DISPATCH.
THEY WERE ABOUT ZOMBIE RIGHTS. YOU DIDN'T DO THEM TO HELP PROMOTE OUR BUSINESS.
BUT IT WORKED, DIDN'T IT? HOW MANY PEOPLE CALL AND ASK SPECIFICALLY FOR ME? HOW MANY PEOPLE SAY THEY'VE SEEN ME IN THE PAPER? HEARD ME ON THE RADIO?
I MAY BE PROMOTING ZOMBIE RIGHTS, BUT IT'S DAMNED GOOD FOR BUSINESS. SO CUT ME SOME SLACK.

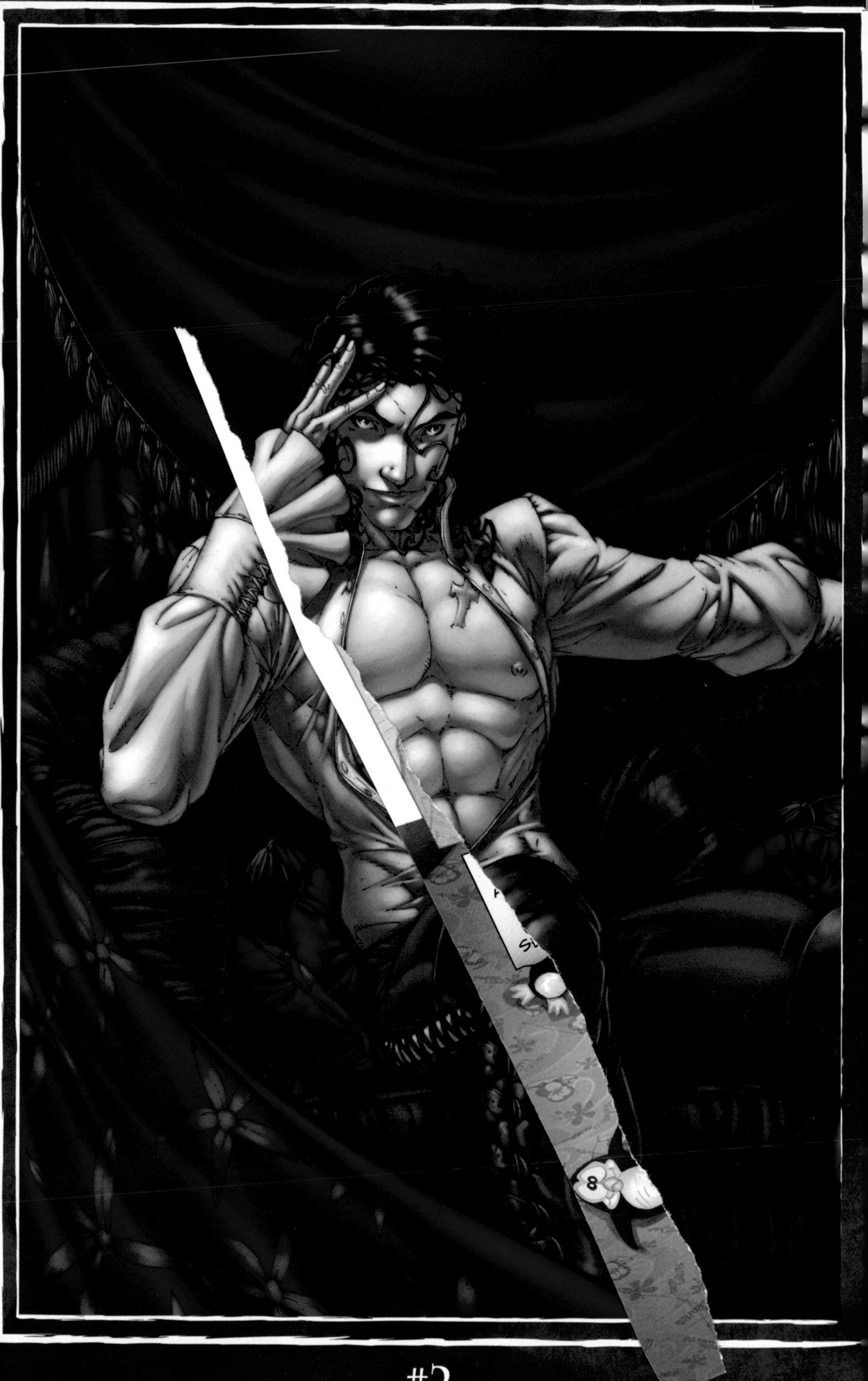

#2

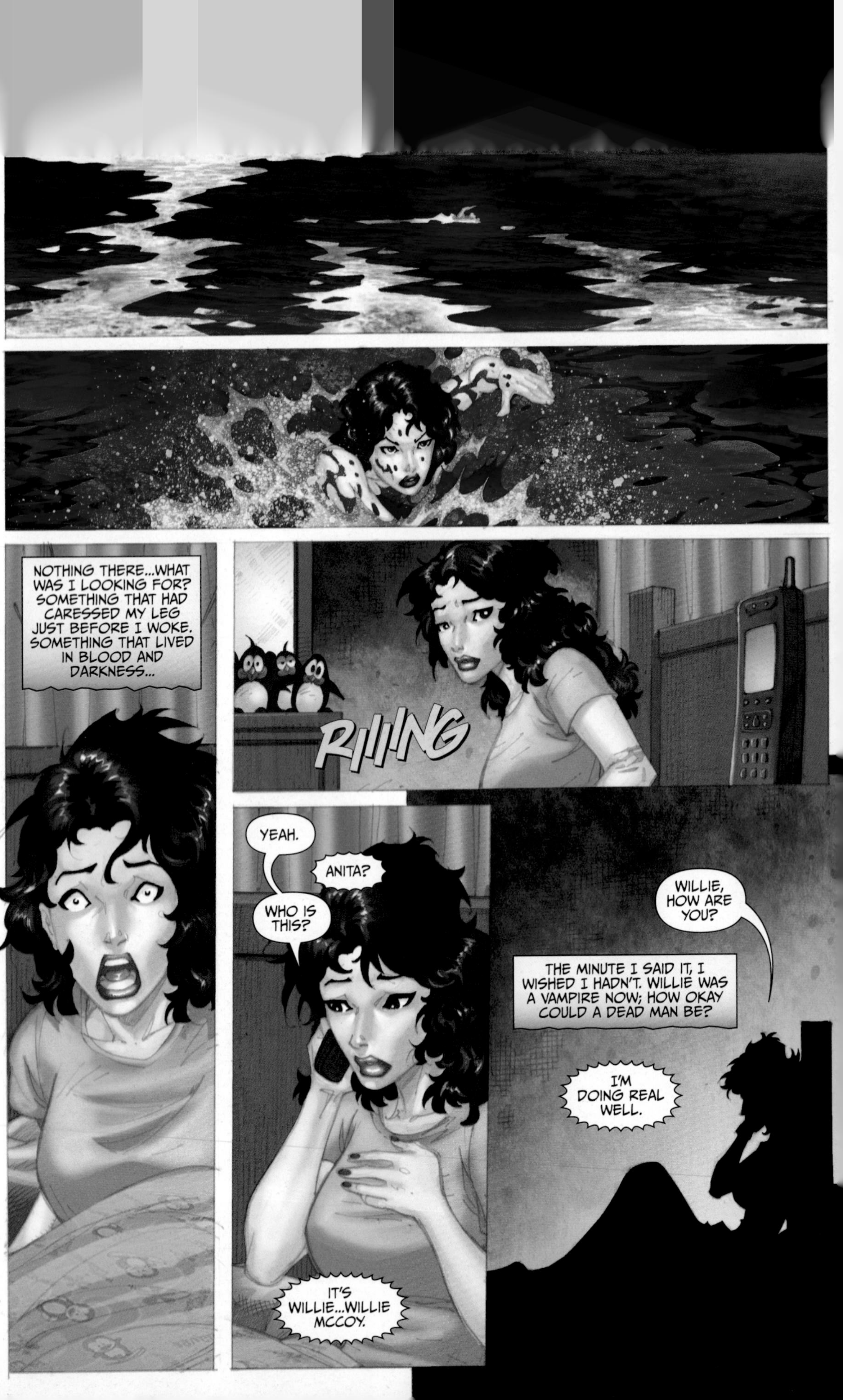
NOTHING THERE...WHAT WAS I LOOKING FOR? SOMETHING THAT HAD CARESSED MY LEG JUST BEFORE I WOKE. SOMETHING THAT LIVED IN BLOOD AND DARKNESS...
RIIING
YEAH.
ANITA?
WHO IS THIS?
IT'S WILLIE...WILLIE MCCOY.
WILLIE, HOW ARE YOU?
THE MINUTE I SAID IT, I WISHED I HADN'T. WILLIE WAS A VAMPIRE NOW; HOW OKAY COULD A DEAD MAN BE?
I'M DOING REAL WELL.

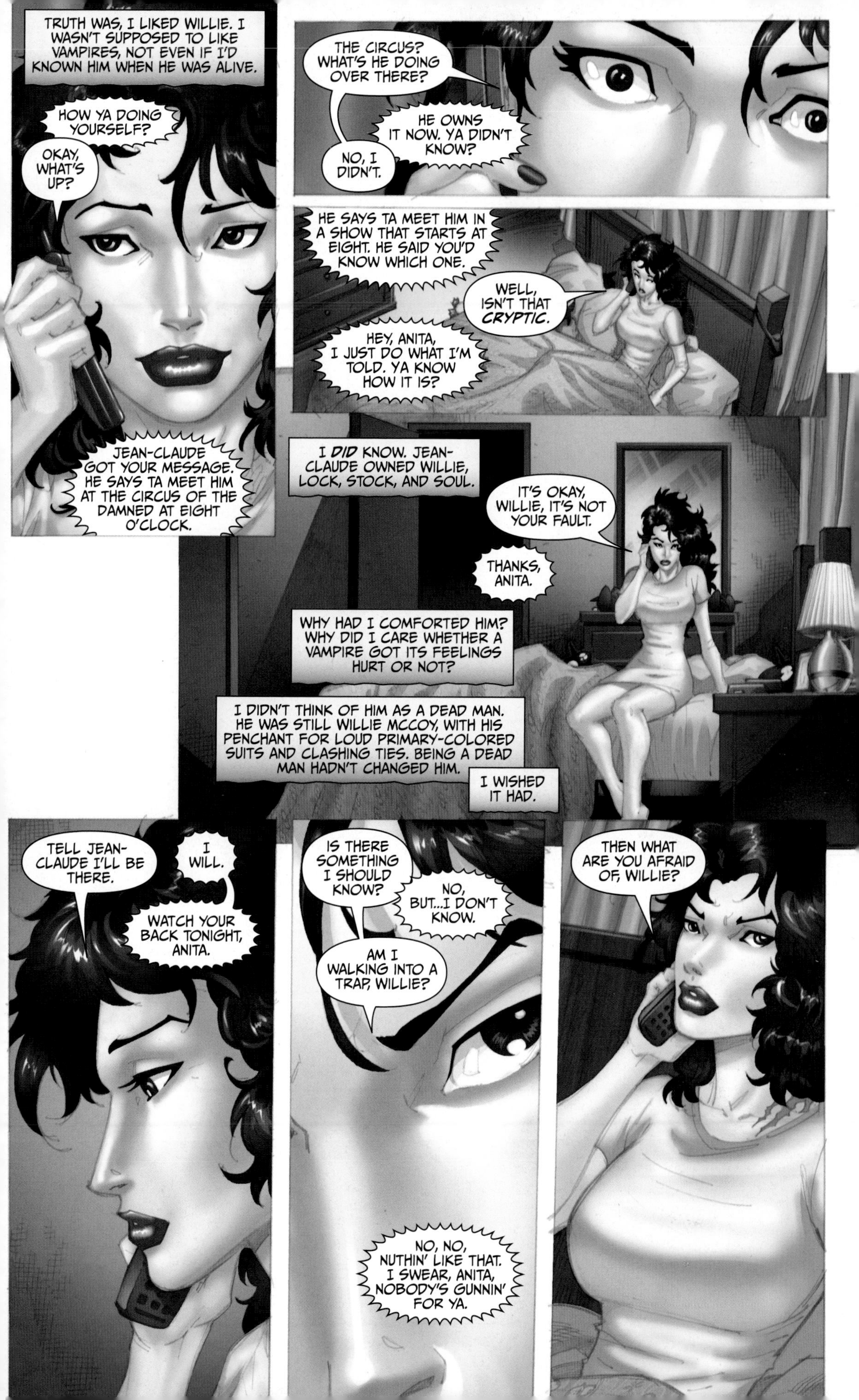

TRUTH WAS, I LIKED WILLIE. I WASN'T SUPPOSED TO LIKE VAMPIRES, NOT EVEN IF I'D KNOWN HIM WHEN HE WAS ALIVE.
HOW YA DOING YOURSELF?
OKAY, WHAT'S UP?
JEAN-CLAUDE GOT YOUR MESSAGE. HE SAYS TA MEET HIM AT THE CIRCUS OF THE DAMNED AT EIGHT O'CLOCK.
THE CIRCUS? WHAT'S HE DOING OVER THERE?
HE OWNS IT NOW. YA DIDN'T KNOW?
NO, I DIDN'T.
HE SAYS TA MEET HIM IN A SHOW THAT STARTS AT EIGHT. HE SAID YOU'D KNOW WHICH ONE.
WELL, ISN'T THAT *CRYPTIC*.
HEY, ANITA, I JUST DO WHAT I'M TOLD. YA KNOW HOW IT IS?
I *DID* KNOW. JEAN-CLAUDE OWNED WILLIE, LOCK, STOCK, AND SOUL.
IT'S OKAY, WILLIE, IT'S NOT YOUR FAULT.
THANKS, ANITA.
WHY HAD I COMFORTED HIM? WHY DID I CARE WHETHER A VAMPIRE GOT ITS FEELINGS HURT OR NOT?
I DIDN'T THINK OF HIM AS A DEAD MAN. HE WAS STILL WILLIE MCCOY, WITH HIS PENCHANT FOR LOUD PRIMARY-COLORED SUITS AND CLASHING TIES. BEING A DEAD MAN HADN'T CHANGED HIM.
I WISHED IT HAD.
TELL JEAN-CLAUDE I'LL BE THERE.
I WILL.
WATCH YOUR BACK TONIGHT, ANITA.
IS THERE SOMETHING I SHOULD KNOW?
NO, BUT...I DON'T KNOW.
AM I WALKING INTO A TRAP, WILLIE?
NO, NO, NUTHIN' LIKE THAT. I SWEAR, ANITA, NOBODY'S GUNNIN' FOR YA.
THEN WHAT ARE YOU AFRAID OF, WILLIE?

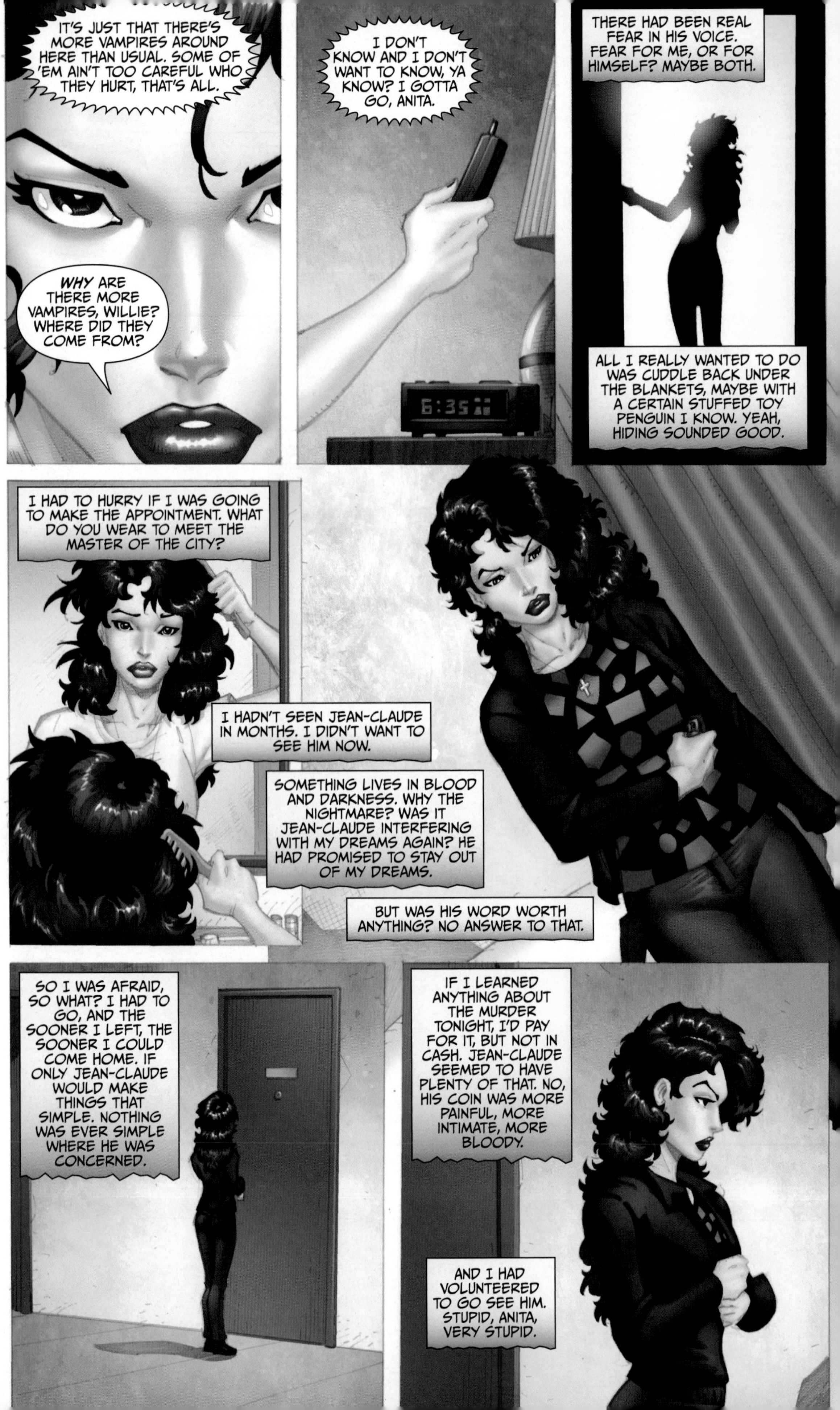
IT'S JUST THAT THERE'S MORE VAMPIRES AROUND HERE THAN USUAL. SOME OF 'EM AIN'T TOO CAREFUL WHO THEY HURT, THAT'S ALL.
WHY ARE THERE MORE VAMPIRES, WILLIE? WHERE DID THEY COME FROM?
I DON'T KNOW AND I DON'T WANT TO KNOW, YA KNOW? I GOTTA GO, ANITA.
6:35
THERE HAD BEEN REAL FEAR IN HIS VOICE. FEAR FOR ME, OR FOR HIMSELF? MAYBE BOTH.
ALL I REALLY WANTED TO DO WAS CUDDLE BACK UNDER THE BLANKETS, MAYBE WITH A CERTAIN STUFFED TOY PENGUIN I KNOW. YEAH, HIDING SOUNDED GOOD.
I HAD TO HURRY IF I WAS GOING TO MAKE THE APPOINTMENT. WHAT DO YOU WEAR TO MEET THE MASTER OF THE CITY?
I HADN'T SEEN JEAN-CLAUDE IN MONTHS. I DIDN'T WANT TO SEE HIM NOW.
SOMETHING LIVES IN BLOOD AND DARKNESS. WHY THE NIGHTMARE? WAS IT JEAN-CLAUDE INTERFERING WITH MY DREAMS AGAIN? HE HAD PROMISED TO STAY OUT OF MY DREAMS.
BUT WAS HIS WORD WORTH ANYTHING? NO ANSWER TO THAT.
SO I WAS AFRAID, SO WHAT? I HAD TO GO, AND THE SOONER I LEFT, THE SOONER I COULD COME HOME. IF ONLY JEAN-CLAUDE WOULD MAKE THINGS THAT SIMPLE. NOTHING WAS EVER SIMPLE WHERE HE WAS CONCERNED.
IF I LEARNED ANYTHING ABOUT THE MURDER TONIGHT, I'D PAY FOR IT, BUT NOT IN CASH. JEAN-CLAUDE SEEMED TO HAVE PLENTY OF THAT. NO, HIS COIN WAS MORE PAINFUL, MORE INTIMATE, MORE BLOODY.
AND I HAD VOLUNTEERED TO GO SEE HIM. STUPID, ANITA, VERY STUPID.

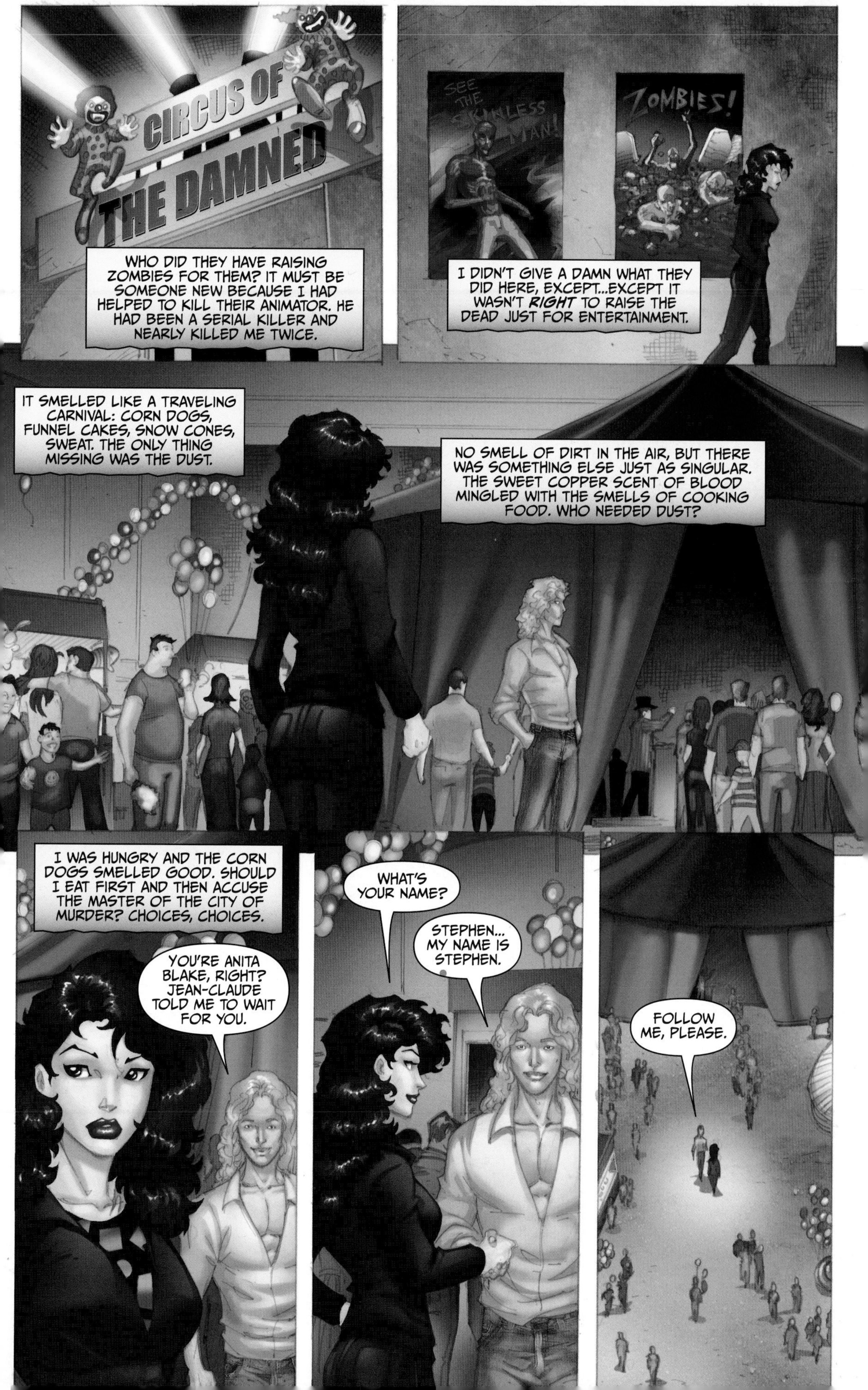
CIRCUS OF
THE DAMNED
WHO DID THEY HAVE RAISING ZOMBIES FOR THEM? IT MUST BE SOMEONE NEW BECAUSE I HAD HELPED TO KILL THEIR ANIMATOR. HE HAD BEEN A SERIAL KILLER AND NEARLY KILLED ME TWICE.
SEE THE SKINLESS MAN!
ZOMBIES!
I DIDN'T GIVE A DAMN WHAT THEY DID HERE, EXCEPT...EXCEPT IT WASN'T *RIGHT* TO RAISE THE DEAD JUST FOR ENTERTAINMENT.
IT SMELLED LIKE A TRAVELING CARNIVAL: CORN DOGS, FUNNEL CAKES, SNOW CONES, SWEAT. THE ONLY THING MISSING WAS THE DUST.
NO SMELL OF DIRT IN THE AIR, BUT THERE WAS SOMETHING ELSE JUST AS SINGULAR. THE SWEET COPPER SCENT OF BLOOD MINGLED WITH THE SMELLS OF COOKING FOOD. WHO NEEDED DUST?
I WAS HUNGRY AND THE CORN DOGS SMELLED GOOD. SHOULD I EAT FIRST AND THEN ACCUSE THE MASTER OF THE CITY OF MURDER? CHOICES, CHOICES.
YOU'RE ANITA BLAKE, RIGHT? JEAN-CLAUDE TOLD ME TO WAIT FOR YOU.
WHAT'S YOUR NAME?
STEPHEN... MY NAME IS STEPHEN.
FOLLOW ME, PLEASE.

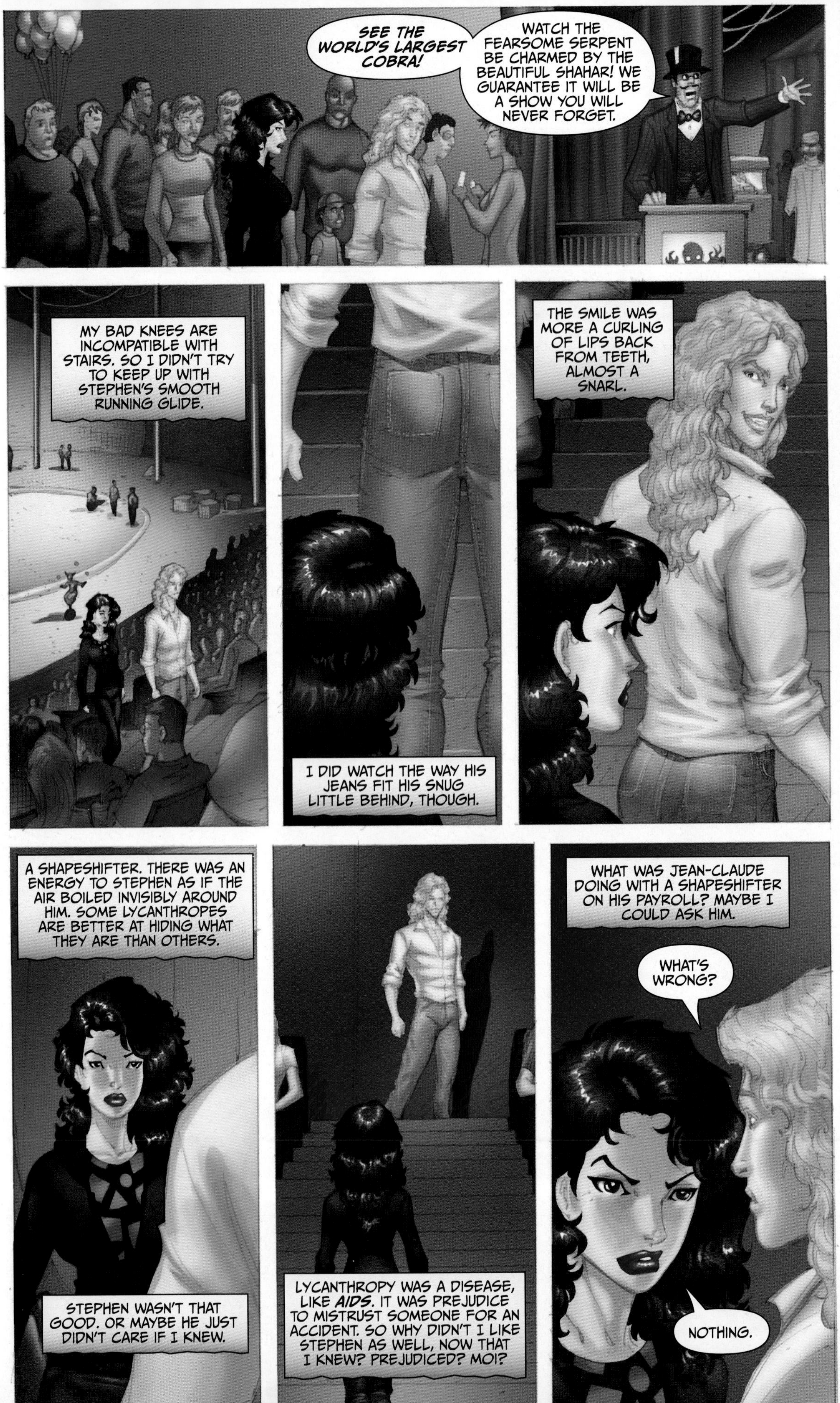
SEE THE WORLD'S LARGEST COBRA!
WATCH THE FEARSOME SERPENT BE CHARMED BY THE BEAUTIFUL SHAHAR! WE GUARANTEE IT WILL BE A SHOW YOU WILL NEVER FORGET.
MY BAD KNEES ARE INCOMPATIBLE WITH STAIRS. SO I DIDN'T TRY TO KEEP UP WITH STEPHEN'S SMOOTH RUNNING GLIDE.
I DID WATCH THE WAY HIS JEANS FIT HIS SNUG LITTLE BEHIND, THOUGH.
THE SMILE WAS MORE A CURLING OF LIPS BACK FROM TEETH, ALMOST A SNARL.
A SHAPESHIFTER. THERE WAS AN ENERGY TO STEPHEN AS IF THE AIR BOILED INVISIBLY AROUND HIM. SOME LYCANTHROPES ARE BETTER AT HIDING WHAT THEY ARE THAN OTHERS.
STEPHEN WASN'T THAT GOOD. OR MAYBE HE JUST DIDN'T CARE IF I KNEW.
LYCANTHROPY WAS A DISEASE, LIKE AIDS. IT WAS PREJUDICE TO MISTRUST SOMEONE FOR AN ACCIDENT. SO WHY DIDN'T I LIKE STEPHEN AS WELL, NOW THAT I KNEW? PREJUDICED? MOI?
WHAT WAS JEAN-CLAUDE DOING WITH A SHAPESHIFTER ON HIS PAYROLL? MAYBE I COULD ASK HIM.
WHAT'S WRONG?
NOTHING.

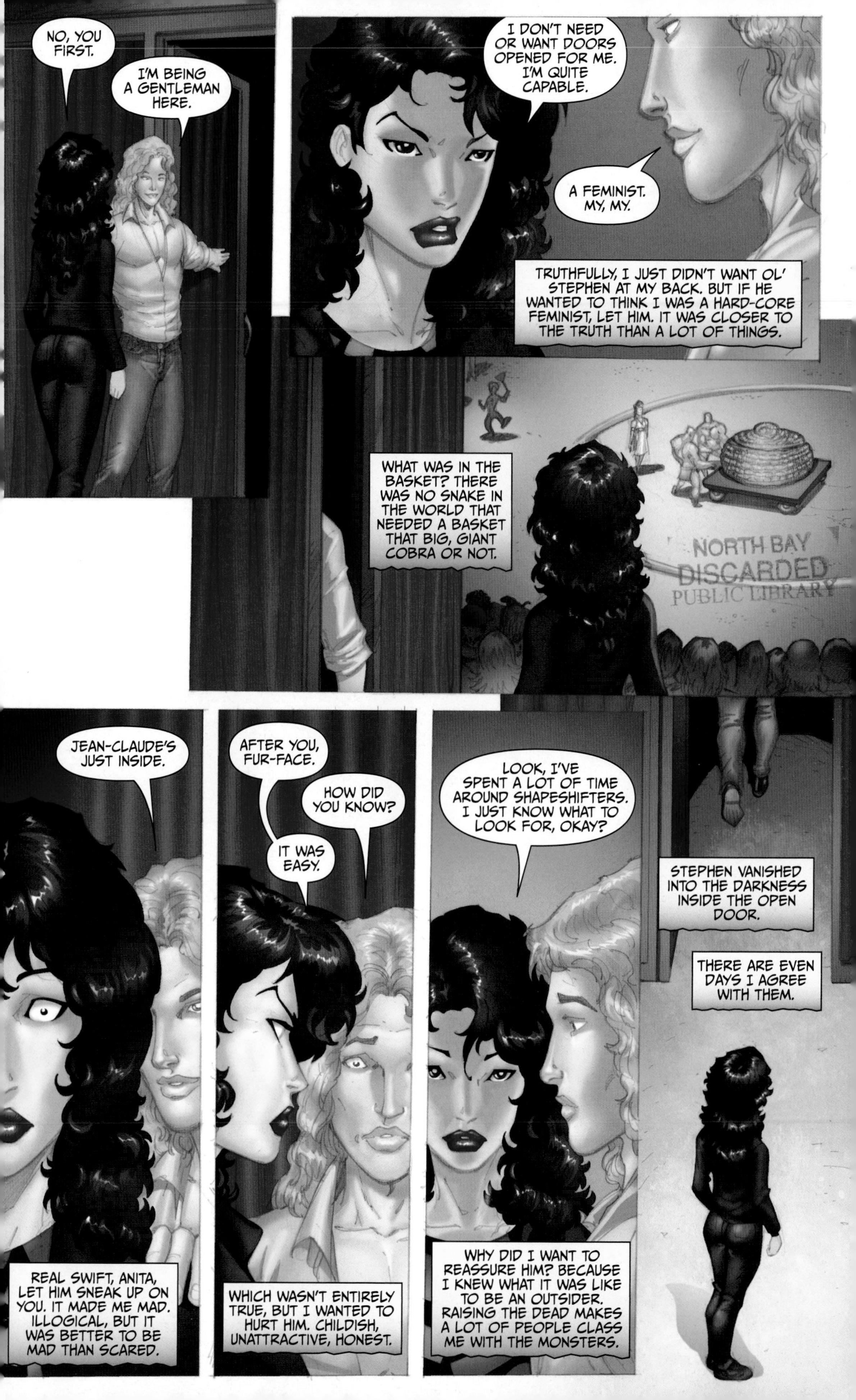
NO, YOU FIRST.
I'M BEING A GENTLEMAN HERE.
I DON'T NEED OR WANT DOORS OPENED FOR ME. I'M QUITE CAPABLE.
A FEMINIST. MY, MY.
TRUTHFULLY, I JUST DIDN'T WANT OL' STEPHEN AT MY BACK. BUT IF HE WANTED TO THINK I WAS A HARD-CORE FEMINIST, LET HIM. IT WAS CLOSER TO THE TRUTH THAN A LOT OF THINGS.
WHAT WAS IN THE BASKET? THERE WAS NO SNAKE IN THE WORLD THAT NEEDED A BASKET THAT BIG, GIANT COBRA OR NOT.
NORTH BAY
DISCARDED
PUBLIC LIBRARY
JEAN-CLAUDE'S JUST INSIDE.
REAL SWIFT, ANITA, LET HIM SNEAK UP ON YOU. IT MADE ME MAD. ILLOGICAL, BUT IT WAS BETTER TO BE MAD THAN SCARED.
AFTER YOU, FUR-FACE.
HOW DID YOU KNOW?
IT WAS EASY.
WHICH WASN'T ENTIRELY TRUE, BUT I WANTED TO HURT HIM. CHILDISH, UNATTRACTIVE, HONEST.
LOOK, I'VE SPENT A LOT OF TIME AROUND SHAPESHIFTERS. I JUST KNOW WHAT TO LOOK FOR, OKAY?
WHY DID I WANT TO REASSURE HIM? BECAUSE I KNEW WHAT IT WAS LIKE TO BE AN OUTSIDER. RAISING THE DEAD MAKES A LOT OF PEOPLE CLASS ME WITH THE MONSTERS.
STEPHEN VANISHED INTO THE DARKNESS INSIDE THE OPEN DOOR.
THERE ARE EVEN DAYS I AGREE WITH THEM.

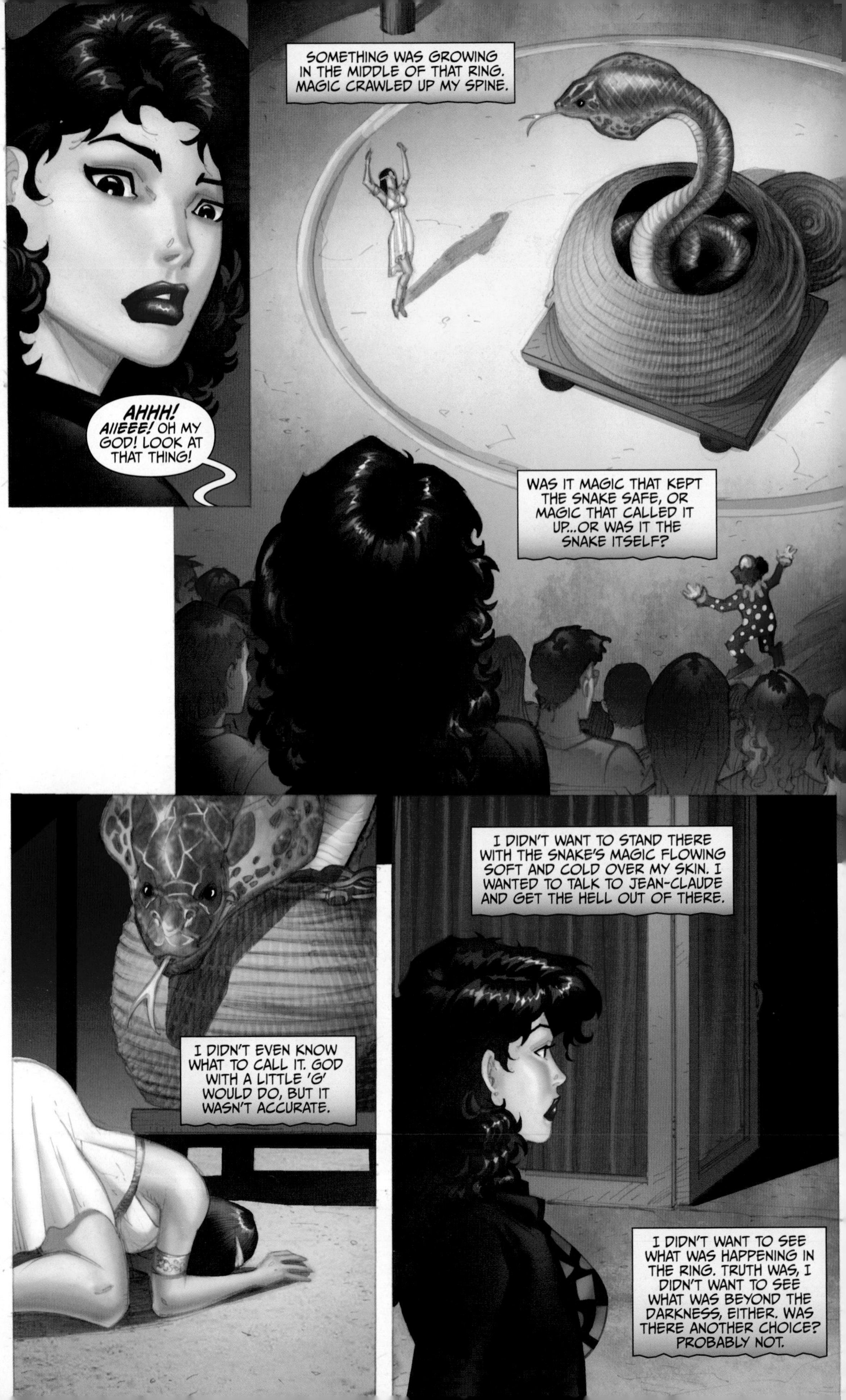
SOMETHING WAS GROWING IN THE MIDDLE OF THAT RING. MAGIC CRAWLED UP MY SPINE.
AHHH! AIIEEE! OH MY GOD! LOOK AT THAT THING!
WAS IT MAGIC THAT KEPT THE SNAKE SAFE, OR MAGIC THAT CALLED IT UP...OR WAS IT THE SNAKE ITSELF?
I DIDN'T EVEN KNOW WHAT TO CALL IT. GOD WITH A LITTLE 'G' WOULD DO, BUT IT WASN'T ACCURATE.
I DIDN'T WANT TO STAND THERE WITH THE SNAKE'S MAGIC FLOWING SOFT AND COLD OVER MY SKIN. I WANTED TO TALK TO JEAN-CLAUDE AND GET THE HELL OUT OF THERE.
I DIDN'T WANT TO SEE WHAT WAS HAPPENING IN THE RING. TRUTH WAS, I DIDN'T WANT TO SEE WHAT WAS BEYOND THE DARKNESS, EITHER. WAS THERE ANOTHER CHOICE? PROBABLY NOT.

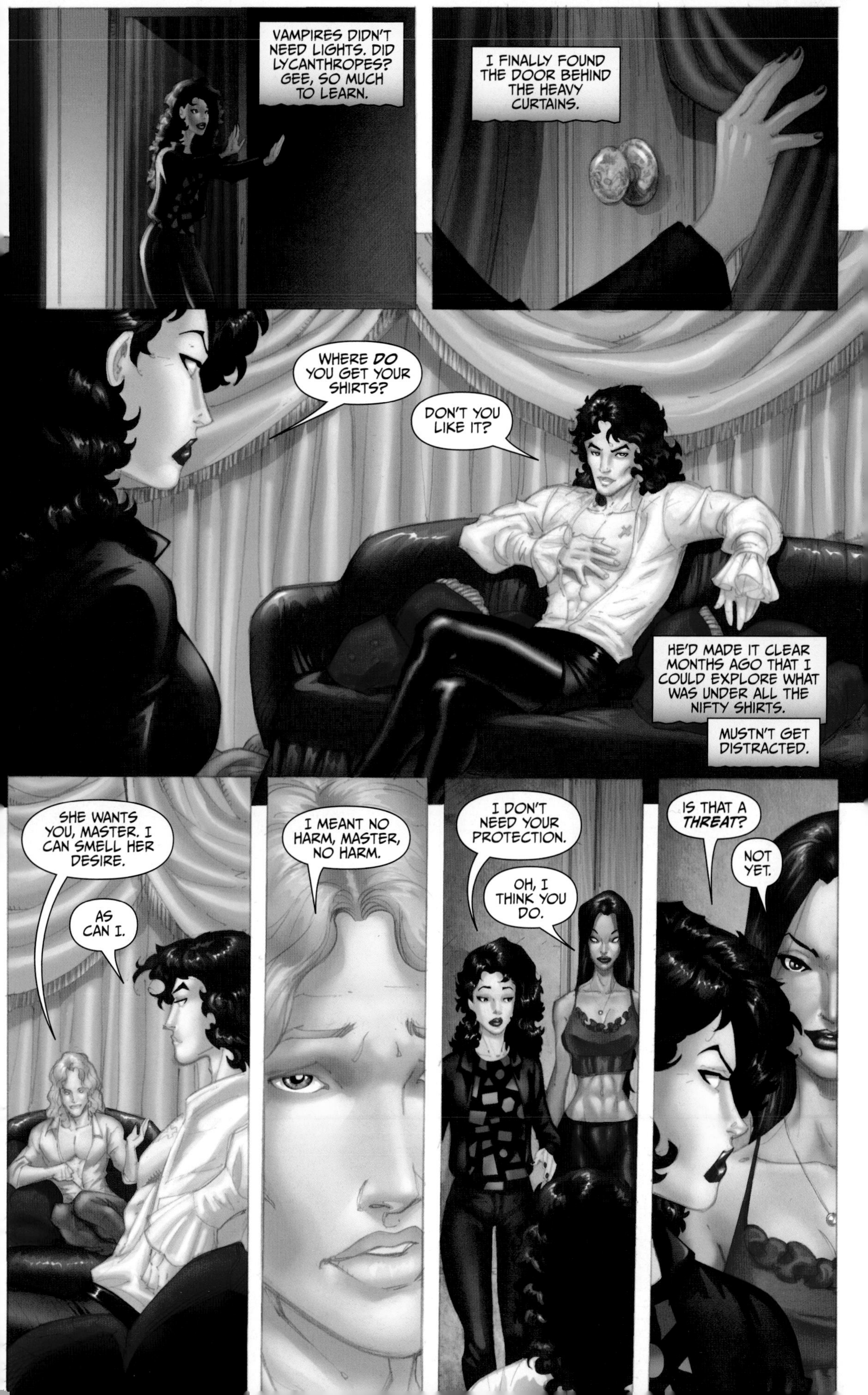
VAMPIRES DIDN'T NEED LIGHTS. DID LYCANTHROPES? GEE, SO MUCH TO LEARN.
I FINALLY FOUND THE DOOR BEHIND THE HEAVY CURTAINS.
WHERE *DO* YOU GET YOUR SHIRTS?
DON'T YOU LIKE IT?
HE'D MADE IT CLEAR MONTHS AGO THAT I COULD EXPLORE WHAT WAS UNDER ALL THE NIFTY SHIRTS.
MUSTN'T GET DISTRACTED.
SHE WANTS YOU, MASTER. I CAN SMELL HER DESIRE.
AS CAN I.
I MEANT NO HARM, MASTER, NO HARM.
I DON'T NEED YOUR PROTECTION.
OH, I THINK YOU DO.
IS THAT A *THREAT*?
NOT YET.

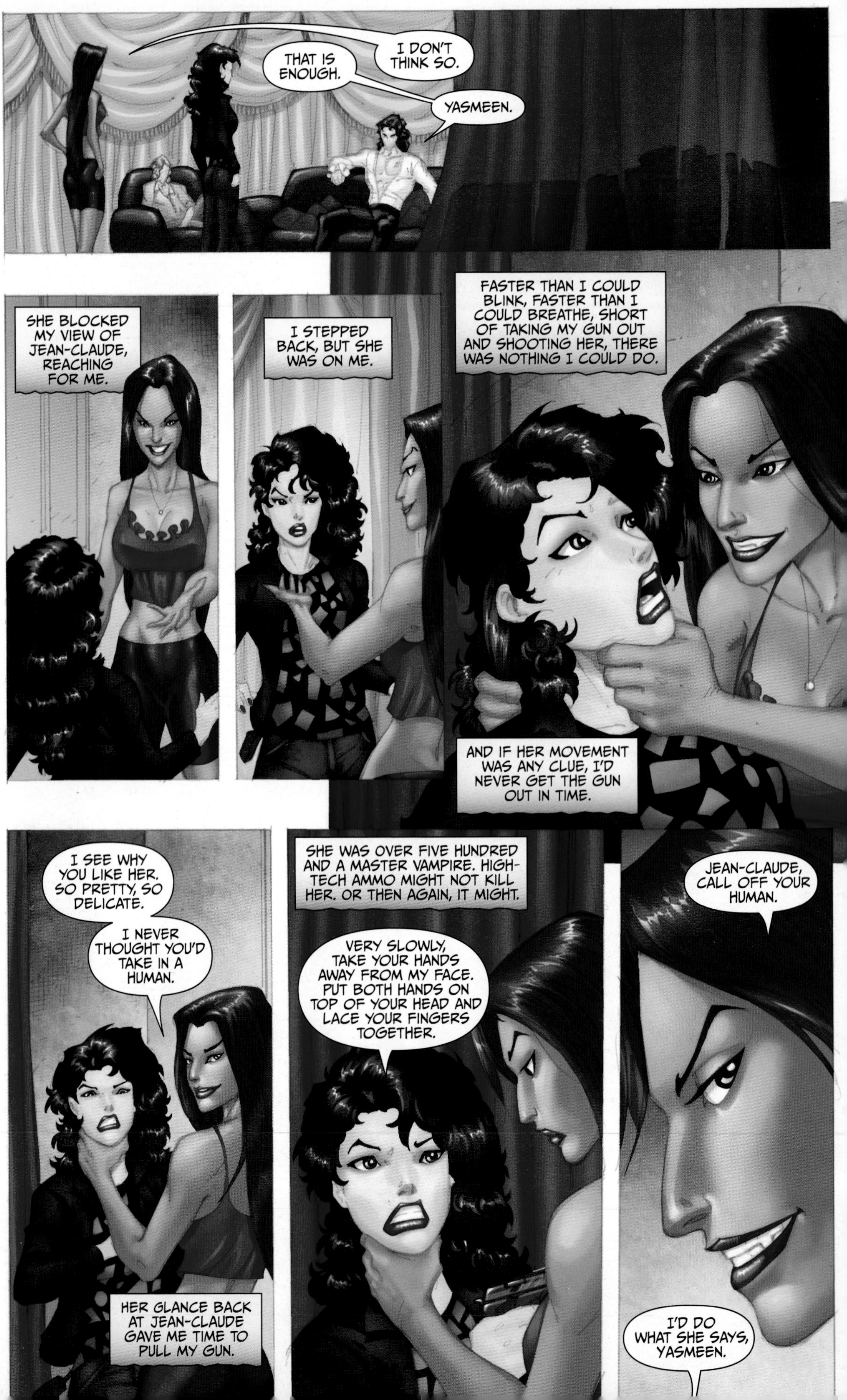
THAT IS ENOUGH.
I DON'T THINK SO.
YASMEEN.
SHE BLOCKED MY VIEW OF JEAN-CLAUDE, REACHING FOR ME.
I STEPPED BACK, BUT SHE WAS ON ME.
FASTER THAN I COULD BLINK, FASTER THAN I COULD BREATHE, SHORT OF TAKING MY GUN OUT AND SHOOTING HER, THERE WAS NOTHING I COULD DO.
AND IF HER MOVEMENT WAS ANY CLUE, I'D NEVER GET THE GUN OUT IN TIME.
I SEE WHY YOU LIKE HER. SO PRETTY, SO DELICATE.
I NEVER THOUGHT YOU'D TAKE IN A HUMAN.
HER GLANCE BACK AT JEAN-CLAUDE GAVE ME TIME TO PULL MY GUN.
SHE WAS OVER FIVE HUNDRED AND A MASTER VAMPIRE. HIGH-TECH AMMO MIGHT NOT KILL HER. OR THEN AGAIN, IT MIGHT.
VERY SLOWLY, TAKE YOUR HANDS AWAY FROM MY FACE. PUT BOTH HANDS ON TOP OF YOUR HEAD AND LACE YOUR FINGERS TOGETHER.
JEAN-CLAUDE, CALL OFF YOUR HUMAN.
I'D DO WHAT SHE SAYS, YASMEEN.

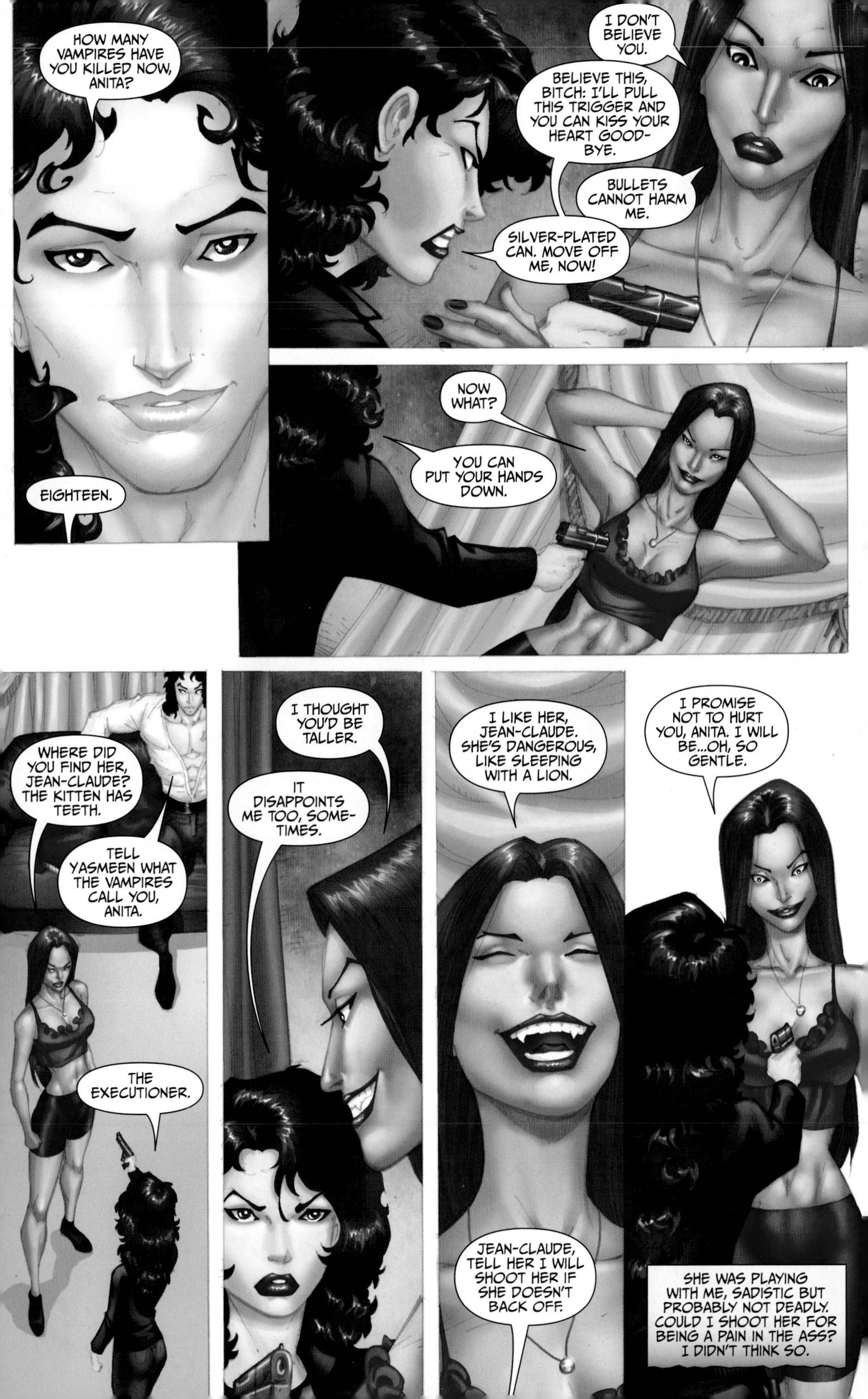
HOW MANY VAMPIRES HAVE YOU KILLED NOW, ANITA?
EIGHTEEN.
I DON'T BELIEVE YOU.
BELIEVE THIS, BITCH: I'LL PULL THIS TRIGGER AND YOU CAN KISS YOUR HEART GOOD-BYE.
BULLETS CANNOT HARM ME.
SILVER-PLATED CAN. MOVE OFF ME, NOW!
NOW WHAT?
YOU CAN PUT YOUR HANDS DOWN.
WHERE DID YOU FIND HER, JEAN-CLAUDE? THE KITTEN HAS TEETH.
TELL YASMEEN WHAT THE VAMPIRES CALL YOU, ANITA.
THE EXECUTIONER.
I THOUGHT YOU'D BE TALLER.
IT DISAPPOINTS ME TOO, SOME-TIMES.
I LIKE HER, JEAN-CLAUDE. SHE'S DANGEROUS, LIKE SLEEPING WITH A LION.
JEAN-CLAUDE, TELL HER I WILL SHOOT HER IF SHE DOESN'T BACK OFF.
I PROMISE NOT TO HURT YOU, ANITA. I WILL BE...OH, SO GENTLE.
SHE WAS PLAYING WITH ME, SADISTIC BUT PROBABLY NOT DEADLY. COULD I SHOOT HER FOR BEING A PAIN IN THE ASS? I DIDN'T THINK SO.

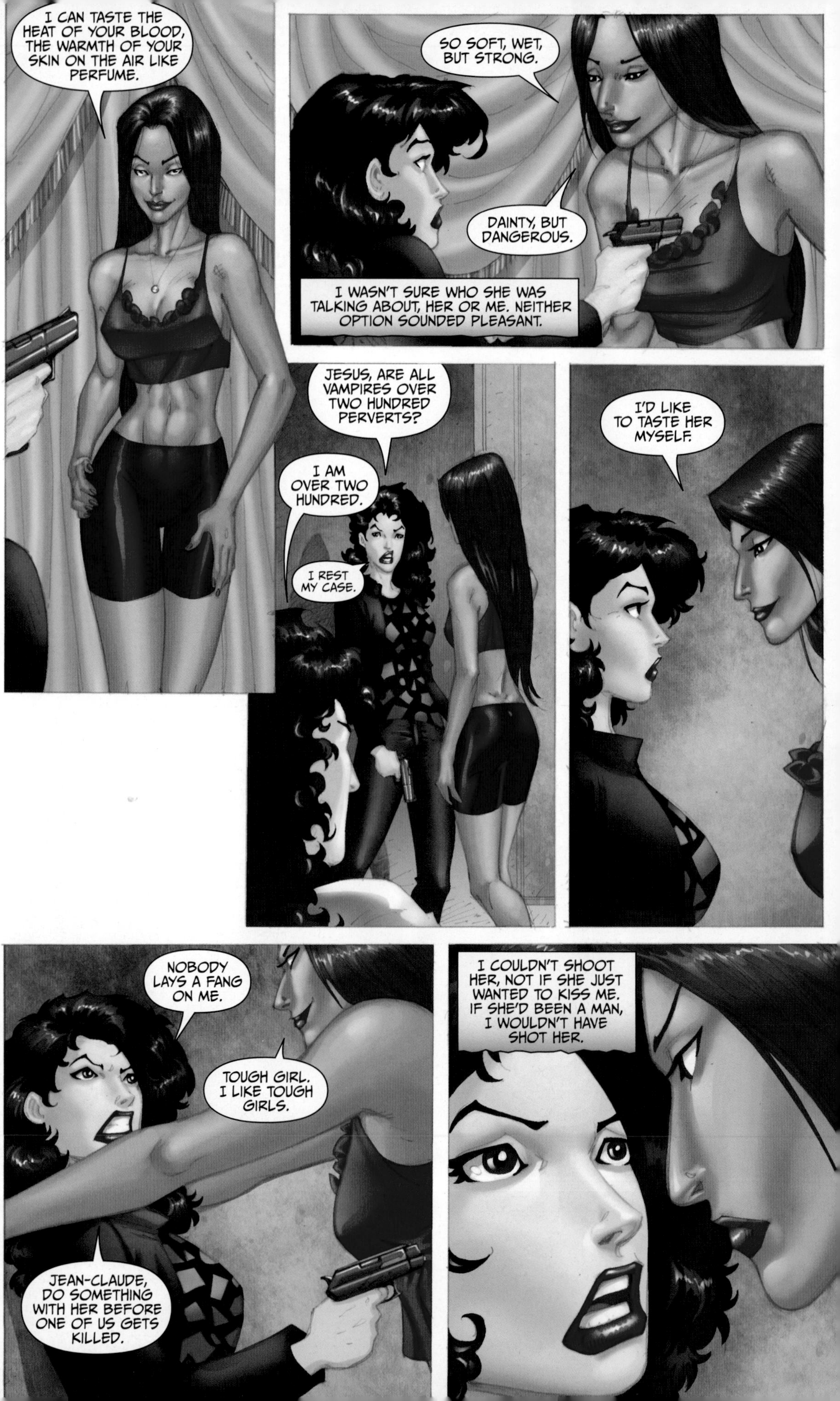
I CAN TASTE THE HEAT OF YOUR BLOOD, THE WARMTH OF YOUR SKIN ON THE AIR LIKE PERFUME.
SO SOFT, WET, BUT STRONG.
DAINTY, BUT DANGEROUS.
I WASN'T SURE WHO SHE WAS TALKING ABOUT, HER OR ME. NEITHER OPTION SOUNDED PLEASANT.
JESUS, ARE ALL VAMPIRES OVER TWO HUNDRED PERVERTS?
I AM OVER TWO HUNDRED.
I REST MY CASE.
I'D LIKE TO TASTE HER MYSELF.
NOBODY LAYS A FANG ON ME.
TOUGH GIRL. I LIKE TOUGH GIRLS.
JEAN-CLAUDE, DO SOMETHING WITH HER BEFORE ONE OF US GETS KILLED.
I COULDN'T SHOOT HER, NOT IF SHE JUST WANTED TO KISS ME. IF SHE'D BEEN A MAN, I WOULDN'T HAVE SHOT HER.

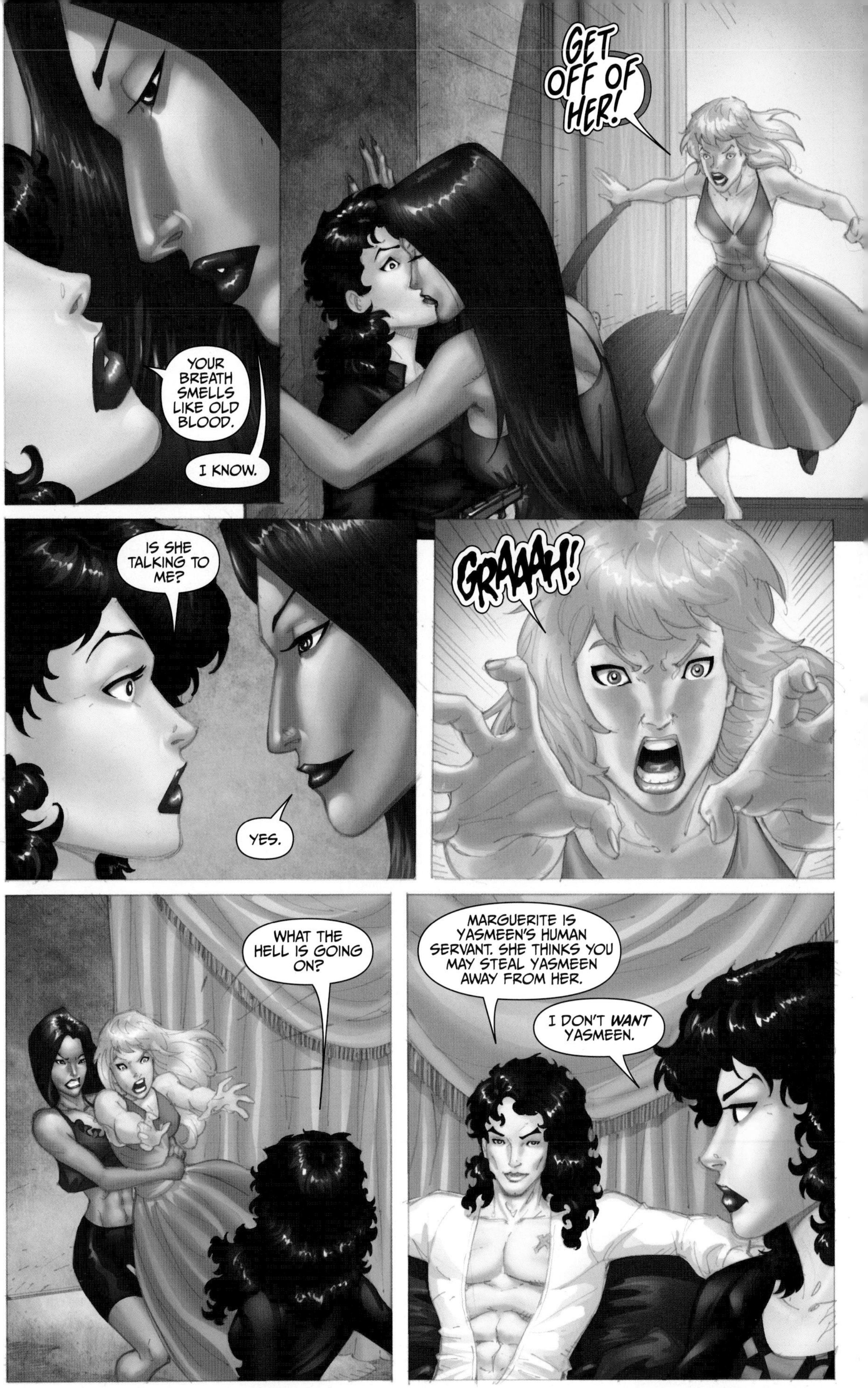
GET OFF OF HER!
YOUR BREATH SMELLS LIKE OLD BLOOD.
I KNOW.
IS SHE TALKING TO ME?
YES.
GRAAAH!
WHAT THE HELL IS GOING ON?
MARGUERITE IS YASMEEN'S HUMAN SERVANT. SHE THINKS YOU MAY STEAL YASMEEN AWAY FROM HER.
I DON'T *WANT* YASMEEN.

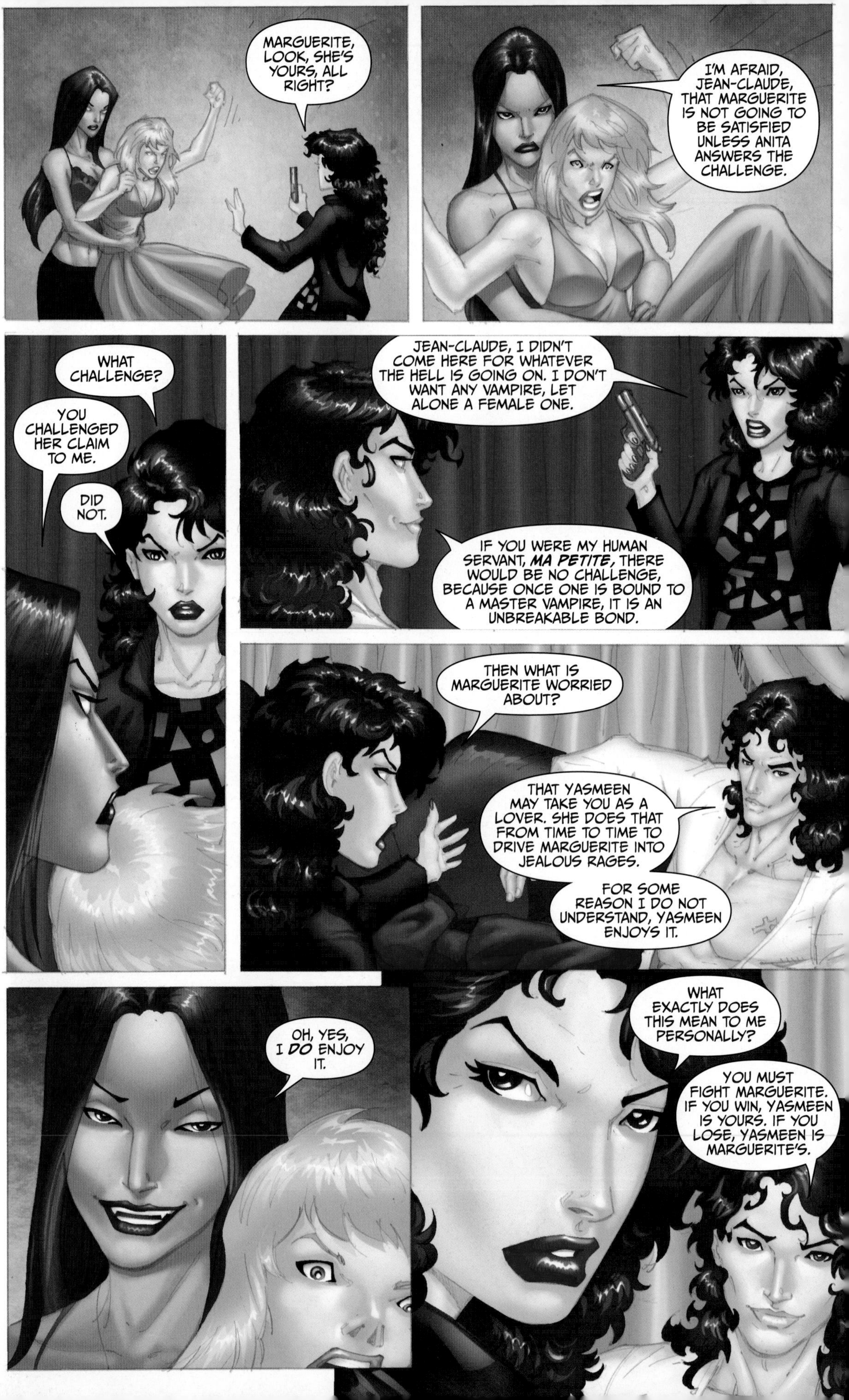
MARGUERITE, LOOK, SHE'S YOURS, ALL RIGHT?
I'M AFRAID, JEAN-CLAUDE, THAT MARGUERITE IS NOT GOING TO BE SATISFIED UNLESS ANITA ANSWERS THE CHALLENGE.
WHAT CHALLENGE?
YOU CHALLENGED HER CLAIM TO ME.
DID NOT.
JEAN-CLAUDE, I DIDN'T COME HERE FOR WHATEVER THE HELL IS GOING ON. I DON'T WANT ANY VAMPIRE, LET ALONE A FEMALE ONE.
IF YOU WERE MY HUMAN SERVANT, *MA PETITE,* THERE WOULD BE NO CHALLENGE, BECAUSE ONCE ONE IS BOUND TO A MASTER VAMPIRE, IT IS AN UNBREAKABLE BOND.
THEN WHAT IS MARGUERITE WORRIED ABOUT?
THAT YASMEEN MAY TAKE YOU AS A LOVER. SHE DOES THAT FROM TIME TO TIME TO DRIVE MARGUERITE INTO JEALOUS RAGES.
FOR SOME REASON I DO NOT UNDERSTAND, YASMEEN ENJOYS IT.
OH, YES, I *DO* ENJOY IT.
WHAT EXACTLY DOES THIS MEAN TO ME PERSONALLY?
YOU MUST FIGHT MARGUERITE. IF YOU WIN, YASMEEN IS YOURS. IF YOU LOSE, YASMEEN IS MARGUERITE'S.

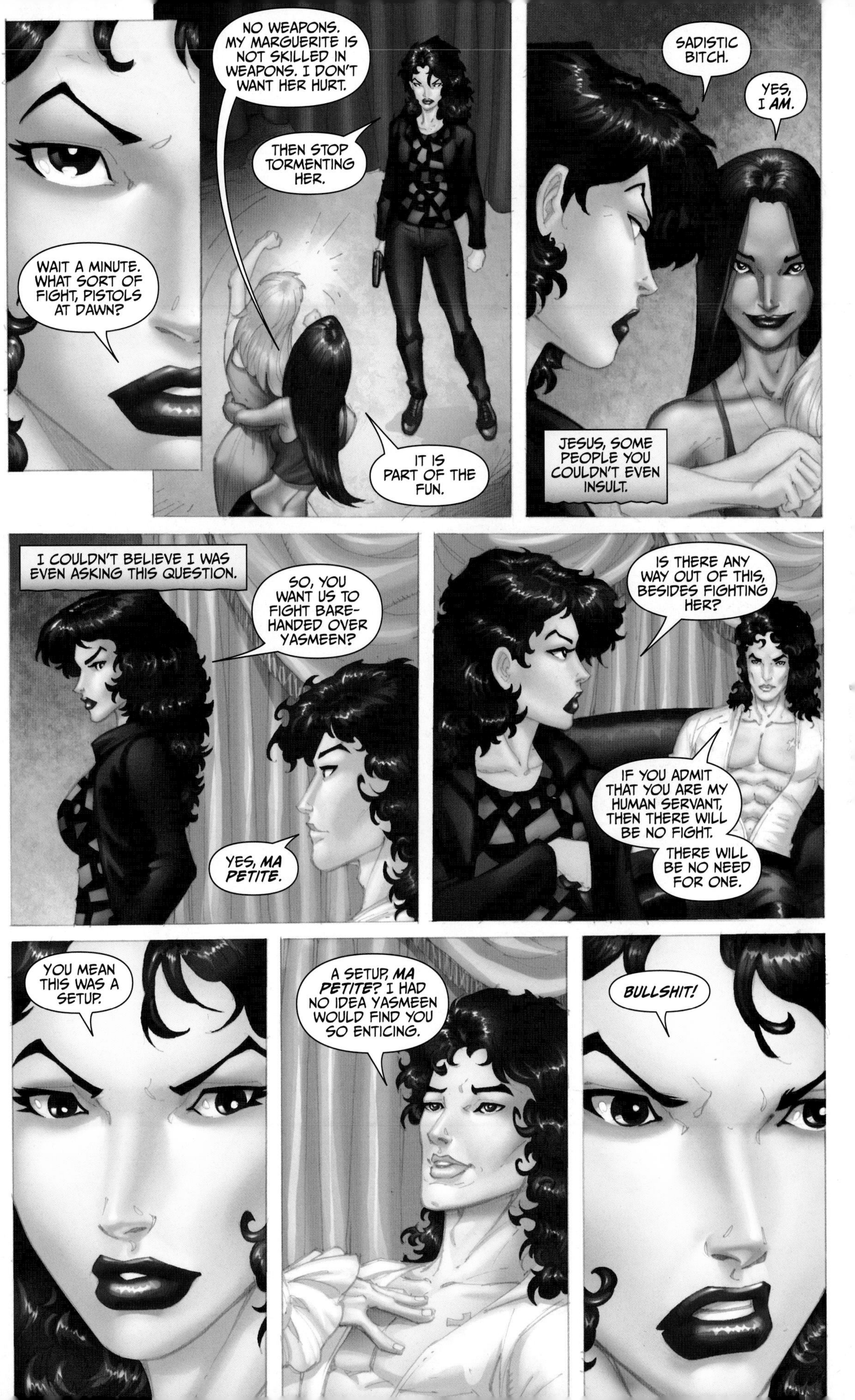
WAIT A MINUTE. WHAT SORT OF FIGHT, PISTOLS AT DAWN?
NO WEAPONS. MY MARGUERITE IS NOT SKILLED IN WEAPONS. I DON'T WANT HER HURT.
THEN STOP TORMENTING HER.
IT IS PART OF THE FUN.
SADISTIC BITCH.
YES, I *AM*.
JESUS, SOME PEOPLE YOU COULDN'T EVEN INSULT.
I COULDN'T BELIEVE I WAS EVEN ASKING THIS QUESTION.
SO, YOU WANT US TO FIGHT BARE-HANDED OVER YASMEEN?
YES, *MA PETITE*.
IS THERE ANY WAY OUT OF THIS, BESIDES FIGHTING HER?
IF YOU ADMIT THAT YOU ARE MY HUMAN SERVANT, THEN THERE WILL BE NO FIGHT.
THERE WILL BE NO NEED FOR ONE.
YOU MEAN THIS WAS A SETUP.
A SETUP, *MA PETITE*? I HAD NO IDEA YASMEEN WOULD FIND YOU SO ENTICING.
BULLSHIT!

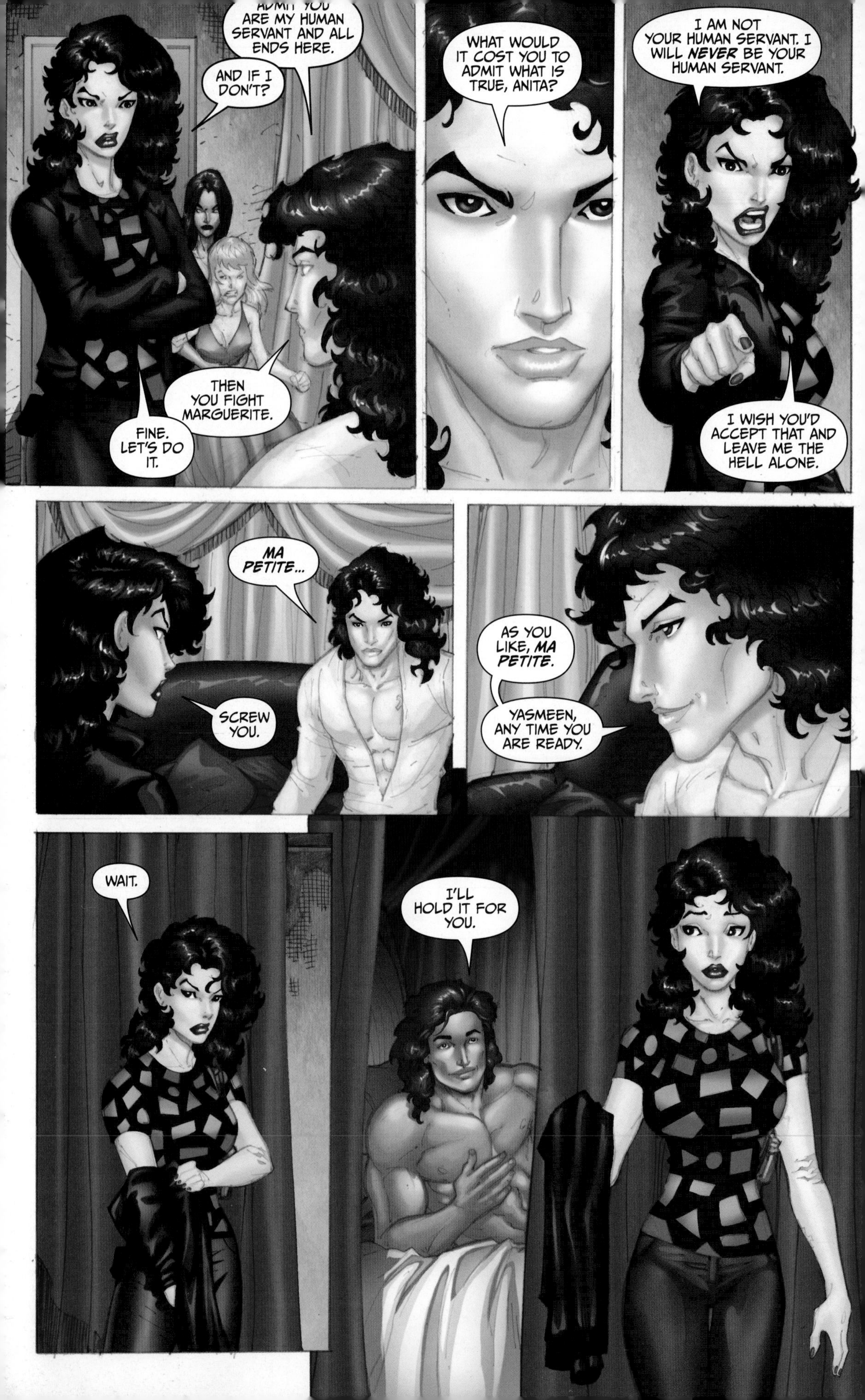
ADMIT YOU ARE MY HUMAN SERVANT AND ALL ENDS HERE.
AND IF I DON'T?
THEN YOU FIGHT MARGUERITE.
FINE. LET'S DO IT.
WHAT WOULD IT COST YOU TO ADMIT WHAT IS TRUE, ANITA?
I AM NOT YOUR HUMAN SERVANT. I WILL *NEVER* BE YOUR HUMAN SERVANT.
I WISH YOU'D ACCEPT THAT AND LEAVE ME THE HELL ALONE.
MA PETITE...
SCREW YOU.
AS YOU LIKE, *MA PETITE*.
YASMEEN, ANY TIME YOU ARE READY.
WAIT.
I'LL HOLD IT FOR YOU.

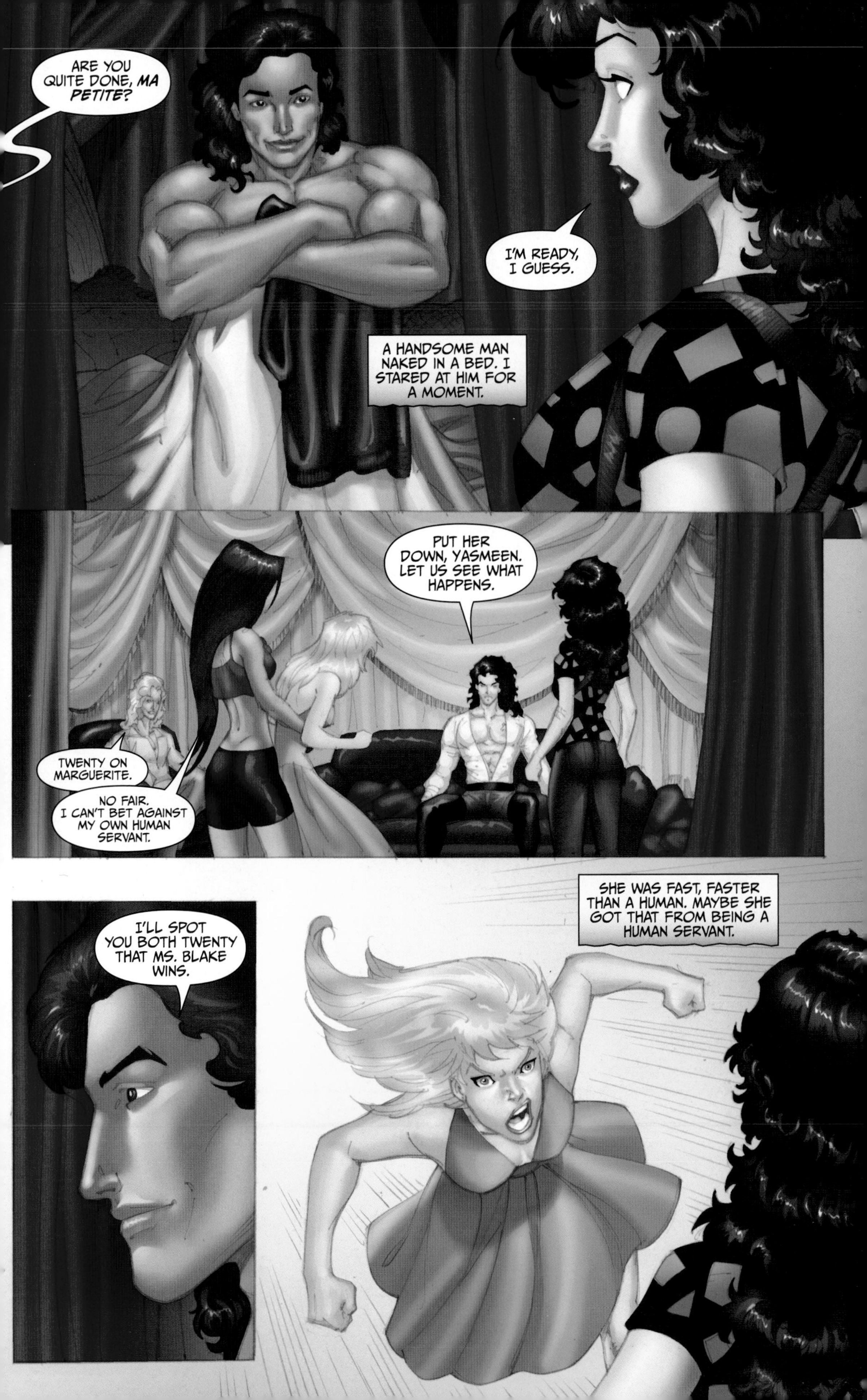
ARE YOU QUITE DONE, *MA PETITE*?
I'M READY, I GUESS.
A HANDSOME MAN NAKED IN A BED. I STARED AT HIM FOR A MOMENT.
PUT HER DOWN, YASMEEN. LET US SEE WHAT HAPPENS.
TWENTY ON MARGUERITE.
NO FAIR. I CAN'T BET AGAINST MY OWN HUMAN SERVANT.
I'LL SPOT YOU BOTH TWENTY THAT MS. BLAKE WINS.
SHE WAS FAST, FASTER THAN A HUMAN. MAYBE SHE GOT THAT FROM BEING A HUMAN SERVANT.

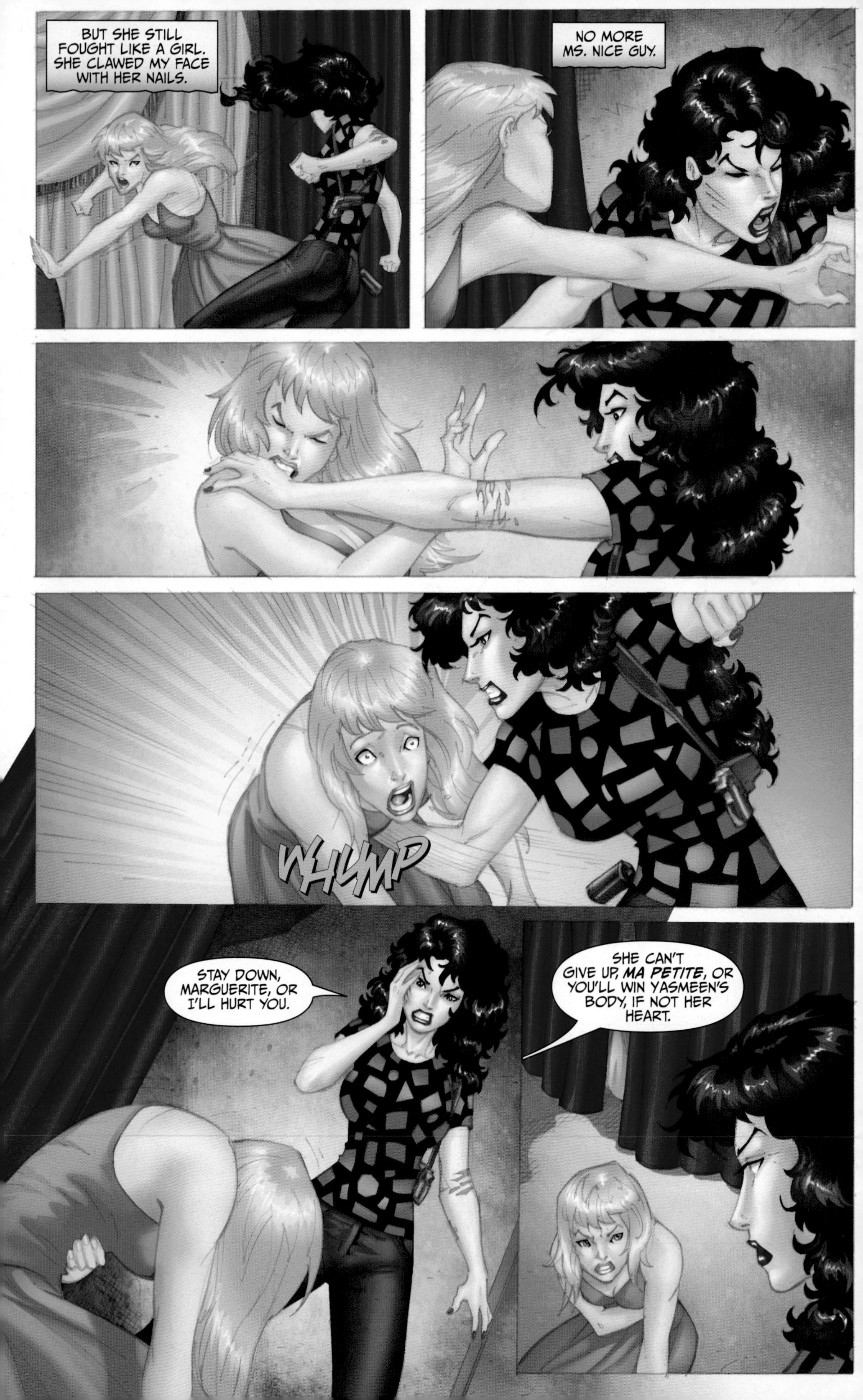
BUT SHE STILL FOUGHT LIKE A GIRL. SHE CLAWED MY FACE WITH HER NAILS.
NO MORE MS. NICE GUY.
WHUMP
STAY DOWN, MARGUERITE, OR I'LL HURT YOU.
SHE CAN'T GIVE UP, *MA PETITE*, OR YOU'LL WIN YASMEEN'S BODY, IF NOT HER HEART.

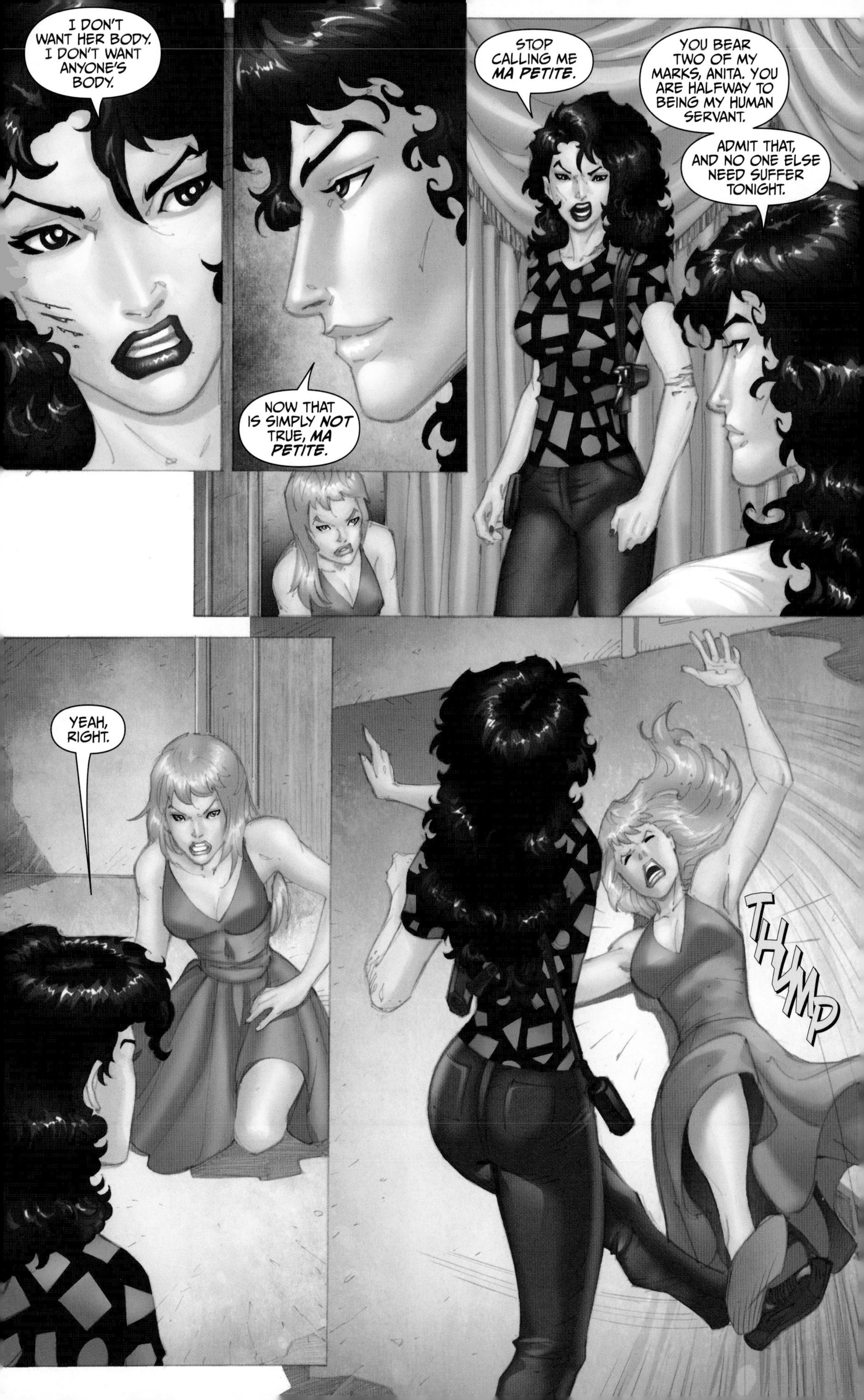

I DON'T WANT HER BODY. I DON'T WANT ANYONE'S BODY.
NOW THAT IS SIMPLY *NOT* TRUE, *MA PETITE*.
STOP CALLING ME *MA PETITE*.
YOU BEAR TWO OF MY MARKS, ANITA. YOU ARE HALFWAY TO BEING MY HUMAN SERVANT.
ADMIT THAT, AND NO ONE ELSE NEED SUFFER TONIGHT.
YEAH, RIGHT.
THUMP

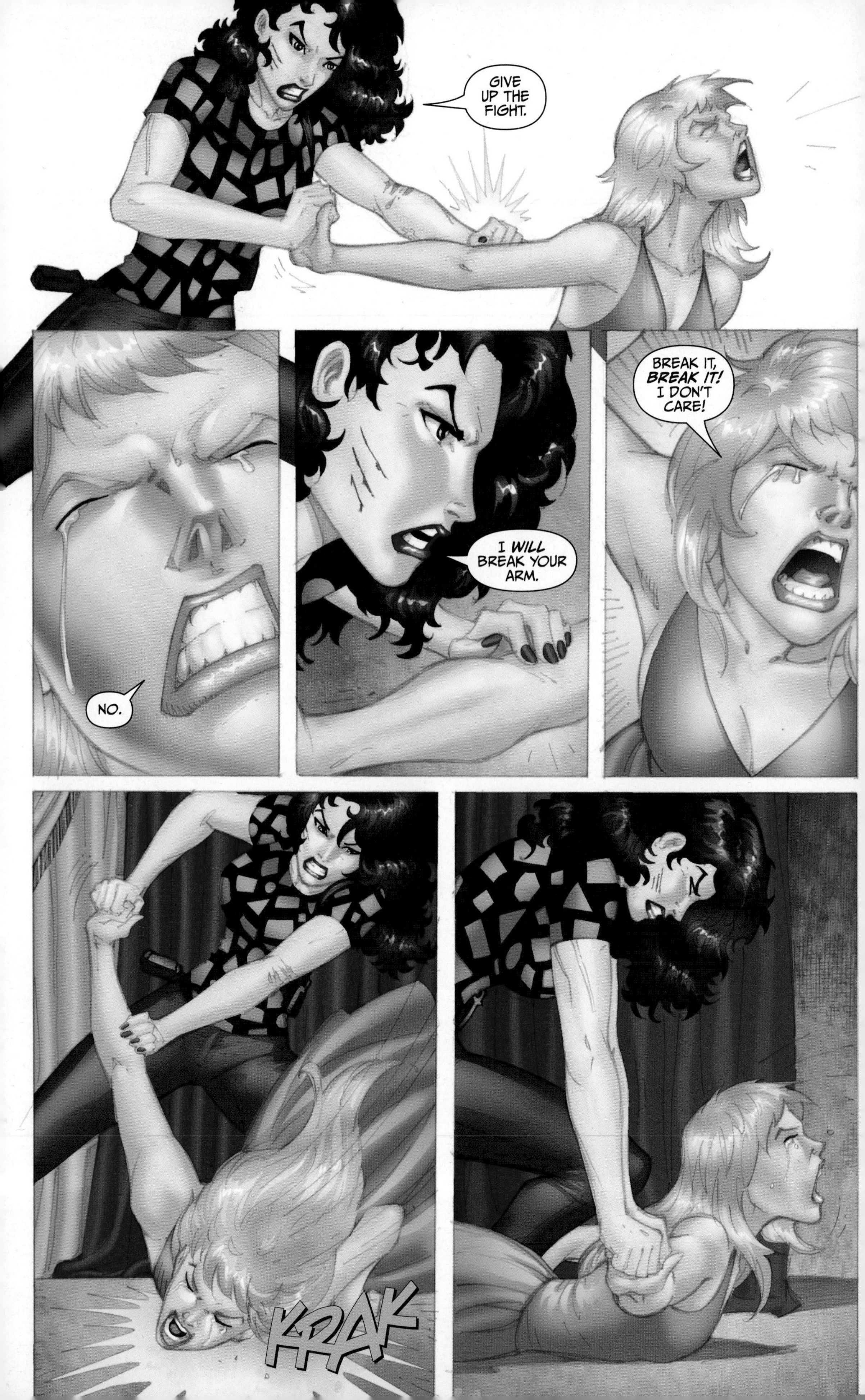
GIVE UP THE FIGHT.
NO.
I WILL BREAK YOUR ARM.
BREAK IT, BREAK IT! I DON'T CARE!
KRAK

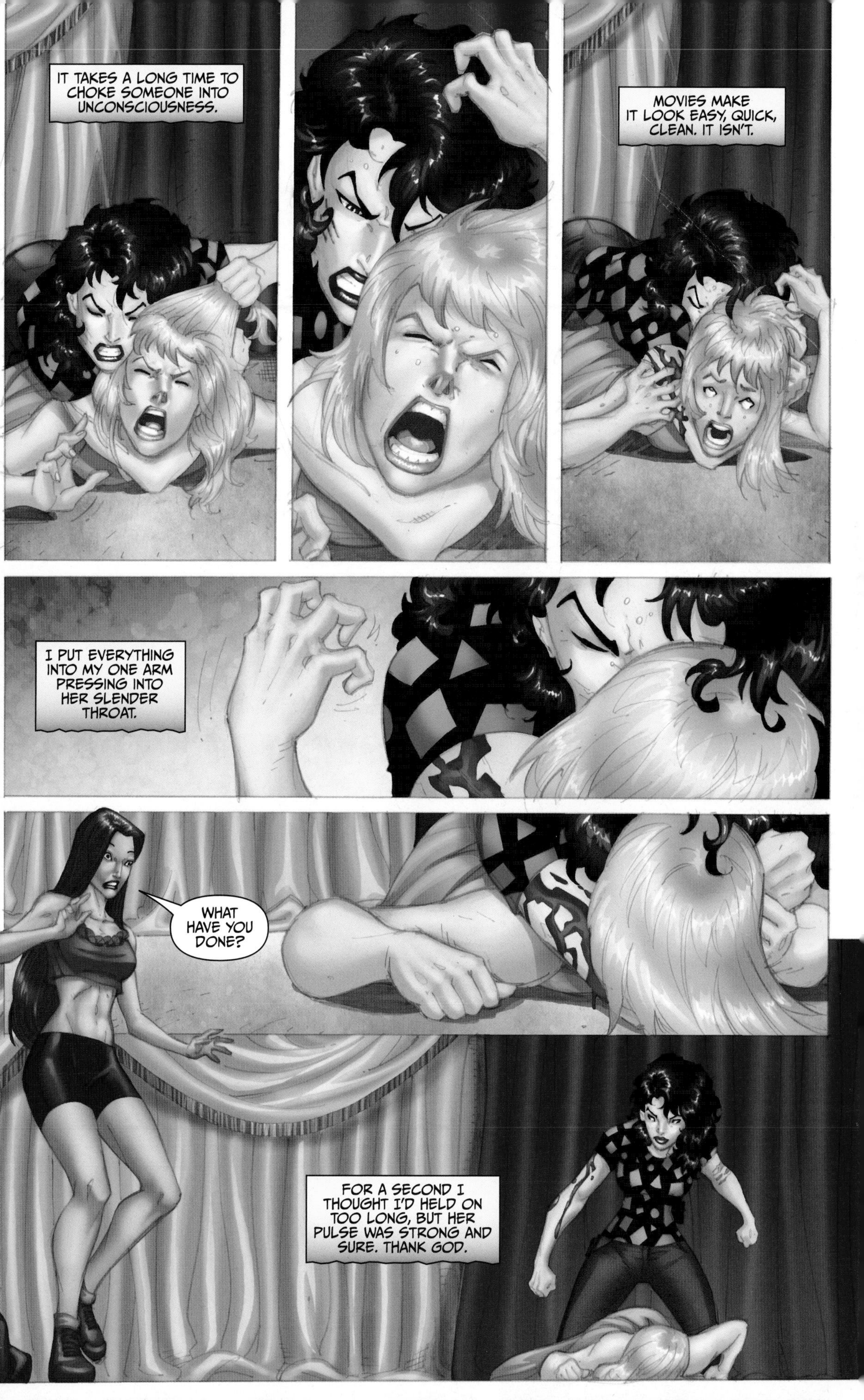
IT TAKES A LONG TIME TO CHOKE SOMEONE INTO UNCONSCIOUSNESS.
MOVIES MAKE IT LOOK EASY, QUICK, CLEAN. IT ISN'T.
I PUT EVERYTHING INTO MY ONE ARM PRESSING INTO HER SLENDER THROAT.
WHAT HAVE YOU DONE?
FOR A SECOND I THOUGHT I'D HELD ON TOO LONG, BUT HER PULSE WAS STRONG AND SURE. THANK GOD.

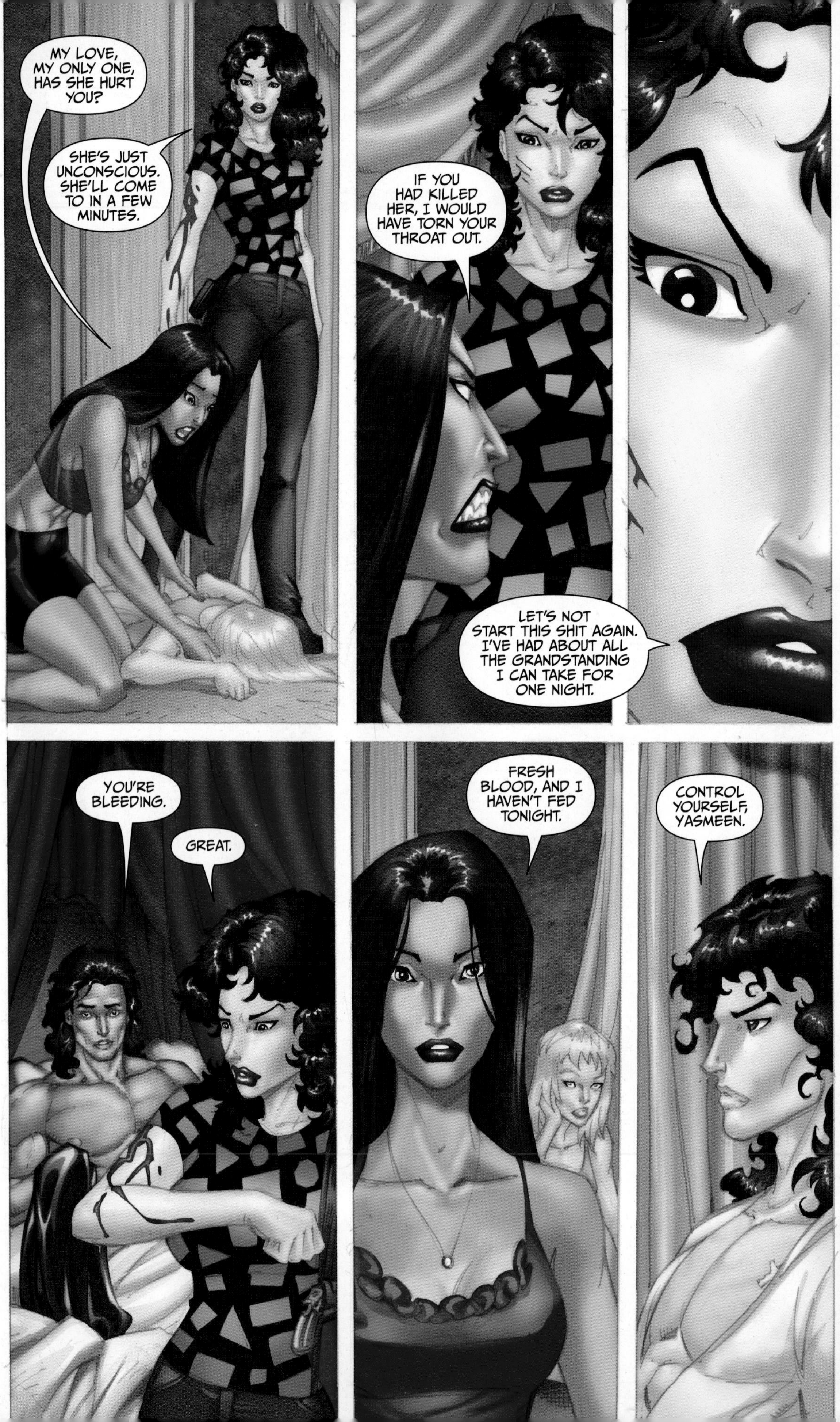
MY LOVE, MY ONLY ONE, HAS SHE HURT YOU?
SHE'S JUST UNCONSCIOUS. SHE'LL COME TO IN A FEW MINUTES.
IF YOU HAD KILLED HER, I WOULD HAVE TORN YOUR THROAT OUT.
LET'S NOT START THIS SHIT AGAIN. I'VE HAD ABOUT ALL THE GRANDSTANDING I CAN TAKE FOR ONE NIGHT.
YOU'RE BLEEDING.
GREAT.
FRESH BLOOD, AND I HAVEN'T FED TONIGHT.
CONTROL YOURSELF, YASMEEN.

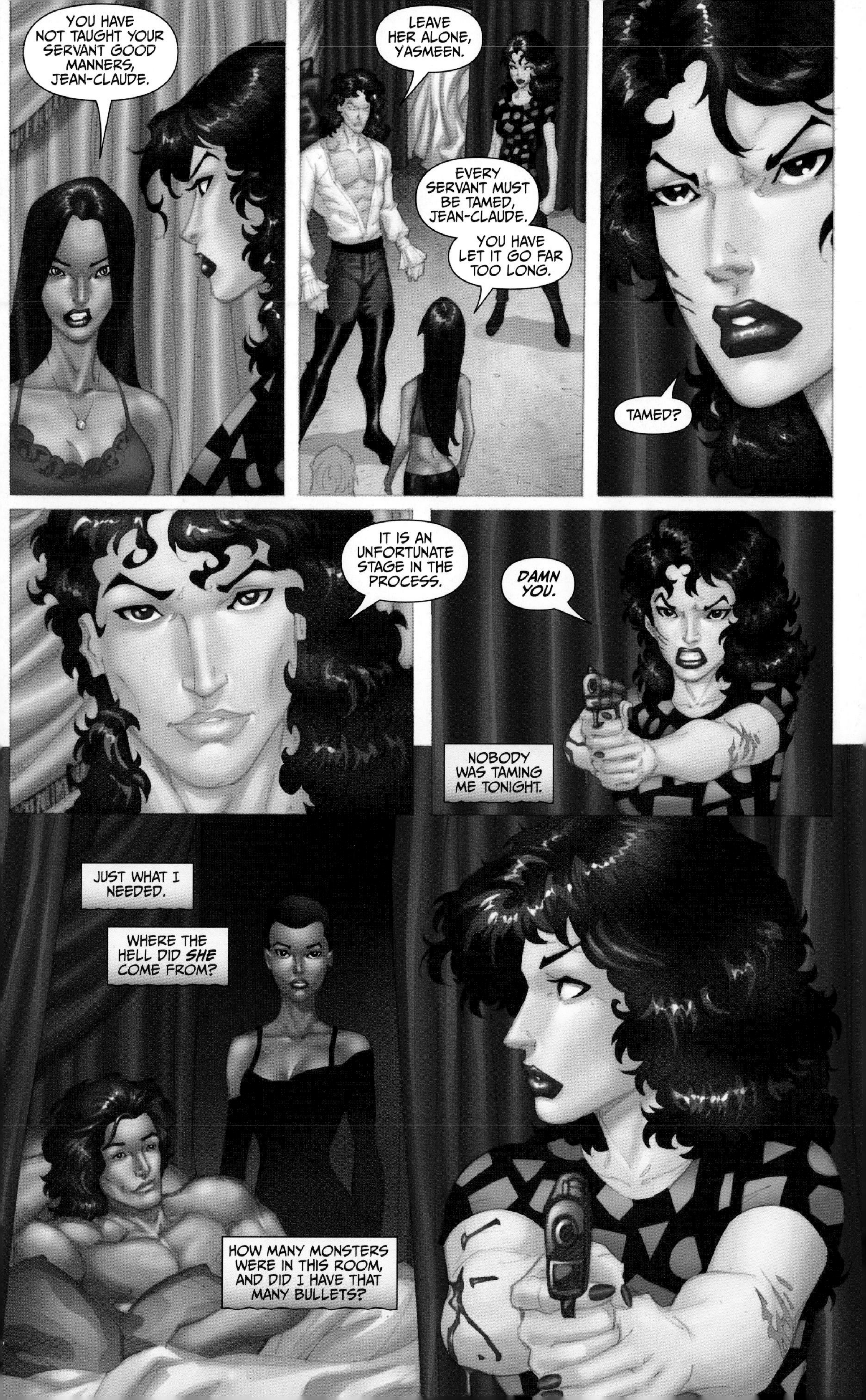
YOU HAVE NOT TAUGHT YOUR SERVANT GOOD MANNERS, JEAN-CLAUDE.
LEAVE HER ALONE, YASMEEN.
EVERY SERVANT MUST BE TAMED, JEAN-CLAUDE.
YOU HAVE LET IT GO FAR TOO LONG.
TAMED?
IT IS AN UNFORTUNATE STAGE IN THE PROCESS.
DAMN YOU.
NOBODY WAS TAMING ME TONIGHT.
JUST WHAT I NEEDED.
WHERE THE HELL DID SHE COME FROM?
HOW MANY MONSTERS WERE IN THIS ROOM, AND DID I HAVE THAT MANY BULLETS?

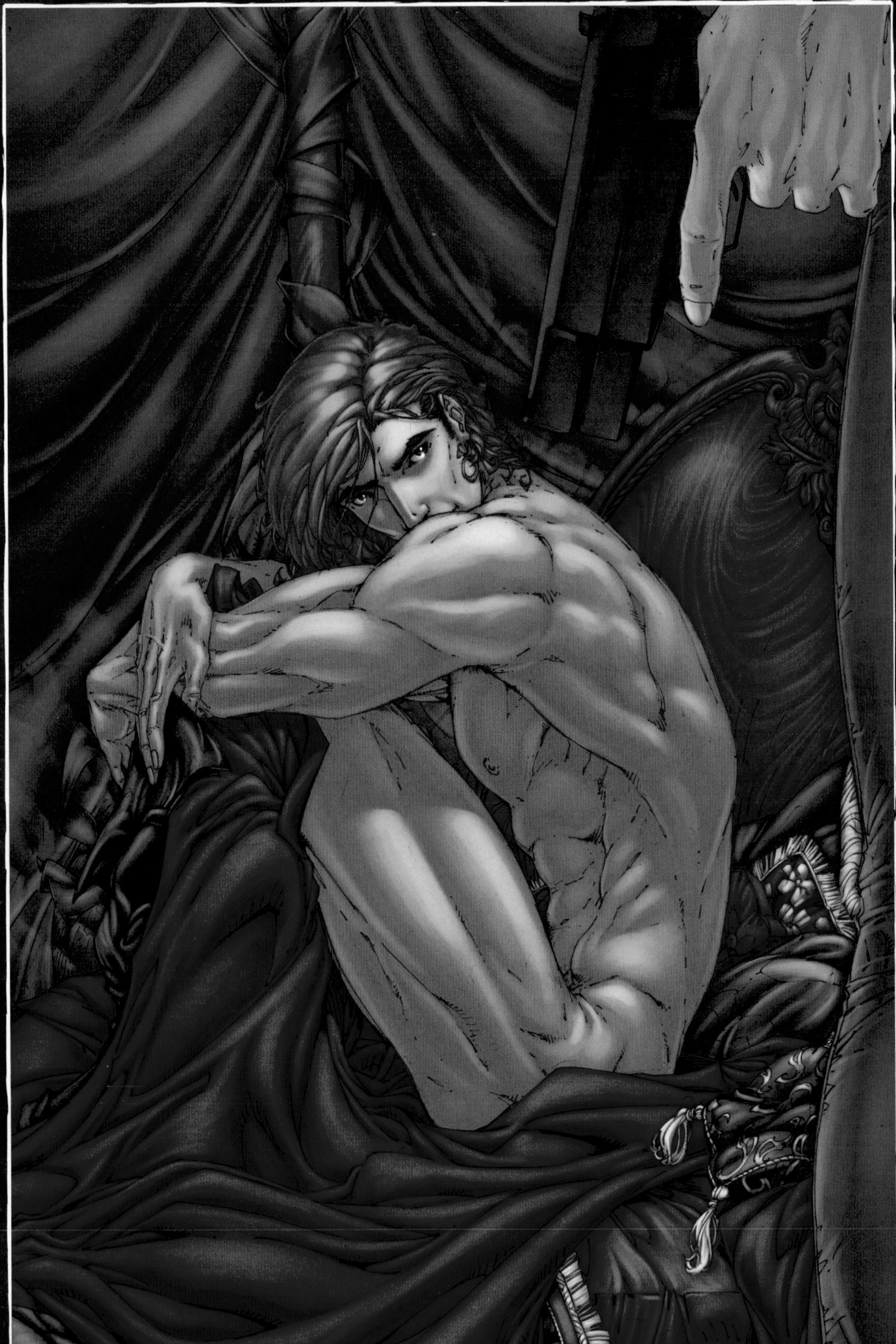

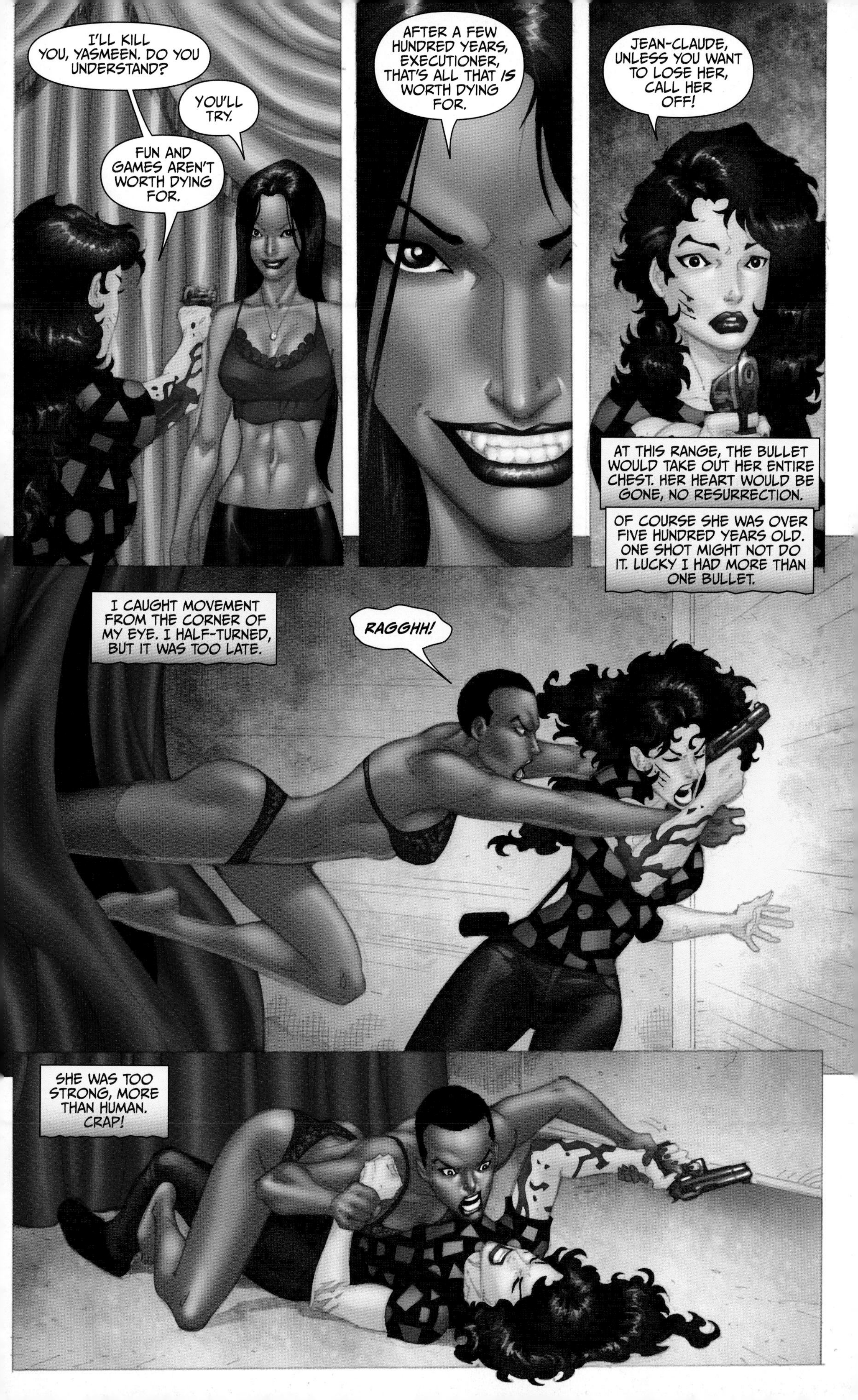
I'LL KILL YOU, YASMEEN. DO YOU UNDERSTAND?
YOU'LL TRY.
FUN AND GAMES AREN'T WORTH DYING FOR.
AFTER A FEW HUNDRED YEARS, EXECUTIONER, THAT'S ALL THAT *IS* WORTH DYING FOR.
JEAN-CLAUDE, UNLESS YOU WANT TO LOSE HER, CALL HER OFF!
AT THIS RANGE, THE BULLET WOULD TAKE OUT HER ENTIRE CHEST. HER HEART WOULD BE GONE, NO RESURRECTION.
OF COURSE SHE WAS OVER FIVE HUNDRED YEARS OLD. ONE SHOT MIGHT NOT DO IT. LUCKY I HAD MORE THAN ONE BULLET.
I CAUGHT MOVEMENT FROM THE CORNER OF MY EYE. I HALF-TURNED, BUT IT WAS TOO LATE.
RAGGHH!
SHE WAS TOO STRONG, MORE THAN HUMAN. CRAP!

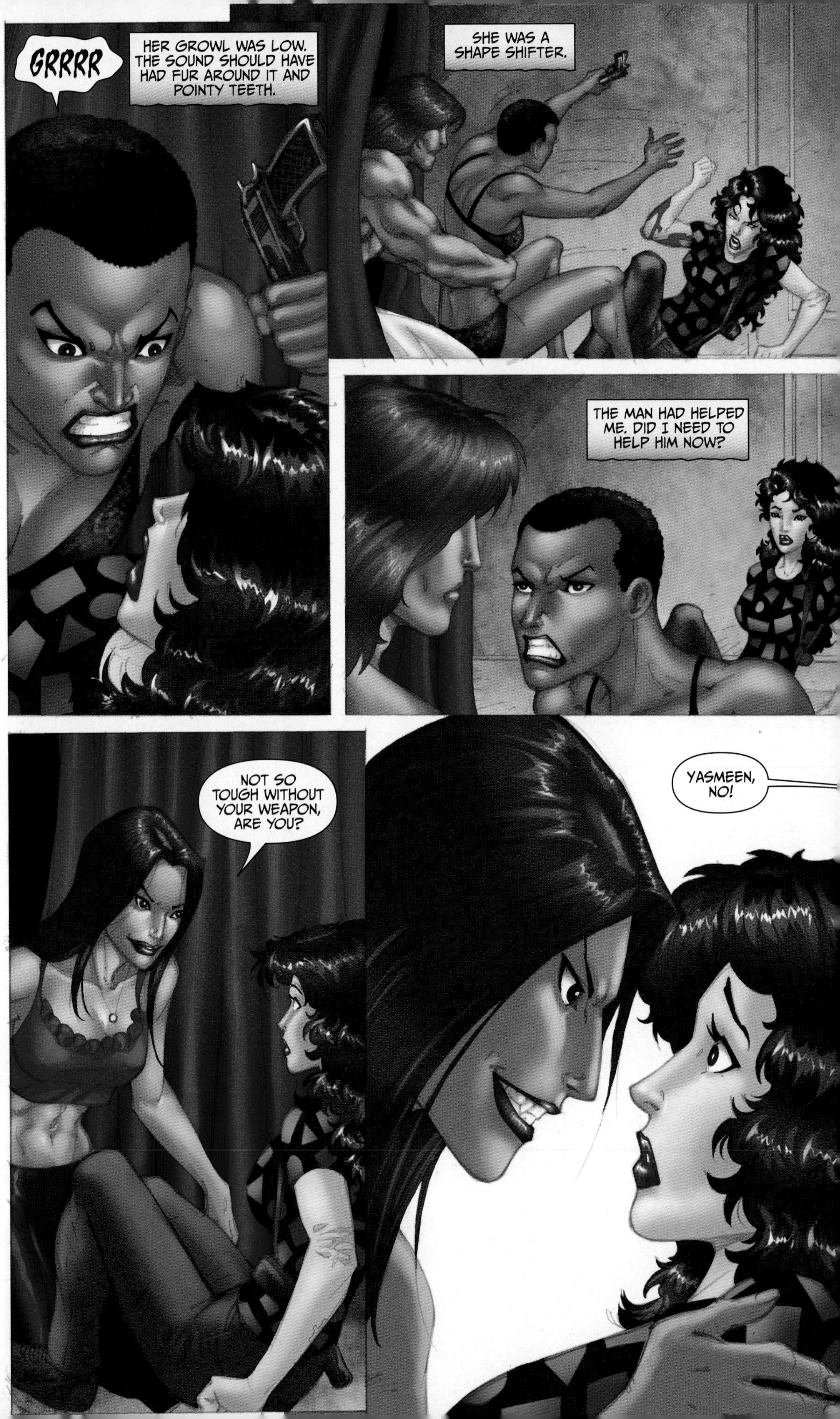
GRRRR
HER GROWL WAS LOW. THE SOUND SHOULD HAVE HAD FUR AROUND IT AND POINTY TEETH.
SHE WAS A SHAPE SHIFTER.
THE MAN HAD HELPED ME. DID I NEED TO HELP HIM NOW?
NOT SO TOUGH WITHOUT YOUR WEAPON, ARE YOU?
YASMEEN, NO!

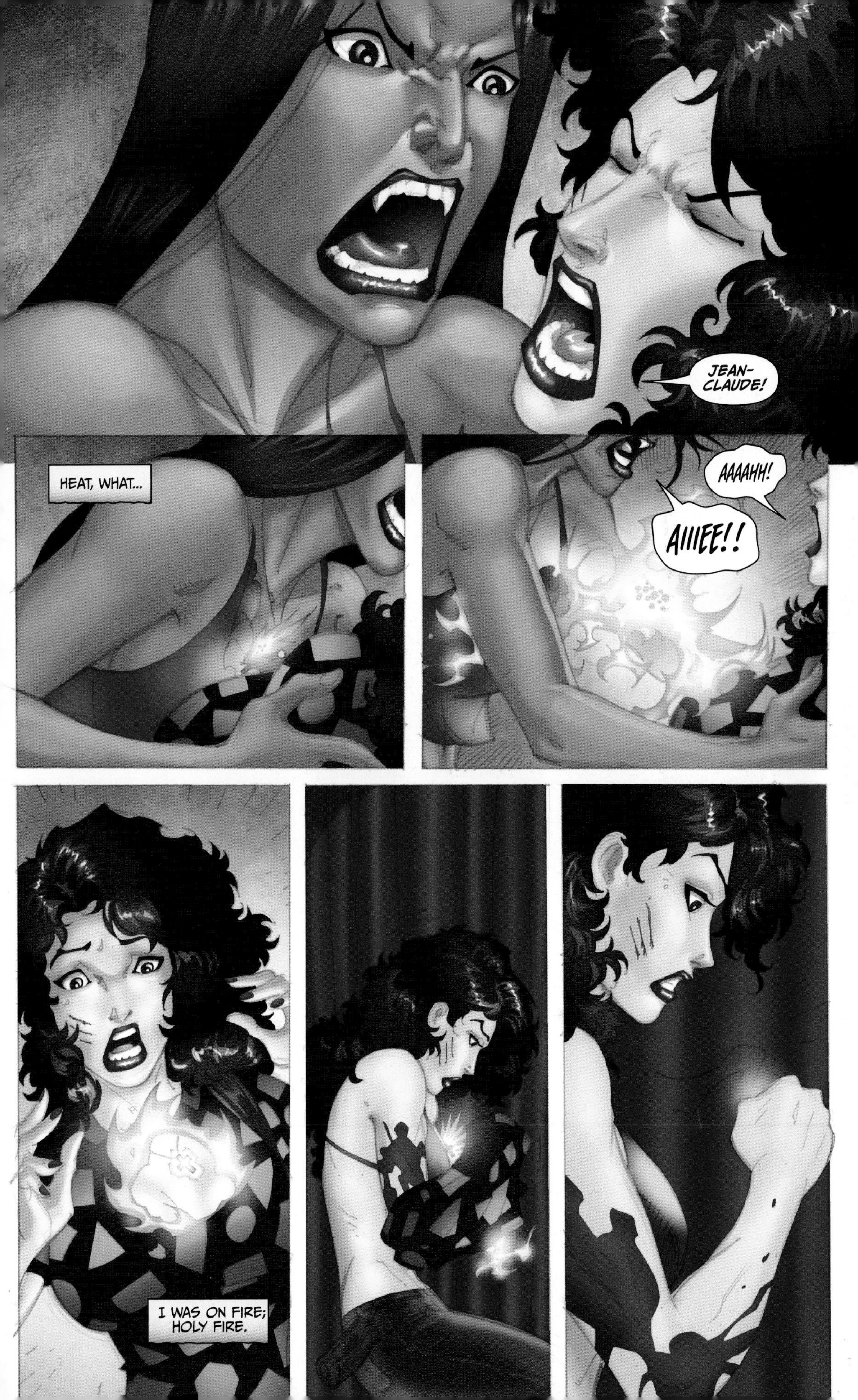
JEAN-CLAUDE!
HEAT, WHAT...
AAAAHH!
AIIIEE!!
I WAS ON FIRE; HOLY FIRE.

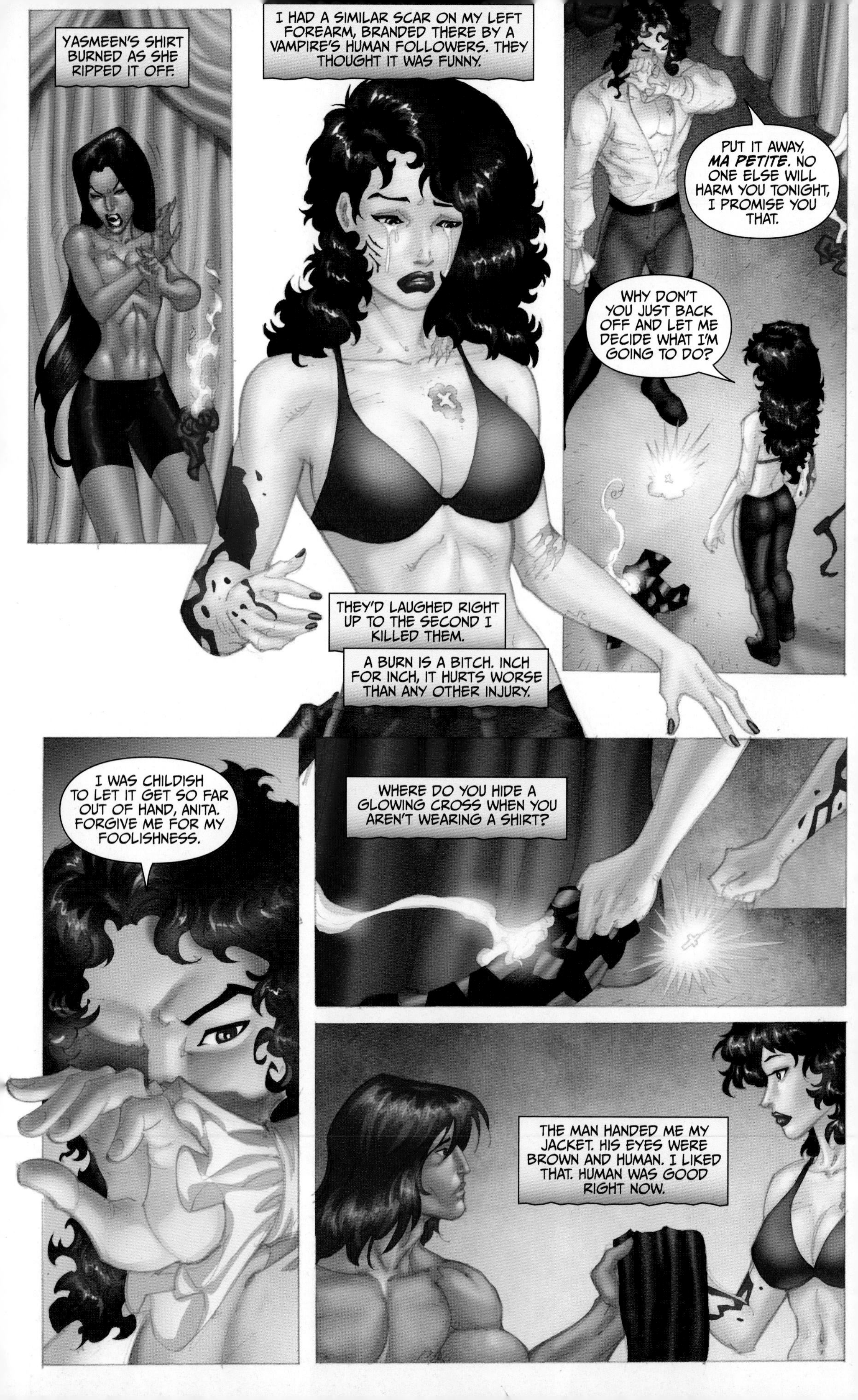
YASMEEN'S SHIRT BURNED AS SHE RIPPED IT OFF.
I HAD A SIMILAR SCAR ON MY LEFT FOREARM, BRANDED THERE BY A VAMPIRE'S HUMAN FOLLOWERS. THEY THOUGHT IT WAS FUNNY.
THEY'D LAUGHED RIGHT UP TO THE SECOND I KILLED THEM.
A BURN IS A BITCH. INCH FOR INCH, IT HURTS WORSE THAN ANY OTHER INJURY.
PUT IT AWAY, MA PETITE. NO ONE ELSE WILL HARM YOU TONIGHT, I PROMISE YOU THAT.
WHY DON'T YOU JUST BACK OFF AND LET ME DECIDE WHAT I'M GOING TO DO?
I WAS CHILDISH TO LET IT GET SO FAR OUT OF HAND, ANITA. FORGIVE ME FOR MY FOOLISHNESS.
WHERE DO YOU HIDE A GLOWING CROSS WHEN YOU AREN'T WEARING A SHIRT?
THE MAN HANDED ME MY JACKET. HIS EYES WERE BROWN AND HUMAN. I LIKED THAT. HUMAN WAS GOOD RIGHT NOW.

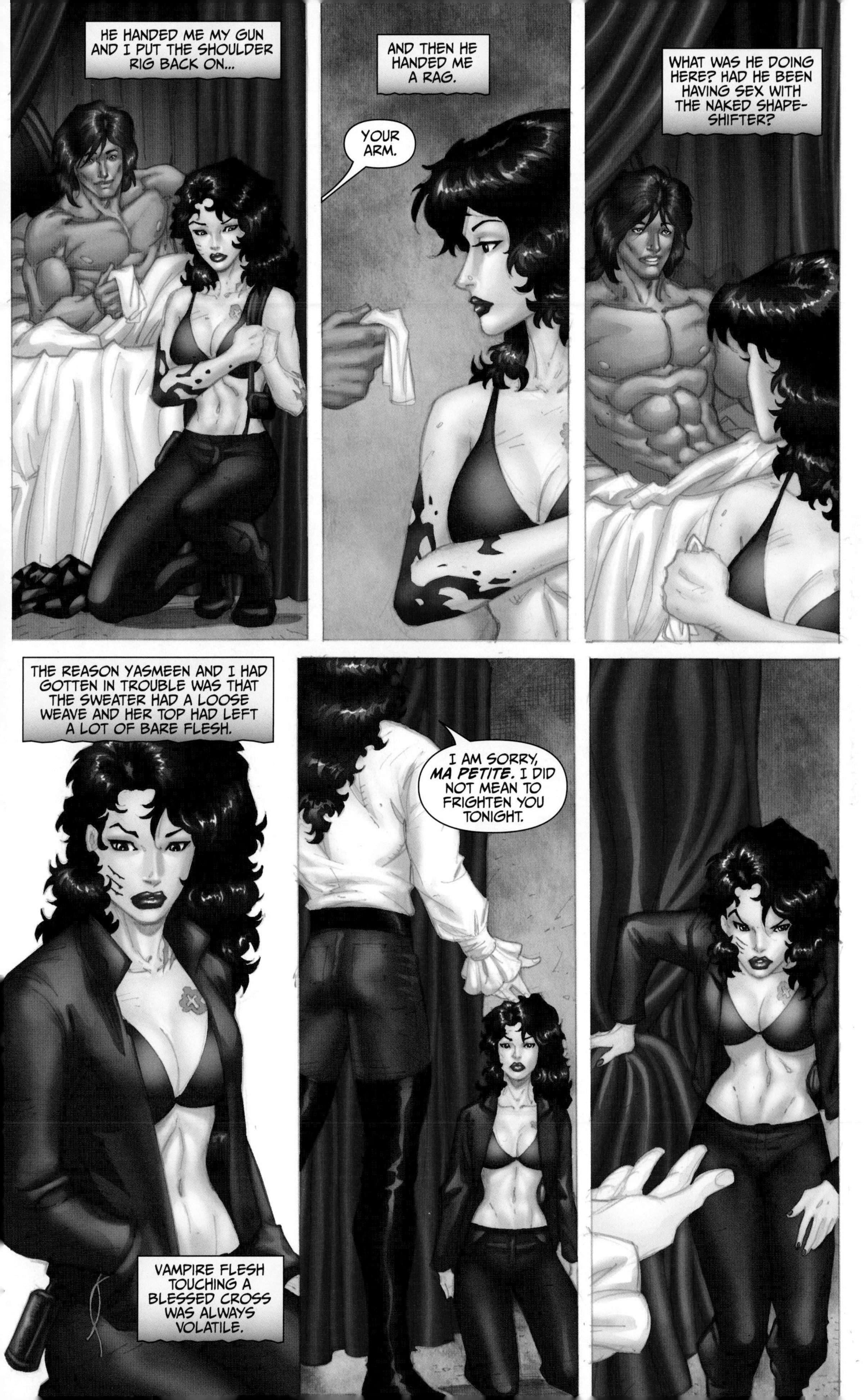
HE HANDED ME MY GUN AND I PUT THE SHOULDER RIG BACK ON...
AND THEN HE HANDED ME A RAG.
YOUR ARM.
WHAT WAS HE DOING HERE? HAD HE BEEN HAVING SEX WITH THE NAKED SHAPE-SHIFTER?
THE REASON YASMEEN AND I HAD GOTTEN IN TROUBLE WAS THAT THE SWEATER HAD A LOOSE WEAVE AND HER TOP HAD LEFT A LOT OF BARE FLESH.
VAMPIRE FLESH TOUCHING A BLESSED CROSS WAS ALWAYS VOLATILE.
I AM SORRY, MA PETITE. I DID NOT MEAN TO FRIGHTEN YOU TONIGHT.

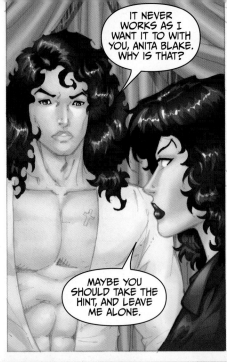

IT NEVER WORKS AS I WANT IT TO WITH YOU, ANITA BLAKE. WHY IS THAT?

MAYBE YOU SHOULD TAKE THE HINT, AND LEAVE ME ALONE.

I'M AFRAID IT IS TOO LATE FOR THAT.

WHAT'S *THAT* SUPPOSED TO MEAN?

JEAN-CLAUDE...THE SNAKE...

WHAT ABOUT THE SNAKE?

IT'S GONE CRAZY. IT ATTACKED SHAHAR, ITS TRAINER. SHE'S DEAD.

IS IT IN THE CROWD?

NOT YET.

WE WILL HAVE TO FINISH THIS DISCUSSION LATER, *MA PETITE.*

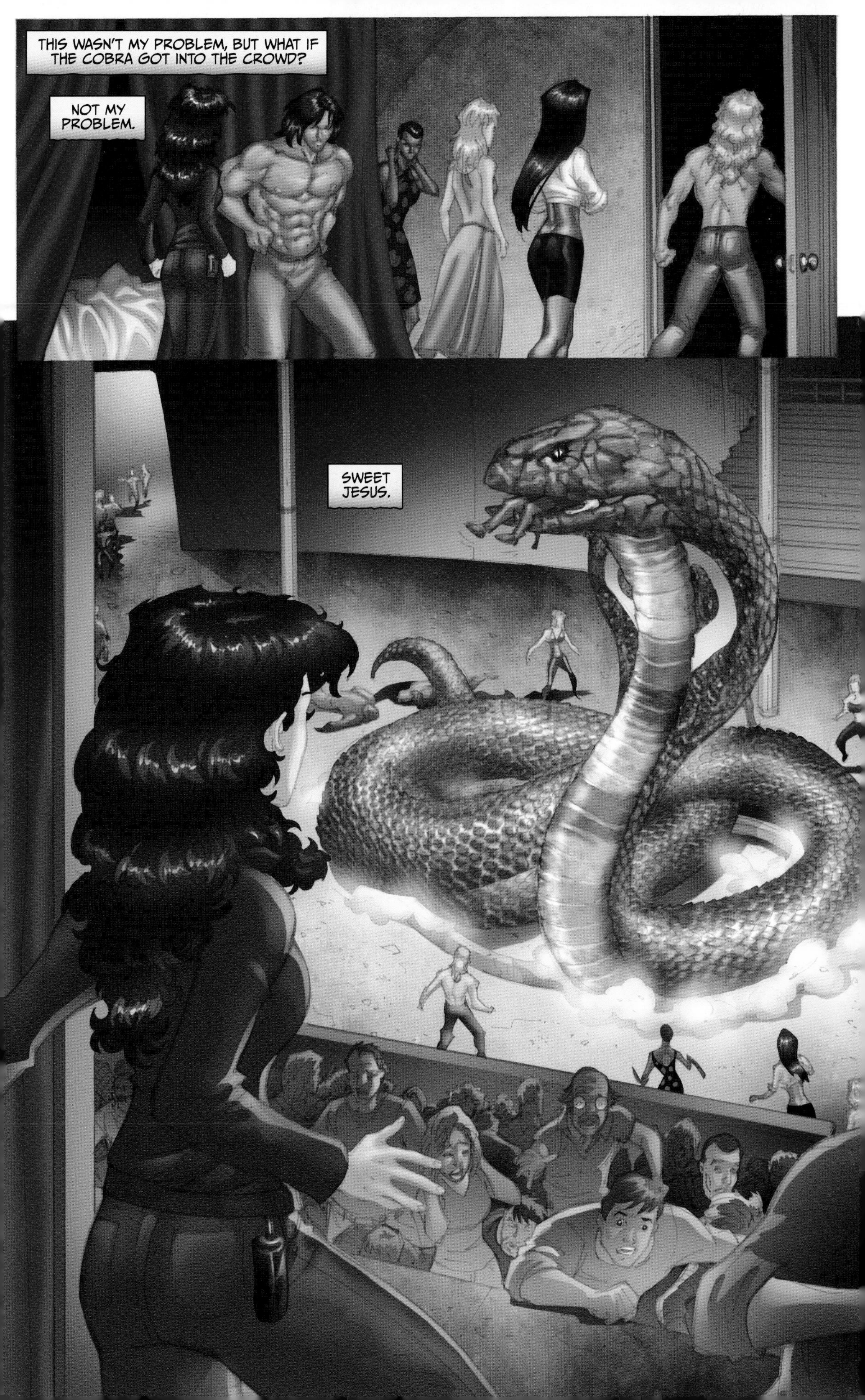
THIS WASN'T MY PROBLEM, BUT WHAT IF THE COBRA GOT INTO THE CROWD?
NOT MY PROBLEM.
SWEET JESUS.

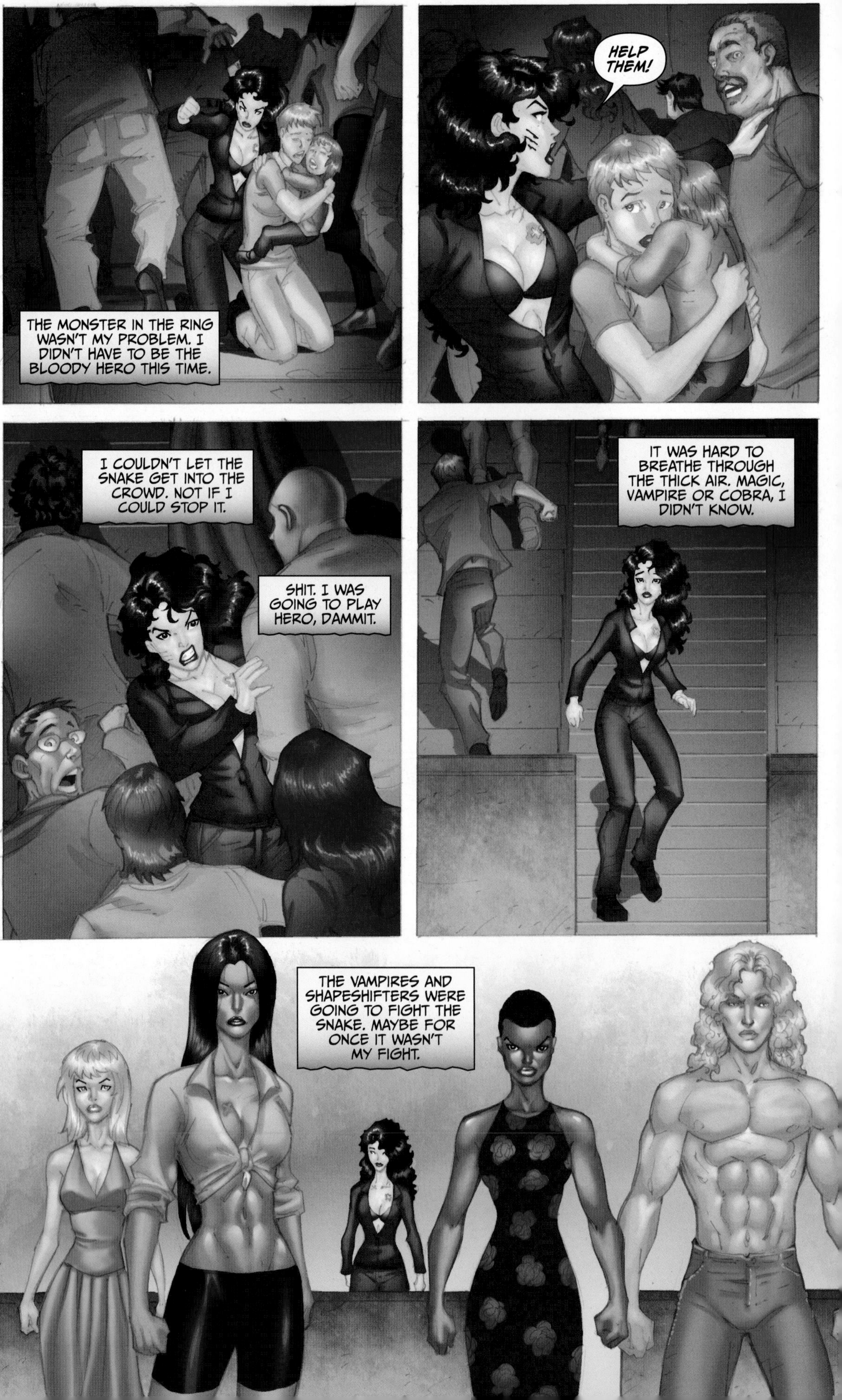
THE MONSTER IN THE RING WASN'T MY PROBLEM. I DIDN'T HAVE TO BE THE BLOODY HERO THIS TIME.
HELP THEM!
I COULDN'T LET THE SNAKE GET INTO THE CROWD. NOT IF I COULD STOP IT.
SHIT. I WAS GOING TO PLAY HERO, DAMMIT.
IT WAS HARD TO BREATHE THROUGH THE THICK AIR. MAGIC, VAMPIRE OR COBRA, I DIDN'T KNOW.
THE VAMPIRES AND SHAPESHIFTERS WERE GOING TO FIGHT THE SNAKE. MAYBE FOR ONCE IT WASN'T MY FIGHT.

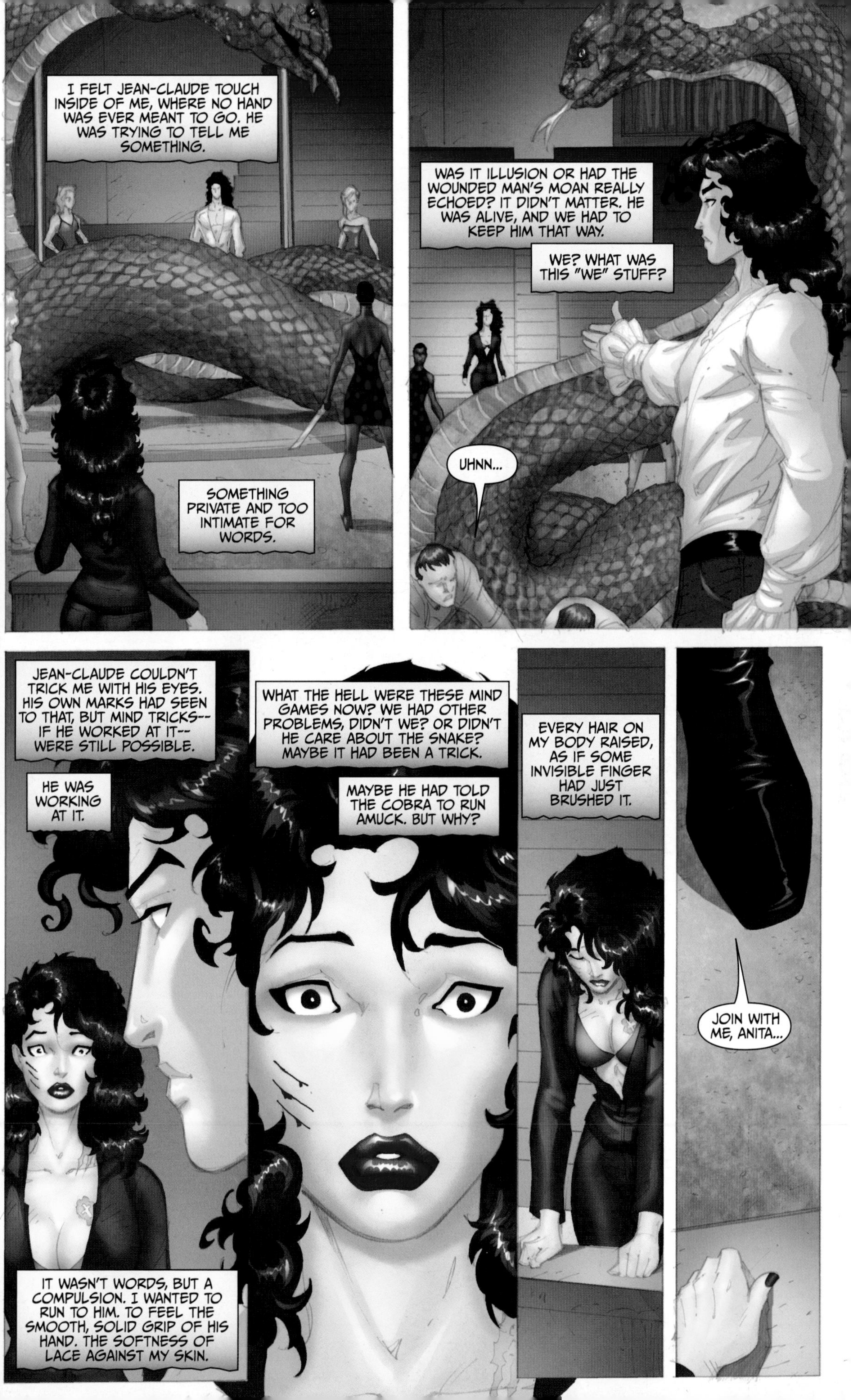
I FELT JEAN-CLAUDE TOUCH INSIDE OF ME, WHERE NO HAND WAS EVER MEANT TO GO. HE WAS TRYING TO TELL ME SOMETHING.
SOMETHING PRIVATE AND TOO INTIMATE FOR WORDS.
WAS IT ILLUSION OR HAD THE WOUNDED MAN'S MOAN REALLY ECHOED? IT DIDN'T MATTER. HE WAS ALIVE, AND WE HAD TO KEEP HIM THAT WAY.
WE? WHAT WAS THIS "WE" STUFF?
UHNN...
JEAN-CLAUDE COULDN'T TRICK ME WITH HIS EYES. HIS OWN MARKS HAD SEEN TO THAT, BUT MIND TRICKS-- IF HE WORKED AT IT-- WERE STILL POSSIBLE.
HE WAS WORKING AT IT.
IT WASN'T WORDS, BUT A COMPULSION. I WANTED TO RUN TO HIM. TO FEEL THE SMOOTH, SOLID GRIP OF HIS HAND. THE SOFTNESS OF LACE AGAINST MY SKIN.
WHAT THE HELL WERE THESE MIND GAMES NOW? WE HAD OTHER PROBLEMS, DIDN'T WE? OR DIDN'T HE CARE ABOUT THE SNAKE? MAYBE IT HAD BEEN A TRICK.
MAYBE HE HAD TOLD THE COBRA TO RUN AMUCK. BUT WHY?
EVERY HAIR ON MY BODY RAISED, AS IF SOME INVISIBLE FINGER HAD JUST BRUSHED IT.
JOIN WITH ME, ANITA...

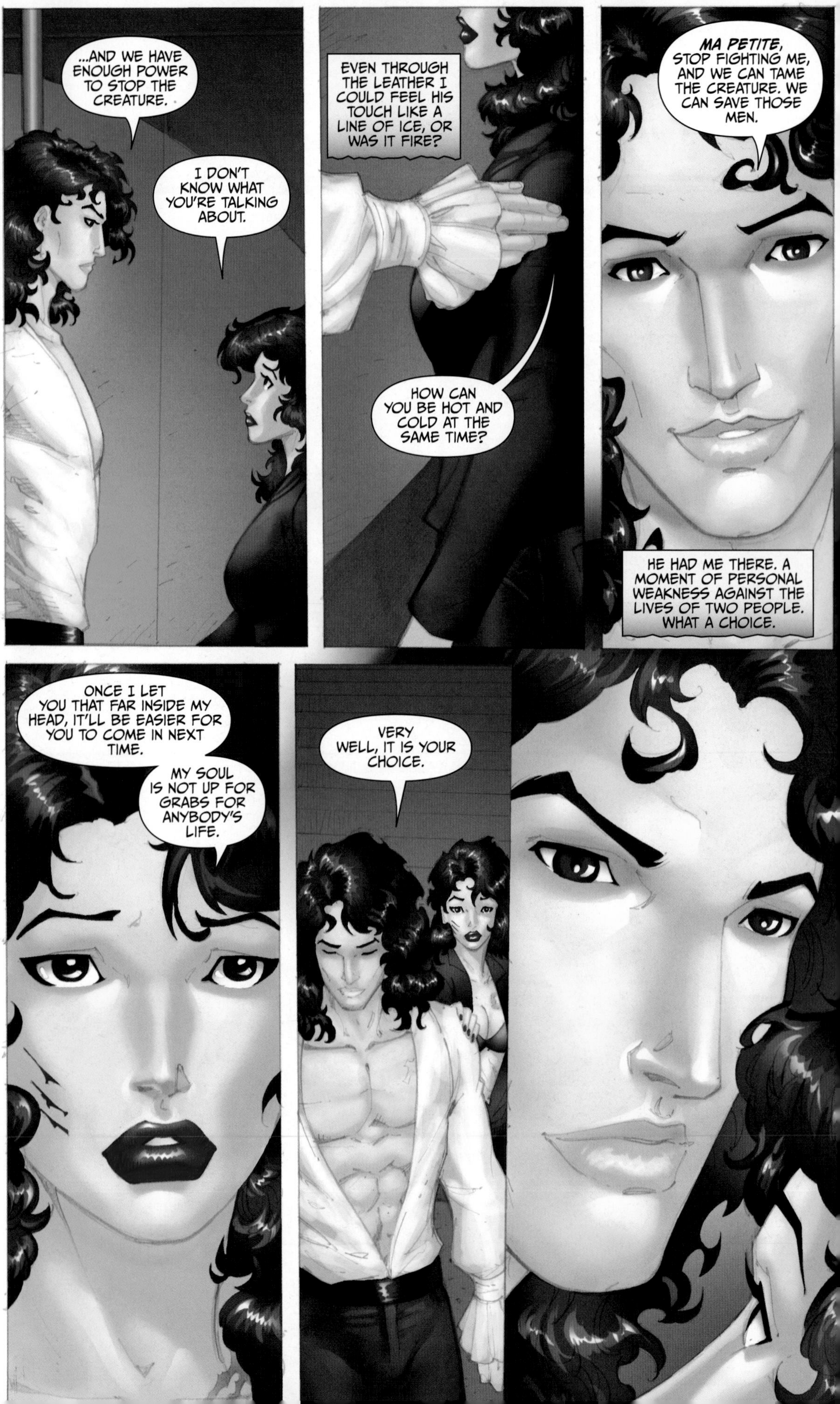
...AND WE HAVE ENOUGH POWER TO STOP THE CREATURE.
I DON'T KNOW WHAT YOU'RE TALKING ABOUT.
EVEN THROUGH THE LEATHER I COULD FEEL HIS TOUCH LIKE A LINE OF ICE, OR WAS IT FIRE?
HOW CAN YOU BE HOT AND COLD AT THE SAME TIME?
MA PETITE, STOP FIGHTING ME, AND WE CAN TAME THE CREATURE. WE CAN SAVE THOSE MEN.
HE HAD ME THERE. A MOMENT OF PERSONAL WEAKNESS AGAINST THE LIVES OF TWO PEOPLE. WHAT A CHOICE.
ONCE I LET YOU THAT FAR INSIDE MY HEAD, IT'LL BE EASIER FOR YOU TO COME IN NEXT TIME.
MY SOUL IS NOT UP FOR GRABS FOR ANYBODY'S LIFE.
VERY WELL, IT IS YOUR CHOICE.

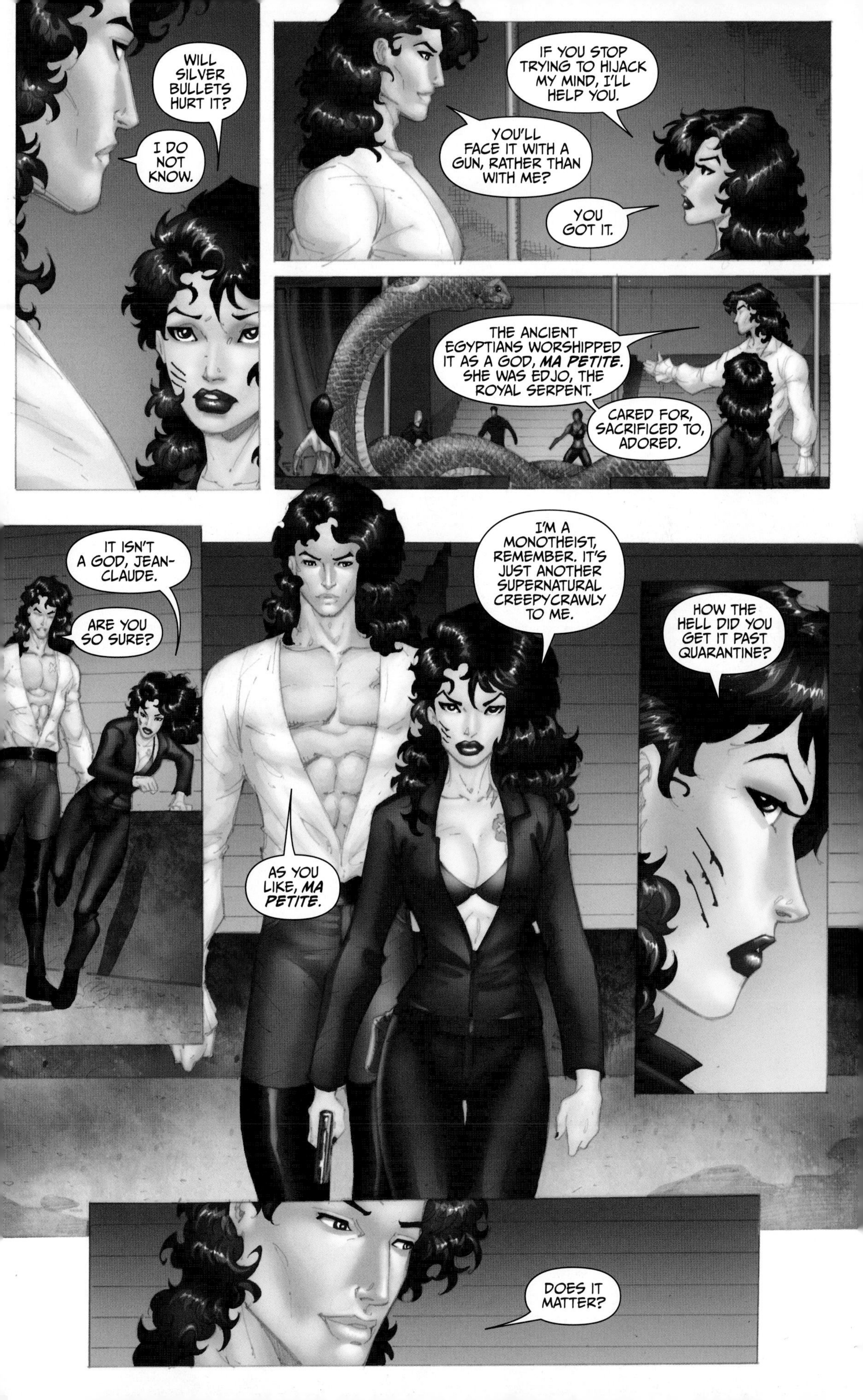
WILL SILVER BULLETS HURT IT?
I DO NOT KNOW.
IF YOU STOP TRYING TO HIJACK MY MIND, I'LL HELP YOU.
YOU'LL FACE IT WITH A GUN, RATHER THAN WITH ME?
YOU GOT IT.
THE ANCIENT EGYPTIANS WORSHIPPED IT AS A GOD, *MA PETITE*. SHE WAS EDJO, THE ROYAL SERPENT.
CARED FOR, SACRIFICED TO, ADORED.
IT ISN'T A GOD, JEAN-CLAUDE.
ARE YOU SO SURE?
I'M A MONOTHEIST, REMEMBER. IT'S JUST ANOTHER SUPERNATURAL CREEPYCRAWLY TO ME.
AS YOU LIKE, *MA PETITE*.
HOW THE HELL DID YOU GET IT PAST QUARANTINE?
DOES IT MATTER?

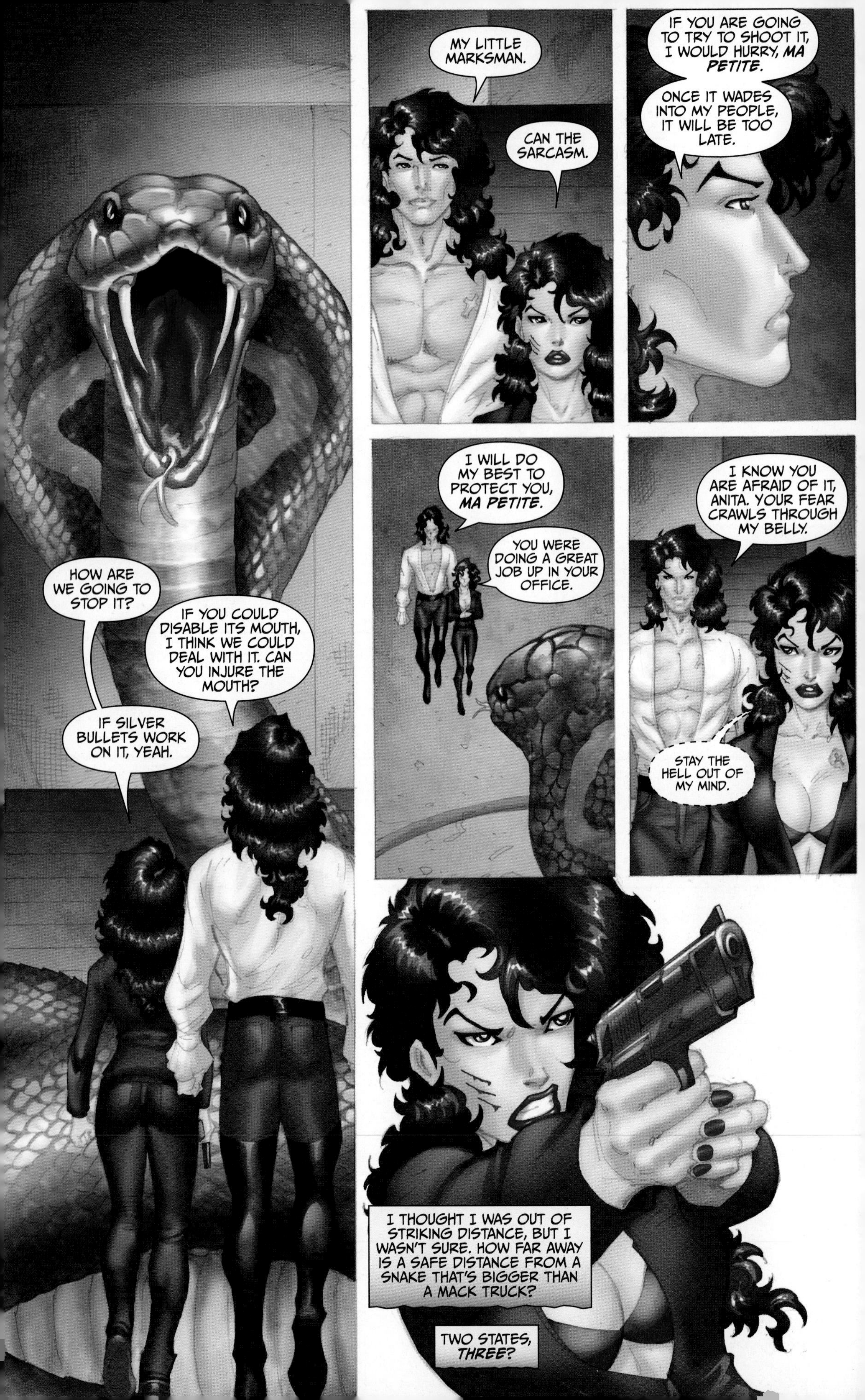
HOW ARE WE GOING TO STOP IT?
IF YOU COULD DISABLE ITS MOUTH, I THINK WE COULD DEAL WITH IT. CAN YOU INJURE THE MOUTH?
IF SILVER BULLETS WORK ON IT, YEAH.
MY LITTLE MARKSMAN.
CAN THE SARCASM.
IF YOU ARE GOING TO TRY TO SHOOT IT, I WOULD HURRY, *MA PETITE*.
ONCE IT WADES INTO MY PEOPLE, IT WILL BE TOO LATE.
I WILL DO MY BEST TO PROTECT YOU, *MA PETITE*.
YOU WERE DOING A GREAT JOB UP IN YOUR OFFICE.
I KNOW YOU ARE AFRAID OF IT, ANITA. YOUR FEAR CRAWLS THROUGH MY BELLY.
STAY THE HELL OUT OF MY MIND.
I THOUGHT I WAS OUT OF STRIKING DISTANCE, BUT I WASN'T SURE. HOW FAR AWAY IS A SAFE DISTANCE FROM A SNAKE THAT'S BIGGER THAN A MACK TRUCK?
TWO STATES, *THREE?*

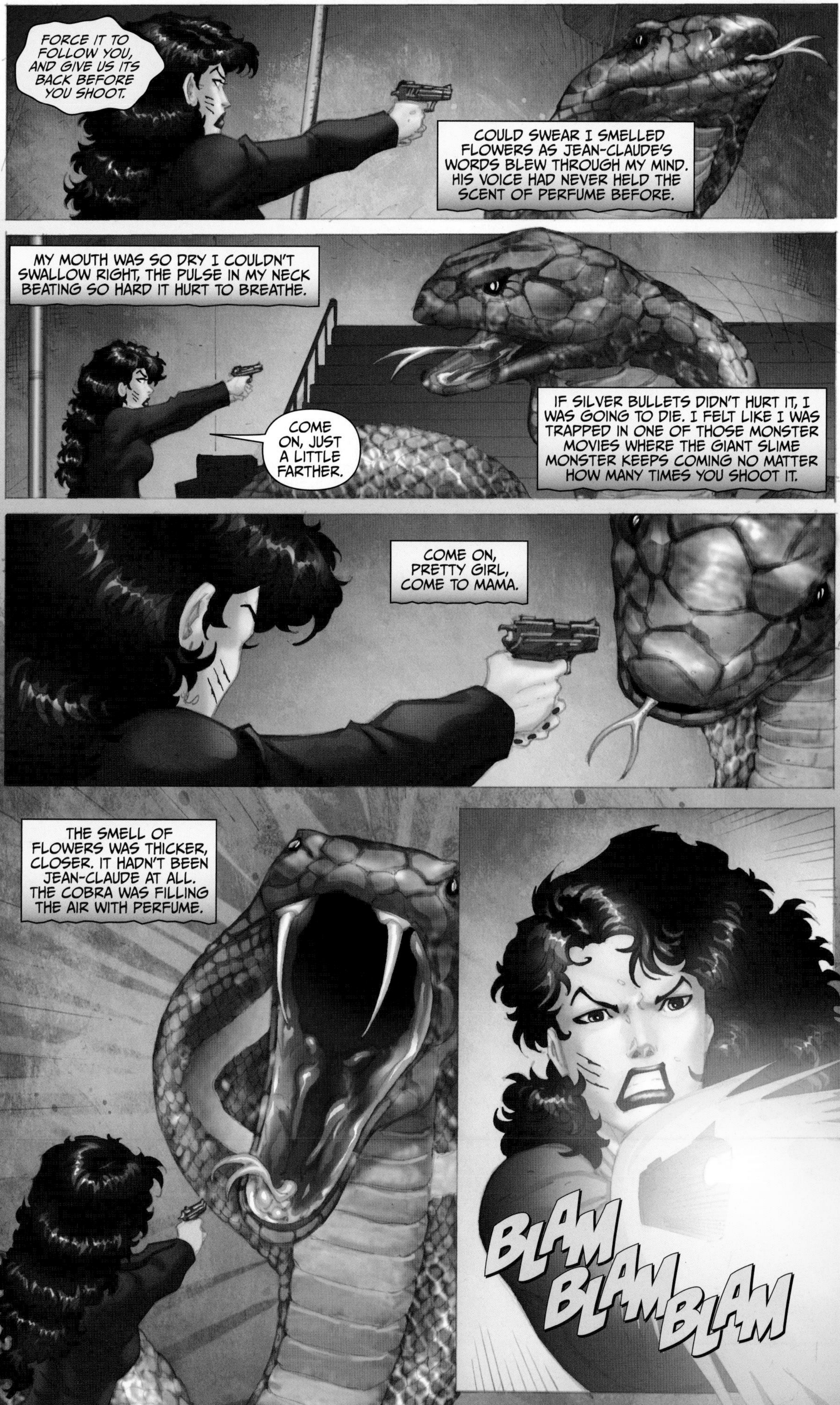
FORCE IT TO FOLLOW YOU, AND GIVE US ITS BACK BEFORE YOU SHOOT.
COULD SWEAR I SMELLED FLOWERS AS JEAN-CLAUDE'S WORDS BLEW THROUGH MY MIND. HIS VOICE HAD NEVER HELD THE SCENT OF PERFUME BEFORE.
MY MOUTH WAS SO DRY I COULDN'T SWALLOW RIGHT, THE PULSE IN MY NECK BEATING SO HARD IT HURT TO BREATHE.
COME ON, JUST A LITTLE FARTHER.
IF SILVER BULLETS DIDN'T HURT IT, I WAS GOING TO DIE. I FELT LIKE I WAS TRAPPED IN ONE OF THOSE MONSTER MOVIES WHERE THE GIANT SLIME MONSTER KEEPS COMING NO MATTER HOW MANY TIMES YOU SHOOT IT.
COME ON, PRETTY GIRL, COME TO MAMA.
THE SMELL OF FLOWERS WAS THICKER, CLOSER. IT HADN'T BEEN JEAN-CLAUDE AT ALL. THE COBRA WAS FILLING THE AIR WITH PERFUME.
BLAM
BLAM BLAM

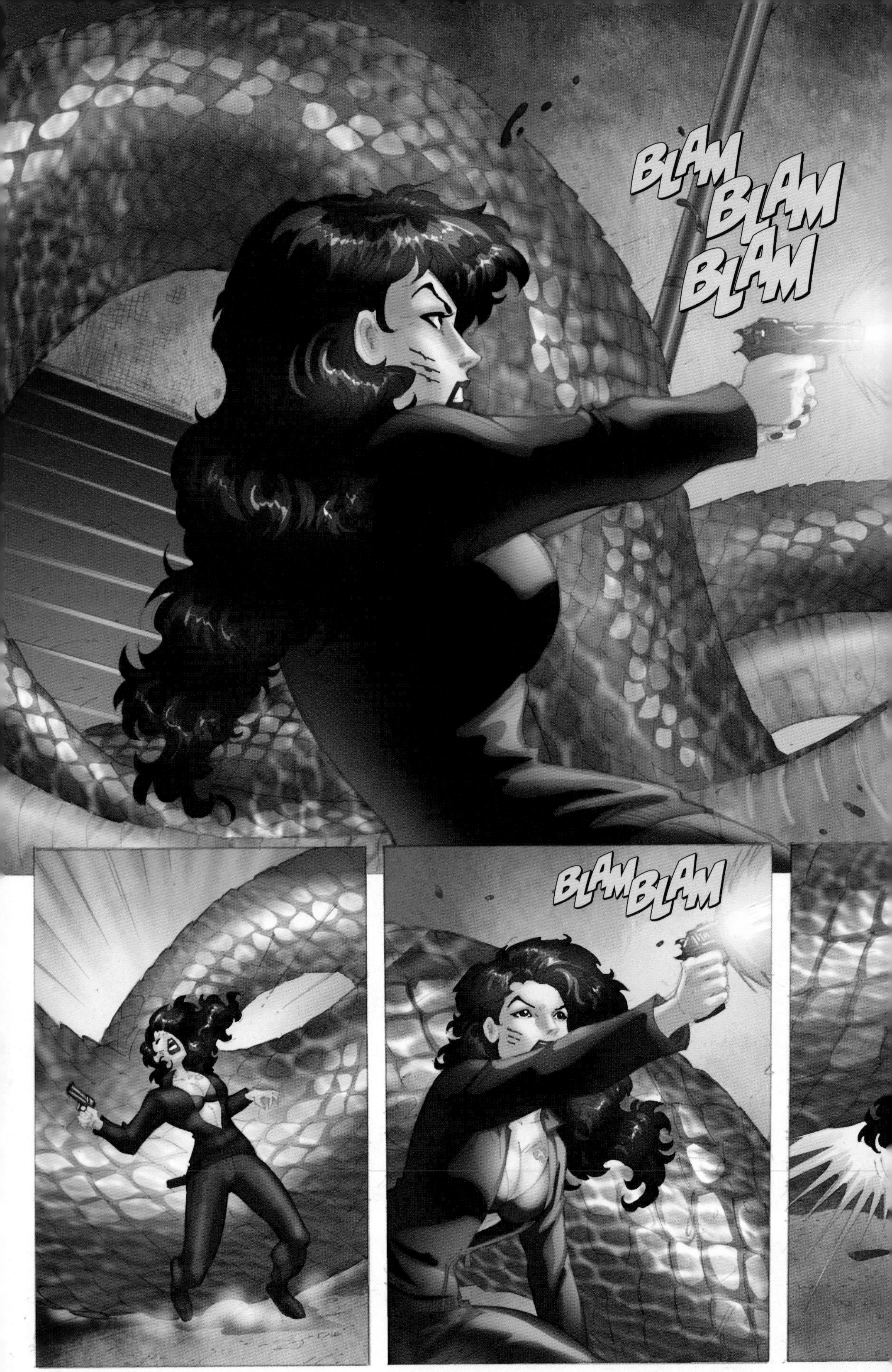
BLAM
BLAM
BLAM
BLAMBLAM

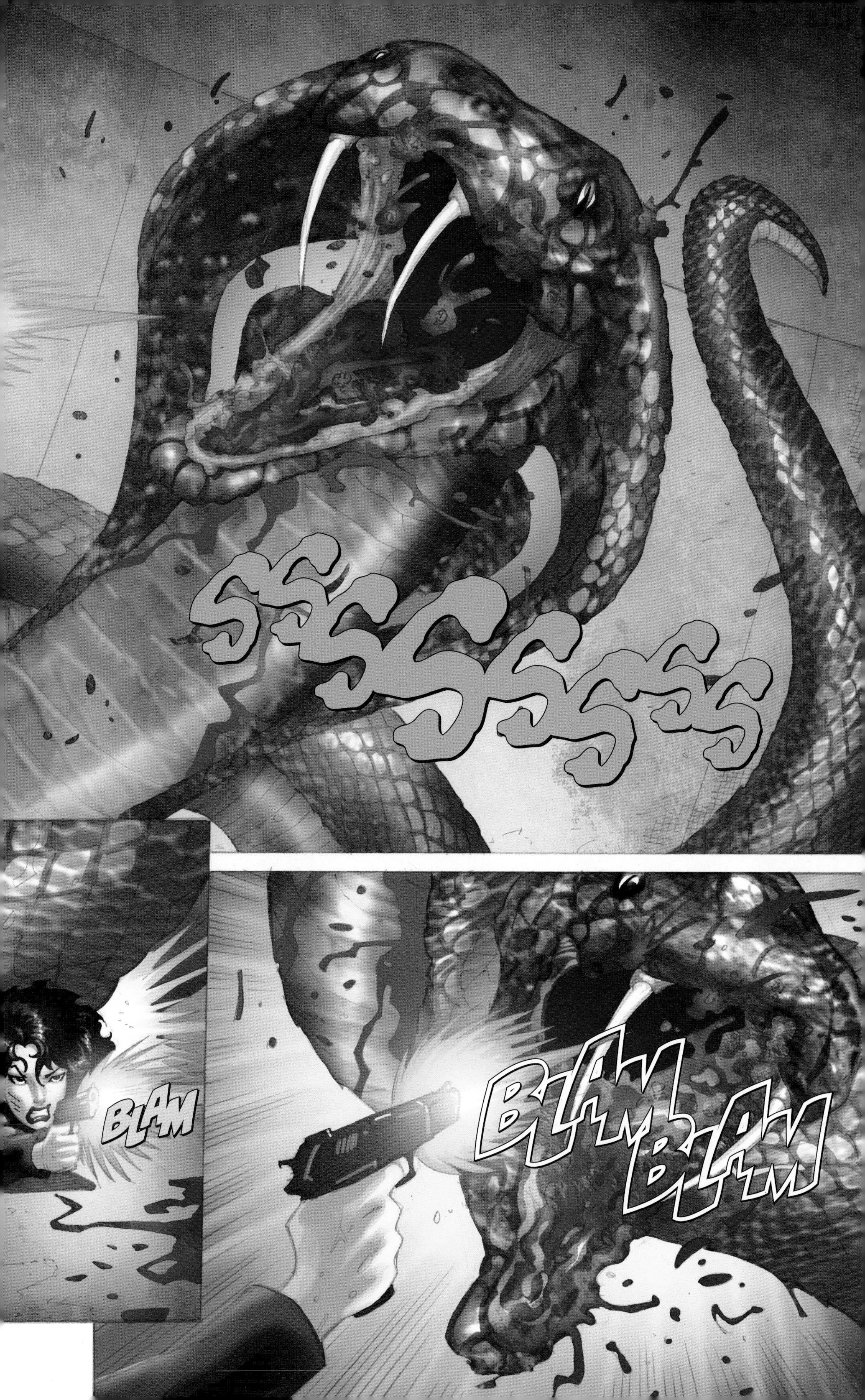
SSSSSSSSSS
BLAM
BLAM BLAM

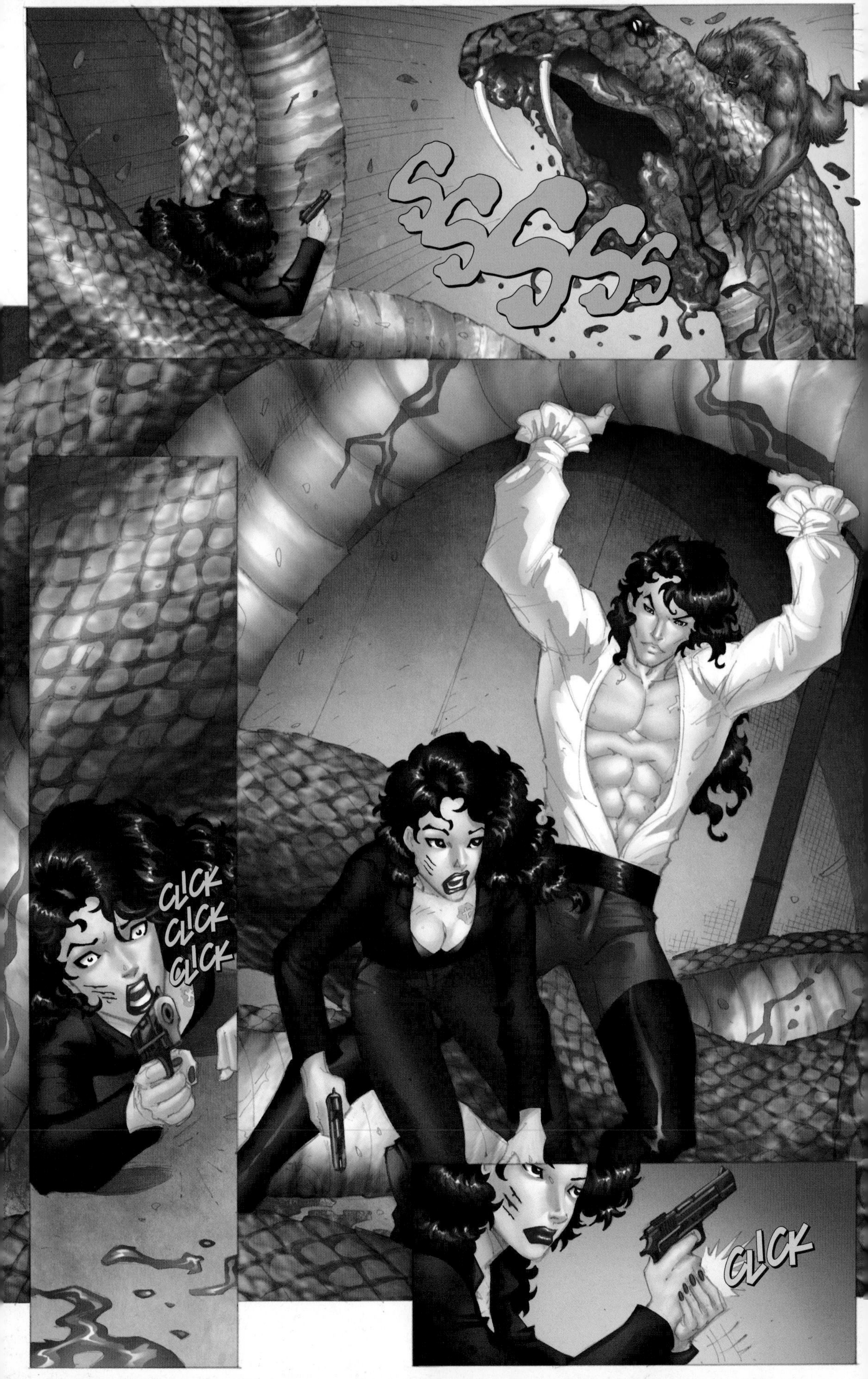
SSSSS
CLICK
CLICK
CLICK
CLICK

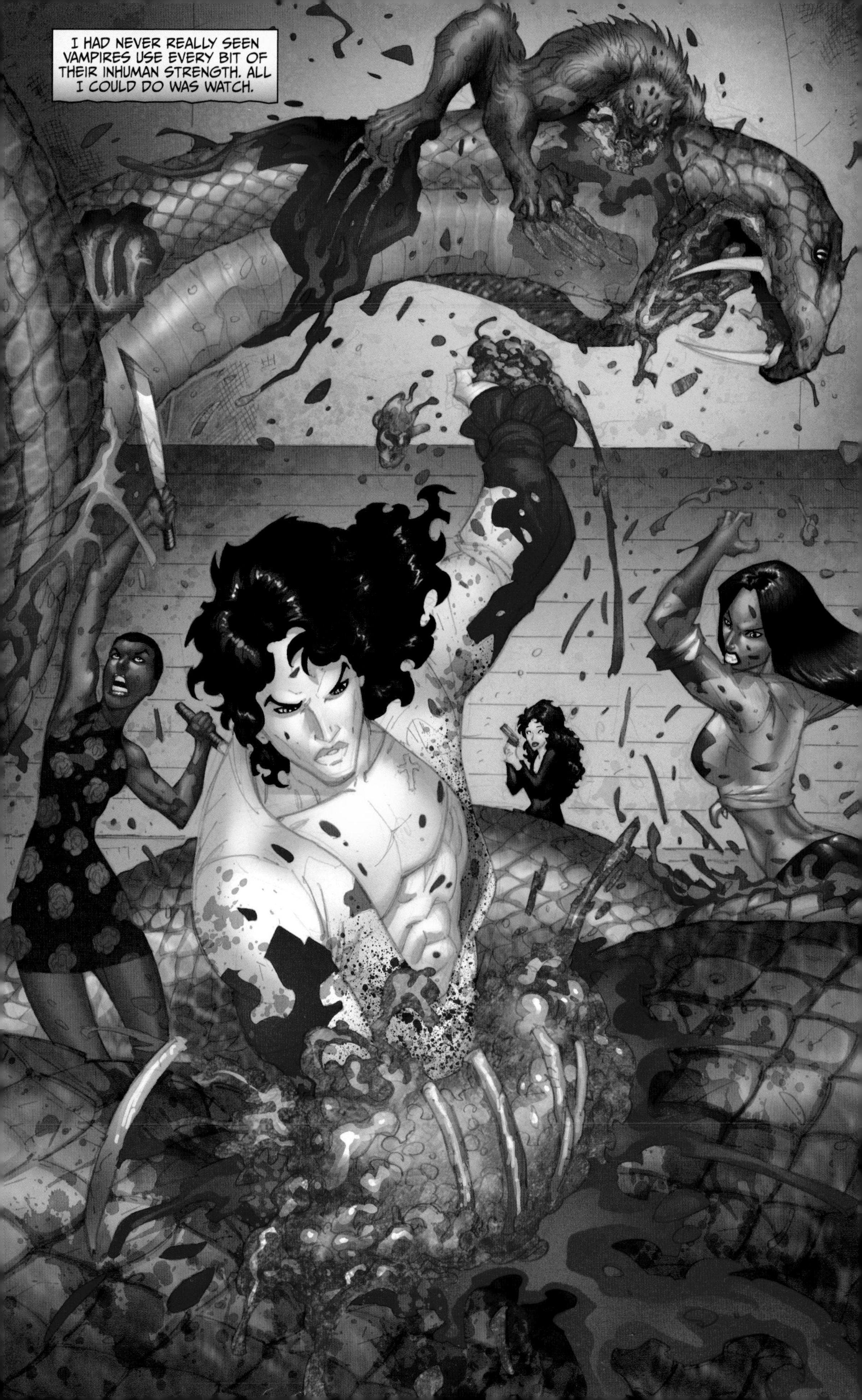
I HAD NEVER REALLY SEEN VAMPIRES USE EVERY BIT OF THEIR INHUMAN STRENGTH. ALL I COULD DO WAS WATCH.

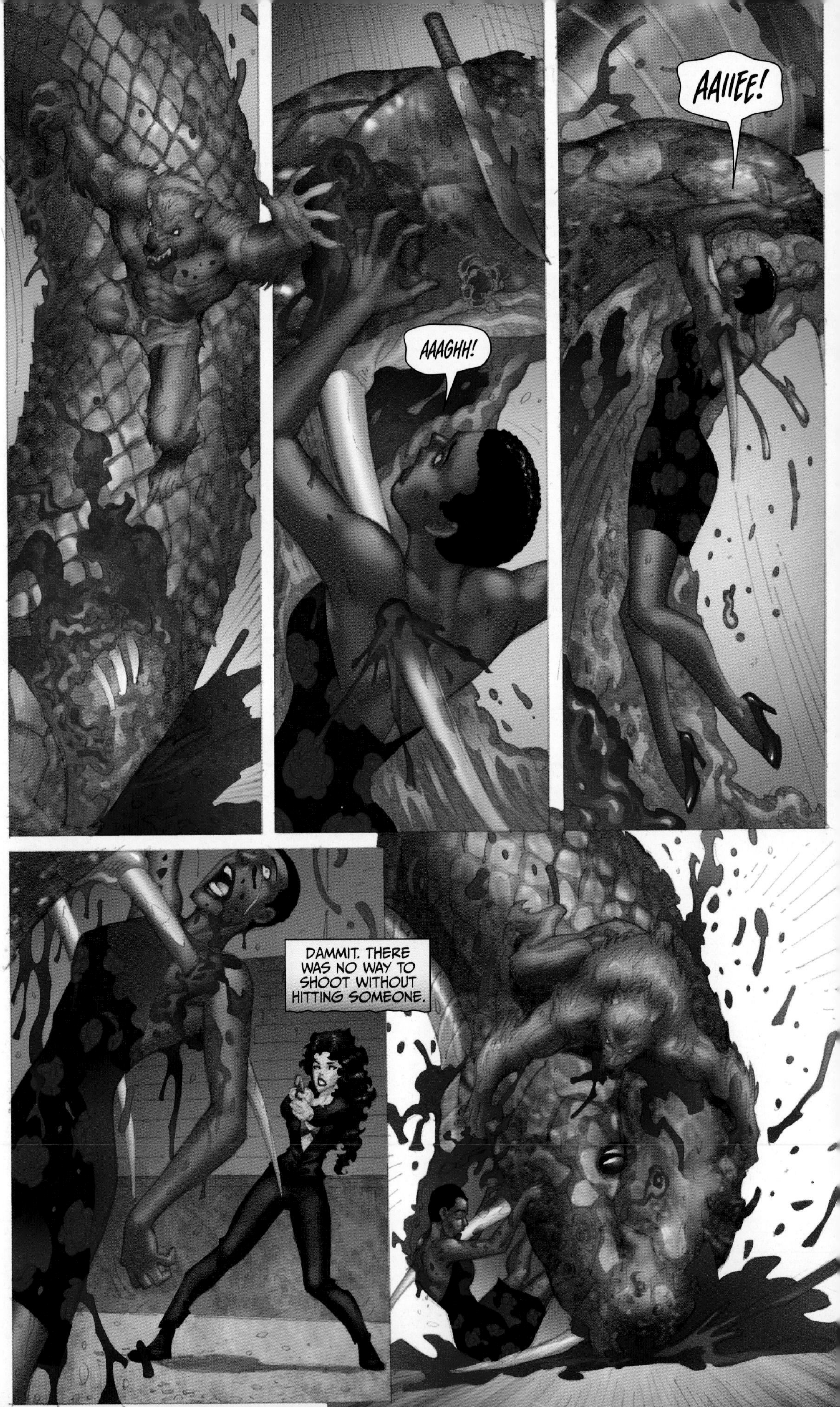
AAAGHH!
AAIIEE!
DAMMIT. THERE WAS NO WAY TO SHOOT WITHOUT HITTING SOMEONE.

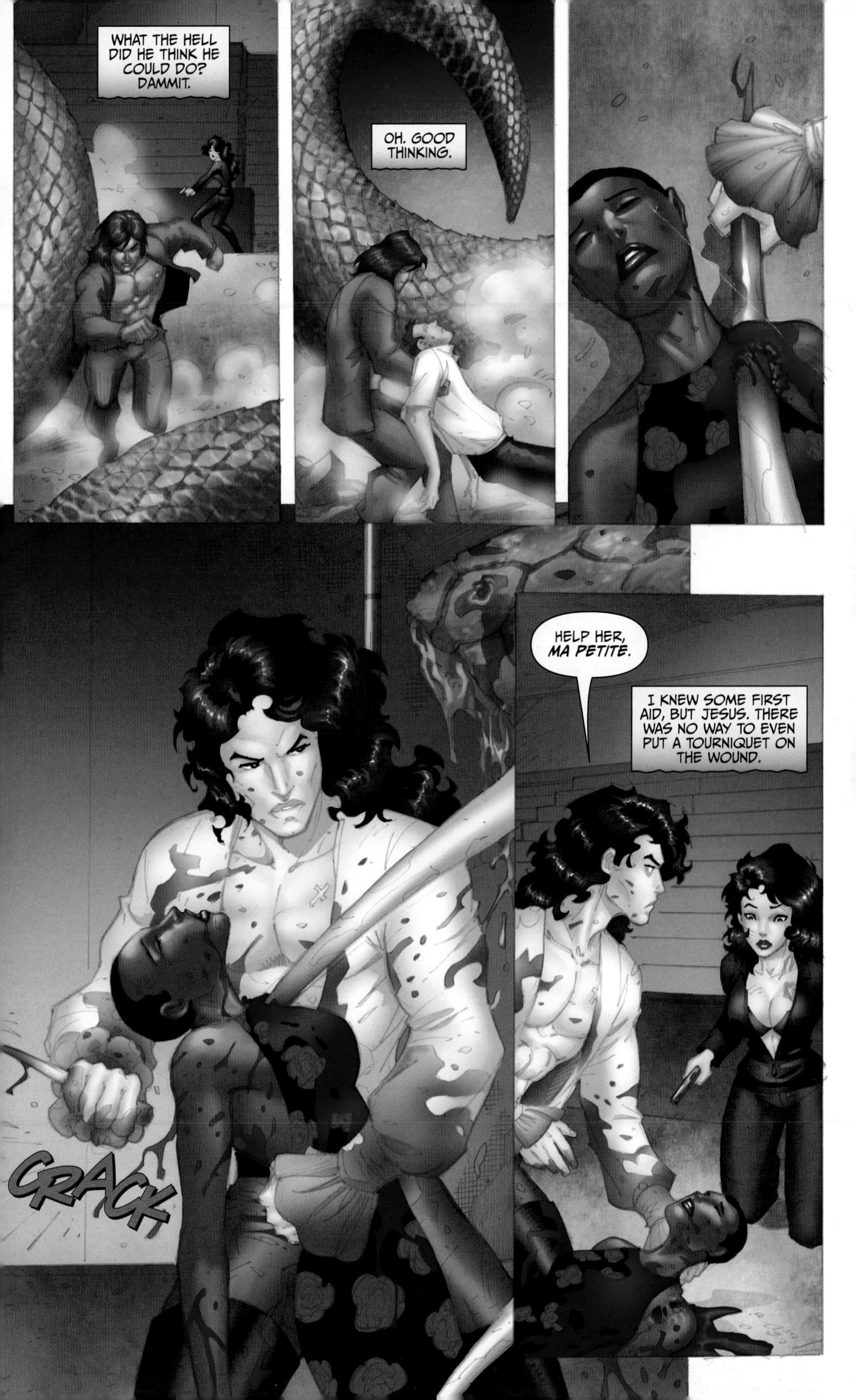
WHAT THE HELL DID HE THINK HE COULD DO? DAMMIT.
OH. GOOD THINKING.
CRACK
HELP HER, *MA PETITE*.
I KNEW SOME FIRST AID, BUT JESUS. THERE WAS NO WAY TO EVEN PUT A TOURNIQUET ON THE WOUND.

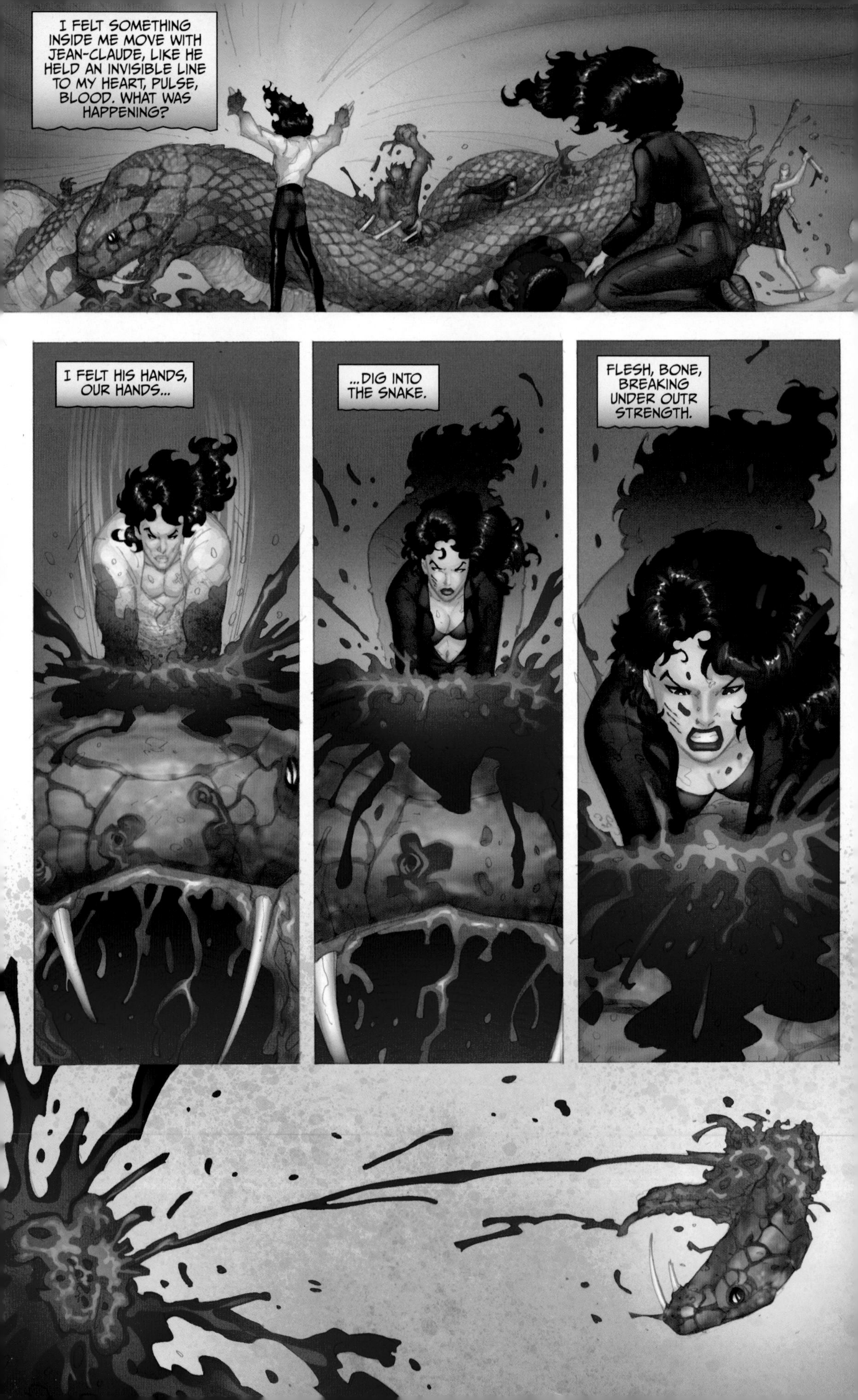
I FELT SOMETHING INSIDE ME MOVE WITH JEAN-CLAUDE, LIKE HE HELD AN INVISIBLE LINE TO MY HEART, PULSE, BLOOD. WHAT WAS HAPPENING?
I FELT HIS HANDS, OUR HANDS...
...DIG INTO THE SNAKE.
FLESH, BONE, BREAKING UNDER OUTR STRENGTH.

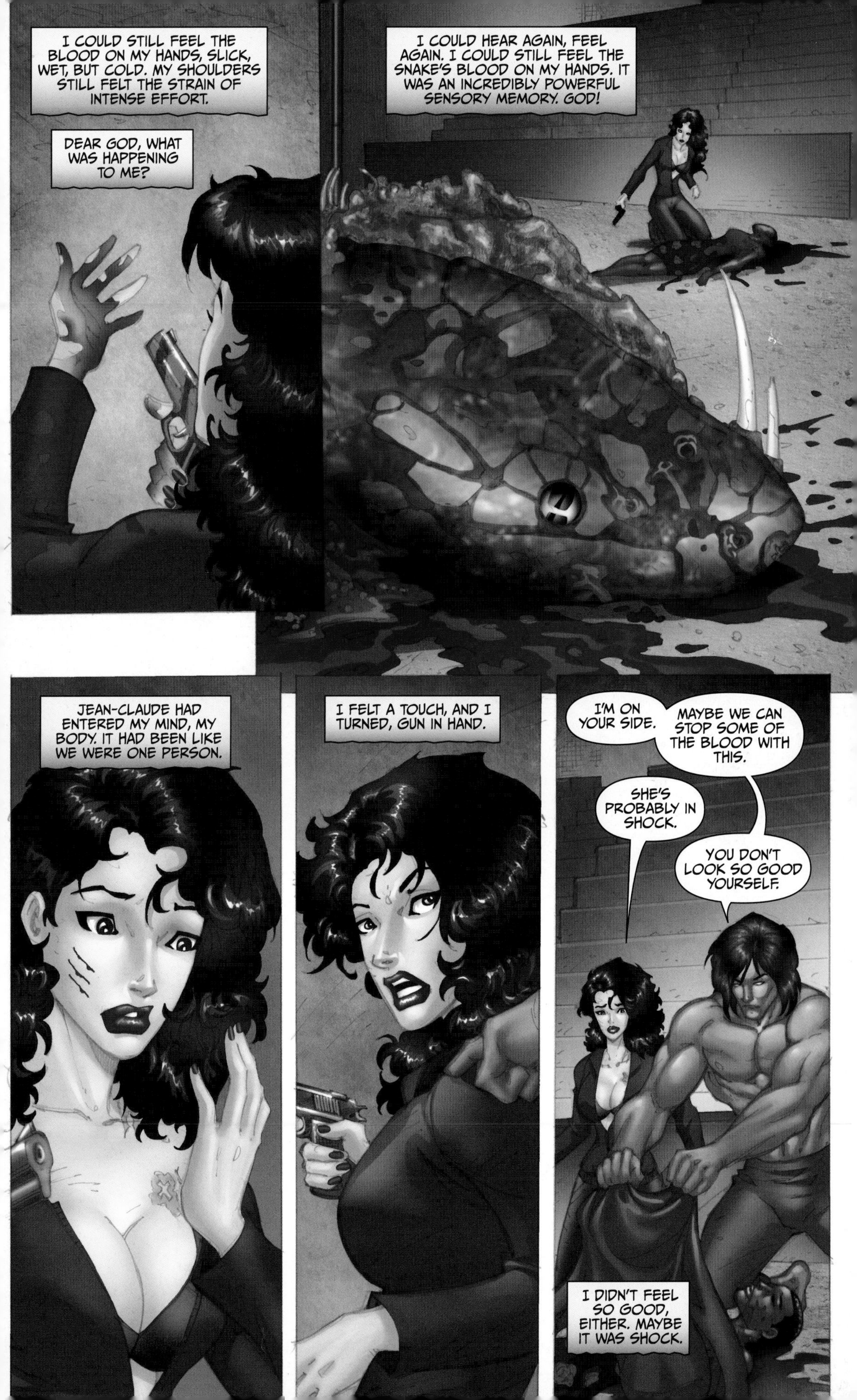
I COULD STILL FEEL THE BLOOD ON MY HANDS, SLICK, WET, BUT COLD. MY SHOULDERS STILL FELT THE STRAIN OF INTENSE EFFORT.
DEAR GOD, WHAT WAS HAPPENING TO ME?
I COULD HEAR AGAIN, FEEL AGAIN. I COULD STILL FEEL THE SNAKE'S BLOOD ON MY HANDS. IT WAS AN INCREDIBLY POWERFUL SENSORY MEMORY. GOD!
JEAN-CLAUDE HAD ENTERED MY MIND, MY BODY. IT HAD BEEN LIKE WE WERE ONE PERSON.
I FELT A TOUCH, AND I TURNED, GUN IN HAND.
I'M ON YOUR SIDE.
MAYBE WE CAN STOP SOME OF THE BLOOD WITH THIS.
SHE'S PROBABLY IN SHOCK.
YOU DON'T LOOK SO GOOD YOURSELF.
I DIDN'T FEEL SO GOOD, EITHER. MAYBE IT WAS SHOCK.

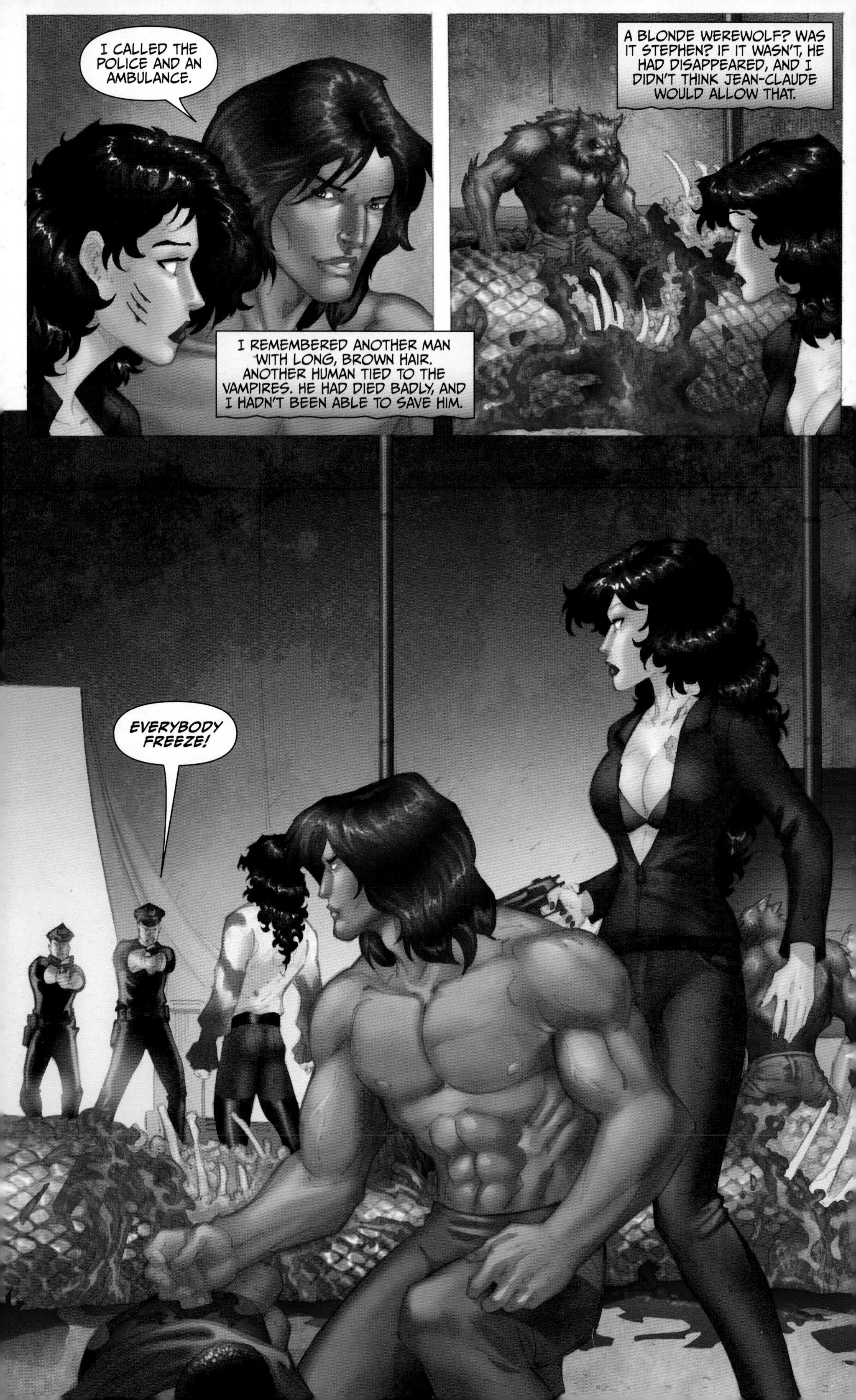
I CALLED THE POLICE AND AN AMBULANCE.
I REMEMBERED ANOTHER MAN WITH LONG, BROWN HAIR. ANOTHER HUMAN TIED TO THE VAMPIRES. HE HAD DIED BADLY, AND I HADN'T BEEN ABLE TO SAVE HIM.
A BLONDE WEREWOLF? WAS IT STEPHEN? IF IT WASN'T, HE HAD DISAPPEARED, AND I DIDN'T THINK JEAN-CLAUDE WOULD ALLOW THAT.
EVERYBODY FREEZE!

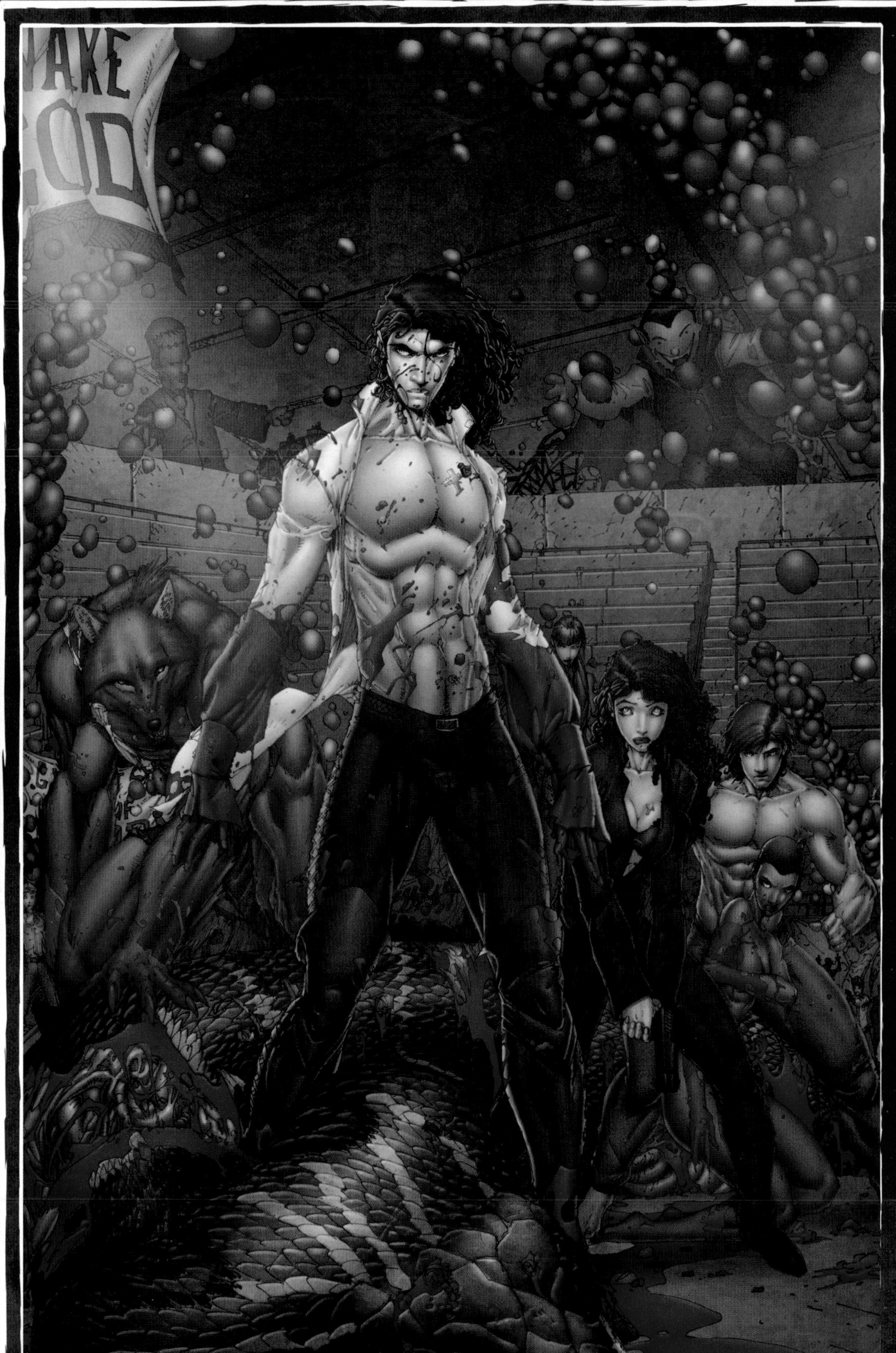

#4

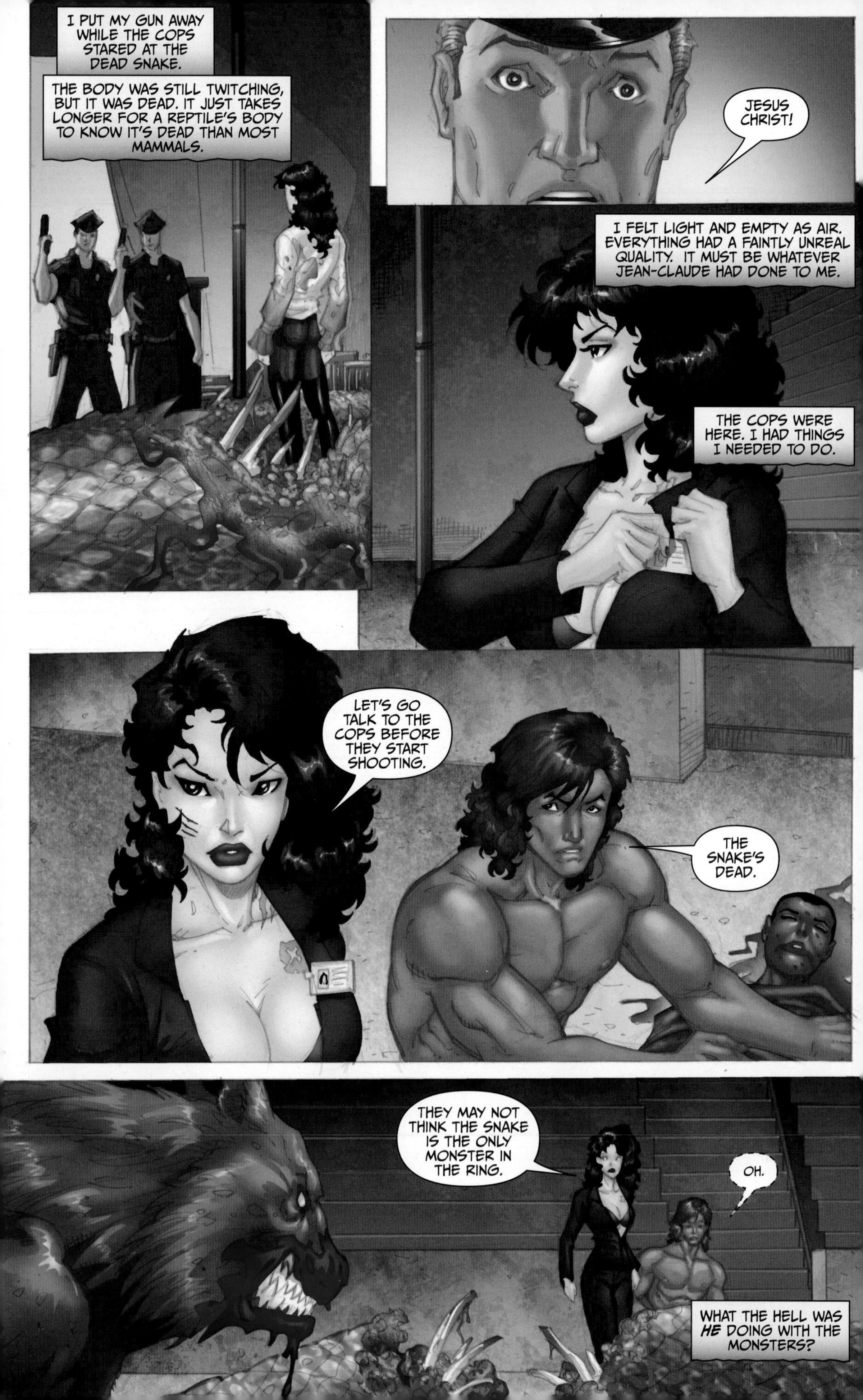
I PUT MY GUN AWAY WHILE THE COPS STARED AT THE DEAD SNAKE.
THE BODY WAS STILL TWITCHING, BUT IT WAS DEAD. IT JUST TAKES LONGER FOR A REPTILE'S BODY TO KNOW IT'S DEAD THAN MOST MAMMALS.
JESUS CHRIST!
I FELT LIGHT AND EMPTY AS AIR. EVERYTHING HAD A FAINTLY UNREAL QUALITY. IT MUST BE WHATEVER JEAN-CLAUDE HAD DONE TO ME.
THE COPS WERE HERE. I HAD THINGS I NEEDED TO DO.
LET'S GO TALK TO THE COPS BEFORE THEY START SHOOTING.
THE SNAKE'S DEAD.
THEY MAY NOT THINK THE SNAKE IS THE ONLY MONSTER IN THE RING.
OH.
WHAT THE HELL WAS *HE* DOING WITH THE MONSTERS?

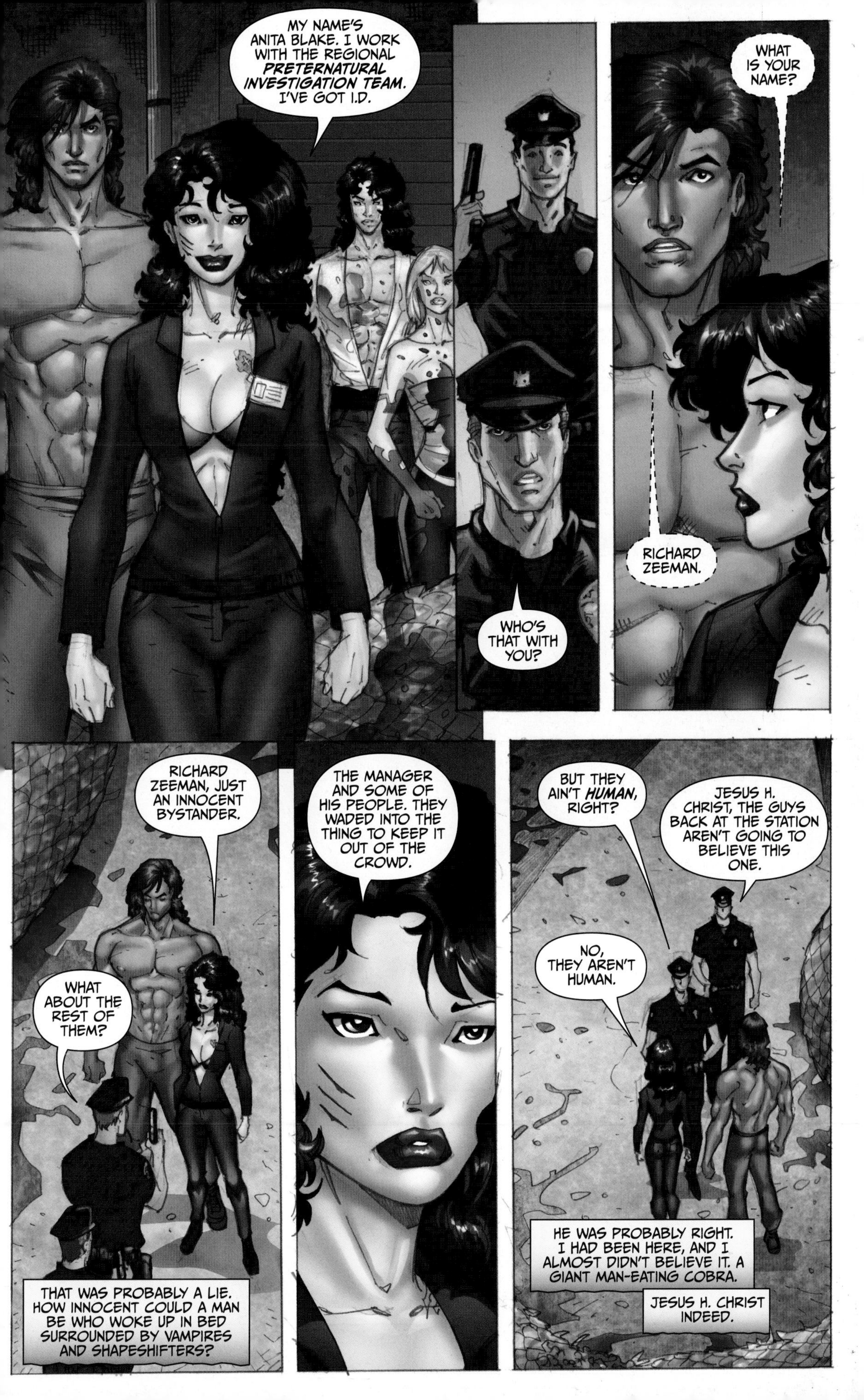
MY NAME'S ANITA BLAKE. I WORK WITH THE REGIONAL *PRETERNATURAL INVESTIGATION TEAM.* I'VE GOT I.D.
WHO'S THAT WITH YOU?
WHAT IS YOUR NAME?
RICHARD ZEEMAN.
RICHARD ZEEMAN, JUST AN INNOCENT BYSTANDER.
WHAT ABOUT THE REST OF THEM?
THAT WAS PROBABLY A LIE. HOW INNOCENT COULD A MAN BE WHO WOKE UP IN BED SURROUNDED BY VAMPIRES AND SHAPESHIFTERS?
THE MANAGER AND SOME OF HIS PEOPLE. THEY WADED INTO THE THING TO KEEP IT OUT OF THE CROWD.
BUT THEY AIN'T *HUMAN*, RIGHT?
NO, THEY AREN'T HUMAN.
JESUS H. CHRIST, THE GUYS BACK AT THE STATION AREN'T GOING TO BELIEVE THIS ONE.
HE WAS PROBABLY RIGHT. I HAD BEEN HERE, AND I ALMOST DIDN'T BELIEVE IT. A GIANT MAN-EATING COBRA.
JESUS H. CHRIST INDEED.

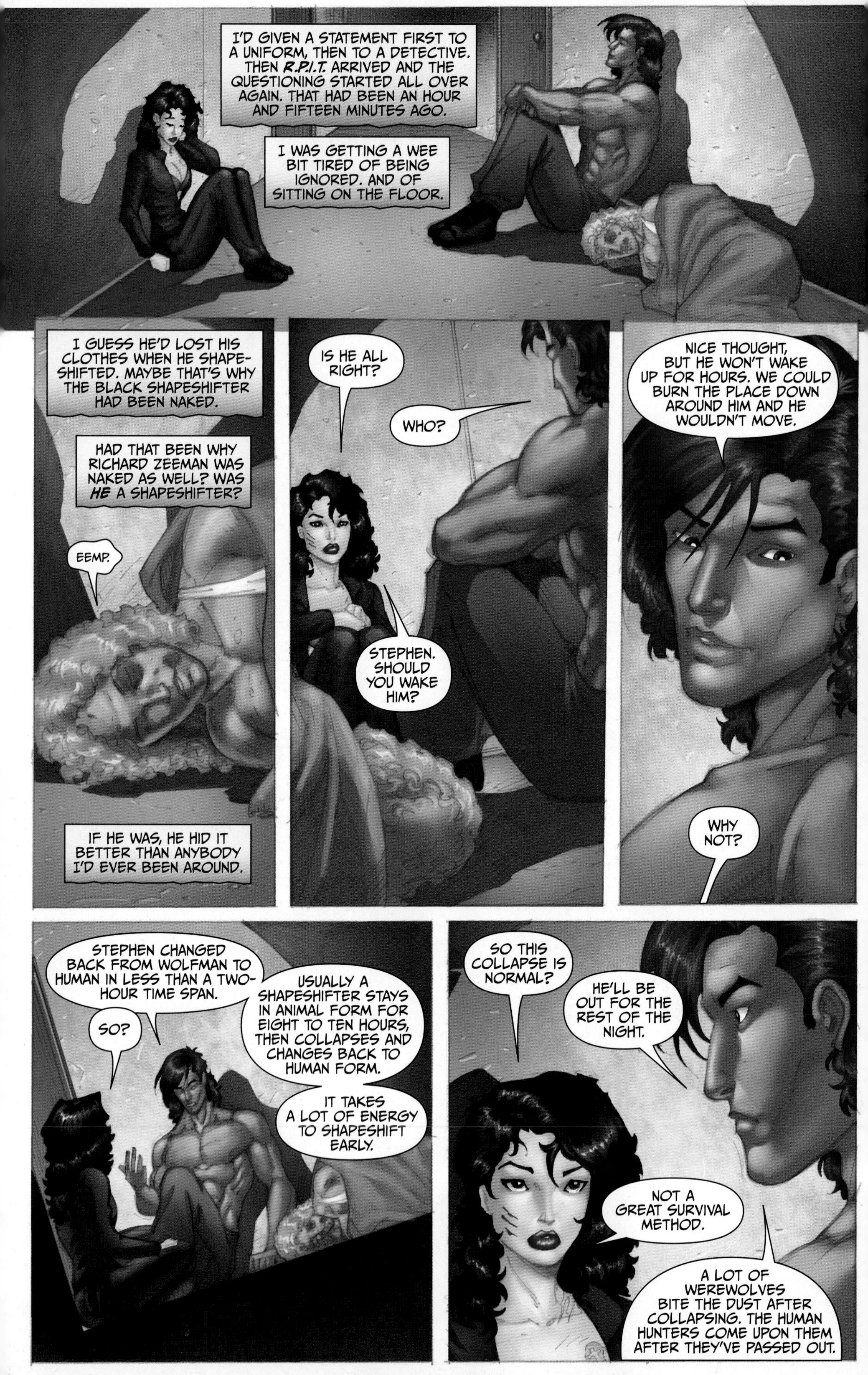
I'D GIVEN A STATEMENT FIRST TO A UNIFORM, THEN TO A DETECTIVE. THEN R.P.I.T. ARRIVED AND THE QUESTIONING STARTED ALL OVER AGAIN. THAT HAD BEEN AN HOUR AND FIFTEEN MINUTES AGO.
I WAS GETTING A WEE BIT TIRED OF BEING IGNORED. AND OF SITTING ON THE FLOOR.
I GUESS HE'D LOST HIS CLOTHES WHEN HE SHAPE-SHIFTED. MAYBE THAT'S WHY THE BLACK SHAPESHIFTER HAD BEEN NAKED.
HAD THAT BEEN WHY RICHARD ZEEMAN WAS NAKED AS WELL? WAS HE A SHAPESHIFTER?
EEMP.
IF HE WAS, HE HID IT BETTER THAN ANYBODY I'D EVER BEEN AROUND.
IS HE ALL RIGHT?
WHO?
STEPHEN. SHOULD YOU WAKE HIM?
NICE THOUGHT, BUT HE WON'T WAKE UP FOR HOURS. WE COULD BURN THE PLACE DOWN AROUND HIM AND HE WOULDN'T MOVE.
WHY NOT?
STEPHEN CHANGED BACK FROM WOLFMAN TO HUMAN IN LESS THAN A TWO-HOUR TIME SPAN.
SO?
USUALLY A SHAPESHIFTER STAYS IN ANIMAL FORM FOR EIGHT TO TEN HOURS, THEN COLLAPSES AND CHANGES BACK TO HUMAN FORM.
IT TAKES A LOT OF ENERGY TO SHAPESHIFT EARLY.
SO THIS COLLAPSE IS NORMAL?
HE'LL BE OUT FOR THE REST OF THE NIGHT.
NOT A GREAT SURVIVAL METHOD.
A LOT OF WEREWOLVES BITE THE DUST AFTER COLLAPSING. THE HUMAN HUNTERS COME UPON THEM AFTER THEY'VE PASSED OUT.

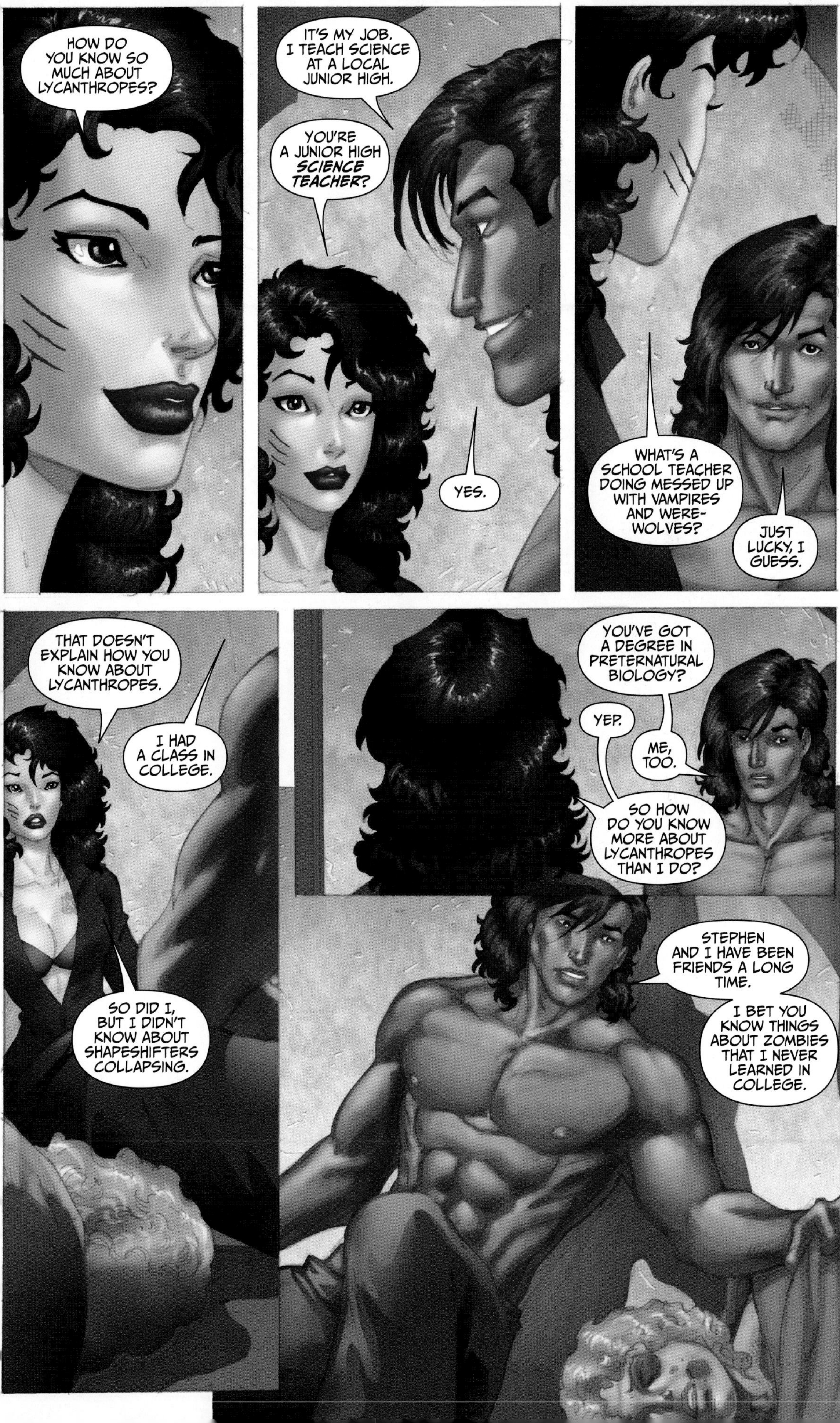
HOW DO YOU KNOW SO MUCH ABOUT LYCANTHROPES?
IT'S MY JOB. I TEACH SCIENCE AT A LOCAL JUNIOR HIGH.
YOU'RE A JUNIOR HIGH *SCIENCE TEACHER?*
YES.
WHAT'S A SCHOOL TEACHER DOING MESSED UP WITH VAMPIRES AND WERE-WOLVES?
JUST LUCKY, I GUESS.
THAT DOESN'T EXPLAIN HOW YOU KNOW ABOUT LYCANTHROPES.
I HAD A CLASS IN COLLEGE.
SO DID I, BUT I DIDN'T KNOW ABOUT SHAPESHIFTERS COLLAPSING.
YOU'VE GOT A DEGREE IN PRETERNATURAL BIOLOGY?
YEP.
ME, TOO.
SO HOW DO YOU KNOW MORE ABOUT LYCANTHROPES THAN I DO?
STEPHEN AND I HAVE BEEN FRIENDS A LONG TIME.
I BET YOU KNOW THINGS ABOUT ZOMBIES THAT I NEVER LEARNED IN COLLEGE.

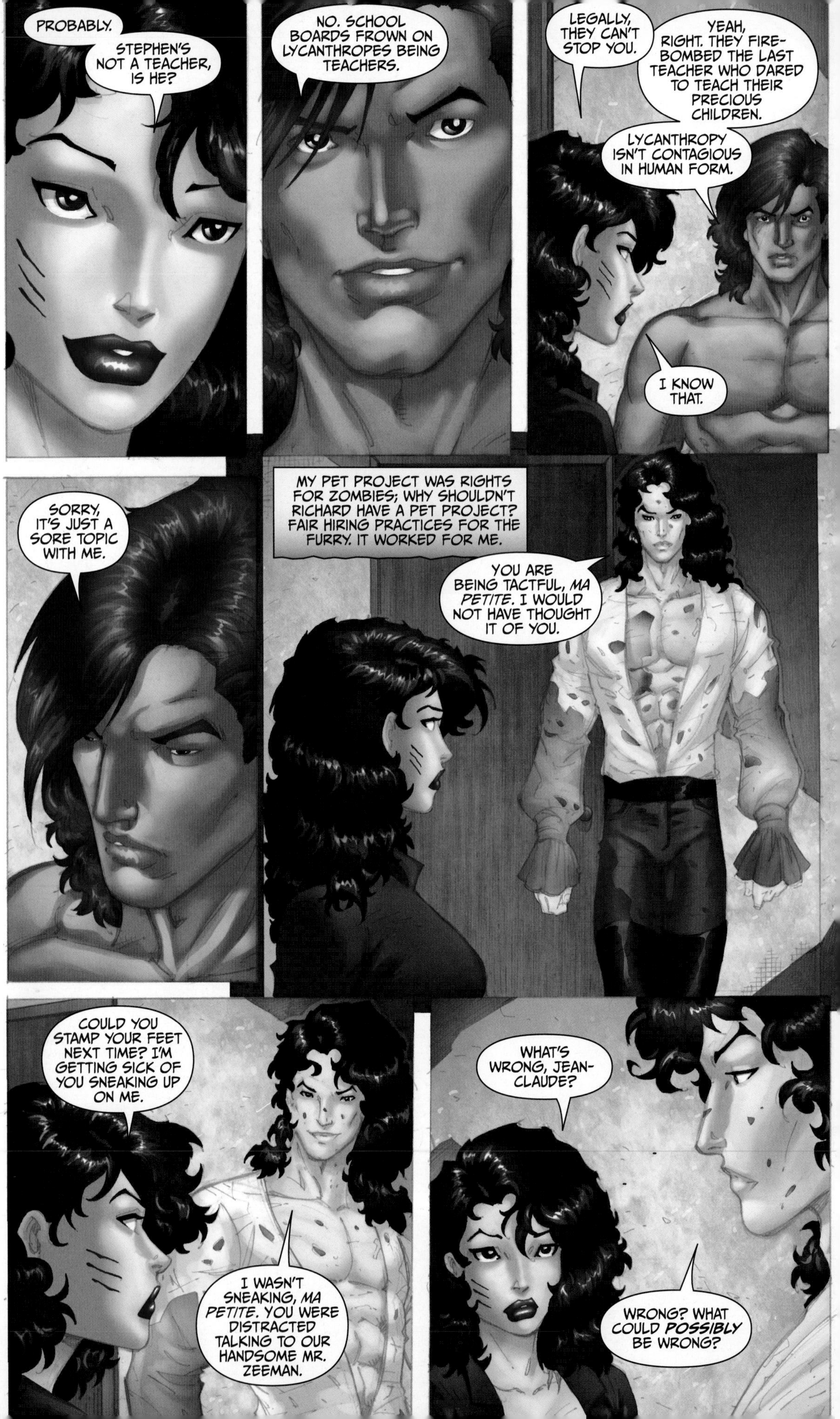
PROBABLY.
STEPHEN'S NOT A TEACHER, IS HE?
NO. SCHOOL BOARDS FROWN ON LYCANTHROPES BEING TEACHERS.
LEGALLY, THEY CAN'T STOP YOU.
YEAH, RIGHT. THEY FIRE-BOMBED THE LAST TEACHER WHO DARED TO TEACH THEIR PRECIOUS CHILDREN.
LYCANTHROPY ISN'T CONTAGIOUS IN HUMAN FORM.
I KNOW THAT.
SORRY, IT'S JUST A SORE TOPIC WITH ME.
MY PET PROJECT WAS RIGHTS FOR ZOMBIES; WHY SHOULDN'T RICHARD HAVE A PET PROJECT? FAIR HIRING PRACTICES FOR THE FURRY. IT WORKED FOR ME.
YOU ARE BEING TACTFUL, *MA PETITE*. I WOULD NOT HAVE THOUGHT IT OF YOU.
COULD YOU STAMP YOUR FEET NEXT TIME? I'M GETTING SICK OF YOU SNEAKING UP ON ME.
I WASN'T SNEAKING, *MA PETITE*. YOU WERE DISTRACTED TALKING TO OUR HANDSOME MR. ZEEMAN.
WHAT'S WRONG, JEAN-CLAUDE?
WRONG? WHAT COULD ***POSSIBLY*** BE WRONG?

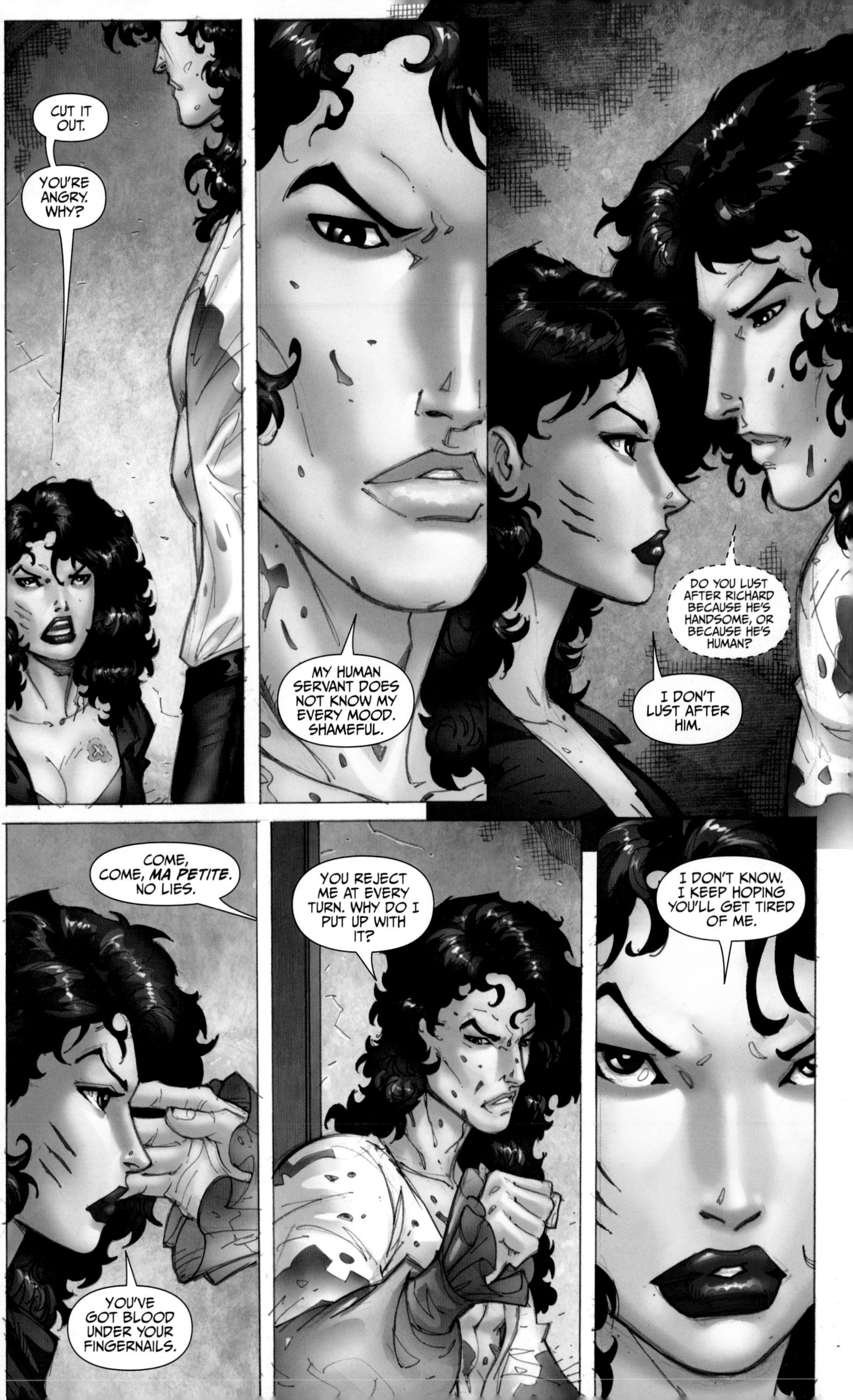
CUT IT OUT.
YOU'RE ANGRY. WHY?
MY HUMAN SERVANT DOES NOT KNOW MY EVERY MOOD. SHAMEFUL.
DO YOU LUST AFTER RICHARD BECAUSE HE'S HANDSOME, OR BECAUSE HE'S HUMAN?
I DON'T LUST AFTER HIM.
COME, COME, MA PETITE. NO LIES.
YOU'VE GOT BLOOD UNDER YOUR FINGERNAILS.
YOU REJECT ME AT EVERY TURN. WHY DO I PUT UP WITH IT?
I DON'T KNOW. I KEEP HOPING YOU'LL GET TIRED OF ME.

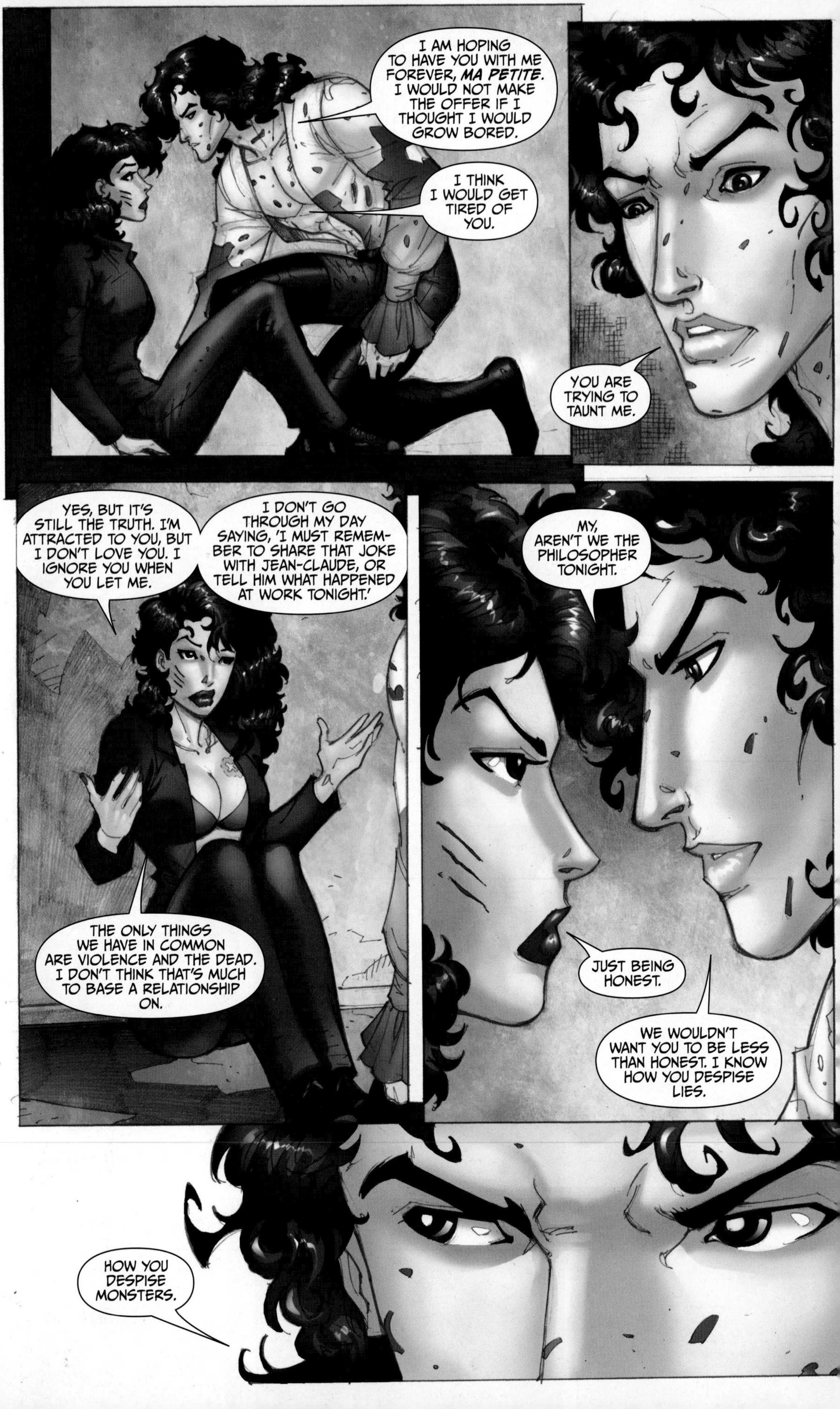
I AM HOPING TO HAVE YOU WITH ME FOREVER, *MA PETITE*. I WOULD NOT MAKE THE OFFER IF I THOUGHT I WOULD GROW BORED.
I THINK I WOULD GET TIRED OF YOU.
YOU ARE TRYING TO TAUNT ME.
YES, BUT IT'S STILL THE TRUTH. I'M ATTRACTED TO YOU, BUT I DON'T LOVE YOU. I IGNORE YOU WHEN YOU LET ME.
I DON'T GO THROUGH MY DAY SAYING, 'I MUST REMEMBER TO SHARE THAT JOKE WITH JEAN-CLAUDE, OR TELL HIM WHAT HAPPENED AT WORK TONIGHT.'
THE ONLY THINGS WE HAVE IN COMMON ARE VIOLENCE AND THE DEAD. I DON'T THINK THAT'S MUCH TO BASE A RELATIONSHIP ON.
MY, AREN'T WE THE PHILOSOPHER TONIGHT.
JUST BEING HONEST.
WE WOULDN'T WANT YOU TO BE LESS THAN HONEST. I KNOW HOW YOU DESPISE LIES.
HOW YOU DESPISE MONSTERS.

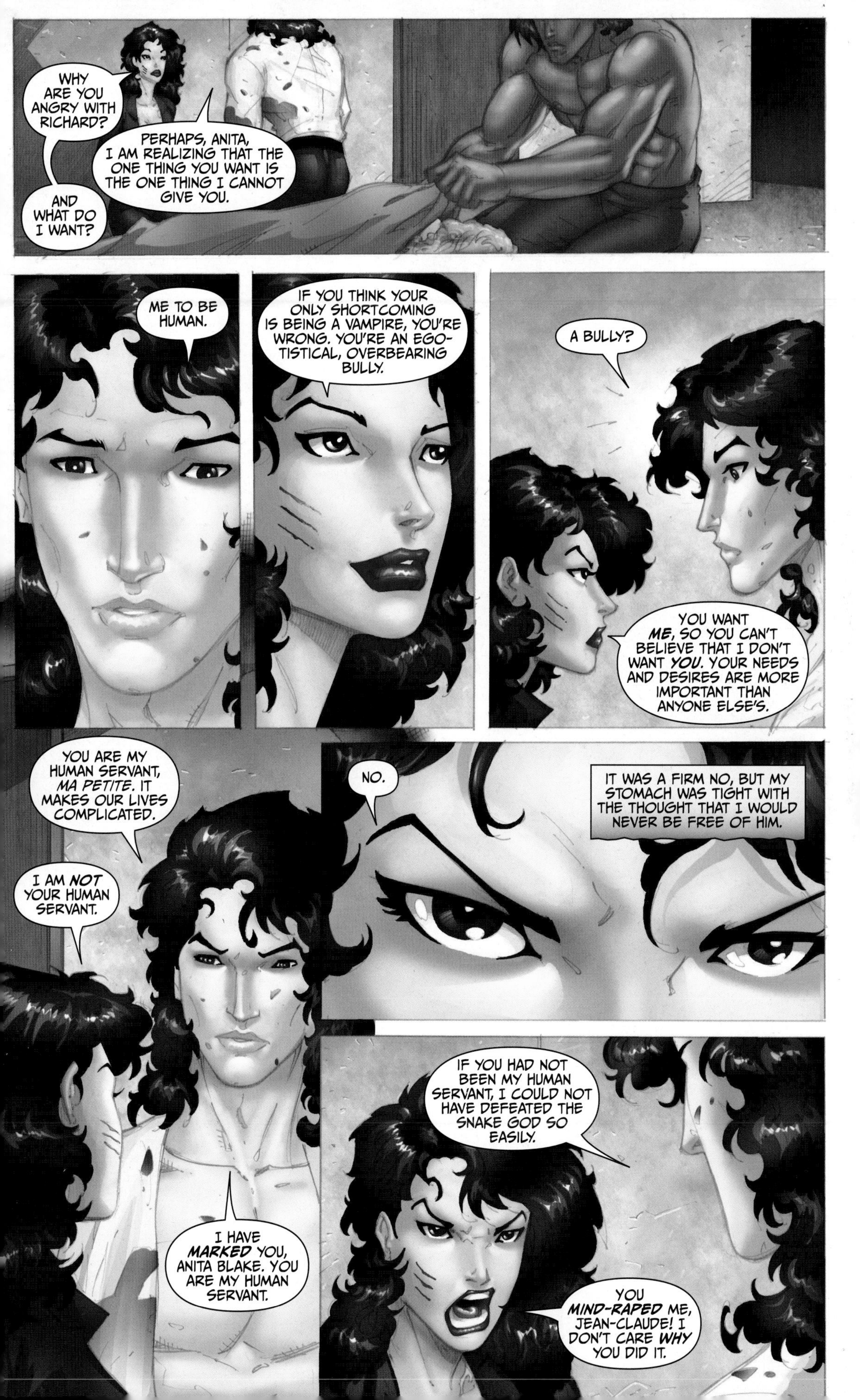
WHY ARE YOU ANGRY WITH RICHARD?
PERHAPS, ANITA, I AM REALIZING THAT THE ONE THING YOU WANT IS THE ONE THING I CANNOT GIVE YOU.
AND WHAT DO I WANT?
ME TO BE HUMAN.
IF YOU THINK YOUR ONLY SHORTCOMING IS BEING A VAMPIRE, YOU'RE WRONG. YOU'RE AN EGOTISTICAL, OVERBEARING BULLY.
A BULLY?
YOU WANT *ME*, SO YOU CAN'T BELIEVE THAT I DON'T WANT *YOU*. YOUR NEEDS AND DESIRES ARE MORE IMPORTANT THAN ANYONE ELSE'S.
YOU ARE MY HUMAN SERVANT, *MA PETITE*. IT MAKES OUR LIVES COMPLICATED.
I AM *NOT* YOUR HUMAN SERVANT.
I HAVE *MARKED* YOU, ANITA BLAKE. YOU ARE MY HUMAN SERVANT.
NO.
IT WAS A FIRM NO, BUT MY STOMACH WAS TIGHT WITH THE THOUGHT THAT I WOULD NEVER BE FREE OF HIM.
IF YOU HAD NOT BEEN MY HUMAN SERVANT, I COULD NOT HAVE DEFEATED THE SNAKE GOD SO EASILY.
YOU *MIND-RAPED* ME, JEAN-CLAUDE! I DON'T CARE *WHY* YOU DID IT.

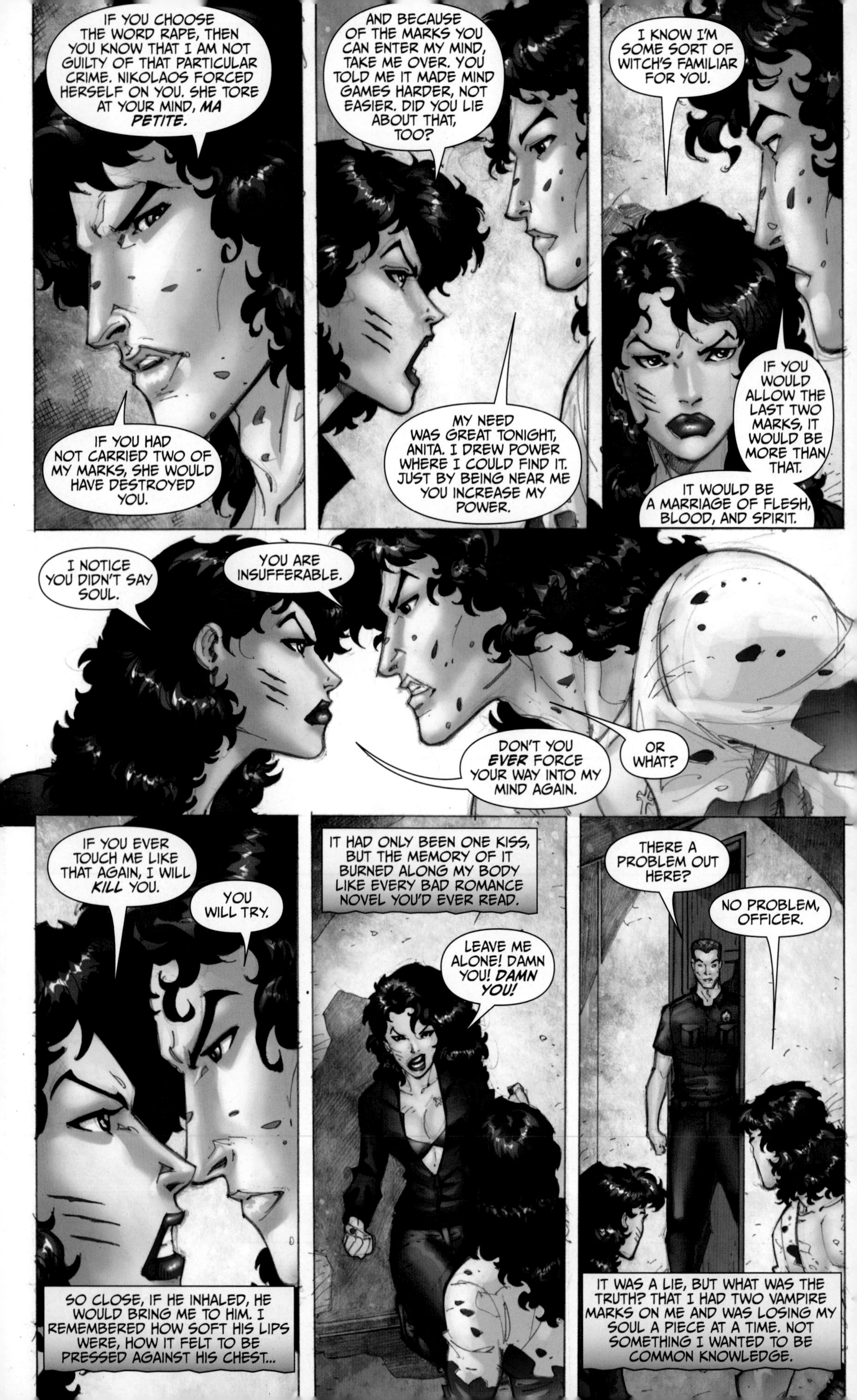
IF YOU CHOOSE THE WORD RAPE, THEN YOU KNOW THAT I AM NOT GUILTY OF THAT PARTICULAR CRIME. NIKOLAOS FORCED HERSELF ON YOU. SHE TORE AT YOUR MIND, *MA PETITE.*
IF YOU HAD NOT CARRIED TWO OF MY MARKS, SHE WOULD HAVE DESTROYED YOU.
AND BECAUSE OF THE MARKS YOU CAN ENTER MY MIND, TAKE ME OVER. YOU TOLD ME IT MADE MIND GAMES HARDER, NOT EASIER. DID YOU LIE ABOUT THAT, TOO?
MY NEED WAS GREAT TONIGHT, ANITA. I DREW POWER WHERE I COULD FIND IT. JUST BY BEING NEAR ME YOU INCREASE MY POWER.
I KNOW I'M SOME SORT OF WITCH'S FAMILIAR FOR YOU.
IF YOU WOULD ALLOW THE LAST TWO MARKS, IT WOULD BE MORE THAN THAT.
IT WOULD BE A MARRIAGE OF FLESH, BLOOD, AND SPIRIT.
I NOTICE YOU DIDN'T SAY SOUL.
YOU ARE INSUFFERABLE.
DON'T YOU *EVER* FORCE YOUR WAY INTO MY MIND AGAIN.
OR WHAT?
IF YOU EVER TOUCH ME LIKE THAT AGAIN, I WILL *KILL* YOU.
YOU WILL TRY.
SO CLOSE, IF HE INHALED, HE WOULD BRING ME TO HIM. I REMEMBERED HOW SOFT HIS LIPS WERE, HOW IT FELT TO BE PRESSED AGAINST HIS CHEST...
IT HAD ONLY BEEN ONE KISS, BUT THE MEMORY OF IT BURNED ALONG MY BODY LIKE EVERY BAD ROMANCE NOVEL YOU'D EVER READ.
LEAVE ME ALONE! DAMN YOU! *DAMN YOU!*
THERE A PROBLEM OUT HERE?
NO PROBLEM, OFFICER.
IT WAS A LIE, BUT WHAT WAS THE TRUTH? THAT I HAD TWO VAMPIRE MARKS ON ME AND WAS LOSING MY SOUL A PIECE AT A TIME. NOT SOMETHING I WANTED TO BE COMMON KNOWLEDGE.

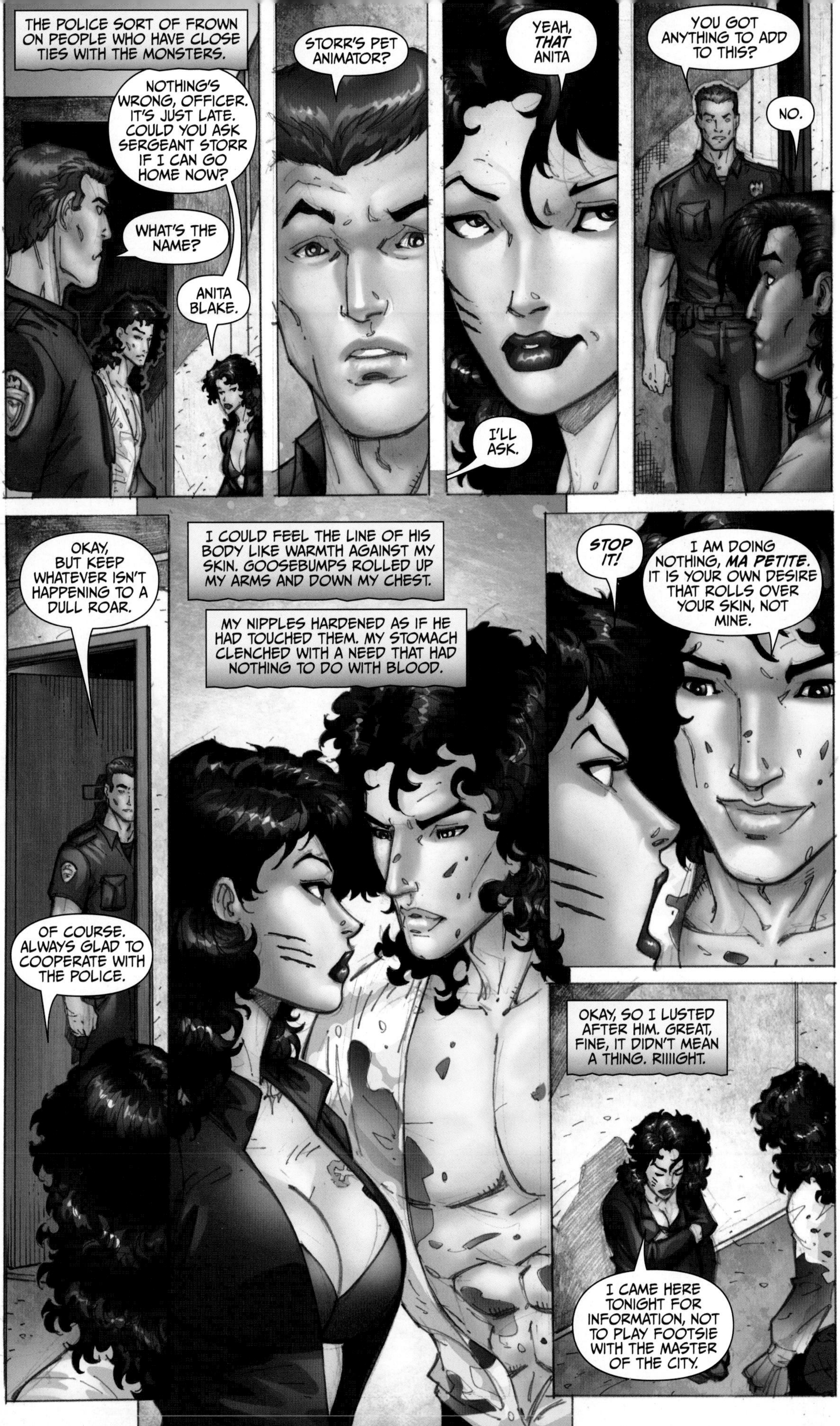
THE POLICE SORT OF FROWN ON PEOPLE WHO HAVE CLOSE TIES WITH THE MONSTERS.
NOTHING'S WRONG, OFFICER. IT'S JUST LATE. COULD YOU ASK SERGEANT STORR IF I CAN GO HOME NOW?
WHAT'S THE NAME?
ANITA BLAKE.
STORR'S PET ANIMATOR?
YEAH, *THAT* ANITA
I'LL ASK.
YOU GOT ANYTHING TO ADD TO THIS?
NO.
OKAY, BUT KEEP WHATEVER ISN'T HAPPENING TO A DULL ROAR.
OF COURSE. ALWAYS GLAD TO COOPERATE WITH THE POLICE.
I COULD FEEL THE LINE OF HIS BODY LIKE WARMTH AGAINST MY SKIN. GOOSEBUMPS ROLLED UP MY ARMS AND DOWN MY CHEST.
MY NIPPLES HARDENED AS IF HE HAD TOUCHED THEM. MY STOMACH CLENCHED WITH A NEED THAT HAD NOTHING TO DO WITH BLOOD.
STOP IT!
I AM DOING NOTHING, *MA PETITE*. IT IS YOUR OWN DESIRE THAT ROLLS OVER YOUR SKIN, NOT MINE.
OKAY, SO I LUSTED AFTER HIM. GREAT, FINE, IT DIDN'T MEAN A THING. RIIIIGHT.
I CAME HERE TONIGHT FOR INFORMATION, NOT TO PLAY FOOTSIE WITH THE MASTER OF THE CITY.

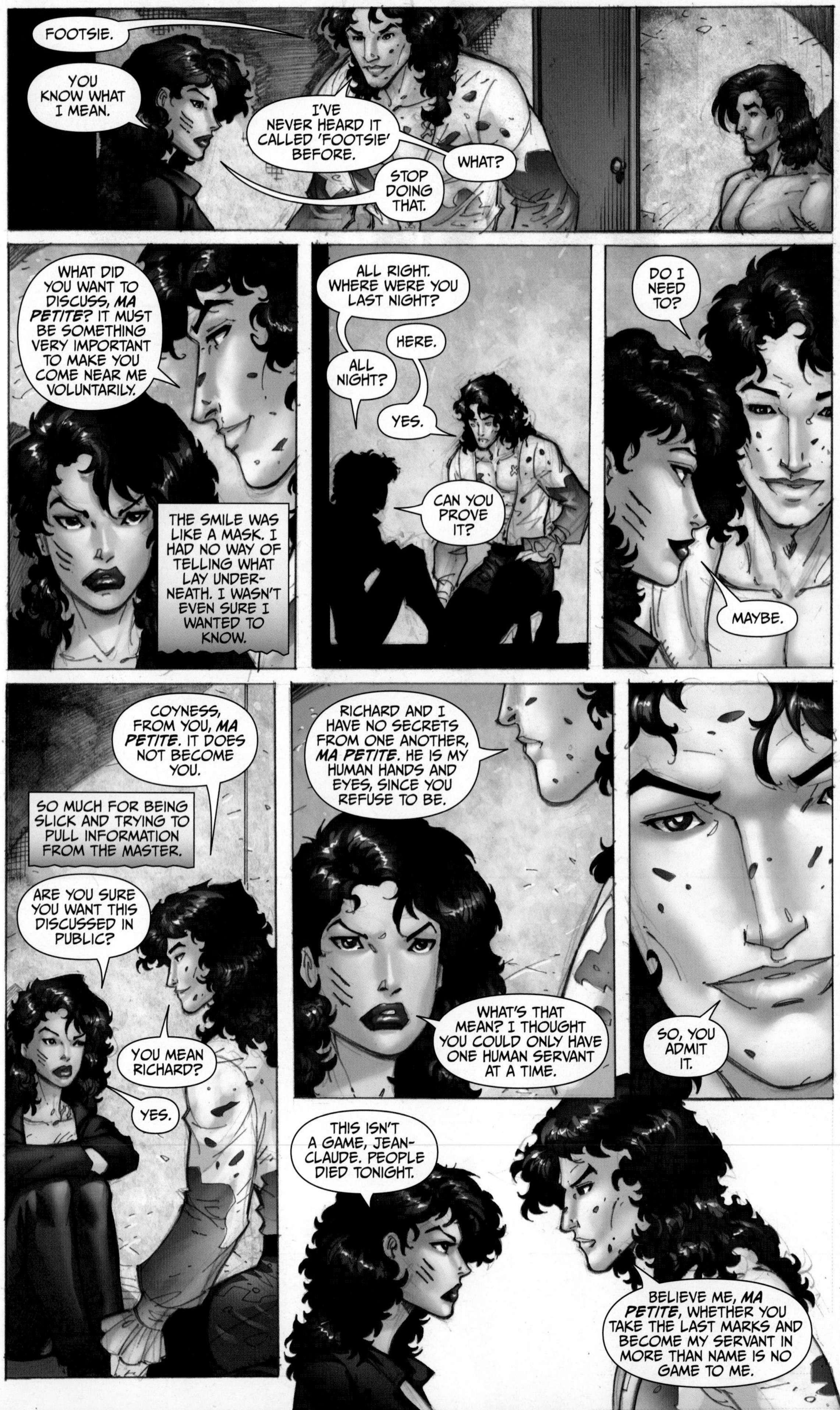

FOOTSIE.
YOU KNOW WHAT I MEAN.
I'VE NEVER HEARD IT CALLED 'FOOTSIE' BEFORE.
WHAT?
STOP DOING THAT.
WHAT DID YOU WANT TO DISCUSS, MA PETITE? IT MUST BE SOMETHING VERY IMPORTANT TO MAKE YOU COME NEAR ME VOLUNTARILY.
THE SMILE WAS LIKE A MASK. I HAD NO WAY OF TELLING WHAT LAY UNDERNEATH. I WASN'T EVEN SURE I WANTED TO KNOW.
ALL RIGHT. WHERE WERE YOU LAST NIGHT?
HERE.
ALL NIGHT?
YES.
CAN YOU PROVE IT?
DO I NEED TO?
MAYBE.
COYNESS, FROM YOU, MA PETITE. IT DOES NOT BECOME YOU.
SO MUCH FOR BEING SLICK AND TRYING TO PULL INFORMATION FROM THE MASTER.
ARE YOU SURE YOU WANT THIS DISCUSSED IN PUBLIC?
YOU MEAN RICHARD?
YES.
RICHARD AND I HAVE NO SECRETS FROM ONE ANOTHER, MA PETITE. HE IS MY HUMAN HANDS AND EYES, SINCE YOU REFUSE TO BE.
WHAT'S THAT MEAN? I THOUGHT YOU COULD ONLY HAVE ONE HUMAN SERVANT AT A TIME.
SO, YOU ADMIT IT.
THIS ISN'T A GAME, JEAN-CLAUDE. PEOPLE DIED TONIGHT.
BELIEVE ME, MA PETITE, WHETHER YOU TAKE THE LAST MARKS AND BECOME MY SERVANT IN MORE THAN NAME IS NO GAME TO ME.

THERE WAS A MURDER LAST NIGHT.

AND?

IT WAS A VAMPIRE VICTIM.

AH, MY PART IN THIS BECOMES CLEAR.

I'M GLAD YOU FIND IT FUNNY.

DYING FROM VAMPIRE BITES IS ONLY TEMPORARILY FATAL, *MA PETITE*. WAIT UNTIL THE THIRD NIGHT WHEN THE VICTIM RISES, THEN QUESTION HIM.

WHAT IS IT THAT YOU ARE NOT TELLING ME?

I FOUND FIVE DIFFERENT BITE RADIUSES ON THE VICTIM.

SO YOU ARE LOOKING FOR A ROGUE MASTER VAMPIRE.

YEP. KNOW ANY?

I REMEMBERED A BENGAL TIGER I'D SEEN ONCE IN A ZOO. SOME GENIUS HAD PUT ONE BARRED WALL SO CLOSE TO THE FENCE, I COULD HAVE REACHED THROUGH AND TOUCHED THE TIGER EASILY. IT WAS SO CLOSE, SO BEAUTIFUL, SO WILD, SO...TEMPTING.

THERE WAS THAT SMALL PART OF ME THAT REGRETTED NOT REACHING THROUGH THE BARS. I FELT JEAN-CLAUDE'S LAUGHTER RUNNING LIKE VELVET DOWN MY SPINE. WOULD PART OF ME ALWAYS WONDER WHAT WOULD HAVE BEEN LIKE IF I HAD JUST SAID YES?

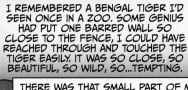

AHHAHA HAHA!

PROBABLY. BUT I COULD LIVE WITH IT.

WHAT ARE YOU THINKING, *MA PETITE*?

I DON'T KNOW ANYTHING ABOUT YOU, JEAN-CLAUDE, NOT A BLOODY THING.

YOU KNOW MORE ABOUT ME THAN ANYONE ELSE IN THE CITY.

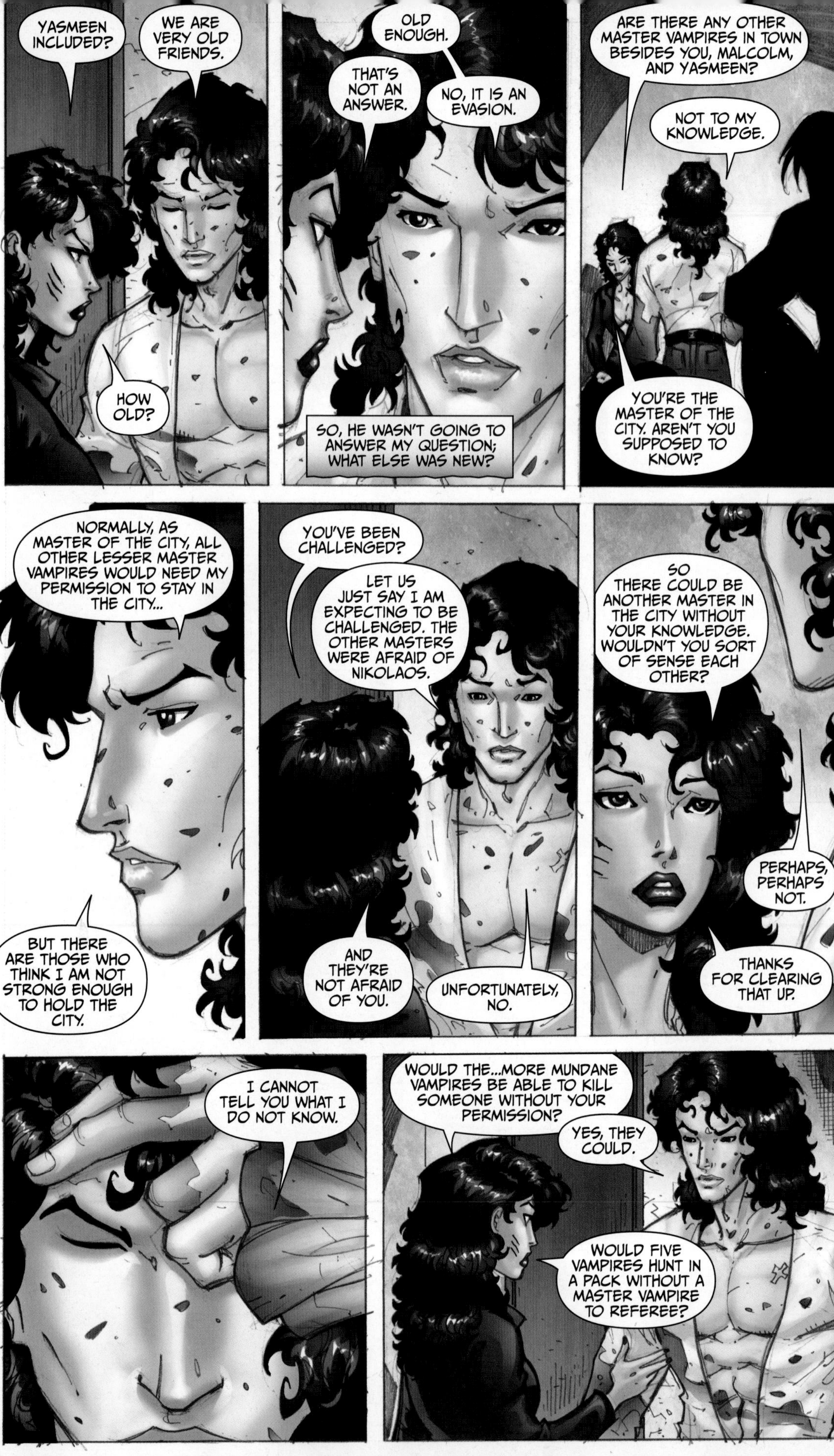
YASMEEN INCLUDED?
WE ARE VERY OLD FRIENDS.
HOW OLD?
OLD ENOUGH.
THAT'S NOT AN ANSWER.
NO, IT IS AN EVASION.
SO, HE WASN'T GOING TO ANSWER MY QUESTION; WHAT ELSE WAS NEW?
ARE THERE ANY OTHER MASTER VAMPIRES IN TOWN BESIDES YOU, MALCOLM, AND YASMEEN?
NOT TO MY KNOWLEDGE.
YOU'RE THE MASTER OF THE CITY. AREN'T YOU SUPPOSED TO KNOW?
NORMALLY, AS MASTER OF THE CITY, ALL OTHER LESSER MASTER VAMPIRES WOULD NEED MY PERMISSION TO STAY IN THE CITY...
BUT THERE ARE THOSE WHO THINK I AM NOT STRONG ENOUGH TO HOLD THE CITY.
YOU'VE BEEN CHALLENGED?
LET US JUST SAY I AM EXPECTING TO BE CHALLENGED. THE OTHER MASTERS WERE AFRAID OF NIKOLAOS.
AND THEY'RE NOT AFRAID OF YOU.
UNFORTUNATELY, NO.
SO THERE COULD BE ANOTHER MASTER IN THE CITY WITHOUT YOUR KNOWLEDGE. WOULDN'T YOU SORT OF SENSE EACH OTHER?
PERHAPS, PERHAPS NOT.
THANKS FOR CLEARING THAT UP.
I CANNOT TELL YOU WHAT I DO NOT KNOW.
WOULD THE...MORE MUNDANE VAMPIRES BE ABLE TO KILL SOMEONE WITHOUT YOUR PERMISSION?
YES, THEY COULD.
WOULD FIVE VAMPIRES HUNT IN A PACK WITHOUT A MASTER VAMPIRE TO REFEREE?

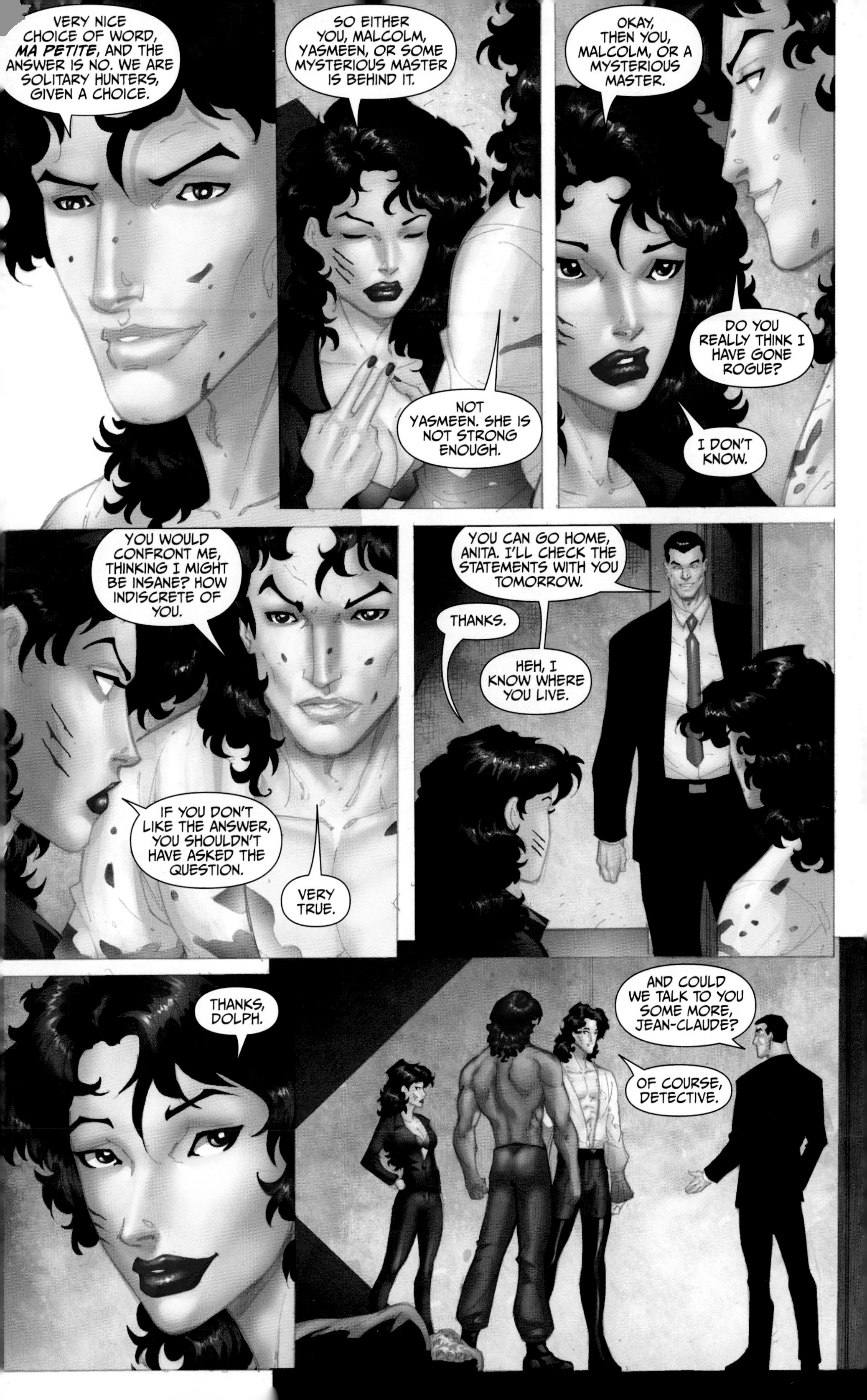
VERY NICE CHOICE OF WORD, ***MA PETITE***, AND THE ANSWER IS NO. WE ARE SOLITARY HUNTERS, GIVEN A CHOICE.
SO EITHER YOU, MALCOLM, YASMEEN, OR SOME MYSTERIOUS MASTER IS BEHIND IT.
NOT YASMEEN. SHE IS NOT STRONG ENOUGH.
OKAY, THEN YOU, MALCOLM, OR A MYSTERIOUS MASTER.
DO YOU REALLY THINK I HAVE GONE ROGUE?
I DON'T KNOW.
YOU WOULD CONFRONT ME, THINKING I MIGHT BE INSANE? HOW INDISCRETE OF YOU.
IF YOU DON'T LIKE THE ANSWER, YOU SHOULDN'T HAVE ASKED THE QUESTION.
VERY TRUE.
YOU CAN GO HOME, ANITA. I'LL CHECK THE STATEMENTS WITH YOU TOMORROW.
THANKS.
HEH, I KNOW WHERE YOU LIVE.
THANKS, DOLPH.
AND COULD WE TALK TO YOU SOME MORE, JEAN-CLAUDE?
OF COURSE, DETECTIVE.

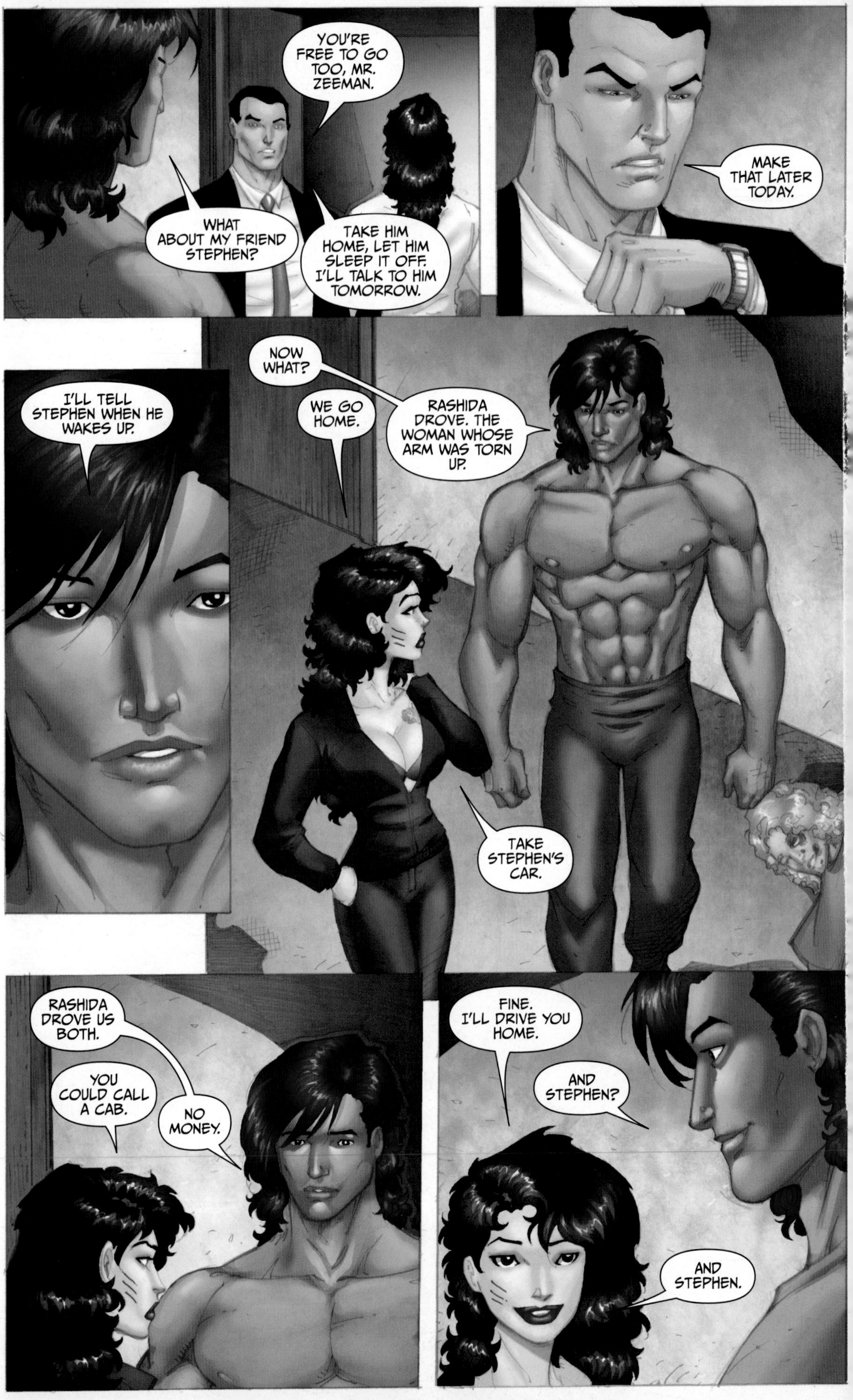
YOU'RE FREE TO GO TOO, MR. ZEEMAN.
WHAT ABOUT MY FRIEND STEPHEN?
TAKE HIM HOME, LET HIM SLEEP IT OFF. I'LL TALK TO HIM TOMORROW.
MAKE THAT LATER TODAY.
I'LL TELL STEPHEN WHEN HE WAKES UP.
NOW WHAT?
WE GO HOME.
RASHIDA DROVE. THE WOMAN WHOSE ARM WAS TORN UP.
TAKE STEPHEN'S CAR.
RASHIDA DROVE US BOTH.
YOU COULD CALL A CAB.
NO MONEY.
FINE. I'LL DRIVE YOU HOME.
AND STEPHEN?
AND STEPHEN.

YOU DON'T EVEN KNOW WHERE I LIVE. IT COULD BE KANSAS CITY.

IF IT'S A TEN HOUR DRIVE, YOU'RE ON YOUR OWN. IF IT'S REASONABLE, I'LL DRIVE YOU.

IS MERAMEC HEIGHTS REASONABLE?

SURE.

LET ME GET MY COAT.

I'LL WAIT HERE.

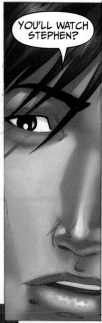

YOU'LL WATCH STEPHEN?

WHAT ARE YOU AFRAID OF?

AIRPLANES, GUNS, LARGE PREDATORS, AND MASTER VAMPIRES.

I AGREE WITH TWO OUT OF FOUR.

I'LL GO GET MY COAT.

MY, MY, GRANDMOTHER, WHAT STRONG ARMS YOU HAVE.

IS MY LINE, 'THE BETTER TO HOLD YOU WITH'?

YOU WANT A RIDE, OR NOT?

I WANT A RIDE.

THEN CAN THE SARCASM.

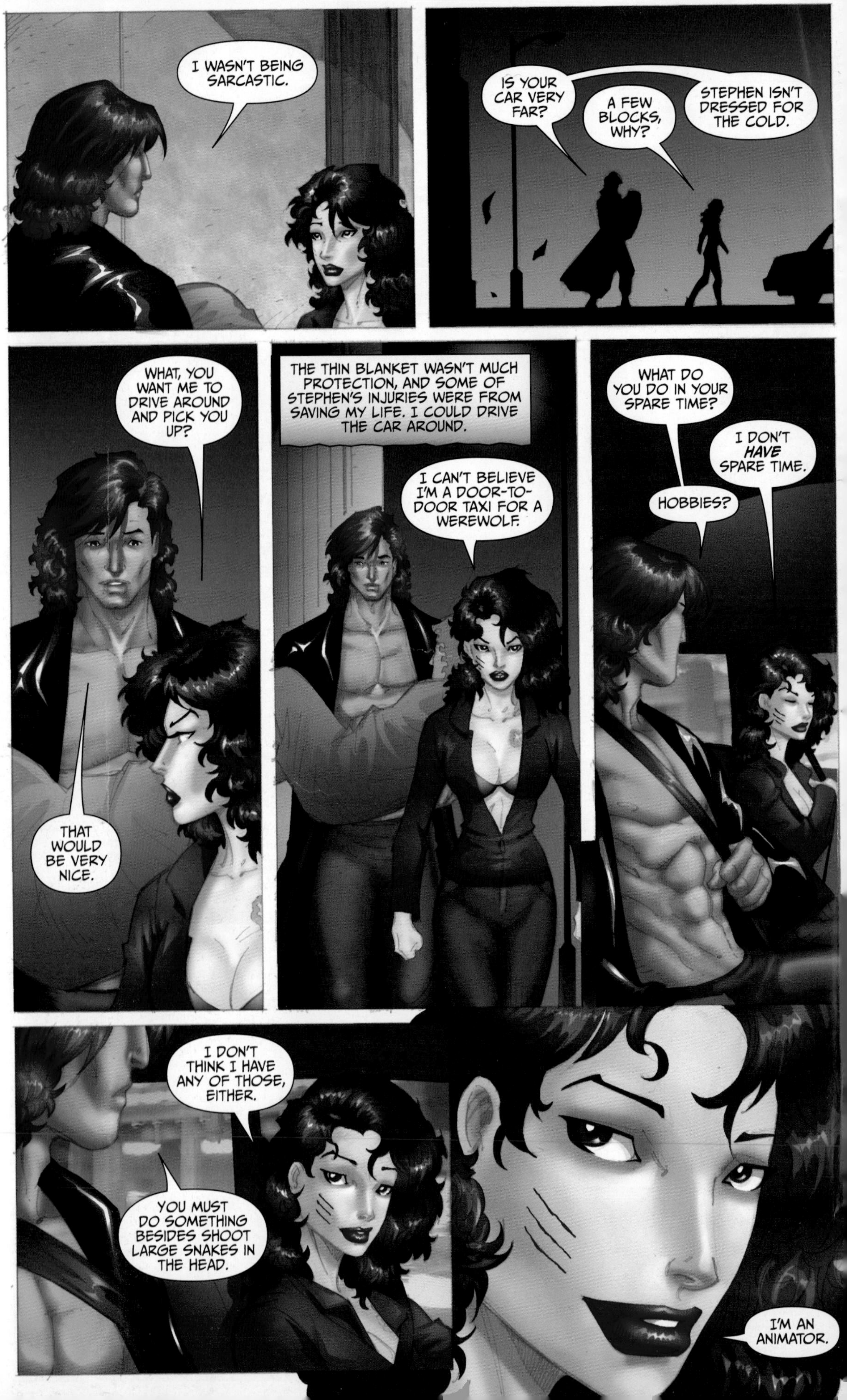

I WASN'T BEING SARCASTIC.
IS YOUR CAR VERY FAR?
A FEW BLOCKS, WHY?
STEPHEN ISN'T DRESSED FOR THE COLD.
WHAT, YOU WANT ME TO DRIVE AROUND AND PICK YOU UP?
THAT WOULD BE VERY NICE.
THE THIN BLANKET WASN'T MUCH PROTECTION, AND SOME OF STEPHEN'S INJURIES WERE FROM SAVING MY LIFE. I COULD DRIVE THE CAR AROUND.
I CAN'T BELIEVE I'M A DOOR-TO-DOOR TAXI FOR A WEREWOLF.
WHAT DO YOU DO IN YOUR SPARE TIME?
I DON'T HAVE SPARE TIME.
HOBBIES?
I DON'T THINK I HAVE ANY OF THOSE, EITHER.
YOU MUST DO SOMETHING BESIDES SHOOT LARGE SNAKES IN THE HEAD.
I'M AN ANIMATOR.

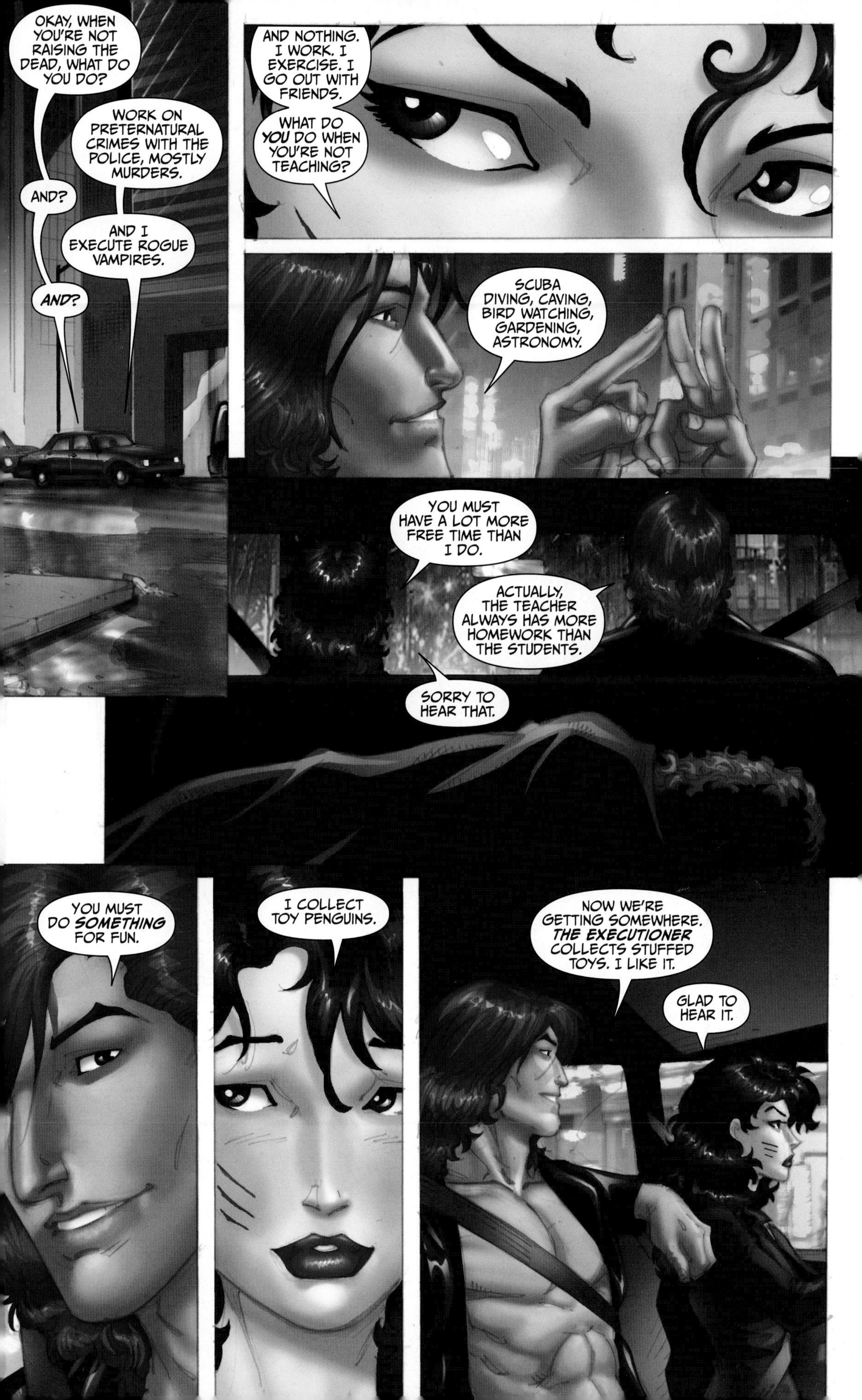
OKAY, WHEN YOU'RE NOT RAISING THE DEAD, WHAT DO YOU DO?
WORK ON PRETERNATURAL CRIMES WITH THE POLICE, MOSTLY MURDERS.
AND?
AND I EXECUTE ROGUE VAMPIRES.
AND?
AND NOTHING. I WORK. I EXERCISE. I GO OUT WITH FRIENDS.
WHAT DO YOU DO WHEN YOU'RE NOT TEACHING?
SCUBA DIVING, CAVING, BIRD WATCHING, GARDENING, ASTRONOMY.
YOU MUST HAVE A LOT MORE FREE TIME THAN I DO.
ACTUALLY, THE TEACHER ALWAYS HAS MORE HOMEWORK THAN THE STUDENTS.
SORRY TO HEAR THAT.
YOU MUST DO SOMETHING FOR FUN.
I COLLECT TOY PENGUINS.
NOW WE'RE GETTING SOMEWHERE. THE EXECUTIONER COLLECTS STUFFED TOYS. I LIKE IT.
GLAD TO HEAR IT.

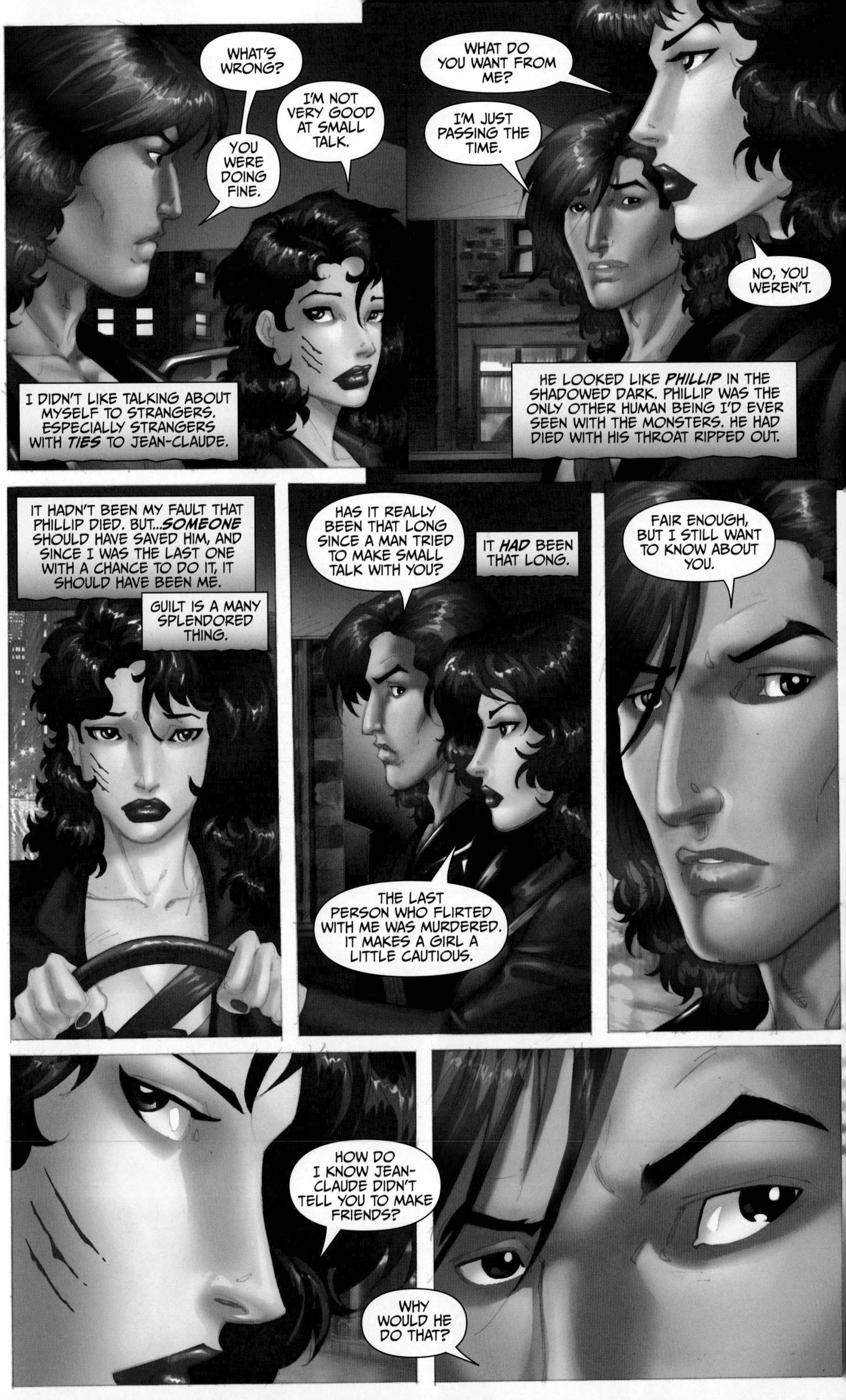
WHAT'S WRONG?
I'M NOT VERY GOOD AT SMALL TALK.
YOU WERE DOING FINE.
I DIDN'T LIKE TALKING ABOUT MYSELF TO STRANGERS. ESPECIALLY STRANGERS WITH *TIES* TO JEAN-CLAUDE.
WHAT DO YOU WANT FROM ME?
I'M JUST PASSING THE TIME.
NO, YOU WEREN'T.
HE LOOKED LIKE *PHILLIP* IN THE SHADOWED DARK. PHILLIP WAS THE ONLY OTHER HUMAN BEING I'D EVER SEEN WITH THE MONSTERS. HE HAD DIED WITH HIS THROAT RIPPED OUT.
IT HADN'T BEEN MY FAULT THAT PHILLIP DIED. BUT...*SOMEONE* SHOULD HAVE SAVED HIM, AND SINCE I WAS THE LAST ONE WITH A CHANCE TO DO IT, IT SHOULD HAVE BEEN ME.
GUILT IS A MANY SPLENDORED THING.
HAS IT REALLY BEEN THAT LONG SINCE A MAN TRIED TO MAKE SMALL TALK WITH YOU?
IT *HAD* BEEN THAT LONG.
THE LAST PERSON WHO FLIRTED WITH ME WAS MURDERED. IT MAKES A GIRL A LITTLE CAUTIOUS.
FAIR ENOUGH, BUT I STILL WANT TO KNOW ABOUT YOU.
HOW DO I KNOW JEAN-CLAUDE DIDN'T TELL YOU TO MAKE FRIENDS?
WHY WOULD HE DO THAT?

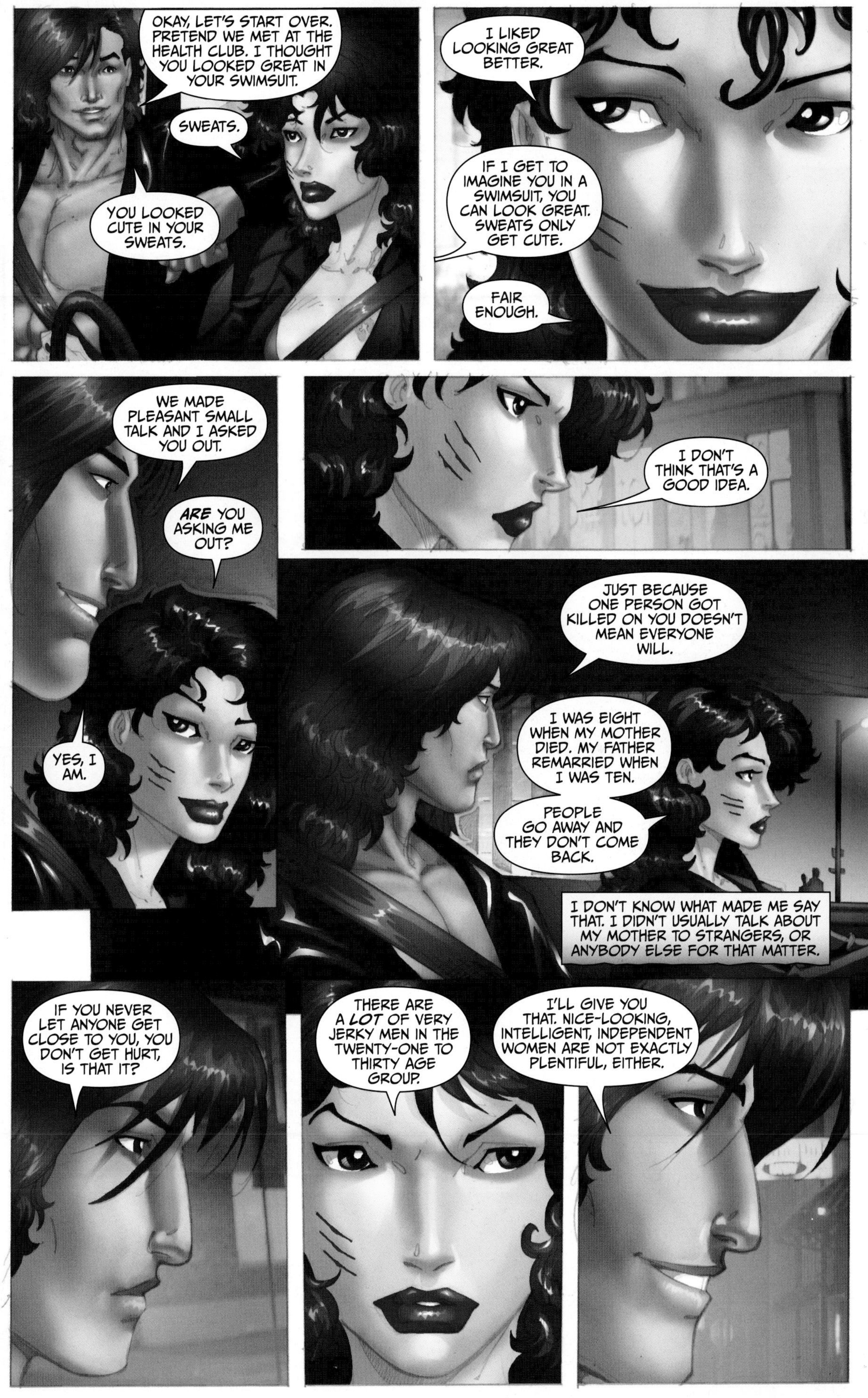

OKAY, LET'S START OVER. PRETEND WE MET AT THE HEALTH CLUB. I THOUGHT YOU LOOKED GREAT IN YOUR SWIMSUIT.
SWEATS.
YOU LOOKED CUTE IN YOUR SWEATS.
I LIKED LOOKING GREAT BETTER.
IF I GET TO IMAGINE YOU IN A SWIMSUIT, YOU CAN LOOK GREAT. SWEATS ONLY GET CUTE.
FAIR ENOUGH.
WE MADE PLEASANT SMALL TALK AND I ASKED YOU OUT.
ARE YOU ASKING ME OUT?
YES, I AM.
I DON'T THINK THAT'S A GOOD IDEA.
JUST BECAUSE ONE PERSON GOT KILLED ON YOU DOESN'T MEAN EVERYONE WILL.
I WAS EIGHT WHEN MY MOTHER DIED. MY FATHER REMARRIED WHEN I WAS TEN.
PEOPLE GO AWAY AND THEY DON'T COME BACK.
I DON'T KNOW WHAT MADE ME SAY THAT. I DIDN'T USUALLY TALK ABOUT MY MOTHER TO STRANGERS, OR ANYBODY ELSE FOR THAT MATTER.
IF YOU NEVER LET ANYONE GET CLOSE TO YOU, YOU DON'T GET HURT, IS THAT IT?
THERE ARE A *LOT* OF VERY JERKY MEN IN THE TWENTY-ONE TO THIRTY AGE GROUP.
I'LL GIVE YOU THAT. NICE-LOOKING, INTELLIGENT, INDEPENDENT WOMEN ARE NOT EXACTLY PLENTIFUL, EITHER.

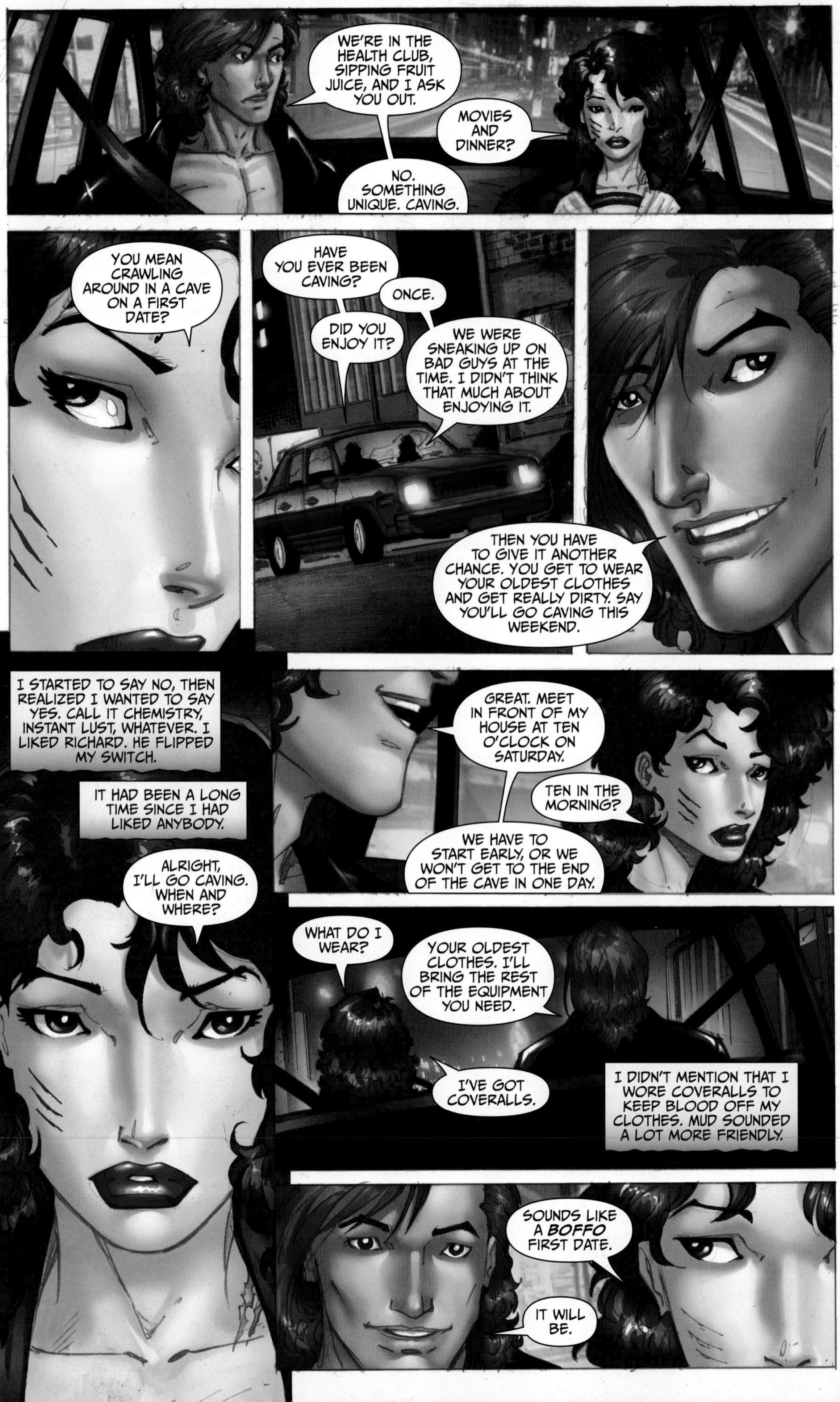
WE'RE IN THE HEALTH CLUB, SIPPING FRUIT JUICE, AND I ASK YOU OUT.
MOVIES AND DINNER?
NO. SOMETHING UNIQUE. CAVING.
YOU MEAN CRAWLING AROUND IN A CAVE ON A FIRST DATE?
HAVE YOU EVER BEEN CAVING?
ONCE.
DID YOU ENJOY IT?
WE WERE SNEAKING UP ON BAD GUYS AT THE TIME. I DIDN'T THINK THAT MUCH ABOUT ENJOYING IT.
THEN YOU HAVE TO GIVE IT ANOTHER CHANCE. YOU GET TO WEAR YOUR OLDEST CLOTHES AND GET REALLY DIRTY. SAY YOU'LL GO CAVING THIS WEEKEND.
I STARTED TO SAY NO, THEN REALIZED I WANTED TO SAY YES. CALL IT CHEMISTRY, INSTANT LUST, WHATEVER. I LIKED RICHARD. HE FLIPPED MY SWITCH.
IT HAD BEEN A LONG TIME SINCE I HAD LIKED ANYBODY.
ALRIGHT, I'LL GO CAVING. WHEN AND WHERE?
GREAT. MEET IN FRONT OF MY HOUSE AT TEN O'CLOCK ON SATURDAY.
TEN IN THE MORNING?
WE HAVE TO START EARLY, OR WE WON'T GET TO THE END OF THE CAVE IN ONE DAY.
WHAT DO I WEAR?
YOUR OLDEST CLOTHES. I'LL BRING THE REST OF THE EQUIPMENT YOU NEED.
I'VE GOT COVERALLS.
I DIDN'T MENTION THAT I WORE COVERALLS TO KEEP BLOOD OFF MY CLOTHES. MUD SOUNDED A LOT MORE FRIENDLY.
SOUNDS LIKE A *BOFFO* FIRST DATE.
IT WILL BE.

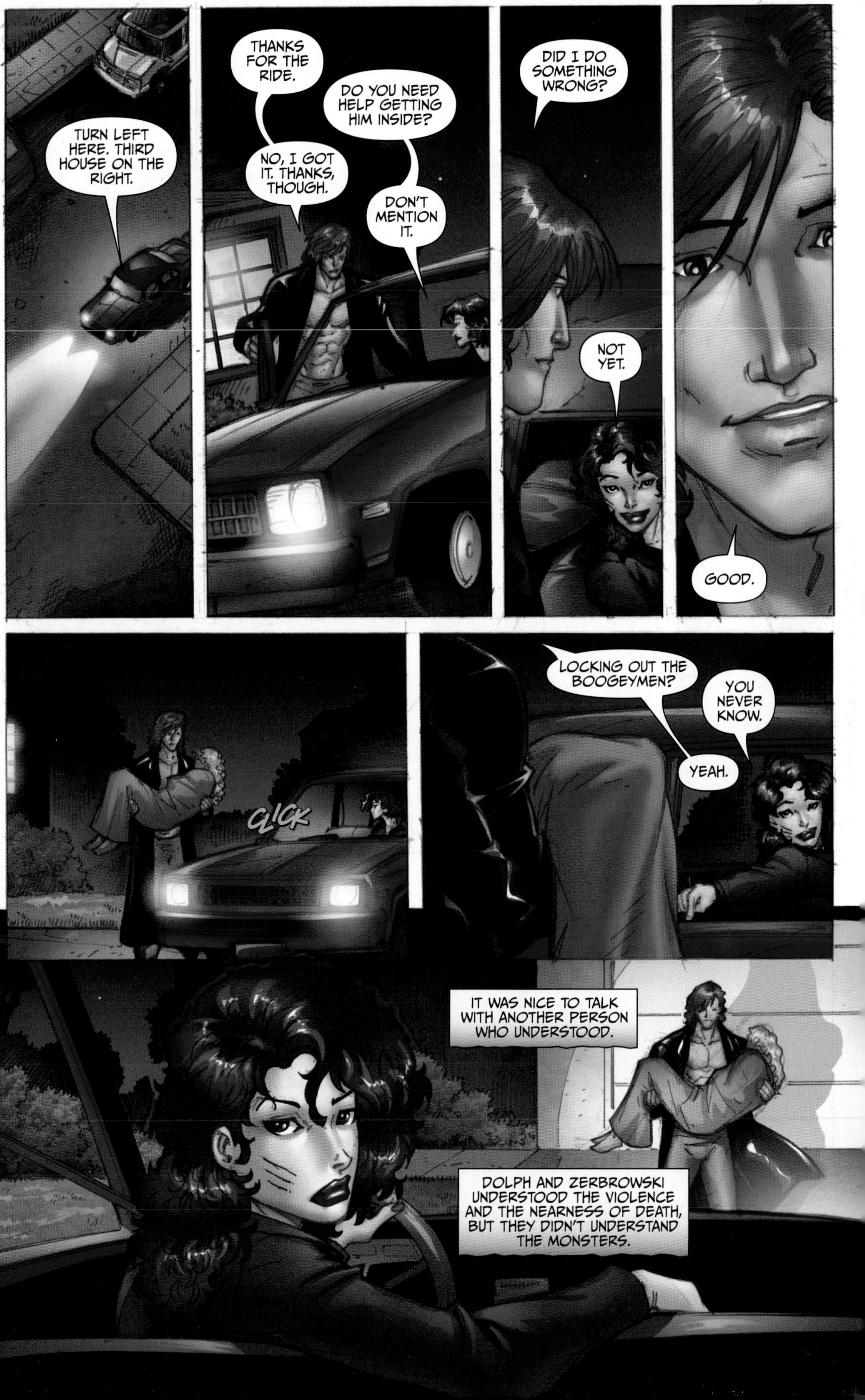
TURN LEFT HERE. THIRD HOUSE ON THE RIGHT.
THANKS FOR THE RIDE.
DO YOU NEED HELP GETTING HIM INSIDE?
NO, I GOT IT. THANKS, THOUGH.
DON'T MENTION IT.
DID I DO SOMETHING WRONG?
NOT YET.
GOOD.
CLICK
LOCKING OUT THE BOOGEYMEN?
YEAH.
YOU NEVER KNOW.
IT WAS NICE TO TALK WITH ANOTHER PERSON WHO UNDERSTOOD.
DOLPH AND ZERBROWSKI UNDERSTOOD THE VIOLENCE AND THE NEARNESS OF DEATH, BUT THEY DIDN'T UNDERSTAND THE MONSTERS.

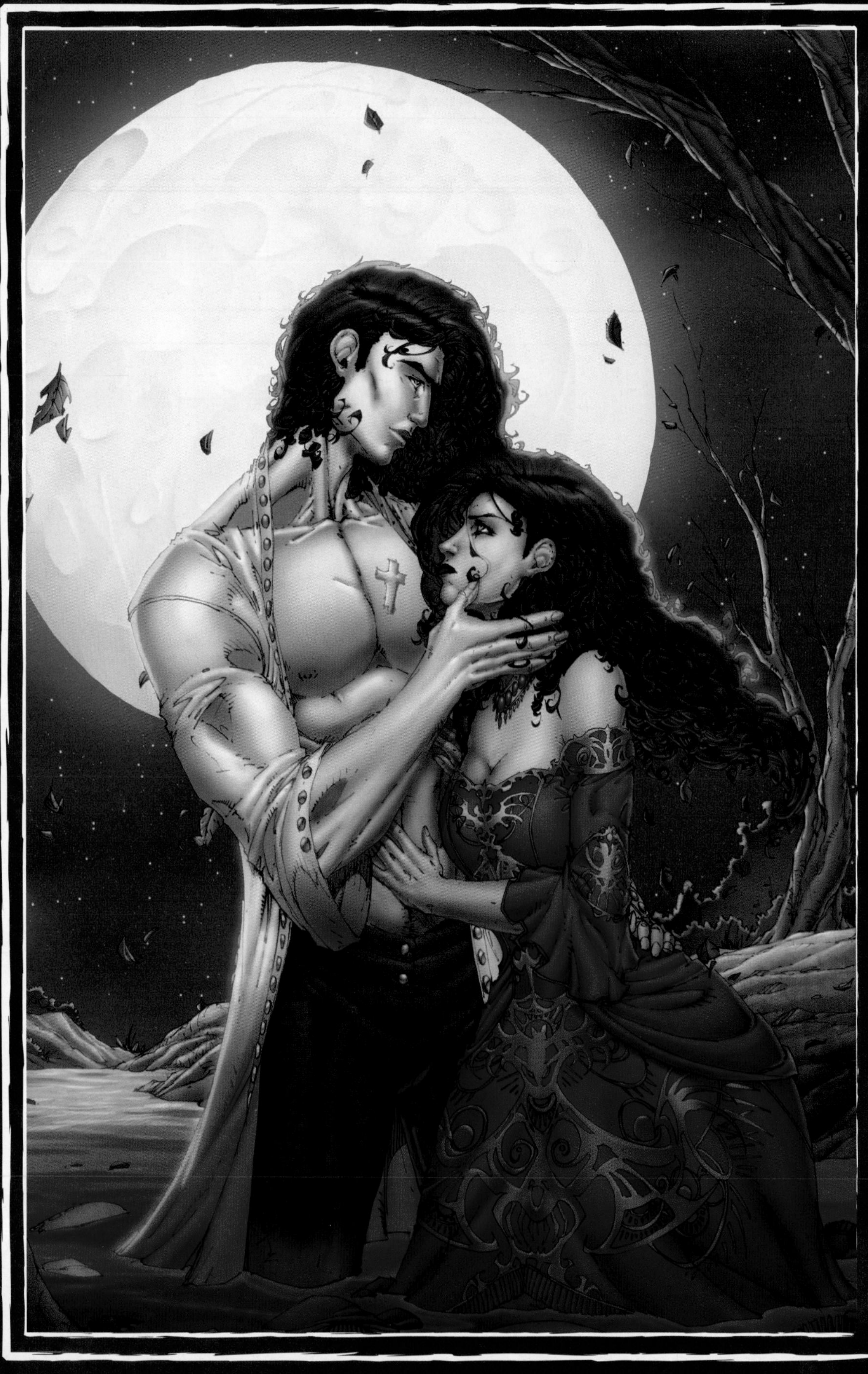

#5

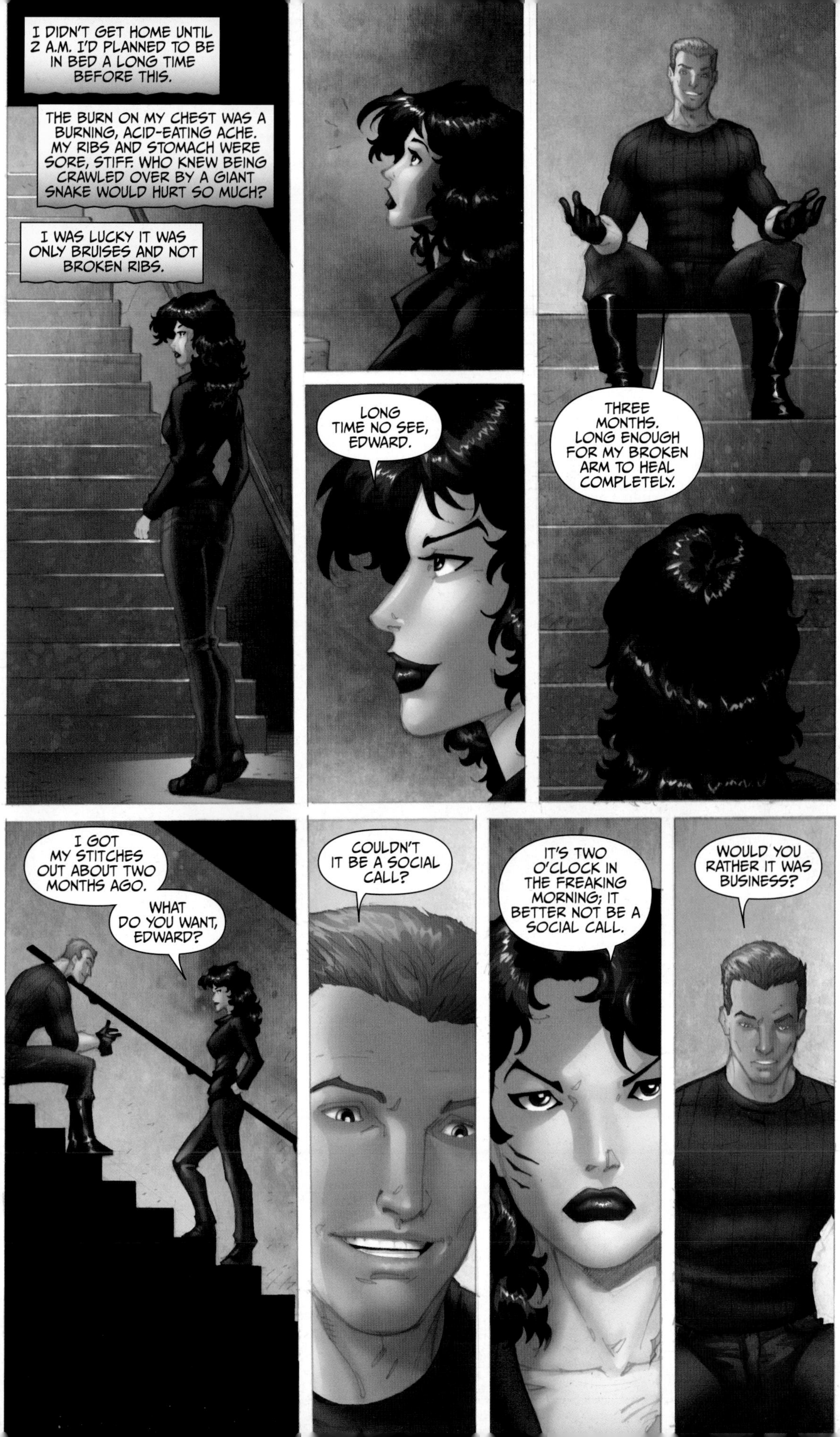
I DIDN'T GET HOME UNTIL 2 A.M. I'D PLANNED TO BE IN BED A LONG TIME BEFORE THIS.
THE BURN ON MY CHEST WAS A BURNING, ACID-EATING ACHE. MY RIBS AND STOMACH WERE SORE, STIFF. WHO KNEW BEING CRAWLED OVER BY A GIANT SNAKE WOULD HURT SO MUCH?
I WAS LUCKY IT WAS ONLY BRUISES AND NOT BROKEN RIBS.
LONG TIME NO SEE, EDWARD.
THREE MONTHS. LONG ENOUGH FOR MY BROKEN ARM TO HEAL COMPLETELY.
I GOT MY STITCHES OUT ABOUT TWO MONTHS AGO.
WHAT DO YOU WANT, EDWARD?
COULDN'T IT BE A SOCIAL CALL?
IT'S TWO O'CLOCK IN THE FREAKING MORNING; IT BETTER NOT BE A SOCIAL CALL.
WOULD YOU RATHER IT WAS BUSINESS?

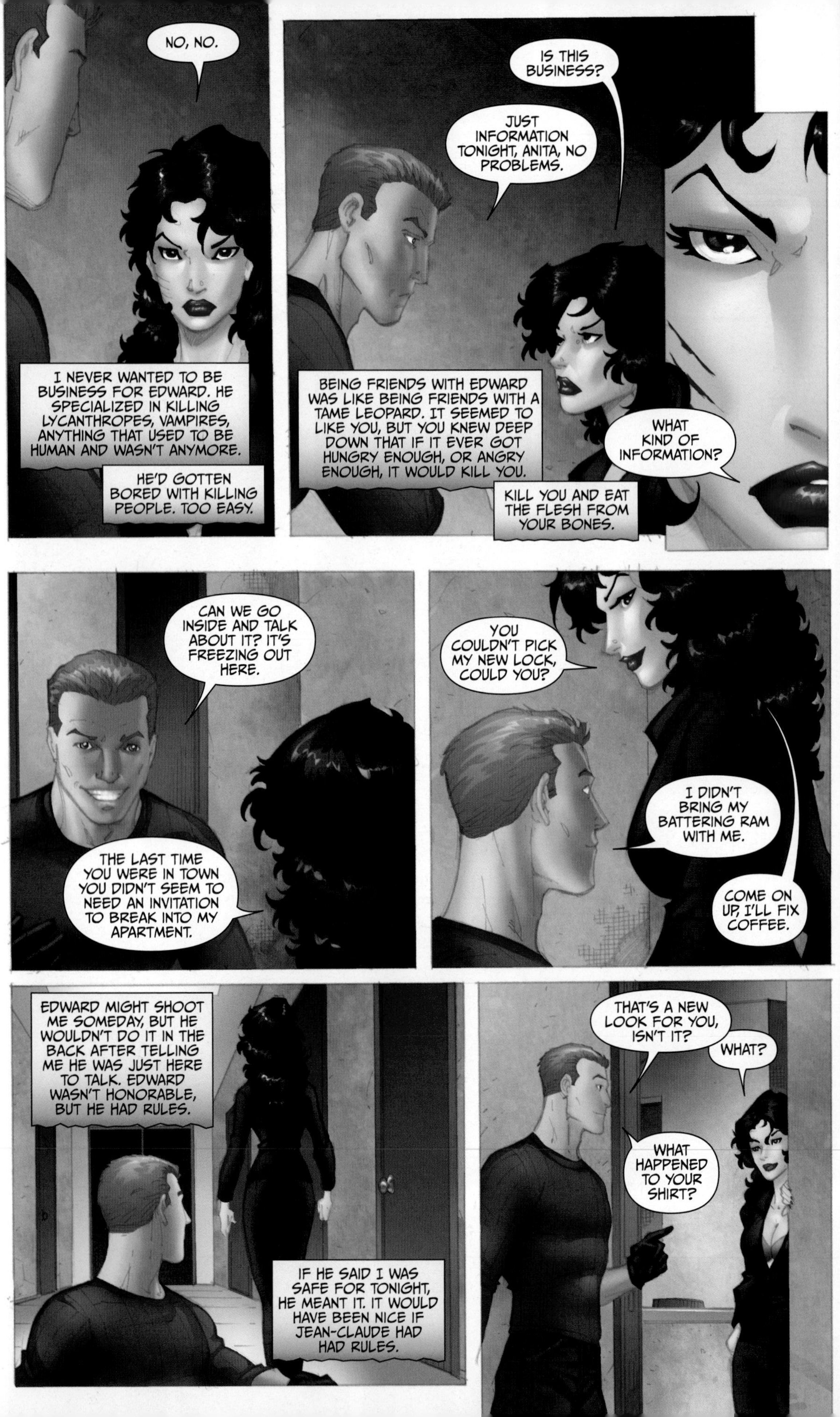
NO, NO.
I NEVER WANTED TO BE BUSINESS FOR EDWARD. HE SPECIALIZED IN KILLING LYCANTHROPES, VAMPIRES, ANYTHING THAT USED TO BE HUMAN AND WASN'T ANYMORE.
HE'D GOTTEN BORED WITH KILLING PEOPLE. TOO EASY.
IS THIS BUSINESS?
JUST INFORMATION TONIGHT, ANITA, NO PROBLEMS.
BEING FRIENDS WITH EDWARD WAS LIKE BEING FRIENDS WITH A TAME LEOPARD. IT SEEMED TO LIKE YOU, BUT YOU KNEW DEEP DOWN THAT IF IT EVER GOT HUNGRY ENOUGH, OR ANGRY ENOUGH, IT WOULD KILL YOU.
KILL YOU AND EAT THE FLESH FROM YOUR BONES.
WHAT KIND OF INFORMATION?
CAN WE GO INSIDE AND TALK ABOUT IT? IT'S FREEZING OUT HERE.
THE LAST TIME YOU WERE IN TOWN YOU DIDN'T SEEM TO NEED AN INVITATION TO BREAK INTO MY APARTMENT.
YOU COULDN'T PICK MY NEW LOCK, COULD YOU?
I DIDN'T BRING MY BATTERING RAM WITH ME.
COME ON UP, I'LL FIX COFFEE.
EDWARD MIGHT SHOOT ME SOMEDAY, BUT HE WOULDN'T DO IT IN THE BACK AFTER TELLING ME HE WAS JUST HERE TO TALK. EDWARD WASN'T HONORABLE, BUT HE HAD RULES.
IF HE SAID I WAS SAFE FOR TONIGHT, HE MEANT IT. IT WOULD HAVE BEEN NICE IF JEAN-CLAUDE HAD HAD RULES.
THAT'S A NEW LOOK FOR YOU, ISN'T IT?
WHAT?
WHAT HAPPENED TO YOUR SHIRT?

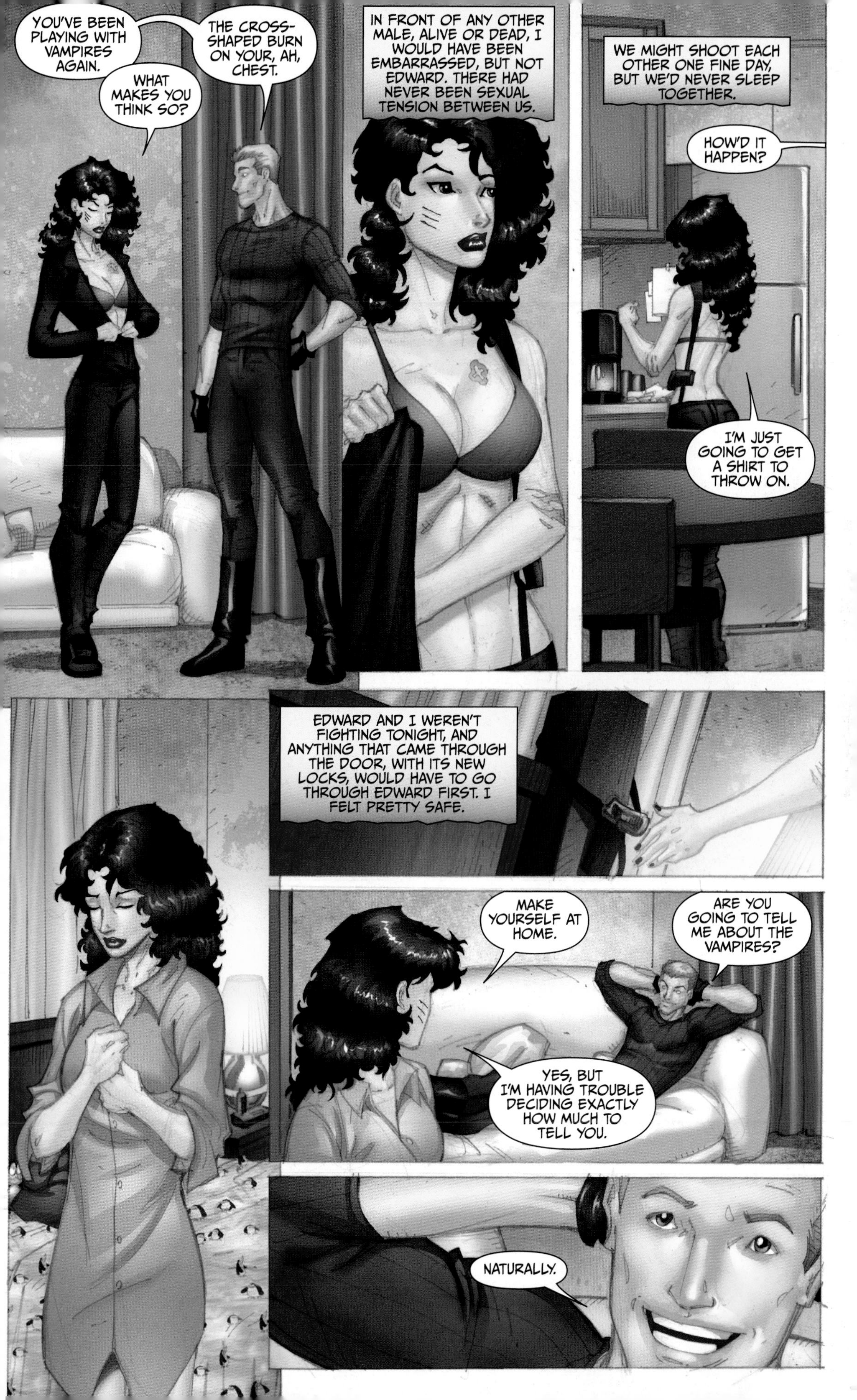

YOU'VE BEEN PLAYING WITH VAMPIRES AGAIN.
WHAT MAKES YOU THINK SO?
THE CROSS-SHAPED BURN ON YOUR, AH, CHEST.
IN FRONT OF ANY OTHER MALE, ALIVE OR DEAD, I WOULD HAVE BEEN EMBARRASSED, BUT NOT EDWARD. THERE HAD NEVER BEEN SEXUAL TENSION BETWEEN US.
WE MIGHT SHOOT EACH OTHER ONE FINE DAY, BUT WE'D NEVER SLEEP TOGETHER.
HOW'D IT HAPPEN?
I'M JUST GOING TO GET A SHIRT TO THROW ON.
EDWARD AND I WEREN'T FIGHTING TONIGHT, AND ANYTHING THAT CAME THROUGH THE DOOR, WITH ITS NEW LOCKS, WOULD HAVE TO GO THROUGH EDWARD FIRST. I FELT PRETTY SAFE.
MAKE YOURSELF AT HOME.
ARE YOU GOING TO TELL ME ABOUT THE VAMPIRES?
YES, BUT I'M HAVING TROUBLE DECIDING EXACTLY HOW MUCH TO TELL YOU.
NATURALLY.

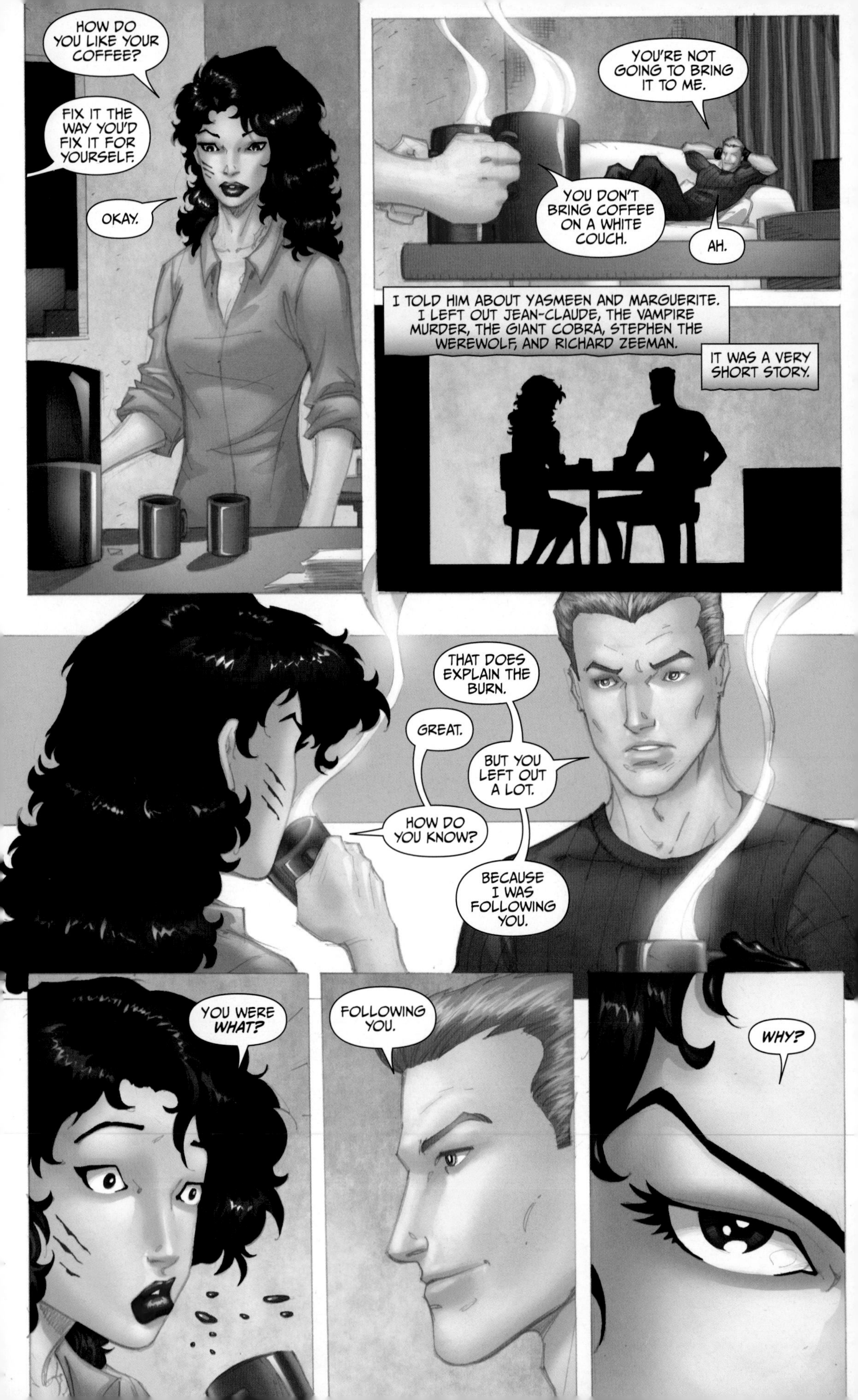
HOW DO YOU LIKE YOUR COFFEE?
FIX IT THE WAY YOU'D FIX IT FOR YOURSELF.
OKAY.
YOU'RE NOT GOING TO BRING IT TO ME.
YOU DON'T BRING COFFEE ON A WHITE COUCH.
AH.
I TOLD HIM ABOUT YASMEEN AND MARGUERITE. I LEFT OUT JEAN-CLAUDE, THE VAMPIRE MURDER, THE GIANT COBRA, STEPHEN THE WEREWOLF, AND RICHARD ZEEMAN.
IT WAS A VERY SHORT STORY.
THAT DOES EXPLAIN THE BURN.
GREAT.
BUT YOU LEFT OUT A LOT.
HOW DO YOU KNOW?
BECAUSE I WAS FOLLOWING YOU.
YOU WERE *WHAT?*
FOLLOWING YOU.
WHY?

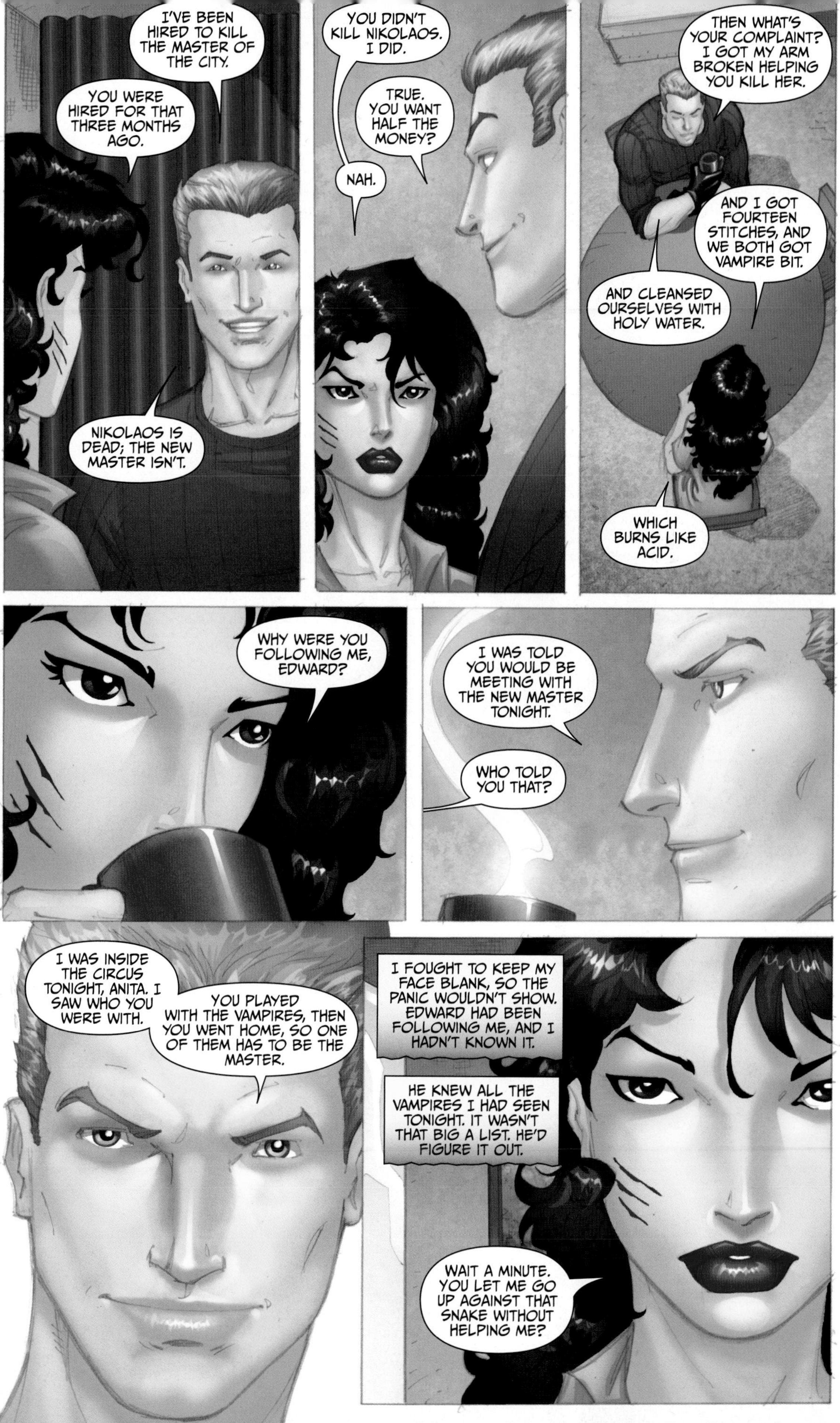
I'VE BEEN HIRED TO KILL THE MASTER OF THE CITY.
YOU WERE HIRED FOR THAT THREE MONTHS AGO.
NIKOLAOS IS DEAD; THE NEW MASTER ISN'T.
YOU DIDN'T KILL NIKOLAOS. I DID.
TRUE. YOU WANT HALF THE MONEY?
NAH.
THEN WHAT'S YOUR COMPLAINT? I GOT MY ARM BROKEN HELPING YOU KILL HER.
AND I GOT FOURTEEN STITCHES, AND WE BOTH GOT VAMPIRE BIT.
AND CLEANSED OURSELVES WITH HOLY WATER.
WHICH BURNS LIKE ACID.
WHY WERE YOU FOLLOWING ME, EDWARD?
I WAS TOLD YOU WOULD BE MEETING WITH THE NEW MASTER TONIGHT.
WHO TOLD YOU THAT?
I WAS INSIDE THE CIRCUS TONIGHT, ANITA. I SAW WHO YOU WERE WITH.
YOU PLAYED WITH THE VAMPIRES, THEN YOU WENT HOME, SO ONE OF THEM HAS TO BE THE MASTER.
I FOUGHT TO KEEP MY FACE BLANK, SO THE PANIC WOULDN'T SHOW. EDWARD HAD BEEN FOLLOWING ME, AND I HADN'T KNOWN IT.
HE KNEW ALL THE VAMPIRES I HAD SEEN TONIGHT. IT WASN'T THAT BIG A LIST. HE'D FIGURE IT OUT.
WAIT A MINUTE. YOU LET ME GO UP AGAINST THAT SNAKE WITHOUT HELPING ME?

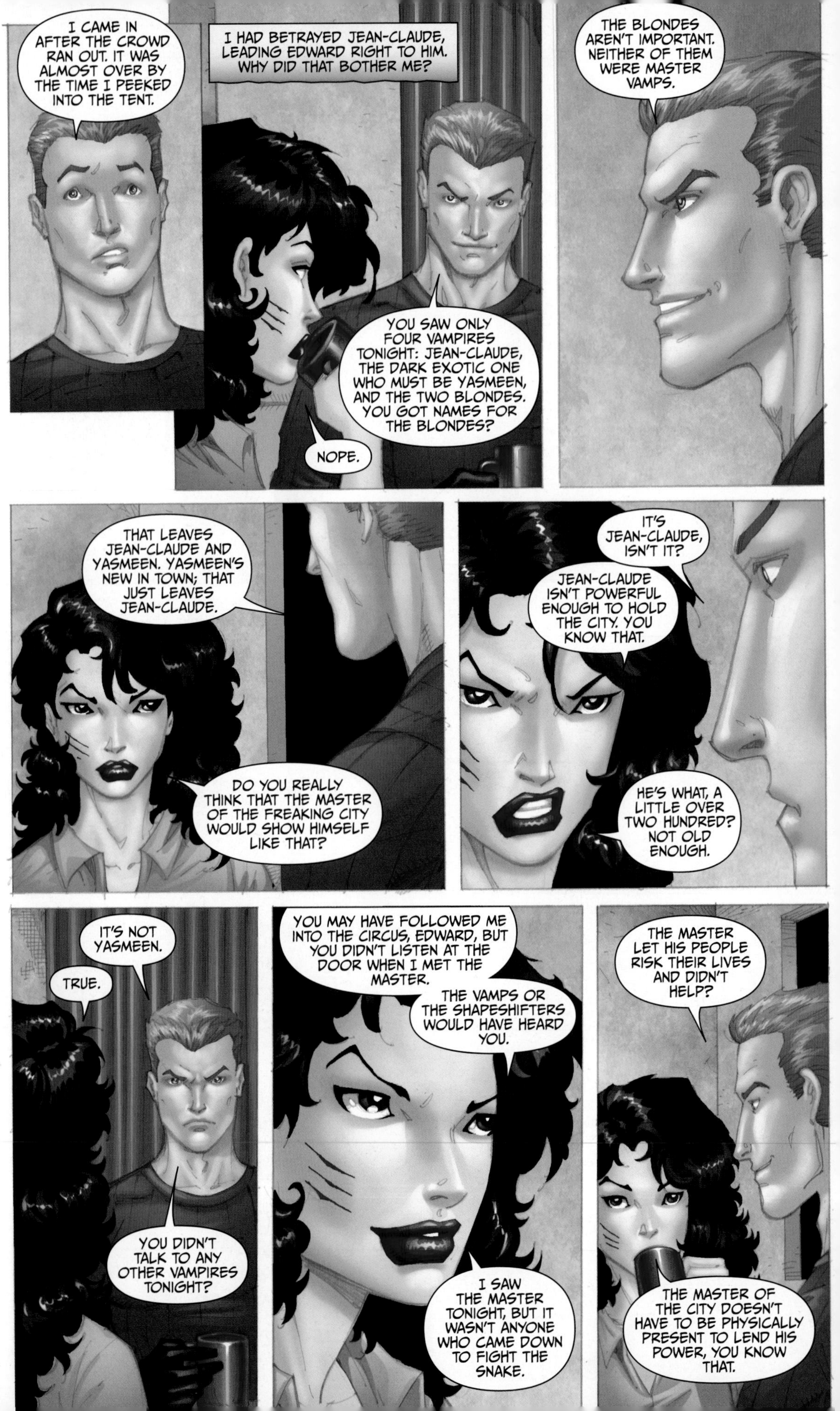

I CAME IN AFTER THE CROWD RAN OUT. IT WAS ALMOST OVER BY THE TIME I PEEKED INTO THE TENT.
I HAD BETRAYED JEAN-CLAUDE, LEADING EDWARD RIGHT TO HIM. WHY DID THAT BOTHER ME?
YOU SAW ONLY FOUR VAMPIRES TONIGHT: JEAN-CLAUDE, THE DARK EXOTIC ONE WHO MUST BE YASMEEN, AND THE TWO BLONDES. YOU GOT NAMES FOR THE BLONDES?
NOPE.
THE BLONDES AREN'T IMPORTANT. NEITHER OF THEM WERE MASTER VAMPS.
THAT LEAVES JEAN-CLAUDE AND YASMEEN. YASMEEN'S NEW IN TOWN; THAT JUST LEAVES JEAN-CLAUDE.
DO YOU REALLY THINK THAT THE MASTER OF THE FREAKING CITY WOULD SHOW HIMSELF LIKE THAT?
IT'S JEAN-CLAUDE, ISN'T IT?
JEAN-CLAUDE ISN'T POWERFUL ENOUGH TO HOLD THE CITY. YOU KNOW THAT.
HE'S WHAT, A LITTLE OVER TWO HUNDRED? NOT OLD ENOUGH.
IT'S NOT YASMEEN.
TRUE.
YOU DIDN'T TALK TO ANY OTHER VAMPIRES TONIGHT?
YOU MAY HAVE FOLLOWED ME INTO THE CIRCUS, EDWARD, BUT YOU DIDN'T LISTEN AT THE DOOR WHEN I MET THE MASTER.
THE VAMPS OR THE SHAPESHIFTERS WOULD HAVE HEARD YOU.
I SAW THE MASTER TONIGHT, BUT IT WASN'T ANYONE WHO CAME DOWN TO FIGHT THE SNAKE.
THE MASTER LET HIS PEOPLE RISK THEIR LIVES AND DIDN'T HELP?
THE MASTER OF THE CITY DOESN'T HAVE TO BE PHYSICALLY PRESENT TO LEND HIS POWER, YOU KNOW THAT.

NO, I DON'T.

BELIEVE IT OR NOT.

PLEASE LET HIM BELIEVE IT.

YOU'RE NOT USUALLY THIS GOOD A LIAR.

I'M NOT LYING.

IF JEAN-CLAUDE ISN'T THE MASTER, THEN YOU KNOW WHO IS?

YES, I KNOW WHO IT IS.

I COULDN'T ANSWER YES TO BOTH QUESTIONS, BUT HELL, WHY STOP LYING NOW?

TELL ME.

THE MASTER WOULD KILL ME IF HE KNEW I TALKED TO YOU.

WE CAN KILL HIM TOGETHER LIKE WE DID THE LAST ONE.

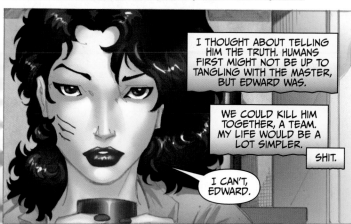

I THOUGHT ABOUT TELLING HIM THE TRUTH. HUMANS FIRST MIGHT NOT BE UP TO TANGLING WITH THE MASTER, BUT EDWARD WAS.

WE COULD KILL HIM TOGETHER, A TEAM. MY LIFE WOULD BE A LOT SIMPLER.

SHIT.

I CAN'T, EDWARD.

WON'T.

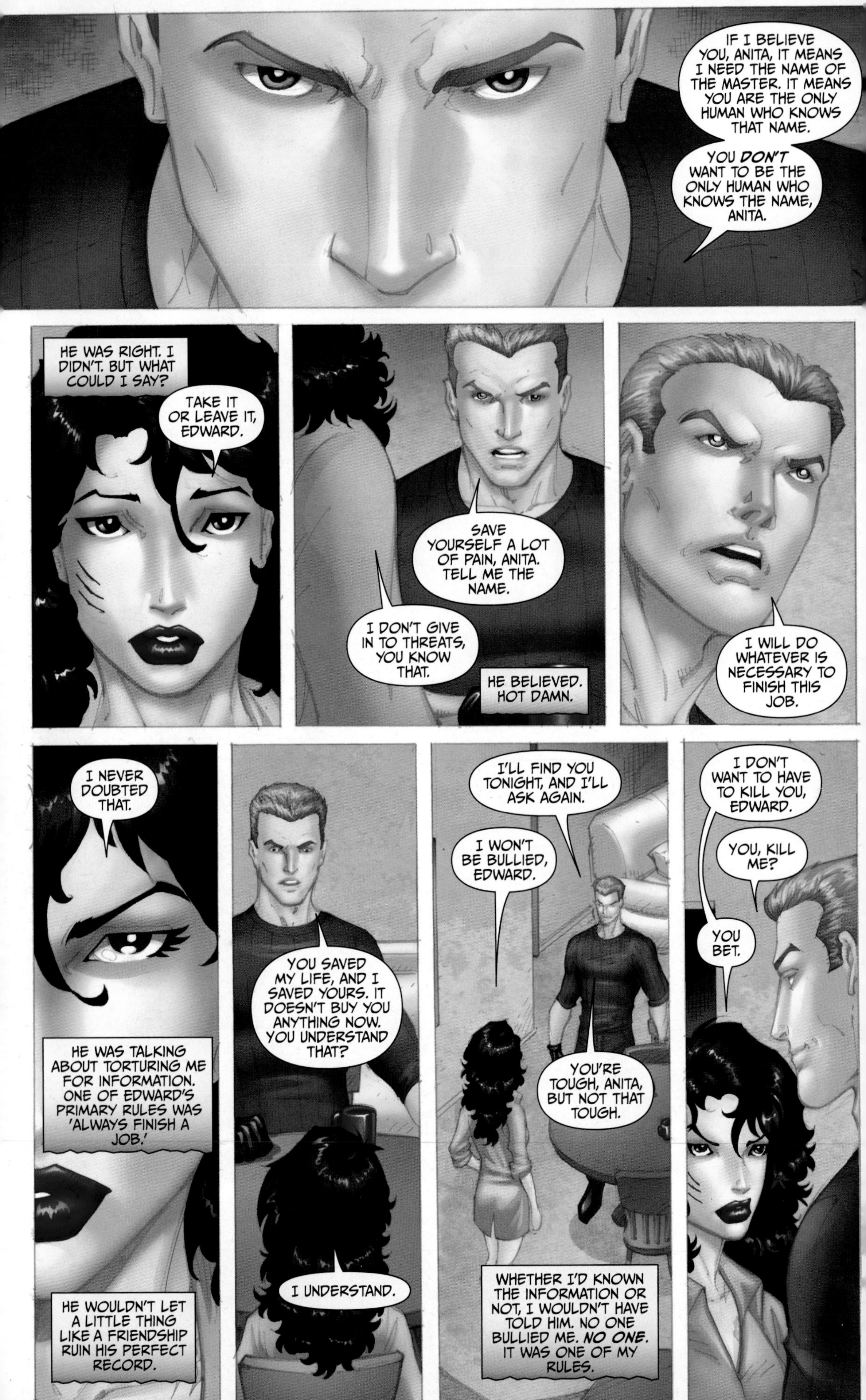
IF I BELIEVE YOU, ANITA, IT MEANS I NEED THE NAME OF THE MASTER. IT MEANS YOU ARE THE ONLY HUMAN WHO KNOWS THAT NAME.
YOU DON'T WANT TO BE THE ONLY HUMAN WHO KNOWS THE NAME, ANITA.
HE WAS RIGHT. I DIDN'T. BUT WHAT COULD I SAY?
TAKE IT OR LEAVE IT, EDWARD.
SAVE YOURSELF A LOT OF PAIN, ANITA. TELL ME THE NAME.
I DON'T GIVE IN TO THREATS, YOU KNOW THAT.
HE BELIEVED. HOT DAMN.
I WILL DO WHATEVER IS NECESSARY TO FINISH THIS JOB.
I NEVER DOUBTED THAT.
HE WAS TALKING ABOUT TORTURING ME FOR INFORMATION. ONE OF EDWARD'S PRIMARY RULES WAS 'ALWAYS FINISH A JOB.'
HE WOULDN'T LET A LITTLE THING LIKE A FRIENDSHIP RUIN HIS PERFECT RECORD.
YOU SAVED MY LIFE, AND I SAVED YOURS. IT DOESN'T BUY YOU ANYTHING NOW. YOU UNDERSTAND THAT?
I UNDERSTAND.
I'LL FIND YOU TONIGHT, AND I'LL ASK AGAIN.
I WON'T BE BULLIED, EDWARD.
YOU'RE TOUGH, ANITA, BUT NOT THAT TOUGH.
WHETHER I'D KNOWN THE INFORMATION OR NOT, I WOULDN'T HAVE TOLD HIM. NO ONE BULLIED ME. NO ONE. IT WAS ONE OF MY RULES.
I DON'T WANT TO HAVE TO KILL YOU, EDWARD.
YOU, KILL ME?
YOU BET.

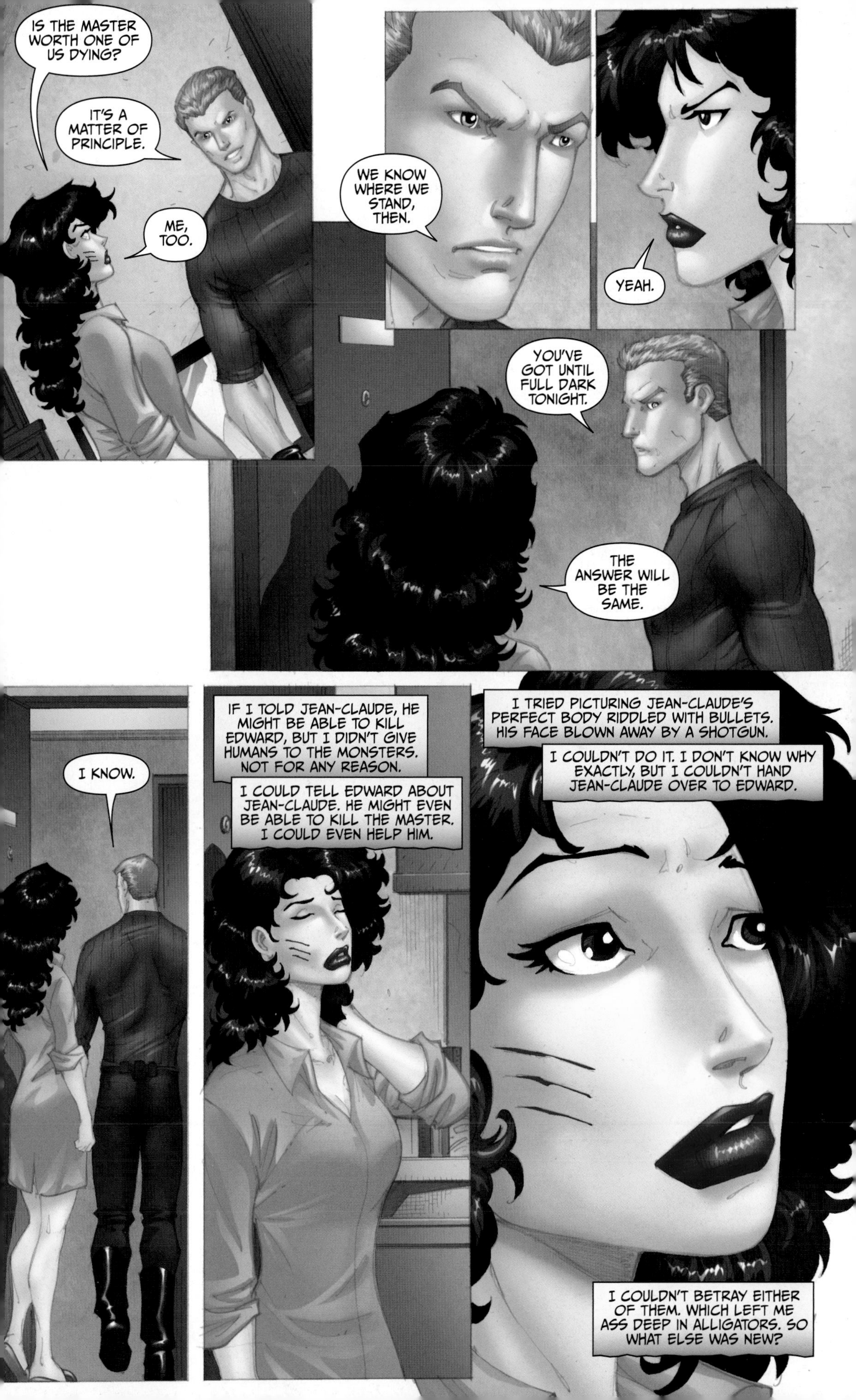
IS THE MASTER WORTH ONE OF US DYING?
IT'S A MATTER OF PRINCIPLE.
ME, TOO.
WE KNOW WHERE WE STAND, THEN.
YEAH.
YOU'VE GOT UNTIL FULL DARK TONIGHT.
THE ANSWER WILL BE THE SAME.
I KNOW.
IF I TOLD JEAN-CLAUDE, HE MIGHT BE ABLE TO KILL EDWARD, BUT I DIDN'T GIVE HUMANS TO THE MONSTERS. NOT FOR ANY REASON.
I COULD TELL EDWARD ABOUT JEAN-CLAUDE. HE MIGHT EVEN BE ABLE TO KILL THE MASTER. I COULD EVEN HELP HIM.
I TRIED PICTURING JEAN-CLAUDE'S PERFECT BODY RIDDLED WITH BULLETS. HIS FACE BLOWN AWAY BY A SHOTGUN.
I COULDN'T DO IT. I DON'T KNOW WHY EXACTLY, BUT I COULDN'T HAND JEAN-CLAUDE OVER TO EDWARD.
I COULDN'T BETRAY EITHER OF THEM. WHICH LEFT ME ASS DEEP IN ALLIGATORS. SO WHAT ELSE WAS NEW?

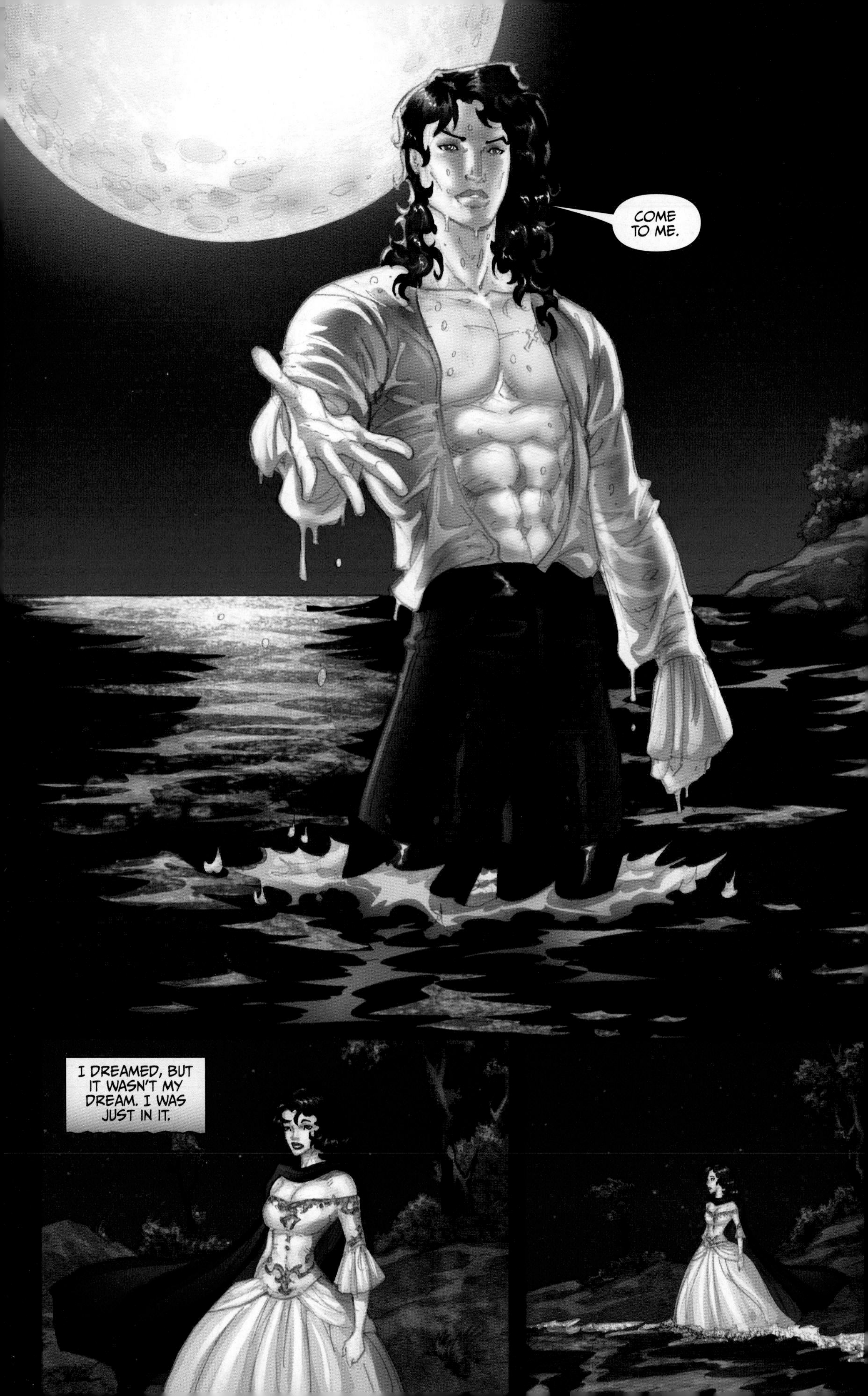
COME TO ME.
I DREAMED, BUT IT WASN'T MY DREAM. I WAS JUST IN IT.

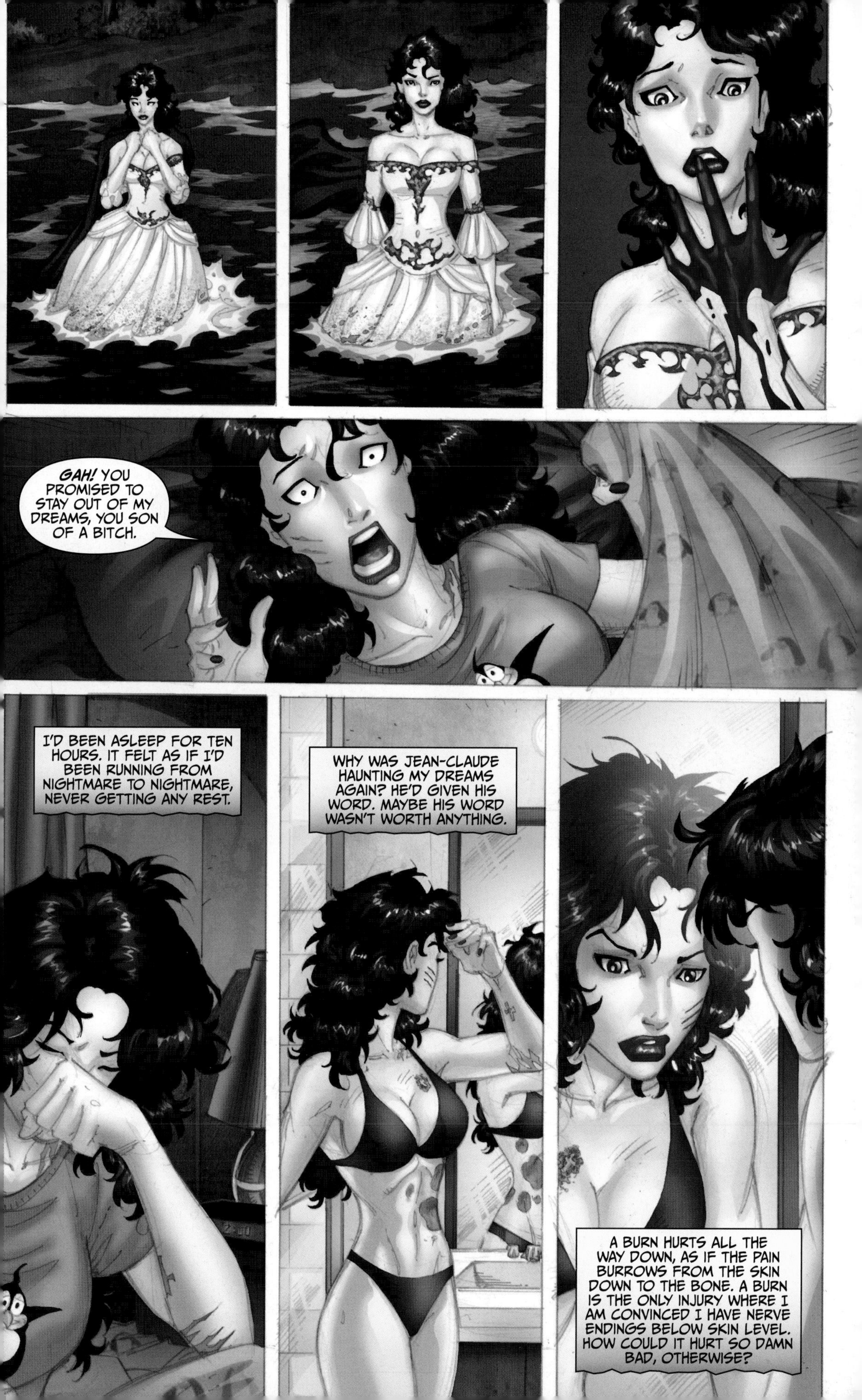
GAH! YOU PROMISED TO STAY OUT OF MY DREAMS, YOU SON OF A BITCH.
I'D BEEN ASLEEP FOR TEN HOURS. IT FELT AS IF I'D BEEN RUNNING FROM NIGHTMARE TO NIGHTMARE, NEVER GETTING ANY REST.
WHY WAS JEAN-CLAUDE HAUNTING MY DREAMS AGAIN? HE'D GIVEN HIS WORD. MAYBE HIS WORD WASN'T WORTH ANYTHING.
A BURN HURTS ALL THE WAY DOWN, AS IF THE PAIN BURROWS FROM THE SKIN DOWN TO THE BONE. A BURN IS THE ONLY INJURY WHERE I AM CONVINCED I HAVE NERVE ENDINGS BELOW SKIN LEVEL. HOW COULD IT HURT SO DAMN BAD, OTHERWISE?

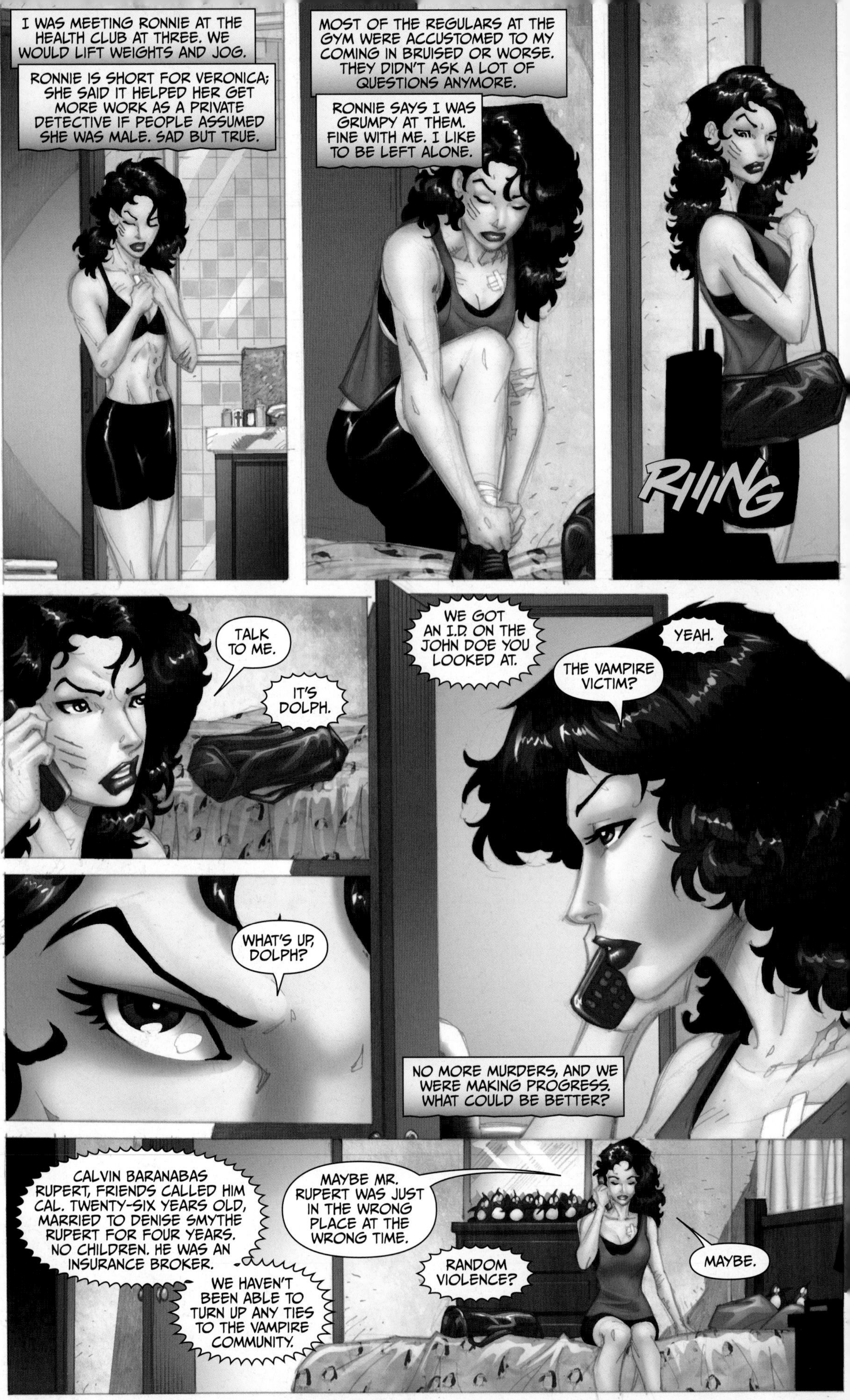
I WAS MEETING RONNIE AT THE HEALTH CLUB AT THREE. WE WOULD LIFT WEIGHTS AND JOG.
RONNIE IS SHORT FOR VERONICA; SHE SAID IT HELPED HER GET MORE WORK AS A PRIVATE DETECTIVE IF PEOPLE ASSUMED SHE WAS MALE. SAD BUT TRUE.
MOST OF THE REGULARS AT THE GYM WERE ACCUSTOMED TO MY COMING IN BRUISED OR WORSE. THEY DIDN'T ASK A LOT OF QUESTIONS ANYMORE.
RONNIE SAYS I WAS GRUMPY AT THEM. FINE WITH ME. I LIKE TO BE LEFT ALONE.
RIIING
TALK TO ME.
IT'S DOLPH.
WHAT'S UP, DOLPH?
WE GOT AN I.D. ON THE JOHN DOE YOU LOOKED AT.
THE VAMPIRE VICTIM?
YEAH.
NO MORE MURDERS, AND WE WERE MAKING PROGRESS. WHAT COULD BE BETTER?
CALVIN BARANABAS RUPERT, FRIENDS CALLED HIM CAL. TWENTY-SIX YEARS OLD, MARRIED TO DENISE SMYTHE RUPERT FOR FOUR YEARS. NO CHILDREN. HE WAS AN INSURANCE BROKER.
WE HAVEN'T BEEN ABLE TO TURN UP ANY TIES TO THE VAMPIRE COMMUNITY.
MAYBE MR. RUPERT WAS JUST IN THE WRONG PLACE AT THE WRONG TIME.
RANDOM VIOLENCE?
MAYBE.

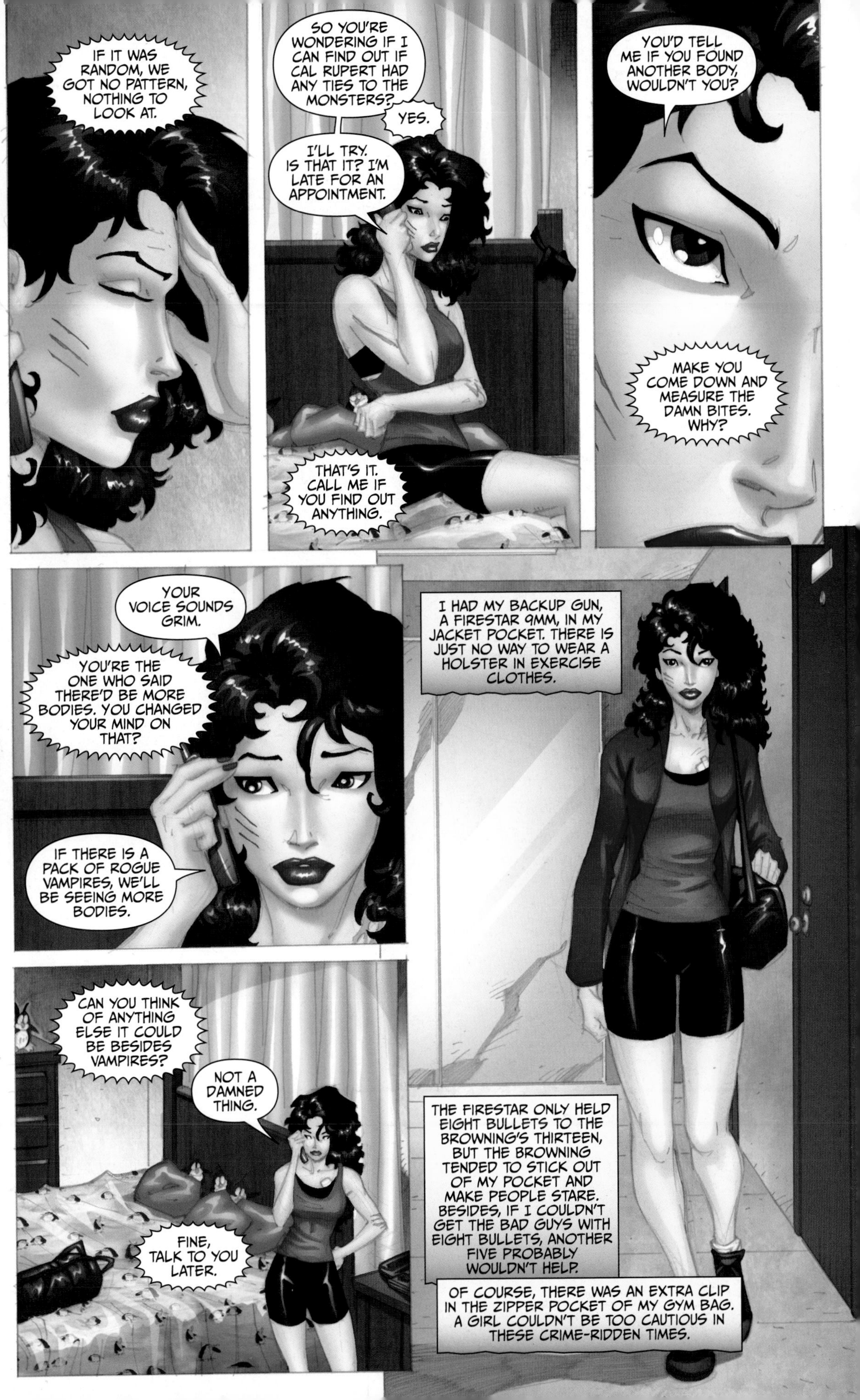
IF IT WAS RANDOM, WE GOT NO PATTERN, NOTHING TO LOOK AT.
SO YOU'RE WONDERING IF I CAN FIND OUT IF CAL RUPERT HAD ANY TIES TO THE MONSTERS?
YES.
I'LL TRY. IS THAT IT? I'M LATE FOR AN APPOINTMENT.
THAT'S IT. CALL ME IF YOU FIND OUT ANYTHING.
YOU'D TELL ME IF YOU FOUND ANOTHER BODY, WOULDN'T YOU?
MAKE YOU COME DOWN AND MEASURE THE DAMN BITES. WHY?
YOUR VOICE SOUNDS GRIM.
YOU'RE THE ONE WHO SAID THERE'D BE MORE BODIES. YOU CHANGED YOUR MIND ON THAT?
IF THERE IS A PACK OF ROGUE VAMPIRES, WE'LL BE SEEING MORE BODIES.
CAN YOU THINK OF ANYTHING ELSE IT COULD BE BESIDES VAMPIRES?
NOT A DAMNED THING.
FINE, TALK TO YOU LATER.
I HAD MY BACKUP GUN, A FIRESTAR 9MM, IN MY JACKET POCKET. THERE IS JUST NO WAY TO WEAR A HOLSTER IN EXERCISE CLOTHES.
THE FIRESTAR ONLY HELD EIGHT BULLETS TO THE BROWNING'S THIRTEEN, BUT THE BROWNING TENDED TO STICK OUT OF MY POCKET AND MAKE PEOPLE STARE. BESIDES, IF I COULDN'T GET THE BAD GUYS WITH EIGHT BULLETS, ANOTHER FIVE PROBABLY WOULDN'T HELP.
OF COURSE, THERE WAS AN EXTRA CLIP IN THE ZIPPER POCKET OF MY GYM BAG. A GIRL COULDN'T BE TOO CAUTIOUS IN THESE CRIME-RIDDEN TIMES.

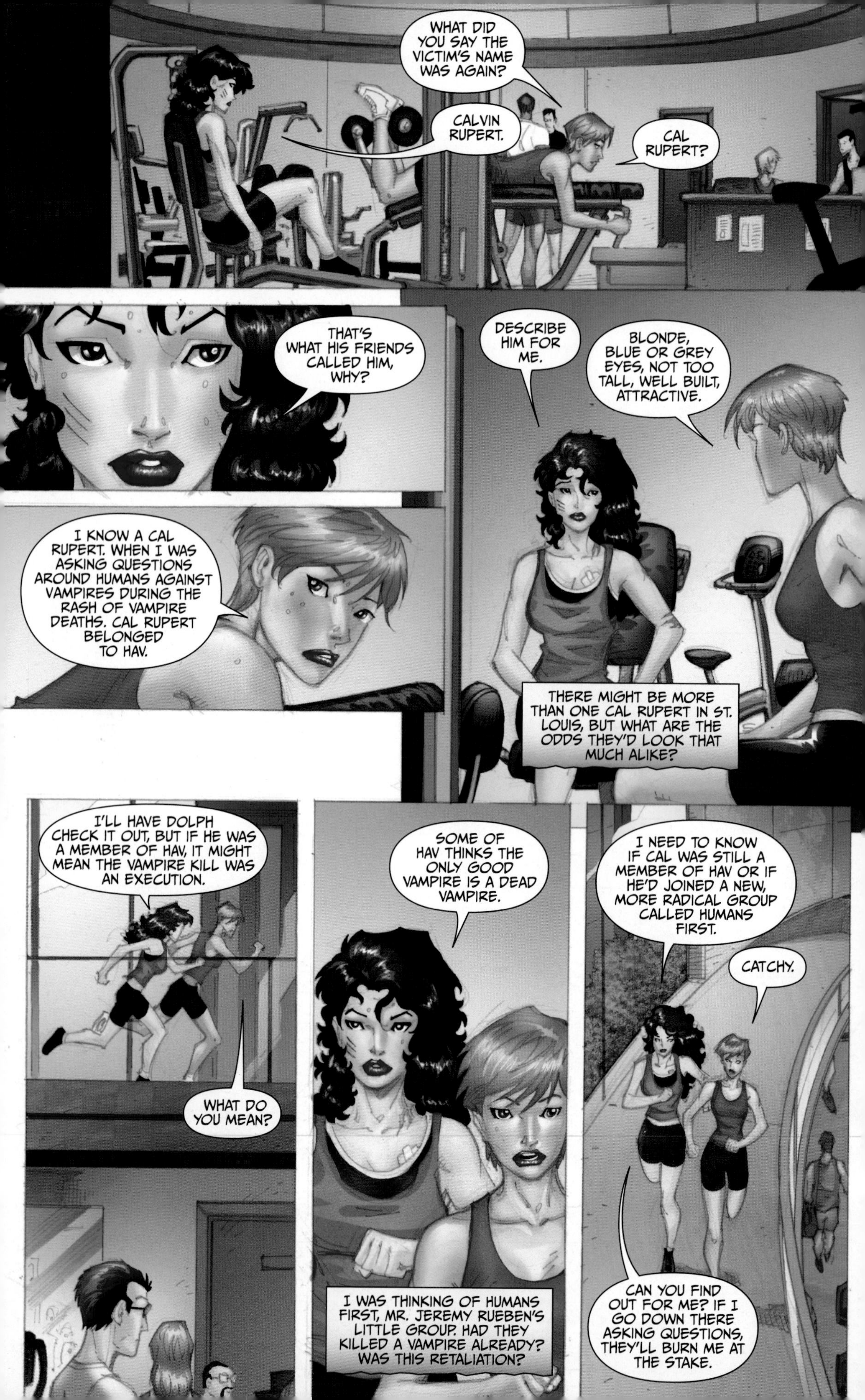
WHAT DID YOU SAY THE VICTIM'S NAME WAS AGAIN?
CALVIN RUPERT.
CAL RUPERT?
THAT'S WHAT HIS FRIENDS CALLED HIM, WHY?
I KNOW A CAL RUPERT. WHEN I WAS ASKING QUESTIONS AROUND HUMANS AGAINST VAMPIRES DURING THE RASH OF VAMPIRE DEATHS. CAL RUPERT BELONGED TO HAV.
DESCRIBE HIM FOR ME.
BLONDE, BLUE OR GREY EYES, NOT TOO TALL, WELL BUILT, ATTRACTIVE.
THERE MIGHT BE MORE THAN ONE CAL RUPERT IN ST. LOUIS, BUT WHAT ARE THE ODDS THEY'D LOOK THAT MUCH ALIKE?
I'LL HAVE DOLPH CHECK IT OUT, BUT IF HE WAS A MEMBER OF HAV, IT MIGHT MEAN THE VAMPIRE KILL WAS AN EXECUTION.
WHAT DO YOU MEAN?
SOME OF HAV THINKS THE ONLY GOOD VAMPIRE IS A DEAD VAMPIRE.
I WAS THINKING OF HUMANS FIRST, MR. JEREMY RUEBEN'S LITTLE GROUP. HAD THEY KILLED A VAMPIRE ALREADY? WAS THIS RETALIATION?
I NEED TO KNOW IF CAL WAS STILL A MEMBER OF HAV OR IF HE'D JOINED A NEW, MORE RADICAL GROUP CALLED HUMANS FIRST.
CATCHY.
CAN YOU FIND OUT FOR ME? IF I GO DOWN THERE ASKING QUESTIONS, THEY'LL BURN ME AT THE STAKE.

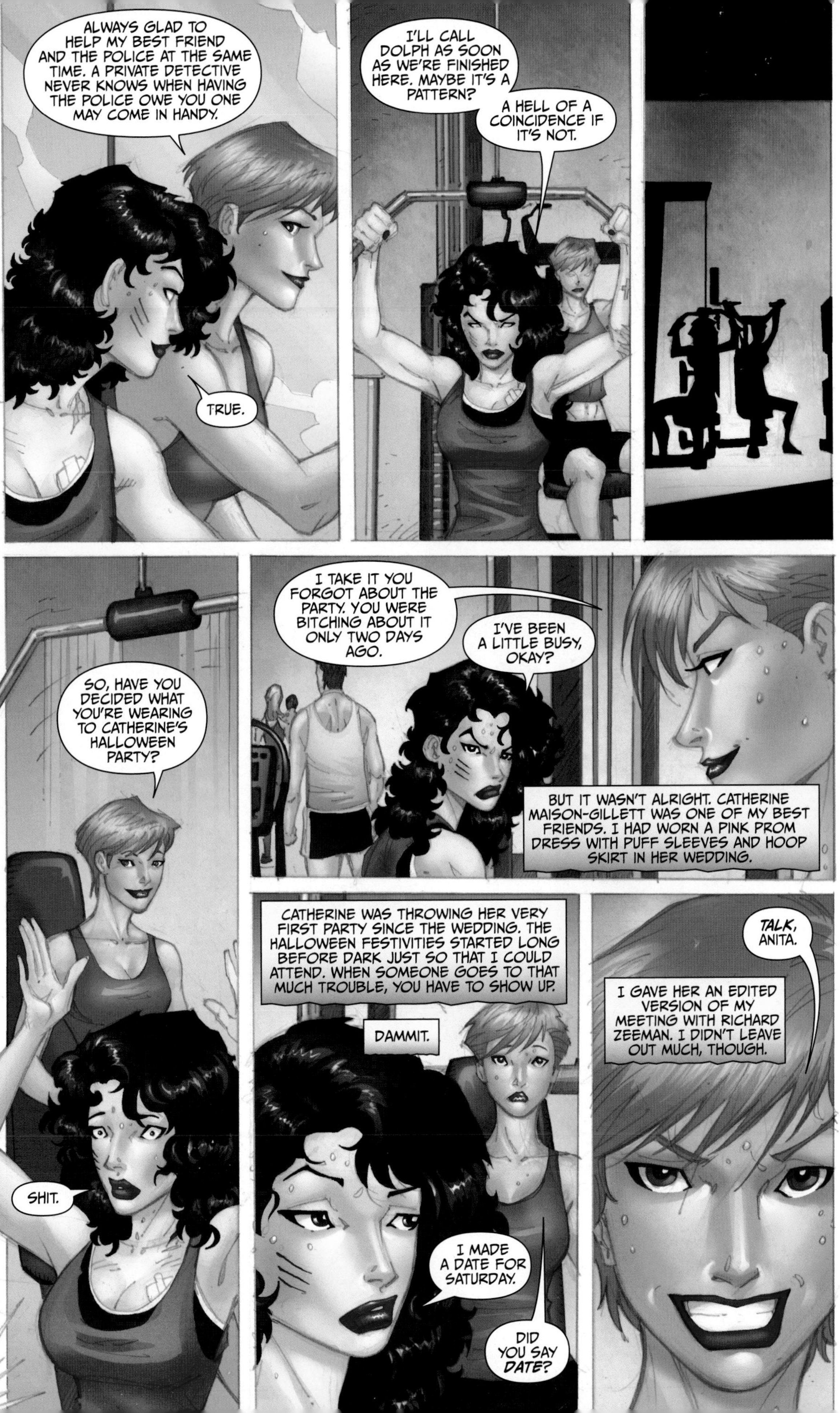
ALWAYS GLAD TO HELP MY BEST FRIEND AND THE POLICE AT THE SAME TIME. A PRIVATE DETECTIVE NEVER KNOWS WHEN HAVING THE POLICE OWE YOU ONE MAY COME IN HANDY.
TRUE.
I'LL CALL DOLPH AS SOON AS WE'RE FINISHED HERE. MAYBE IT'S A PATTERN?
A HELL OF A COINCIDENCE IF IT'S NOT.
SO, HAVE YOU DECIDED WHAT YOU'RE WEARING TO CATHERINE'S HALLOWEEN PARTY?
SHIT.
I TAKE IT YOU FORGOT ABOUT THE PARTY. YOU WERE BITCHING ABOUT IT ONLY TWO DAYS AGO.
I'VE BEEN A LITTLE BUSY, OKAY?
BUT IT WASN'T ALRIGHT. CATHERINE MAISON-GILLETT WAS ONE OF MY BEST FRIENDS. I HAD WORN A PINK PROM DRESS WITH PUFF SLEEVES AND HOOP SKIRT IN HER WEDDING.
CATHERINE WAS THROWING HER VERY FIRST PARTY SINCE THE WEDDING. THE HALLOWEEN FESTIVITIES STARTED LONG BEFORE DARK JUST SO THAT I COULD ATTEND. WHEN SOMEONE GOES TO THAT MUCH TROUBLE, YOU HAVE TO SHOW UP.
DAMMIT.
I MADE A DATE FOR SATURDAY.
DID YOU SAY *DATE*?
TALK, ANITA.
I GAVE HER AN EDITED VERSION OF MY MEETING WITH RICHARD ZEEMAN. I DIDN'T LEAVE OUT MUCH, THOUGH.

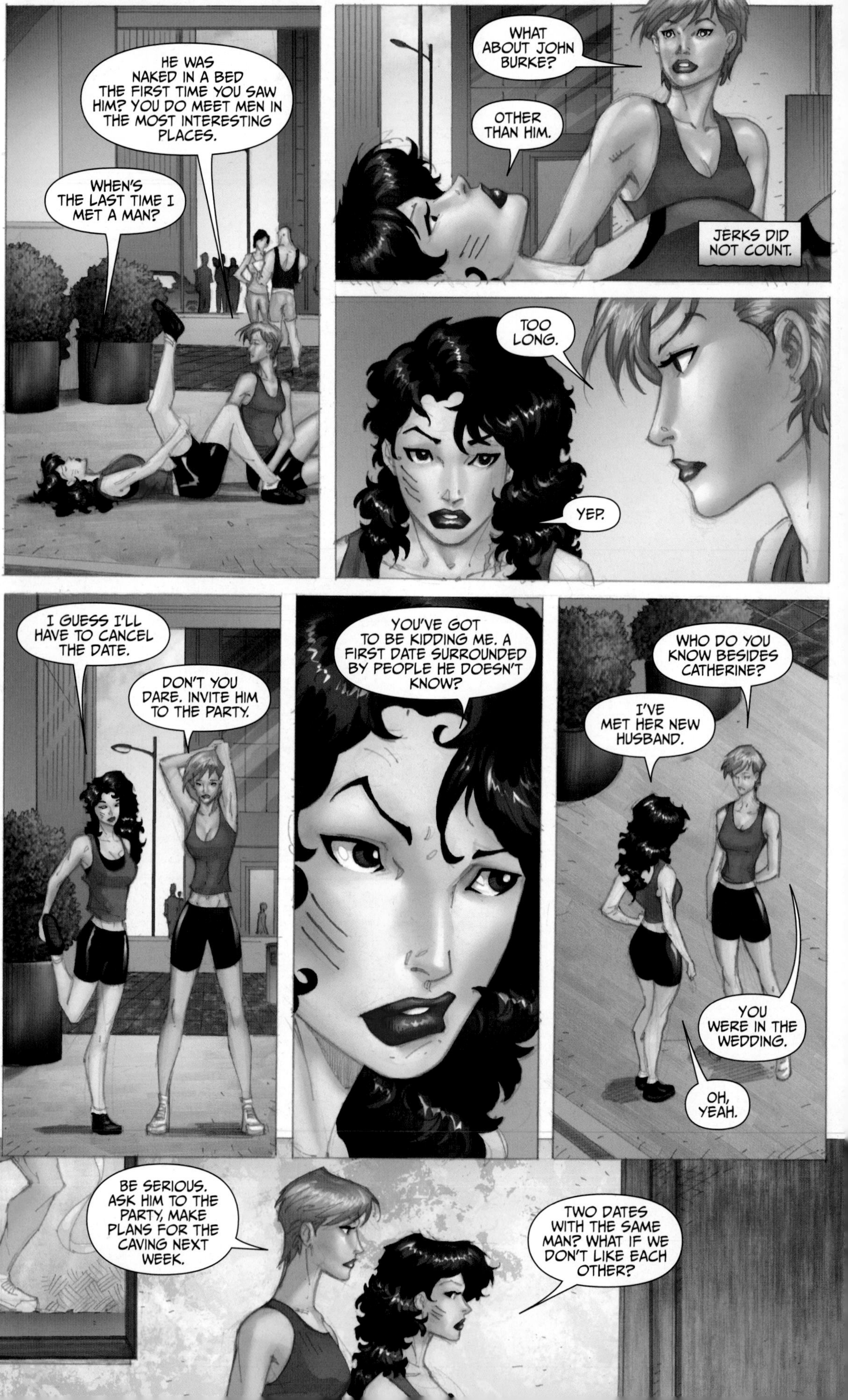
HE WAS NAKED IN A BED THE FIRST TIME YOU SAW HIM? YOU DO MEET MEN IN THE MOST INTERESTING PLACES.
WHEN'S THE LAST TIME I MET A MAN?
WHAT ABOUT JOHN BURKE?
OTHER THAN HIM.
JERKS DID NOT COUNT.
TOO LONG.
YEP.
I GUESS I'LL HAVE TO CANCEL THE DATE.
DON'T YOU DARE. INVITE HIM TO THE PARTY.
YOU'VE GOT TO BE KIDDING ME. A FIRST DATE SURROUNDED BY PEOPLE HE DOESN'T KNOW?
WHO DO YOU KNOW BESIDES CATHERINE?
I'VE MET HER NEW HUSBAND.
YOU WERE IN THE WEDDING.
OH, YEAH.
BE SERIOUS. ASK HIM TO THE PARTY, MAKE PLANS FOR THE CAVING NEXT WEEK.
TWO DATES WITH THE SAME MAN? WHAT IF WE DON'T LIKE EACH OTHER?

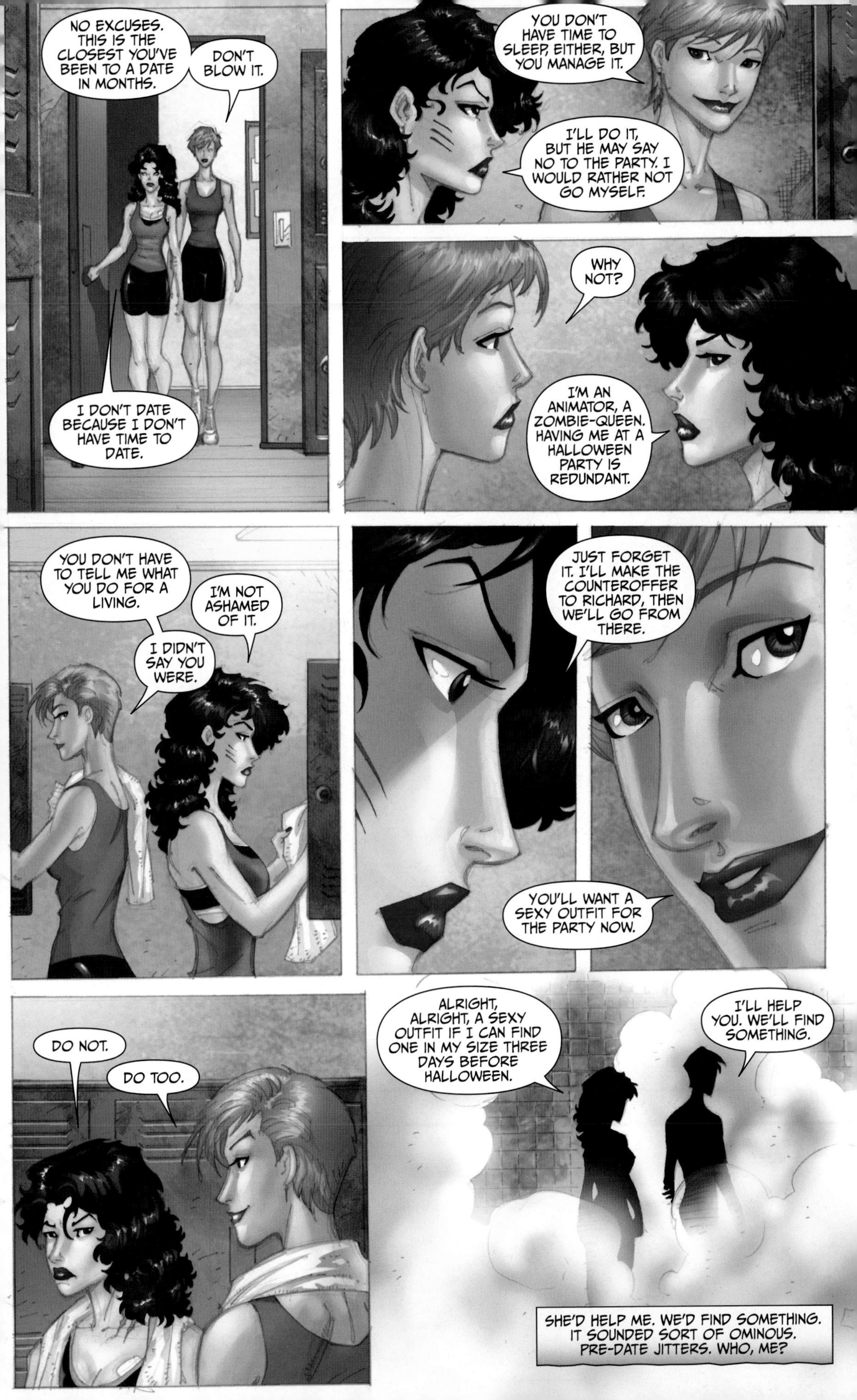
NO EXCUSES. THIS IS THE CLOSEST YOU'VE BEEN TO A DATE IN MONTHS.
DON'T BLOW IT.
I DON'T DATE BECAUSE I DON'T HAVE TIME TO DATE.
YOU DON'T HAVE TIME TO SLEEP, EITHER, BUT YOU MANAGE IT.
I'LL DO IT, BUT HE MAY SAY NO TO THE PARTY. I WOULD RATHER NOT GO MYSELF.
WHY NOT?
I'M AN ANIMATOR, A ZOMBIE-QUEEN. HAVING ME AT A HALLOWEEN PARTY IS REDUNDANT.
YOU DON'T HAVE TO TELL ME WHAT YOU DO FOR A LIVING.
I'M NOT ASHAMED OF IT.
I DIDN'T SAY YOU WERE.
JUST FORGET IT. I'LL MAKE THE COUNTEROFFER TO RICHARD, THEN WE'LL GO FROM THERE.
YOU'LL WANT A SEXY OUTFIT FOR THE PARTY NOW.
DO NOT.
DO TOO.
ALRIGHT, ALRIGHT, A SEXY OUTFIT IF I CAN FIND ONE IN MY SIZE THREE DAYS BEFORE HALLOWEEN.
I'LL HELP YOU. WE'LL FIND SOMETHING.
SHE'D HELP ME. WE'D FIND SOMETHING. IT SOUNDED SORT OF OMINOUS. PRE-DATE JITTERS. WHO, ME?

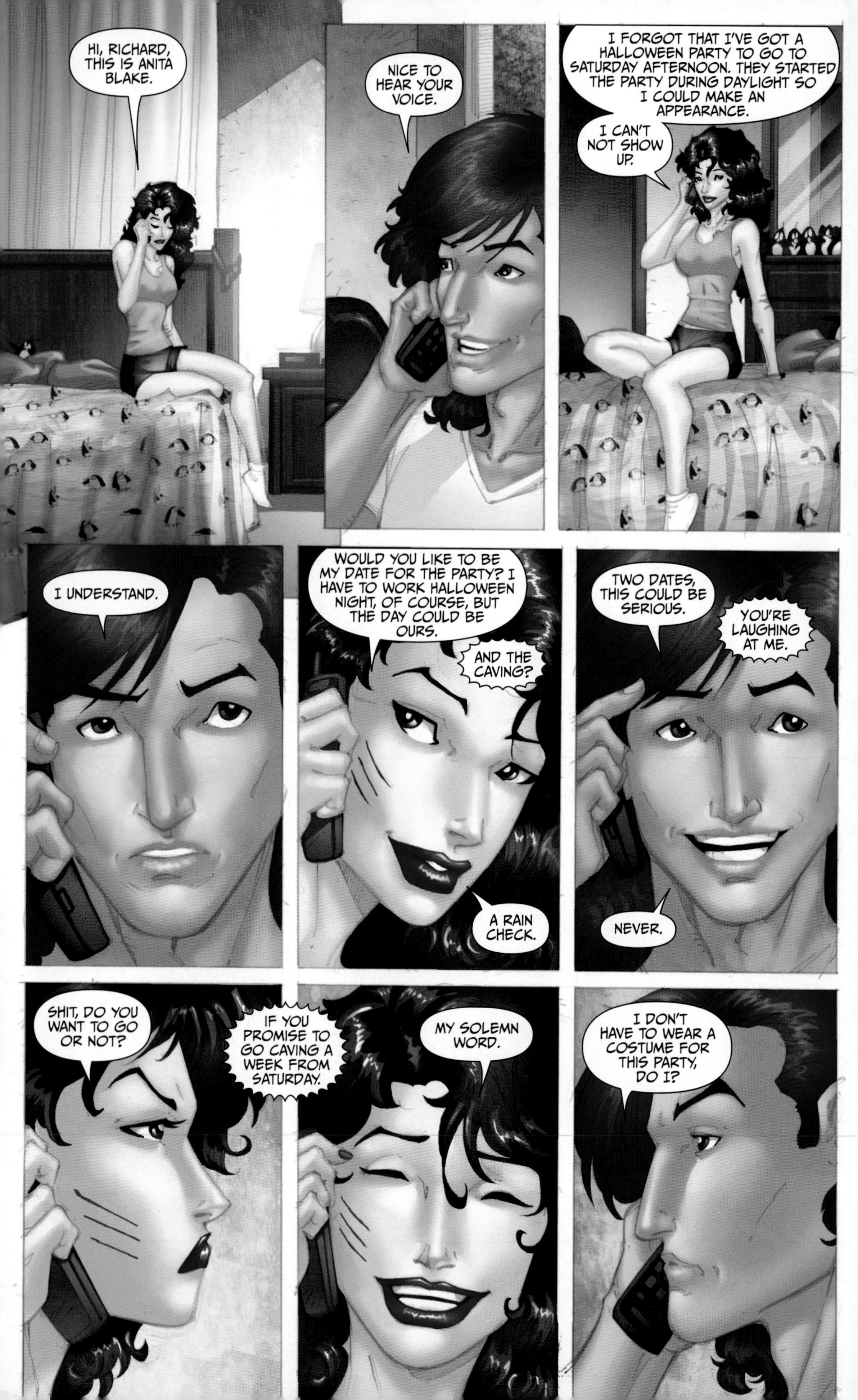
HI, RICHARD, THIS IS ANITA BLAKE.
NICE TO HEAR YOUR VOICE.
I FORGOT THAT I'VE GOT A HALLOWEEN PARTY TO GO TO SATURDAY AFTERNOON. THEY STARTED THE PARTY DURING DAYLIGHT SO I COULD MAKE AN APPEARANCE.
I CAN'T NOT SHOW UP.
I UNDERSTAND.
WOULD YOU LIKE TO BE MY DATE FOR THE PARTY? I HAVE TO WORK HALLOWEEN NIGHT, OF COURSE, BUT THE DAY COULD BE OURS.
AND THE CAVING?
A RAIN CHECK.
TWO DATES, THIS COULD BE SERIOUS.
YOU'RE LAUGHING AT ME.
NEVER.
SHIT, DO YOU WANT TO GO OR NOT?
IF YOU PROMISE TO GO CAVING A WEEK FROM SATURDAY.
MY SOLEMN WORD.
I DON'T HAVE TO WEAR A COSTUME FOR THIS PARTY, DO I?

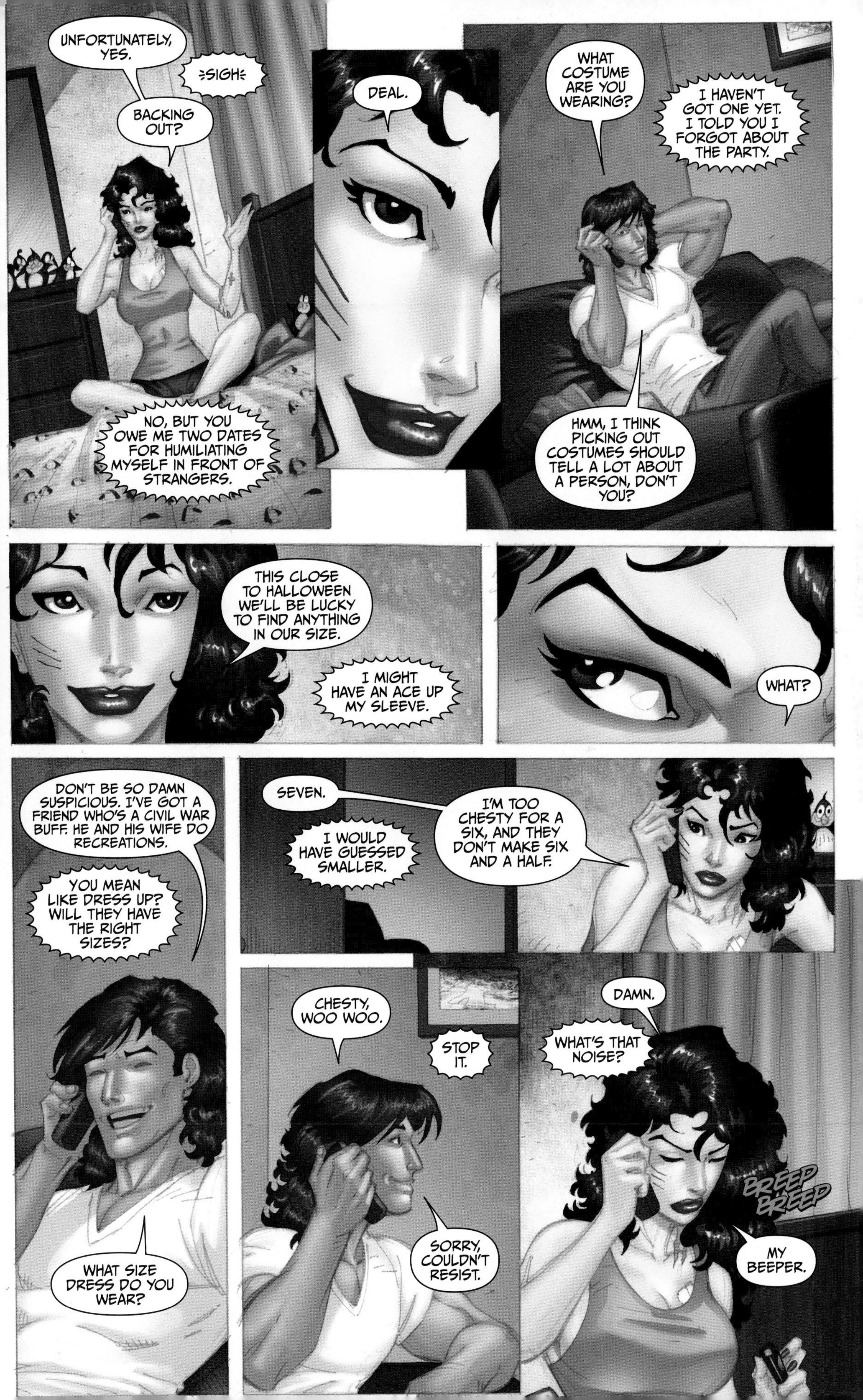
UNFORTUNATELY, YES.
SIGH
BACKING OUT?
NO, BUT YOU OWE ME TWO DATES FOR HUMILIATING MYSELF IN FRONT OF STRANGERS.
DEAL.
WHAT COSTUME ARE YOU WEARING?
I HAVEN'T GOT ONE YET. I TOLD YOU I FORGOT ABOUT THE PARTY.
HMM, I THINK PICKING OUT COSTUMES SHOULD TELL A LOT ABOUT A PERSON, DON'T YOU?
THIS CLOSE TO HALLOWEEN WE'LL BE LUCKY TO FIND ANYTHING IN OUR SIZE.
I MIGHT HAVE AN ACE UP MY SLEEVE.
WHAT?
DON'T BE SO DAMN SUSPICIOUS. I'VE GOT A FRIEND WHO'S A CIVIL WAR BUFF. HE AND HIS WIFE DO RECREATIONS.
YOU MEAN LIKE DRESS UP? WILL THEY HAVE THE RIGHT SIZES?
WHAT SIZE DRESS DO YOU WEAR?
SEVEN.
I WOULD HAVE GUESSED SMALLER.
I'M TOO CHESTY FOR A SIX, AND THEY DON'T MAKE SIX AND A HALF.
CHESTY, WOO WOO.
STOP IT.
SORRY, COULDN'T RESIST.
DAMN.
WHAT'S THAT NOISE?
BREEP BREEP
MY BEEPER.

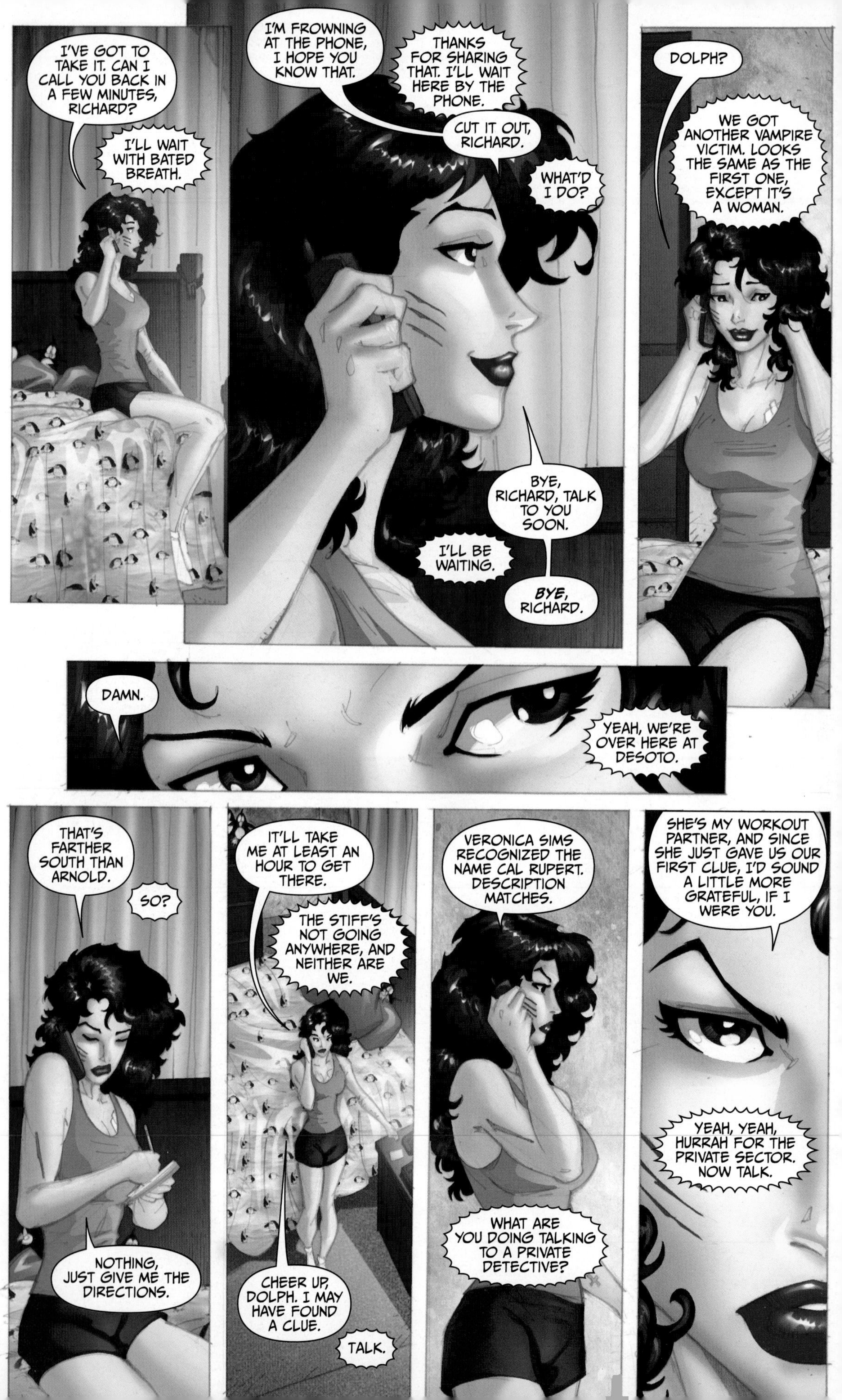

I'VE GOT TO TAKE IT. CAN I CALL YOU BACK IN A FEW MINUTES, RICHARD?
I'LL WAIT WITH BATED BREATH.
I'M FROWNING AT THE PHONE, I HOPE YOU KNOW THAT.
THANKS FOR SHARING THAT. I'LL WAIT HERE BY THE PHONE.
CUT IT OUT, RICHARD.
WHAT'D I DO?
BYE, RICHARD, TALK TO YOU SOON.
I'LL BE WAITING.
BYE, RICHARD.
DOLPH?
WE GOT ANOTHER VAMPIRE VICTIM. LOOKS THE SAME AS THE FIRST ONE, EXCEPT IT'S A WOMAN.
DAMN.
YEAH, WE'RE OVER HERE AT DESOTO.
THAT'S FARTHER SOUTH THAN ARNOLD.
SO?
NOTHING, JUST GIVE ME THE DIRECTIONS.
IT'LL TAKE ME AT LEAST AN HOUR TO GET THERE.
THE STIFF'S NOT GOING ANYWHERE, AND NEITHER ARE WE.
CHEER UP, DOLPH. I MAY HAVE FOUND A CLUE.
TALK.
VERONICA SIMS RECOGNIZED THE NAME CAL RUPERT. DESCRIPTION MATCHES.
WHAT ARE YOU DOING TALKING TO A PRIVATE DETECTIVE?
SHE'S MY WORKOUT PARTNER, AND SINCE SHE JUST GAVE US OUR FIRST CLUE, I'D SOUND A LITTLE MORE GRATEFUL, IF I WERE YOU.
YEAH, YEAH, HURRAH FOR THE PRIVATE SECTOR. NOW TALK.

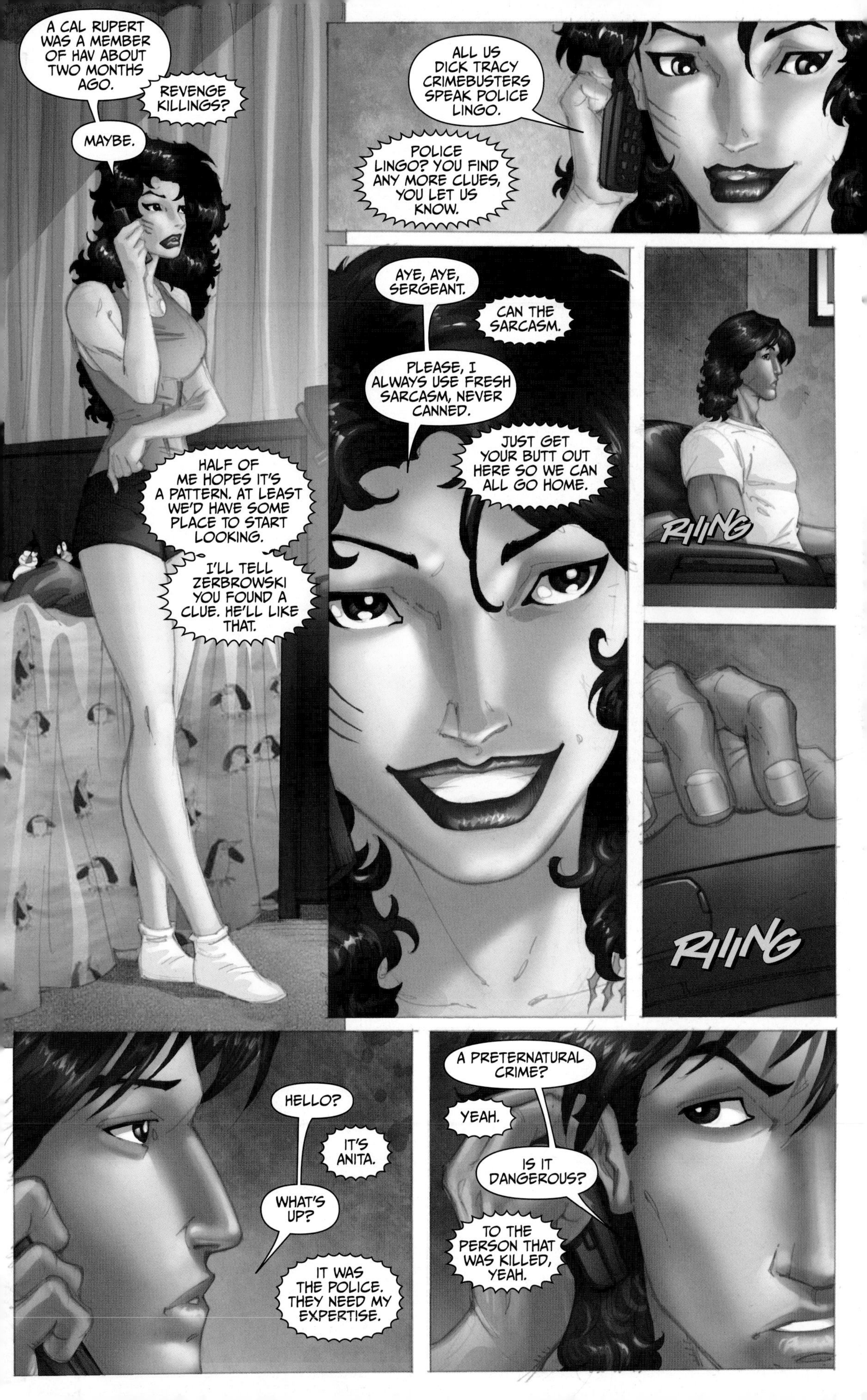
A CAL RUPERT WAS A MEMBER OF HAV ABOUT TWO MONTHS AGO.
REVENGE KILLINGS?
MAYBE.
HALF OF ME HOPES IT'S A PATTERN. AT LEAST WE'D HAVE SOME PLACE TO START LOOKING.
I'LL TELL ZERBROWSKI YOU FOUND A CLUE. HE'LL LIKE THAT.
ALL US DICK TRACY CRIMEBUSTERS SPEAK POLICE LINGO.
POLICE LINGO? YOU FIND ANY MORE CLUES, YOU LET US KNOW.
AYE, AYE, SERGEANT.
CAN THE SARCASM.
PLEASE, I ALWAYS USE FRESH SARCASM, NEVER CANNED.
JUST GET YOUR BUTT OUT HERE SO WE CAN ALL GO HOME.
RIIING
RIIING
HELLO?
IT'S ANITA.
WHAT'S UP?
IT WAS THE POLICE. THEY NEED MY EXPERTISE.
A PRETERNATURAL CRIME?
YEAH.
IS IT DANGEROUS?
TO THE PERSON THAT WAS KILLED, YEAH.

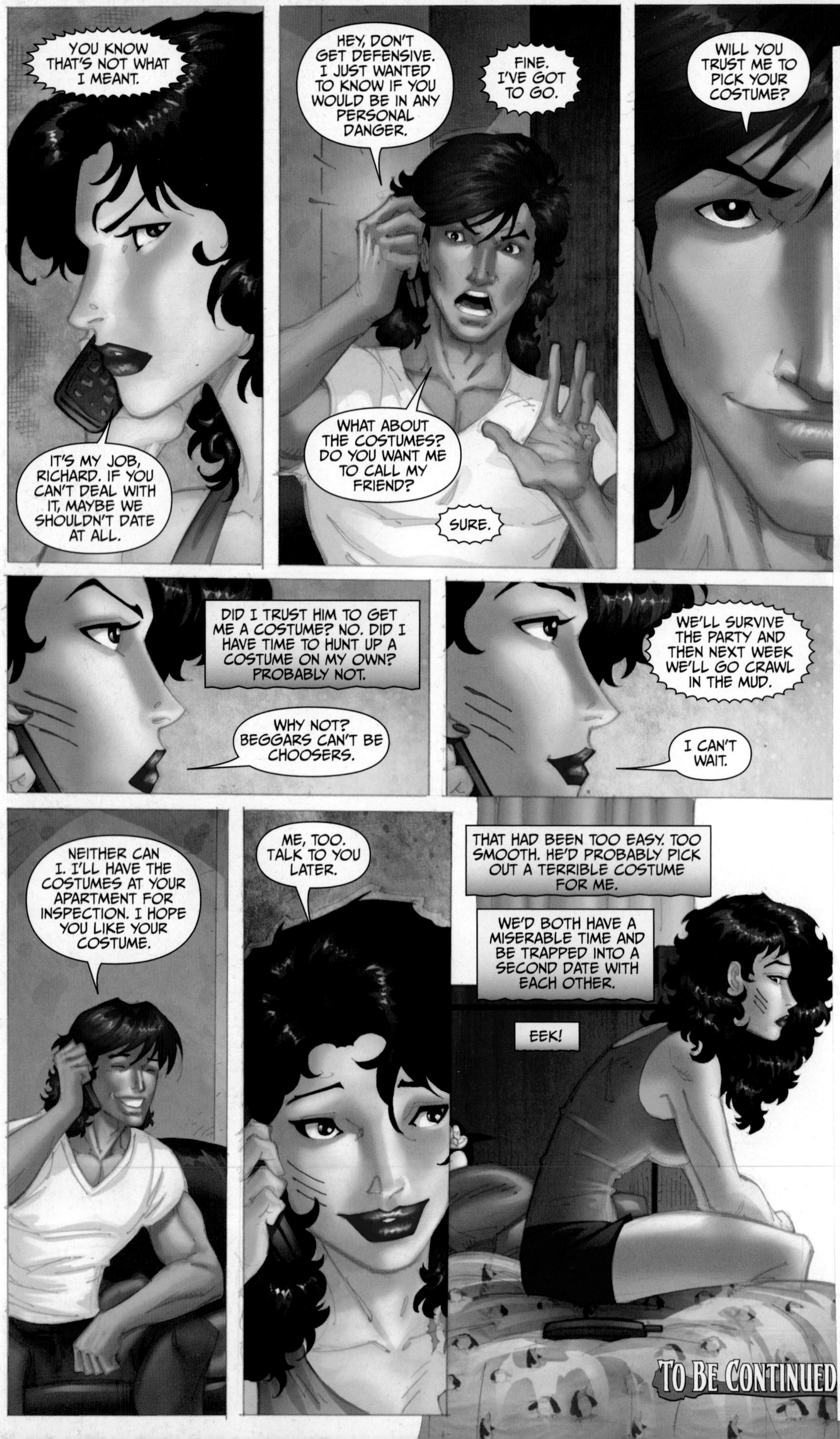
YOU KNOW THAT'S NOT WHAT I MEANT.
IT'S MY JOB, RICHARD. IF YOU CAN'T DEAL WITH IT, MAYBE WE SHOULDN'T DATE AT ALL.
HEY, DON'T GET DEFENSIVE. I JUST WANTED TO KNOW IF YOU WOULD BE IN ANY PERSONAL DANGER.
FINE. I'VE GOT TO GO.
WHAT ABOUT THE COSTUMES? DO YOU WANT ME TO CALL MY FRIEND?
SURE.
WILL YOU TRUST ME TO PICK YOUR COSTUME?
DID I TRUST HIM TO GET ME A COSTUME? NO. DID I HAVE TIME TO HUNT UP A COSTUME ON MY OWN? PROBABLY NOT.
WHY NOT? BEGGARS CAN'T BE CHOOSERS.
WE'LL SURVIVE THE PARTY AND THEN NEXT WEEK WE'LL GO CRAWL IN THE MUD.
I CAN'T WAIT.
NEITHER CAN I. I'LL HAVE THE COSTUMES AT YOUR APARTMENT FOR INSPECTION. I HOPE YOU LIKE YOUR COSTUME.
ME, TOO. TALK TO YOU LATER.
THAT HAD BEEN TOO EASY. TOO SMOOTH. HE'D PROBABLY PICK OUT A TERRIBLE COSTUME FOR ME.
WE'D BOTH HAVE A MISERABLE TIME AND BE TRAPPED INTO A SECOND DATE WITH EACH OTHER.
EEK!
TO BE CONTINUED

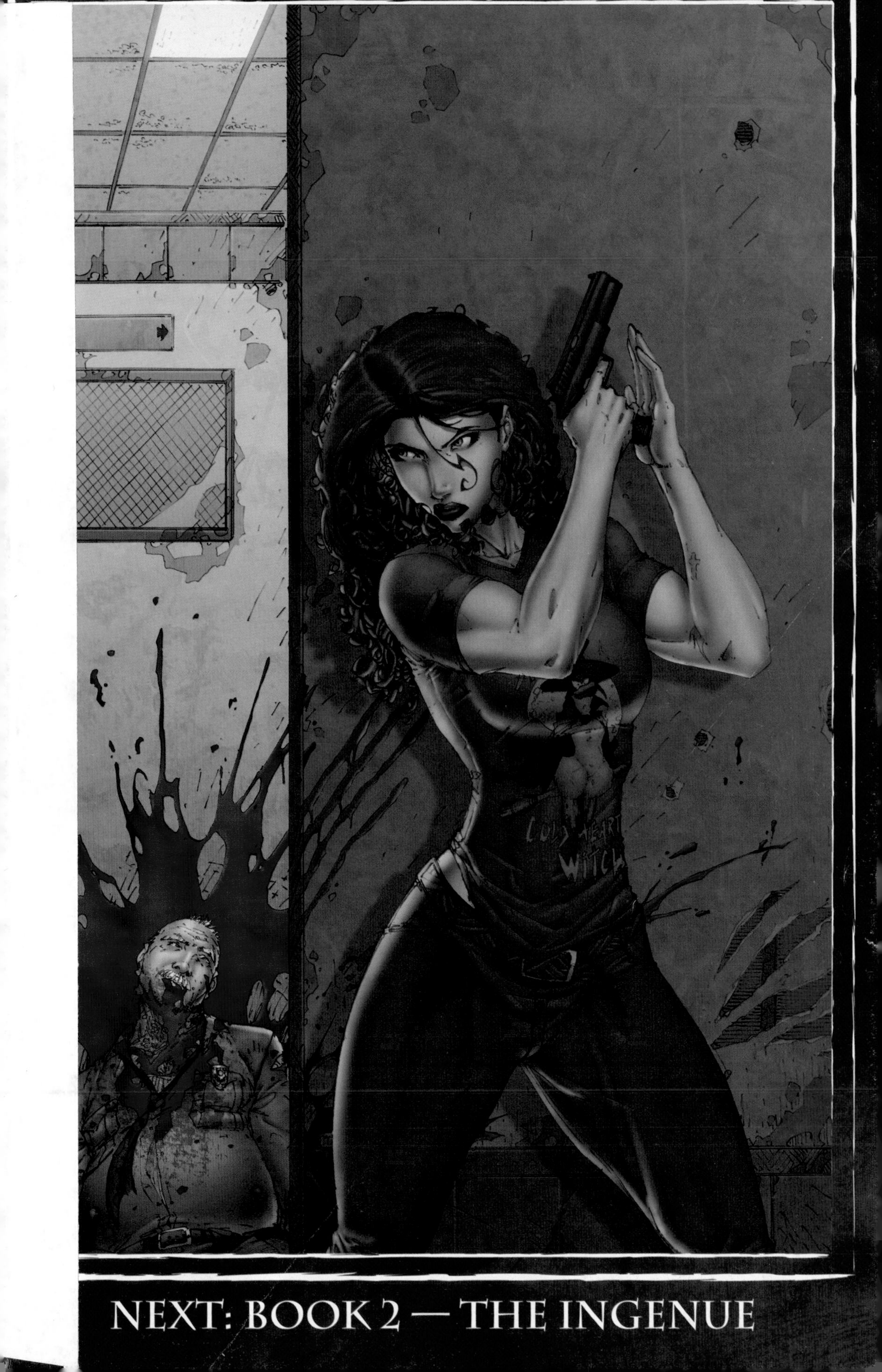

NEXT: BOOK 2 — THE INGENUE